CLASSIC

FICTION

OF THE

HARLEM

RENAISSANCE

CLASSIC

FICTION

OF THE

HARLEM

RENAISSANCE

Edited by

William L. Andrews

New York   Oxford
Oxford University Press
1994

Oxford University Press

Oxford New York Toronto
Delhi Bombay Calcutta Madras Karachi
Kuala Lumpur Singapore Hong Kong Tokyo
Nairobi Dar es Salaam Cape Town
Melbourne Auckland Madrid

and associated companies in
Berlin Ibadan

Library of Congress Cataloging-in-Publication Data
Classic fiction of the Harlem Renaissance / edited by William L. Andrews.
p. cm.   Includes bibliographical references.
ISBN 0-19-508196-X
1. American fiction—Afro-American authors.
2. American fiction—20th century.
3. Afro-Americans—Fiction.
4. Harlem Renaissance.
I. Andrews, William L., 1946– .
PS647.A35C57 1994 813'.5209896073—dc20 93-11023

Frontispiece: Augusta Savage, *Lift Every Voice and Sing*, 1939.
Cast Plaster.
Photograph by Carl Van Vechten.
By Permission of the Estate of Carl Van Vechten,
Joseph Solomon, Executor.

9 8 7 6 5 4 3 2 1

Printed in the United States of America
on acid-free paper

CONTENTS

CLASSIC

FICTION

OF THE

HARLEM

RENAISSANCE

INTRODUCTION

The literary and cultural phenomenon popularly known as the Harlem Renaissance has given rise to more conflicting assessments, more praise and more detraction, than probably any other comparable movement, period, or school of writers has received in African American literary history. As black America's first self-annointed, self-justifying, and self-propagandized artistic and cultural movement, the Harlem Renaissance set grander goals and promised greater results than any group of black artists and thinkers had ever dreamed of before. In the defining text of the Harlem Renaissance, Alain Locke's showcase anthology *The New Negro* (1925), the writers and artists of the renaissance are extolled as "the advance-guard of the African peoples in their contact with Twentieth Century civilization" (14). The arrival of Harlem's New Negroes on the literary and cultural scene is trumpeted as nothing less than black America's "spiritual Coming of Age" (16). Under the auspices of the renaissance's New Negroes, a new generation of African American writers and artists claimed their readiness to dare to imagine what they could do collectively to reorient the meaning and valuation of race so that black people might assume a new stance of assertion rather than accept the old postures of apology and defense.

Yet in Nathan Huggins's *Harlem Renaissance* (1971), the most often-cited scholarly study of the New Negro renaissance in New York, one finds the leaders of the renaissance taken to task for their "cultural elitism" and their vainglorious "naiveté" in believing that through a racially based art they could effect significant social change in white-dominated America (5). Prominent historians of the Harlem Renaissance have joined Huggins in questioning "the success of the 'renaissance' in delivering what it claimed for itself" (9). Seldom, of course, have literary movements in the United States fulfilled the expectations they inspired, especially those movements, like the Harlem Renaissance, that have been predicated on the idea that the responsibility of art is not only to express the views of the artist but also to alter the vision of the nation. Nevertheless, when the New Negroes of Harlem and other major cities of the northern United States asserted their new brand of militancy and declared an end to racial accommodation, when they celebrated their ethnic identity and took seriously their heritage in folk and African cultures, when they insisted that art had a mission to define black people according to their own communally generated aspirations—in all these respects, it is agreed, the Harlem Renaissance *did* signal a revival of African American consciousness that has had lasting reverberations in the twentieth-century United States. The fiction collected in this anthology furnishes compelling testimony to this revival along with new formulations of modern African American consciousness in the 1920s and early 1930s, as portrayed by black writers now considered major contributors to the Harlem Renaissance.

The more critics write about the Harlem Renaissance the harder it has become to define and delimit this historical and literary phenomenon. Today only an uneasy consensus exists among scholars and critics on even so basic a question as whether the Harlem Renaissance is appropriately named. Some have asked if the term *renaissance* doesn't reinforce the self-congratulatory myth of new birth that the promoters of the so-called renaissance invoked to maneuver it (and sometimes themselves) into the public spotlight. In response, most students of the Harlem phenomenon have come to see in it not so much the birth of something new as a *re*newing of modes, styles, and themes that were more deeply rooted in the African American past than the renaissance either knew or wanted to acknowledge. Instead of the familiar metaphors of new birth and revitalized spirit, the Harlem Renaissance might be more aptly thought of as an outpouring, an efflorescence, of creative expression that had long been bottled up within black America by the constraints of segregation. To a significant degree the creative flame that burned with unprecedented brightness among the younger leaders of the renaissance was lit by torches passed from older and established intellects, such as those of James Weldon Johnson and W. E. B. Du Bois. Various social, political, and economic developments in the second and third decades of the twentieth century—the end of World War I and the return of black veterans, the cresting tides of African American migrations from the South to the urban North, the formation of civil rights organizations such as the National Association for the Advancement of Colored People (NAACP) and black solidarity movements like Marcus Garvey's Universal Negro Improvement Association, and the new sense of economic, social, and cultural potential that attended the ascendance of Harlem as the "Negro capital of the world"—all served to trigger an eruption in literature and the arts that had been reaching a critical mass for some time. Although the Harlem Renaissance has often been called the prelude to later twentieth-century black artistic movements, there is good reason to understand it as the final phase of trends originating in the segregation era of the 1890s rather than the initiating phase of cultural developments that culminated in the Civil Rights era of the 1960s.

Even if one clings to the term *renaissance* for no other reason than that it serves as a tacitly accepted reference to a place and a time in which something remarkable happened in African American arts and letters, doubts about calling it a "Harlem Renaissance" still abound. Should Harlem get sole credit for engendering a renaissance? After all, similar though less publicized cultural developments were taking place in black communities in Philadelphia and Washington, D.C.— not to mention international centers such as Paris—during the second and third decades of the twentieth century. As Sterling Brown, one of the most knowledgeable observers of the New Negro movement, has stressed: "Most of the writers [in the Harlem Renaissance] were not Harlemites; much of the best writing was not about Harlem, which was the show-window, the cashier's till but no more Negro America than New York is America" (57). Harlem, in other words, may provide a useful focal point for the mythic capitol of the so-called renaissance, but it should not be used to localize the purview of the writers who participated in that renaissance.

Perhaps the most easily granted challenge to the reliability of the term *Harlem Renaissance* concerns the typical linkage of the renaissance to the decade of the 1920s. Few historians of the renaissance attempt to gauge when it actually began, for the obvious reason that social, cultural, and economic factors are too complexly interwoven to single out one for special originating status. Books, plays, and artistic works are equally problematic as originating texts because they may be as much symptomatic of something already underway as the initiators of something new. In view of these factors, few today argue over who or what launched the so-called renaissance of African American arts and letters or what brought it to an end. While the onset of the Depression is often blamed for the collapse and dispersal of the Harlem Renaissance, writers such as Langston Hughes, Zora Neale Hurston, and Arna Bontemps (all three made their initial fame as part of the Harlem school in the 1920s) did not abandon their work or repudiate their cultural commitments during the 1930s. The flamboyant spirit of the renaissance may have withered in the bleak atmosphere of the Depression. Nevertheless, key figures like Hughes and Hurston adapted their core convictions to the new realities of the 1930s and went on with their lives and their art, leading what has been judged by some critics as a "second generation" of the renaissance through the Depression era and beyond.

Questions about the character, locale, or time frame of the Harlem Renaissance have given rise to alternative labels—New Negro movement, Negro renaissance, Black renaissance—that may seem more valid indicators of the sociopolitical agenda, geographical breadth, and cultural orientation of the extraordinary developments in African American arts and letters that claimed international attention in the 1920s. Certainly the renaissance of African American art forms in 1920s Harlem cannot be interpreted apart from the contemporary resurgence of black consciousness expressed in a movement for greater intellectual autonomy and sociopolitical aggressiveness that many associate with the term *New Negro*. Whether the renaissance in Harlem evolved out of the New Negro movement or the New Negroes of the 1920s learned to recognize themselves in the art of the renaissance is the sort of chicken-and-egg question that points to the complex intersection of the many intellectual, sociopolitical, artistic, and cultural trends that profoundly changed African American life in the early twentieth century. Granting the relevance of the New Negro movement and the revolutionary new ideas of blackness that arose along with, if not because of, the Harlem Renaissance, the reader of this anthology should not be surprised to find the fiction of the Harlem Renaissance as engaging, challenging, controversial, and continually fascinating as the era itself.

"The 1920's were the years of Manhattan's black Renaissance," Langston Hughes states flatly at the outset of "Black Renaissance," the third section of his autobiography *The Big Sea* (1940 p. 223). No modern African American writer was better situated historically or better suited temperamentally to assess what the "Black Renaissance" was all about than Hughes. Like the 100,000 southern and midwestern blacks who migrated to Harlem in the decade after World War I, Hughes arrived in New York in 1921 looking for the new social and economic opportunities and the freely expressive black community that had become synonymous with Harlem. As one black New Yorker proudly attested in his contribution to *The New Negro*, Harlem had attained its fabled status because it was

> not merely a Negro colony or community, it is a city within a city, the greatest Negro city in the world. It is not a slum or a fringe. . . . It is

not a "quarter" of dilapidated tenements, but is made up of new-law apartments and handsome dwellings, with well-paved and well-lighted streets. It has its own churches, social and civic centers, shops, theaters and other places of amusement. And it contains more Negroes to the square mile than any other spot on earth (Johnson, 301).

What Hughes discovered in Harlem's unparalleled color and class diversity, in its cabarets and house rent parties, its theaters, churches, and street corner debates; what Hughes learned from the friendships he developed among Harlem's cultural leaders, from his reading of modern literature, and from his travels to Africa and Europe combined to mold him by the mid-1920s into the younger generation's most consistent literary exponent of racial pride and artistic freedom. In *The Big Sea* Hughes turned his distinctively eclectic perspective on the renaissance in Harlem, of which he was both product and in many important ways joint producer. As a personal and cultural history, *The Big Sea* resonates with a mixture of nostalgia and disappointment typical of many reminiscences of Harlem during the Jazz era. Words like "gay," "scintillating," and "fantastic" come to Hughes's mind—along with "dull," "distorted," and "commercial"—to convey what was good and not so good about Harlem life in the 1920s. Anyone seeking an introduction to the Harlem Renaissance should dip into *The Big Sea*, if only to view Hughes's remarkable catalog of poetic and reportorial images of what made Harlem the vogue in the 1920s.

"It was a period," Hughes remembers,

when, at almost every Harlem upper-crust dance or party, one would be introduced to various distinguished white celebrities there as guests. It was a period when almost any Harlem Negro of any social importance at all would be likely to say casually: "As I was remarking the other day to Heywood—," meaning Heywood Broun. Or: "As I said to George—,"referring to George Gershwin. It was a period when local and visiting royalty were not at all uncommon in Harlem. . . . It was a period when Charleston preachers opened up shouting churches as sideshows for white tourists. It was a period when at least one charming colored chorus girl, amber enough to pass for a Latin American, was living in a pent house, with all her bills paid by a gentleman whose name was banker's magic on Wall Street. It was a period when every season there was at least one hit play on Broadway acted by a Negro cast. And when books by Negro authors were being published with much greater frequency and much more publicity than ever before or since in history (227–28).

Looking back on the 1920s in his autobiography *Along This Way* (1933), James Weldon Johnson, the poet, editor, and civil rights leader who best qualifies as the Harlem Renaissance's "renaissance man," paid special tribute to the role of literature in creating, not just reflecting on, what was distinctively "Harlem" about Harlem. The late 1920s was, according to Johnson,

> the era in which was achieved the Harlem of story and song; the era in which Harlem's fame for exotic flavor and colorful sensuousness was spread to all parts of the world; when Harlem was made known as the scene of laughter, singing, dancing, and primitive passions, and as the center of the new Negro literature and art; the era in which it gained its place in the list of famous sections of great cities (380).

"This universal reputation was the work of writers," Johnson concludes, appreciatively.

> The picturesque Harlem was real, but it was the writers who discovered its artistic values and, in giving literary expression to them, actually created the Harlem that caught the world's imagination. . . . The writers who came to parties and went sight-seeing in Harlem found stimulating material for their pens. Then other writers flocked there; many came from [a]far, and depicted it in many ways and in many languages. They still come; the Harlem of story and song still fascinates them (380).

In his autobiography Johnson expresses his conviction that Harlem Renaissance literature had made a brave start but still had a ways to go before it could be said to have grappled with what Johnson calls "the sterner aspects of life" in "commonplace, work-a-day Harlem" (380–81). Hughes was more blunt in assessing the class bases and biases that, as he saw it, both sustained and vitiated the renaissance in Harlem. The elites of Harlem "were sure the New Negro would lead a new life from then on in green pastures of tolerance created by Countee Cullen, Ethel Waters, Claude McKay, Duke Ellington, Bojangles, and Alain Locke." However, Hughes quickly points out, "the ordinary Negroes hadn't heard of the Negro Renaissance" (228). Cullen, its celebrated "poet laureate"; Waters, one of its most popular singers; McKay, its best-selling novelist; Ellington, its most sophisticated musician; Bill "Bojangles" Robinson, its most stylish dancer; and Alain Locke, its intellectual standard-bearer, had excelled as creative individuals. But the collective impact of their work, especially on the real-world situations of the rank-and-file African American, was at best hard to determine and at worst negligible, Hughes decided. As for himself, a participant in and observer of the Black Renaissance in Harlem, Hughes remarks in *The Big Sea* simply and with characteristic understatement: "I was there. I had a swell time while it lasted. But I thought it wouldn't last long. . . . For how could a large and enthusiastic number of people"—by which Hughes meant white people—"be crazy about Negroes forever?" (228).

Portraying the Black renaissance in literature and the visual and performing arts as a temporary "craze" among white thrill-seekers, not unlike dancing the Charleston in a dimly lit uptown Manhattan club, was a familiar diagnosis in the 1930s of what went wrong in Harlem during the 1920s. Hughes was not alone in regretting the heady, in some ways hothouse, ethos of the Harlem Renaissance. Three years before *The Big Sea*, Alain Locke, hailed as the intellectual "midwife" of the renaissance, announced that "flippant exhibitionism" and "social irresponsibility" on the part of writers such as Claude McKay had brought on the demise of "the first decade of the Negro Renaissance" ("Spiritual Truancy," 66). In the wake of such pronouncements, it became fashionable in the 1930s and 1940s to indict the Harlem Renaissance as a self-betrayed "fad," long on style but short on substance, done in by its excessive dependence on and pandering to whites and their prejudices. To these purported failings critics in the 1960s and 1970s added another fault, a politically naive deference to the black bourgeoisie and its aesthetic interests that prevented the renaissance from recognizing its own elitism and its consequent lack of foundation in mass experience.

Most assessments of the Harlem Renaissance as a movement proceed from a conviction, summed up in W. E. B. Du Bois's autobiographical commentary on "the renaissance of Negro literature," that "no authentic group literature can rise save at the demand and with the support of the group which is calling for self-expression" (270). What has not yet been settled, however, is which "group"—the black bourgeoisie? white liberal art patrons? the Harlem cultural elite itself?—was "calling for self-expression" in and through the renaissance. What remains very difficult to define is the notion of an "authentic group literature," which some within the renaissance thought their movement was producing, while others had their doubts. An even larger question is: Should the writing of the Harlem Renaissance be judged on the basis of its success or failure as "group literature," as an authentic or inauthentic representation of *any* group's social agenda and aesthetic aspirations? Is the key issue of responsibility for "self-expression" a matter of which group's interests a given writer seems to have served or tried to serve? Or should we read the classic writers of the Harlem Renaissance more in terms of how they engaged both individual *and* group interests in forms of literary expression that often placed self and group identifications in creative tension?

An attentive reading of the most notable fiction of the renaissance will not yield easy judgments about "success" or "failure" as those terms have sometimes been applied in summary fashion to the renaissance as a whole. What the Harlem Renaissance accomplished or failed to accomplish will likely prove less important to a reader than what individual writers of the renaissance had to say about central issues raised by the renaissance: the meaning of race, the legacy of the folk, the promise of modern life, the potential of art, the building of a nation. It may be that sixty years ago James Weldon Johnson put forward the most balanced appraisal of the successes and failures of the new African American literature of the 1920s. Johnson acknowledged in 1934 "a degree of disillusionment and disappointment for those who a decade ago hailed with loud huzzas the dawn of the Negro literary millenium." But he also admitted, "We expected much; perhaps, too much. I now judge that we ought to be thankful for the half-dozen younger writers who did emerge and make a place for themselves."

Putting aside the questions about what was promised and achieved by, and what could legitimately have been expected of, the Harlem Renaissance, at least one conclusion seems unquestionable today: At least a half-dozen of the younger writers who emerged from the renaissance—Hughes, Hurston, Toomer, McKay, Larsen, and Fisher—did make a lasting place for themselves in American literary history. As fiction writers (though by no means writers solely confined to this genre), these six writers were able to form their own school, characterized by similar themes and allied premises and intentions, that compelled unprecedented notice for African American fiction from the white publishing and reviewing media. As Hugh M. Gloster, a historian of the black American novel, points out, before the 1920s African American fiction was usually a solitary enterprise pursued through self-publication for the edification of a primarily black readership. By contrast, almost all the Harlem Renaissance fiction writers attracted the support of well-funded and highly influential white commercial publishers who willingly used their contacts to obtain extensive critical attention to more than a dozen of the most interesting novels of the renaissance. One should not overestimate the openness and responsiveness of white publishers and reviewers to the younger black fiction writers of the 1920s. But neither should one ignore the fact that the Harlem Renaissance, much more than any previous attempt in African American literary history, forced a serious reassessment of America's, not just black America's, notions about race, modern life, and the interrelationships between the two.

This anthology reprints classic—that is, the most distinctive, influential, and appreciated—novels and short stories by the most famous fiction writers of the Harlem Renaissance: three stories and the concluding novella from Jean Toomer's *Cane* (1923), Zora Neale Hurston's "Sweat" (1926) and "The Gilded Six-Bits" (1933), Claude McKay's *Home to Harlem* (1928), Rudolph Fisher's "Miss Cynthie" (1933), Nella Larsen's *Quicksand* (1928), and Langston Hughes's "The Blues I'm Playing" (1934). This fiction has been selected to reflect those works that are each writer's classic contributions to the Harlem Renaissance; hence two of Hurston's important early short stories appear in this collection but not *Their Eyes Were Watching God* (1937). Also included with the two complete novels, the novella, and the seven short stories in this anthology is a chapter from *Infants of the Spring* (1932), a novel by Wallace Thurman in which virtually all the principal renaissance writers become themselves fictional figures in a no-holds-barred roman à clef about the Harlem Renaissance. To give added flavor and insight into the speech and oral culture of the renaissance, Rudolph Fisher's half tongue-in-cheek "An Introduction to Contemporary Harlemese, Expurgated and Abridged" is appended to this anthology as it originally appeared at the end of Fisher's novel, *The Walls of Jericho* (1928). This text also provides listings of useful book-length critical and historical studies of the renaissance and its fiction as well as of the individual writers whose work is represented in this volume. For general readers, students, and teachers, there can hardly be a more effective or enjoyable way of exploring the intellectual concerns, the socioeconomic perspectives, and the artistic innovations of the Harlem Renaissance than by sampling its classic fiction.

WORKS CITED

Brown, Sterling A. "The New Negro in Literature, 1925–1955." Rayford W. Logan, ed. *The New Negro Thirty Years Afterward*. Washington, D.C.: Howard University Press, 1955. Pp. 57–72.

Du Bois, W. E. B. *Dusk of Dawn*. 1940; New York: Schocken, 1968.

Gloster, Hugh M. *Negro Voices in American Fiction*. Chapel Hill: University of North Carolina Press, 1948.

Huggins, Nathan Irvin. *Harlem Renaissance*. New York: Oxford University Press, 1971.

Hughes, Langston. *The Big Sea*. 1940; New York: Hill and Wang, 1963.

Johnson, James Weldon. *Along This Way*. 1933; New York: Penguin, 1990.

——. "Foreword to *Challenge*, Vol. I (March, 1934)." Nathan Irvin Huggins, ed. *Voices from the Harlem Renaissance*. New York: Oxford University Press, 1976. Pp. 390–91.

Locke, Alain, ed. *The New Negro*. New York: Albert & Charles Boni, 1925.

——. "Spiritual Truancy." Jeffrey C. Stewart, ed. *The Critical Temper of Alain Locke*. New York: Garland, 1983. Pp. 63–66.

SUGGESTIONS FOR FURTHER READING

Anderson, Jervis. *This Was Harlem: A Cultural Portrait, 1900–1950*. New York: Farrar, 1982.

Baker, Houston A., Jr. *Modernism and the Harlem Renaissance*. Chicago: University of Chicago Press, 1991.

Bell, Bernard W. *The Afro-American Novel and Its Tradition*. Amherst: University of Massachusetts Press, 1987.

Bone, Robert A. *The Negro Novel in America*. New Haven: Yale University Press, 1965.

Bontemps, Arna, ed. *The Harlem Renaissance Remembered*. New York: Dodd, 1972.

De Jongh, James. *Vicious Modernism: Black Harlem and the Literary Imagination*. Cambridge: Cambridge University Press, 1990.

Fabre, Michel. *From Harlem to Paris: Black American Writers in France, 1840–1980*. Urbana: University of Illinois Press, 1991.

Gayle, Addison. *The Way of the New World: The Black Novel in America*. Garden City. Anchor Doubleday, 1975.

Hull, Gloria T. *Color, Sex, and Poetry: Three Women Writers of the Harlem Renaissance*. Bloomington: Indiana University Press, 1987.

Kellner, Bruce. *The Harlem Renaissance: An Historical Dictionary for the Era*. Westport, CT: Greenwood, 1984.

Kramer, Victor A., ed. *The Harlem Renaissance Re-examined*. New York: AMS Press, 1987.

Lewis, David Levering. *When Harlem Was in Vogue*. New York: Alfred A. Knopf, 1981.

Perry, Margaret. *The Harlem Renaissance: An Annotated Bibliography and Commentary*. New York: Garland, 1982.

——. *Silence to the Drums: A Survey of the Literature of the Harlem Renaissance*. Westport, CT: Greenwood, 1976.

Singh, Amritjit. *The Novels of the Harlem Renaissance*. University Park: Pennsylvania State University Press, 1976.

Singh, Amritjit, William S. Shriver, and Stanley Brodwin, eds. *The Harlem Renaissance: Reevaluations*. New York: Garland, 1989.

Turner, Darwin T. *In a Minor Chord: Three Afro-American Writers and Their Search for Identity*. Carbondale: Southern Illinois University Press, 1971.

Wheeler, Kenneth W. and Virginia Lee Lussier, eds. *Women, the Arts, and the 1920s in Paris and New York*. New Brunswick, NJ: Transaction Books, 1982.

Young, James O. *Black Writers of the Thirties*. Baton Rouge: Louisiana State University Press, 1973.

JEAN TOOMER
By permission of Fisk University Library Special Collections.

JEAN TOOMER

1894 ГО 1967

To many readers Jean Toomer's *Cane* (1923), a volume of poems, short stories, and a novella that veers sharply away from traditional African American literature and toward new modernist forms and themes, signals the beginning of the literary Harlem Renaissance. Yet the relationships of Toomer and *Cane* to the renaissance have never been easy to pin down. *Cane* appeared at least two years before the New Negro and Harlem culture came into the national spotlight. Toomer never lived in Harlem, and Harlem receives merely a passing reference in *Cane*. Most significant, the introduction to *Cane*, by a white writer and close friend of Toomer's named Waldo Frank, avers that the greatness of *Cane* lies in Toomer's artistic transcendence of race, not in his expression of his own racial identity or a black perspective. According to Toomer's biographer, Nellie McKay, the author of *Cane* was grateful to Frank for recognizing him as an American artist to whom racial designation was secondary to an expression of personal vision. As if to underline a sense of himself as an individual whose art must be understood and judged first on that basis, Toomer refused to allow publicity for *Cane* to mention his African American heritage. Yet in response to an inquiry from the Associated Negro Press just before *Cane* appeared, Toomer stated, "In so far as the old folk-songs, syncopated rhythms, the rich sweet taste of dark-skinned life, in so far as these are Negro, I am, body and soul, Negroid."

Toomer's ambivalence about both his identity and the degree to which his writing should be identified as peculiarly African American has been seen as both a help and a hindrance to his psychological and artistic development. He was born into the so-called "black bourgeoisie," the grandson of P. B. S. Pinchback, a fair-skinned Reconstruction-era politician in Louisiana who had established his family in an affluent part of

Washington, D.C. in the early 1890s. Toomer's mother Nina was a well bred and independent-minded woman who married his father, Nathan Toomer, a gentlemanly figure of uncertain southern background, against her father's wishes in 1894. The marriage ended in divorce in 1898. Light-complexioned and at home on either side of the color line, Jean grew up primarily in the home of his grandfather, earning good marks in school and showing a capacity for leadership in a variety of activities.

After graduation from high school in 1913, Toomer made the first of a series of abrupt breaks with his past, enrolling at the University of Wisconsin to study agriculture. In the next few years he sampled the curricula at a succession of colleges and schools in Massachusetts, Chicago, and New York. He explored various philosophies of living in what he later called a "struggle for myself." In 1919, however, he returned to New York City determined to become a writer. Toomer settled in Greenwich Village and mingled with those who would soon be identified as members of the post-World War I "Lost Generation" of literary iconoclasts. Within a year he was creating poems, stories, and plays inspired by his reading of the verse of Walt Whitman and Robert Frost, the drama of George Bernard Shaw, and Sherwood Anderson's short fiction, particularly *Winesburg, Ohio* (1919). Unfulfilled and restless, however, Toomer accepted in the fall of 1921 an offer to work as a substitute teacher in a black school in a part of rural Georgia where his father had come from. The two months he spent in Sparta, Georgia, introduced Toomer to the liberating life rhythms, the haunting music and healing folk traditions, and the barely submerged fears and frustrations of black people in their struggle to maintain spiritual integrity in the harsh racial climate of the South. On the train back to Washington, Toomer began to write the sketches that appeared two years later in the first section of *Cane*.

Although often called a novel, *Cane* is a three-part work that mixes genres and styles and defies classification. Like T. S. Eliot's *The Waste Land* and several other early modernist literary experiments, *Cane* is made up of fragments but is designed to achieve a unified effect through its impressionistic use of language, the emotional coherence of its imagery, and its recurrent attention to questions of African American identity. The first part of *Cane* evokes the wonder and horror of the rural, segregated South. The focus of this section of the book is on black women's beauty, their seemingly mystical self-possession, and their sexual vulnerability. The middle portion of *Cane* exposes the pathos and futility emanating from the lives of the more sophisticated black men and women who have been drawn to urban centers such as Washington, D.C. These people suffer from the rootlessness, the self-repression, and the various forms of alienation—mind from body, male from female, individual from communal traditions—that are often treated as symptomatic of the modern condition. In the last section of *Cane*, the narrative returns to the rural South, where a northern black schoolteacher and poet, Ralph Kabnis, has come to confront the contradictory essentials of the African American experience in an attempt to resolve the inner conflicts that have prevented him from achieving a sense of wholeness and fulfillment as an artist. Kabnis realizes finally that he is suffering from a sickness of the soul that demands the ministry of the enigmatic Father John, a relic of slavery and the embodiment of the tenacity and wisdom of the African American folk. Yet the conclusion of *Cane* does not state explicitly whether or how Kabnis is spiritually rehabilitated. Rejecting the sense of closure and completion, from the standpoint of both plot and moral purpose, that was traditional in earlier African American fiction, Toomer leaves his reader with the idea that for the modern African American the shaping of a new selfhood will require an ongoing struggle, a continuing evolution and integration of consciousness.

Cane was Jean Toomer's unique contribution to the new fiction of the African American literary renaissance of the 1920s. Even as he was being celebrated as a harbinger of bold new things to come, however, Toomer turned his back on a career in literature in favor of alternate forms of consciousness-raising based in Western adaptations of Eastern mysticism. Between 1922 and the end of the decade he wrote several plays that identified him with the vanguard of the new expressionist drama in the United States, as well as a handful of short stories for prestigious little magazines. But as his writing gravitated increasingly to broadly conceived philosophical and didactic topics, Toomer sacrificed the distinctiveness of style and substance that he had captured in *Cane*. By the end of the 1920s, Toomer decided that he would no longer accept designation as a Negro and would not allow his writing to be included in anthologies of African American literature. Declaring that henceforth he would express himself as simply a member of what he called "the American race," Toomer went on writing in a variety of forms, from aphorisms to autobiography, through the next three decades. But only in a long philosophical poem entitled "The Blue Meridian," a Whitmanesque celebration of the multiethnic essence of American life, did Toomer happily wed his art and theories of identity, society, and progress. Rarely, however, did he find a publisher for his writing. Never again in his lifetime did he attract a national readership.

Benson, Brian Joseph and Mabel Mayle Dillard. *Jean Toomer*. Boston: Twayne, 1980.

Kerman, Cynthia E. and Richard Eldridge. *The Lives of Jean Toomer*. Baton Rouge: Louisiana State University Press, 1989.

McKay, Nellie Y. *Jean Toomer, Artist: A Study of His Literary Life and Work, 1894–1936*. Chapel Hill: University of North Carolina Press, 1984.

O'Daniel, Thurman B., ed. *Jean Toomer: A Critical Evaluation*. Washington, D.C.: Howard University Press, 1988.

Turner, Darwin T., ed. *The Wayward and the Seeking: A Collection of Writings by Jean Toomer*. Washington, D.C.: Howard University Press, 1980.

KARINTHA

Her skin is like dusk on the eastern horizon,
O cant you see it, O cant you see it,
Her skin is like dusk on the eastern horizon
. . . When the sun goes down.

Men had always wanted her, this Karintha, even as a child, Karintha carrying beauty, perfect as dusk when the sun goes down. Old men rode her hobby-horse upon their knees. Young men danced with her at frolics when they should have been dancing with their grown-up girls. God grant us youth, secretly prayed the old men. The young fellows counted the time to pass before she would be old enough to mate with them. This interest of the male, who wishes to ripen a growing thing too soon, could mean no good to her.

Karintha, at twelve, was a wild flash that told the other folks just what it was to live. At sunset, when there was no wind, and the pine-smoke from over by the sawmill hugged the earth, and you couldnt see more than a few feet in front, her sudden darting past you was a bit of vivid color, like a black bird that flashes in light. With the other children one could hear, some distance off, their feet flopping in the two-inch dust. Karintha's running was a whir. It had the sound of the red dust that sometimes makes a spiral in the road. At dusk, during the hush just after the sawmill had closed down, and before any of the women had started their supper-getting-ready songs, her voice, high-pitched, shrill, would put one's ears to itching. But no one ever thought to make her stop because of it. She stoned the cows, and beat her dog, and fought the other children. . . . Even the preacher, who caught her at mischief, told himself that she was as innocently lovely as a November cotton flower. Already, rumors were out about her. Homes in Georgia are most often built on the two-room plan. In one, you cook and eat, in the other you sleep, and there love goes on. Karintha had seen or heard, perhaps she had felt her parents loving. One could but imitate one's parents, for to follow them was the way of God. She played "home" with a small boy who was not afraid to do her bidding. That started the whole thing. Old men could no longer ride her hobby-horse upon their knees. But young men counted faster.

> Her skin is like dusk,
> O cant you see it,
> Her skin is like dusk,
> When the sun goes down.

Karintha is a woman. She who carries beauty, perfect as dusk when the sun goes down. She has been married many times. Old men remind her that a few years back they rode her hobby-horse upon their knees. Karintha smiles, and indulges them when she is in the mood for it. She has contempt for them. Karintha is a woman. Young men run stills to make her money. Young men go to the big cities and run on the road. Young men go away to college. They all want to bring her money. These are the young men who thought that all they had to do was to count time. But Karintha is a woman, and she has had a child. A child fell out of her womb onto a bed of pine-needles in the forest. Pine-needles are smooth and sweet. They are elastic to the feet of rabbits. . . A sawmill was nearby. Its pyramidal sawdust pile smouldered. It is a year before one completely burns. Meanwhile, the smoke curls up and hangs in odd wraiths about the trees, curls up, and spreads itself out over the valley. . . Weeks after Karintha returned home the smoke was so heavy you tasted it in water. Some one made a song:

> Smoke is on the hills. Rise up.
> Smoke is on the hills, O rise
> And take my soul to Jesus.

Karintha is a woman. Men do not know that the soul of her was a growing thing ripened too soon. They will bring their money; they will die not having found it out. . . Karintha at twenty, carrying beauty, perfect as dusk when the sun goes down. Karintha. . .

> Her skin is like dusk on the eastern horizon,
> O cant you see it, O cant you see it,
> Her skin is like dusk on the eastern horizon
> . . . When the sun goes down.

Goes down. . .

BLOOD-BURNING MOON

⌞ ——————————————————————————— ⌟

1

Up from the skeleton stone walls, up from the rotting floor boards and the solid hand-hewn beams of oak of the pre-war cotton factory, dusk came. Up from the dusk the full moon came. Glowing like a fired pine-knot, it illumined the great door and soft showered the Negro shanties aligned along the single street of factory town. The full moon in the great door was an omen. Negro women improvised songs against its spell.

Louisa sang as she came over the crest of the hill from the white folks' kitchen. Her skin was the color of oak leaves on young trees in fall. Her breasts, firm and up-pointed like ripe acorns. And her singing had the low murmur of winds in fig trees. Bob Stone, younger son of the people she worked for, loved her. By the way the world reckons things, he had won her. By measure of that warm glow which came into her mind at thought of him, he had won her. Tom Burwell, whom the whole town called Big Boy, also loved her. But working in the fields all day, and far away from her, gave him no chance to show it. Though often enough of evenings he had tried to. Somehow, he never got along. Strong as he was with hands upon the ax or plow, he found it difficult to hold her. Or so he thought. But the fact was that he held her to factory town more firmly than he thought for. His black balanced, and pulled against, the white of Stone, when she thought of them. And her mind was vaguely upon them as she came over the crest of the hill, coming from the white folks' kitchen. As she sang softly at the evil face of the full moon.

A strange stir was in her. Indolently, she tried to fix upon Bob or Tom as the cause of it. To meet Bob in the canebrake, as she was going to do an hour or so later, was nothing new. And Tom's proposal which she felt on its way to her could be indefinitely put off. Separately, there was no unusual significance to either one. But for some reason, they jumbled when her eyes gazed vacantly at the rising moon. And from the jumble came the stir that was strangely within her. Her lips trembled. The slow rhythm of her song grew agitant and restless. Rusty black and tan spotted hounds, lying in the dark corners of porches or prowling around back yards, put their noses in the air and caught its tremor. They began plaintively to yelp and howl. Chickens woke up and cackled. Intermittently, all over the countryside dogs barked and roosters crowed as if heralding a weird dawn or some ungodly awakening. The women sang lustily. Their songs were cotton-wads to stop their ears. Louisa came down into factory town and sank wearily upon the step before her home. The moon was rising towards a thick cloud-bank which soon would hide it.

> Red nigger moon. Sinner!
> Blood-burning moon. Sinner!
> Come out that fact'ry door.

2

Up from the deep dusk of a cleared spot on the edge of the forest a mellow glow arose and spread fan-wise into the low-hanging heavens. And all around the air was heavy with the scent of boiling cane. A large pile of cane-stalks lay like ribboned shadows upon the ground. A mule, harnessed to a pole, trudged lazily round and round the pivot of the grinder. Beneath a swaying oil lamp, a Negro alternately whipped out at the mule, and fed cane-stalks to the grinder. A fat boy waddled pails of fresh ground juice between the grinder and the boiling stove. Steam came from the copper boiling pan. The scent of cane came from the copper pan and drenched the forest and the hill that sloped to factory town, beneath its fragrance. It drenched the men in circle seated around the stove. Some of them chewed at the white pulp of stalks, but there was no need for them to, if all they wanted was to taste the cane. One tasted it in factory town. And from factory town one could see the soft haze thrown by the glowing stove upon the low-hanging heavens.

Old David Georgia stirred the thickening syrup with a long ladle, and ever so often drew it off. Old David Georgia tended his stove and told tales about the white folks, about moonshining and cotton picking, and about sweet nigger gals, to the men who sat there about his stove to listen to him. Tom Burwell chewed cane-stalk and laughed with the others till some one mentioned Louisa. Till some one said something about Louisa and Bob Stone, about the silk stockings she must have gotten from him. Blood ran up Tom's neck hotter than the glow that flooded from the stove. He sprang up. Glared at the men and said, "She's my gal." Will Manning laughed. Tom strode over to him. Yanked him up and knocked him to the ground. Several of Manning's friends got up to fight for him. Tom whipped out a long knife and would have cut them to shreds if they hadnt ducked into the woods. Tom had had enough. He nodded to Old David Georgia and swung down the path to factory town. Just then, the dogs started barking and the roosters began to crow. Tom felt funny. Away from the fight, away from the stove, chill got to him. He shivered. He shuddered when he saw the full moon rising towards the cloud-bank. He who didnt give a godam for the fears of old women. He forced his mind to fasten on Louisa. Bob Stone. Better not be. He turned into the street and saw Louisa sitting before her home. He went towards her, ambling, touched the brim of a marvelously shaped, spotted, felt hat, said he wanted to say something to her, and then found that he didnt know what he had to say, or if he did, that he couldnt say it. He shoved his big fists in his overalls, grinned, and started to move off.

"Youall want me, Tom?"

"Thats what us wants, sho, Louisa."

"Well, here I am—"

"An here I is, but that aint ahelpin none, all th same."

"You wanted to say something? . ."

"I did that, sho. But words is like th spots on dice: no matter how y fumbles em, there's times when they jes wont come. I dunno why. Seems like th love I feels fo yo done stole m tongue. I got it now. Whee! Louisa, honey, I oughtnt tell y, I feel I oughtnt cause yo is young an goes t church an I has had other gals, but Louisa I sho do love y. Lil gal, Ise watched y from them first days when youall sat right here befo yo door befo th well an sang sometimes in a way that like t broke m heart. Ise carried y with me into th fields, day after day, an after that, an I sho can plow when yo is there, an I can pick cotton. Yassur! Come near beatin Barlo yesterday. I sho did. Yassur! An next year if ole Stone'll trust me, I'll have a farm. My own. My bales will buy yo what y gets from white folks now. Silk stockings an purple dresses—course I dont believe what some folks been whisperin as t how y gets them things now. White folks always did do for niggers what they likes. An they jes cant help alikin yo, Louisa. Bob Stone likes y. Course he does. But not th way folks is awhisperin. Does he, hon?"

"I dont know what you mean, Tom."

"Course y dont. Ise already cut two niggers. Had t hon, t tell em so. Niggers always tryin t make somethin out a nothin. An then besides, white folks aint up t them tricks so much nowadays. Godam better not be. Leastawise not with yo. Cause I wouldnt stand f it. Nassur."

"What would you do, Tom?"

"Cut him jes like I cut a nigger."

"No, Tom—"

"I said I would an there aint no mo to it. But that aint th talk f now. Sing, honey Louisa, an while I'm listenin t y I'll be makin love."

Tom took her hand in his. Against the tough thickness of his own, hers felt soft and small. His huge body slipped down to the step beside her. The full moon sank upward into the deep purple of the cloud-bank. An old woman brought a lighted lamp and hung it on the common well whose bulky shadow squatted in the middle of the road, opposite Tom and Louisa. The old woman lifted the well-lid, took hold the chain, and began drawing up the heavy bucket. As she did so, she sang. Figures shifted, restlesslike, between lamp and window in the front rooms of the shanties. Shadows of the figures fought each other on the gray dust of the road. Figures raised the windows and joined the old woman in song. Louisa and Tom, the whole street, singing:

> Red nigger moon. Sinner!
> Blood-burning moon. Sinner!
> Come out that fact'ry door.

3

Bob Stone sauntered from his veranda out into the gloom of fir trees and magnolias. The clear white of his skin paled, and the flush of his cheeks turned purple. As if to balance this outer change, his mind became consciously a white man's. He passed the house with its huge open hearth which, in the days of slavery, was the plantation cookery. He saw Louisa bent over that hearth. He went in as a master should and took her. Direct, honest, bold. None of this sneaking that he had to go through now. The contrast was repulsive to him. His family had lost ground. Hell no, his family still owned the niggers, practically. Damned if they did, or he wouldnt have to duck around so. What would they think if they knew? His mother? His sister? He shouldnt mention them, shouldnt think of them in this connection. There in the dusk he blushed at doing so. Fellows about town were all right, but how about his friends up North? He could see them incredible, repulsed. They didnt know. The thought first made him laugh. Then, with their eyes still upon him, he began to feel embarrassed. He felt the need of explaining things to them. Explain hell. They wouldnt understand, and moreover, who ever heard of a Southerner getting on his knees to any Yankee, or anyone. No sir. He was going to see Louisa to-night, and love her. She was lovely—in her way. Nigger way. What way was that? Damned if he knew. Must know. He'd known her long enough to know. Was there something about niggers that you couldnt know? Listening to them at church didnt tell you anything. Looking at them didnt tell you anything. Talking to them didnt tell you anything—unless it was gossip, unless they wanted to talk. Of course, about farming, and licker, and craps—but those werent nigger. Nigger was something more. How much more? Something to be afraid of, more? Hell no. Who ever heard of being afraid of a nigger? Tom Burwell. Cartwell had told him that Tom went with Louisa after she reached home. No sir. No nigger had ever been with his girl. He'd like to see one try. Some position for him to be in. Him, Bob Stone, of the old Stone family, in a scrap with a nigger over a nigger girl. In the good old days. . . Ha! Those were the days. His family had lost ground. Not so much, though. Enough for him to have to cut through old Lemon's canefield by way of the woods, that he might meet her. She was worth it. Beautiful nigger gal. Why nigger? Why not, just gal? No, it was because she was nigger that he went to her. Sweet. . . The scent of boiling cane came to him. Then he saw the rich glow of the stove. He heard the voices of the men circled around it. He was about to skirt the clearing when he heard his own name mentioned. He stopped. Quivering. Leaning against a tree, he listened.

"Bad nigger. Yassur, he sho is one bad nigger when he gets started."

"Tom Burwell's been on th gang three times fo cuttin men."

"What y think he's agwine t do t Bob Stone?"

"Dunno yet. He aint found out. When he does—Baby!"

"Aint no tellin."

"Young Stone aint no quitter an I ken tell y that. Blood of th old uns in his veins."

"Thats right. He'll scrap, sho."

"Be gettin too hot f niggers round this away."

"Shut up, nigger. Y dont know what y talkin bout."

Bob Stone's ears burned as though he had been holding them over the stove. Sizzling heat welled up within him. His feet felt as if they rested on red-hot coals. They stung him to quick movement. He circled the fringe of the glowing. Not a twig cracked beneath his feet. He reached the path that led to factory town. Plunged furiously down it. Halfway along, a blindness within him veered him aside. He crashed into the bordering canebrake. Cane leaves cut his face and lips. He tasted blood. He threw himself down and dug his fingers in the ground. The earth was cool. Cane-roots took the fever from his hands. After a long while, or so it seemed to him, the thought came to him that it must be time to see Louisa. He got to his feet and walked calmly to their meeting place. No Louisa. Tom Burwell had her. Veins in his forehead bulged and distended. Saliva moistened the dried blood on his lips. He bit down on his lips. He tasted blood. Not his own blood; Tom Burwell's blood. Bob drove through the cane and out again upon the road. A hound swung down the path before him towards factory town. Bob couldnt see it. The dog loped aside to let him pass. Bob's blind rushing made him stumble over it. He fell with a thud that dazed him. The hound yelped. Answering yelps came from all over the countryside. Chickens cackled. Roosters crowed, heralding the bloodshot eyes of southern awakening. Singers in the town were silenced. They shut their windows down. Palpitant between the rooster crows, a chill hush settled upon the huddled forms of Tom and Louisa. A figure rushed from the shadow and stood before them. Tom popped to his feet.

"Whats y want?"

"I'm Bob Stone."

"Yassur—an I'm Tom Burwell. Whats y want?"

Bob lunged at him. Tom side-stepped, caught him by the shoulder, and flung him to the ground. Straddled him.

"Let me up."

"Yassur—but watch yo doins, Bob Stone."

A few dark figures, drawn by the sound of scuffle, stood about them. Bob sprang to his feet.

"Fight like a man, Tom Burwell, an I'll lick y."

Again he lunged. Tom side-stepped and flung him to the ground. Straddled him.

"Get off me, you godam nigger you."

"Yo sho has started somethin now. Get up."

Tom yanked him up and began hammering at him. Each blow sounded as if it smashed into a precious, irreplaceable soft something. Beneath them, Bob staggered back. He reached in his pocket and whipped out a knife.

"Thats my game, sho."

Blue flash, a steel blade slashed across Bob Stone's throat. He had a sweetish sick feeling. Blood began to flow. Then he felt a sharp twitch of pain. He let his knife drop. He slapped one hand against his neck. He pressed the other on top of his head as if to hold it down. He groaned. He turned, and staggered towards the crest of the hill in the direction of white town. Negroes who had seen the fight slunk into their homes and blew the lamps out. Louisa, dazed, hysterical, refused to go indoors. She slipped, crumbled, her body loosely propped against the woodwork of the well. Tom Burwell leaned against it. He seemed rooted there.

Bob reached Broad Street. White men rushed up to him. He collapsed in their arms.

"Tom Burwell. . . ."

White men like ants upon a forage rushed about. Except for the taut hum of their moving, all was silent. Shotguns, revolvers, rope, kerosene, torches. Two high-powered cars with glaring search-lights. They came together. The taut hum rose to a low roar. Then nothing could be heard but the flop of their feet in the thick dust of the road. The moving body of their silence preceded them over the crest of the hill into factory town. It flattened the Negroes beneath it. It rolled to the wall of the factory, where it stopped. Tom knew that they were coming. He couldnt move. And then he saw the search-lights of the two cars glaring down on him. A quick shock went through him. He stiffened. He started to run. A yell went up from the mob. Tom wheeled about and faced them. They poured down on him. They swarmed. A large man with dead-white face and flabby cheeks came to him and almost jabbed a gun-barrel through his guts.

"Hands behind y, nigger."

Tom's wrists were bound. The big man shoved him to the well. Burn him over it, and when the woodwork caved in, his body would drop to the bottom. Two deaths for a godam nigger. Louisa was driven back. The mob pushed in. Its pressure, its momentum was too great. Drag him to the factory. Wood and stakes already there. Tom moved in the direction indicated. But they had to drag him. They reached the great door. Too many to get in there. The mob divided and flowed around the walls to either side. The big man shoved him through the door. The mob pressed in from the sides. Taut humming. No words. A stake was sunk into the ground. Rotting floor boards piled around it. Kerosene poured on the rotting floor boards. Tom bound to the stake. His breast was bare. Nails' scratches let little lines of blood trickle down and mat into the hair. His face, his eyes were set and stony. Except for irregular breathing, one would have thought him already dead. Torches were flung onto the pile. A great flare muffled in black smoke shot upward. The mob yelled. The mob was silent. Now Tom could be seen within the flames. Only his head, erect, lean, like a blackened stone. Stench of burning flesh soaked the air. Tom's eyes popped. His head settled downward. The mob yelled. Its yell echoed against the skeleton stone walls and sounded like a hundred yells. Like a hundred mobs yelling. Its yell thudded against the thick front wall and fell back. Ghost of a yell slipped through the flames and out the great door of the factory. It fluttered like a dying thing down the single street of factory town. Louisa, upon the step before her home, did not hear it, but her eyes opened slowly. They saw the full moon glowing in the great door. The full moon, an evil thing, an omen, soft showering the homes of folks she knew. Where were they, these people? She'd sing, and perhaps they'd come out and join her. Perhaps Tom Burwell would come. At any rate, the full moon in the great door was an omen which she must sing to:

> Red nigger moon. Sinner!
> Blood-burning moon. Sinner!
> Come out that fact'ry door.

BONA AND PAUL

1

On the school gymnasium floor, young men and women are drilling. They are going to be teachers, and go out into the world . . . thud, thud . . . and give precision to the movements of sick people who all their lives have been drilling. One man is out of step. In step. The teacher glares at him. A girl in bloomers, seated on a mat in the corner because she has told the director that she is sick, sees that the footfalls of the men are rhythmical and syncopated. The dance of his blue-trousered limbs thrills her.

Bona: He is a candle that dances in a grove swung with pale balloons.

Columns of the drillers thud towards her. He is in the front row. He is in no row at all. Bona can look close at him. His red-brown face—

Bona: He is a harvest moon. He is an autumn leaf. He is a nigger. Bona! But dont all the dorm girls say so? And dont you, when you are sane, say so? Thats why I love—Oh, nonsense. You have never loved a man who didnt first love you. Besides—

Columns thud away from her. Come to a halt in line formation. Rigid. The period bell rings, and the teacher dismisses them.

A group collects around Paul. They are choosing sides for basket-ball. Girls against boys. Paul has his. He is limbering up beneath the basket. Bona runs to the girl captain and asks to be chosen. The girls fuss. The director comes to quiet them. He hears what Bona wants.

"But, Miss Hale, you were excused—"

"So I was, Mr. Boynton, but—"

"—you can play basket-ball, but you are too sick to drill."

"If you wish to put it that way."

She swings away from him to the girl captain.

"Helen, I want to play, and you must let me. This is the first time I've asked and I dont see why—"

"Thats just it, Bona. We have our team."

"Well, team or no team, I want to play and thats all there is to it."

She snatches the ball from Helen's hands, and charges down the floor.

Helen shrugs. One of the weaker girls says that she'll drop out. Helen accepts this. The team is formed. The whistle blows. The game starts. Bona, in center, is jumping against Paul. He plays with her. Out-jumps her, makes a quick pass, gets a quick return, and shoots a goal from the middle of the floor. Bona burns crimson. She fights, and tries to guard him. One of her team-mates advises her not to play so hard. Paul shoots his second goal.

Bona begins to feel a little dizzy and all in. She drives on. Almost hugs Paul to guard him. Near the basket, he attempts to shoot, and Bona lunges into his body and tries to beat his arms. His elbow, going up, gives her a sharp crack on the jaw. She whirls. He catches her. Her body stiffens. Then becomes strangely vibrant, and bursts to a swift life within her anger. He is about to give way before her hatred when a new passion flares at him and makes his stomach fall. Bona squeezes him. He suddenly feels stifled, and wonders why in hell the ring of silly gaping faces that's caked about him doesnt make way and give him air. He has a swift illusion that it is himself who has been struck. He looks at Bona. Whir. Whir. They seem to be human distortions spinning tensely in a fog. Spinning . . . dizzy . . . spinning. . . Bona jerks herself free, flushes a startling crimson, breaks through the bewildered teams, and rushes from the hall.

2

Paul is in his room of two windows.

Outside, the South-Side L track cuts them in two.

Bona is one window. One window, Paul.

Hurtling Loop-jammed L trains throw them in swift shadow.

Paul goes to his. Gray slanting roofs of houses are tinted lavender in the setting sun. Paul follows the sun, over the stock-yards where a fresh stench is just arising, across wheat lands that are still waving above their stubble, into the sun. Paul follows the sun to a pine-matted hillock in Georgia. He sees the slanting roofs of gray un-painted cabins tinted lavender. A Negress chants a lullaby beneath the mate-eyes of a southern planter. Her breasts are ample for the suckling of a song. She weans it, and sends it, curiously weaving, among lush melodies of cane and corn. Paul follows the sun into himself in Chicago.

He is at Bona's window.

With his own glow he looks through a dark pane.

Paul's room-mate comes in.

"Say, Paul, I've got a date for you. Come on. Shake a leg, will you?"

His blond hair is combed slick. His vest is snug about him.

He is like the electric light which he snaps on.

"Whatdoysay, Paul? Get a wiggle on. Come on. We havent got much time by the time we eat and dress and everything."

His bustling concentrates on the brushing of his hair.

Art: What in hell's getting into Paul of late, anyway? Christ, but he's getting moony. Its his blood. Dark blood: moony. Doesnt get anywhere unless you boost it. You've got to keep it going—

"Say, Paul!"

—or it'll go to sleep on you. Dark blood; nigger? Thats what those jealous she-hens say. Not Bona though, or she . . . from the South . . . wouldnt want me to fix a date for him and her. Hell of a thing, that Paul's dark: youve got to always be answering questions.

"Say, Paul, for Christ's sake leave that window, cant you?"

"Whats it, Art?"

"Hell, I've told you about fifty times. Got a date for you. Come on."

"With who?"

Art: He didnt use to ask; now he does. Getting up in the air. Getting funny.

"Heres your hat. Want a smoke? Paul! Here. I've got a match. Now come on and I'll tell you all about it on the way to supper."

Paul: He's going to Life this time. No doubt of that. Quit your kidding. Some day, dear Art, I'm going to kick the living slats out of you, and you wont know what I've done it for. And your slats will bring forth Life . . . beautiful woman. . .

Pure Food Restaurant.

"Bring me some soup with a lot of crackers, understand? And then a roast-beef dinner. Same for you, eh, Paul? Now as I was saying, you've got a swell chance with her. And she's game. Best proof: she dont give a damn what the dorm girls say about you and her in the gym, or about the funny looks that Boynton gives her, or about what they say about, well, hell, you know, Paul. And say, Paul, she's a sweetheart. Tall, not puffy and pretty, more serious and deep—the kind you like these days. And they say she's got a car. And say, she's on fire. But you know all about that. She got Helen to fix it up with me. The four of us—remember the last party? Crimson Gardens! Boy!"

Paul's eyes take on a light that Art can settle in.

3

Art has on his patent-leather pumps and fancy vest. A loose fall coat is swung across his arm. His face has been massaged, and over a close shave, powdered. It is a healthy pink the blue of evening tints a purple pallor. Art is happy and confident in the good looks that his mirror gave him. Bubbling over with a joy he must spend now if the night is to contain it all. His bubbles, too, are curiously tinted purple as Paul watches them. Paul, contrary to what he had thought he would be like, is cool like the dusk, and like the dusk, detached. His dark face is a floating shade in evening's shadow. He sees Art, curiously. Art is a purple fluid, carbon-charged, that effervesces beside him. He loves Art. But is it not queer, this pale purple facsimile of a red-blooded Norwegian friend of his? Perhaps for some reason, white skins are not supposed to live at night. Surely, enough nights would transform them fantastically, or kill them. And their red passion? Night paled that too, and made it moony. Moony. Thats what Art thought of him. Bona didnt, even in the daytime. Bona, would she be pale? Impossible. Not that red glow. But the conviction did not set his emotion flowing.

"Come right in, wont you? The young ladies will be right down. Oh, Mr. Carlstrom, do play something for us while you are waiting. We just love to listen to your music. You play so well."

Houses, and dorm sitting-rooms are places where white faces seclude themselves at night. There is a reason. . .

Art sat on the piano and simply tore it down. Jazz. The picture of Our Poets hung perilously.

Paul: I've got to get the kid to play that stuff for me in the day-time. Might be different. More himself. More nigger. Different? There is. Curious, though.

The girls come in. Art stops playing, and almost immediately takes up a petty quarrel, where he had last left it, with Helen.

Bona, black-hair curled staccato, sharply contrasting with Helen's puffy yellow, holds Paul's hand. She squeezes it. Her own emotion supplements the return pressure. And then, for no tangible reason, her spirits drop. Without them, she is nervous, and slightly afraid.

She resents this. Paul's eyes are critical. She resents Paul. She flares at him. She flares to poise and security.

"Shall we be on our way?"

"Yes, Bona, certainly."

The Boulevard is sleek in asphalt, and, with arc-lights and limousines, aglow. Dry leaves scamper behind the whir of cars. The scent of exploded gasoline that mingles with them is faintly sweet. Mellow stone mansions overshadow clapboard homes which now resemble Negro shanties in some southern alley. Bona and Paul, and Art and Helen, move along an island-like, far-stretching strip of leaf-soft ground. Above them, worlds of shadow-planes and solids, silently moving. As if on one of these, Paul looks down on Bona. No doubt of it: her face is pale. She is talking. Her words have no feel to them. One sees them. They are pink petals that fall upon velvet cloth. Bona is soft, and pale, and beautiful.

"Paul, tell me something about yourself—or would you rather wait?"

"I'll tell you anything you'd like to know."

"Not what I want to know, Paul; what you want to tell me."

"You have the beauty of a gem fathoms under sea."

"I feel that, but I dont want to be. I want to be near you. Perhaps I will be if I tell you something. Paul, I love you."

The sea casts up its jewel into his hands, and burns them furiously. To tuck her arm under his and hold her hand will ease the burn.

"What can I say to you, brave dear woman—I cant talk love. Love is a dry grain in my mouth unless it is wet with kisses."

"You would dare? right here on the Boulevard? before Arthur and Helen?"

"Before myself? I dare."

"Here then."

Bona, in the slim shadow of a tree trunk, pulls Paul to her. Suddenly she stiffens. Stops.

"But you have not said you love me."

"I cant—yet—Bona."

"Ach, you never will. Youre cold. Cold."

Bona: Colored; cold. Wrong somewhere.

She hurries and catches up with Art and Helen.

4

Crimson Gardens. Hurrah! So one feels. People . . . University of Chicago students, members of the stock exchange, a large Negro in crimson uniform who guards the door . . . had watched them enter. Had leaned towards each other over ash-smeared tablecloths and highballs and whispered: What is he, a Spaniard, an Indian, an Italian, a Mexican, a Hindu, or a Japanese? Art had at first fidgeted under their stares . . . what are *you* looking at, you godam pack of owl-eyed hyenas? . . . but soon settled into his fuss with Helen, and forgot them. A strange thing happened to Paul. Suddenly he knew that he was apart from the people around him. Apart from the pain which they had unconsciously caused. Suddenly he knew that people saw, not attractiveness in his dark skin, but difference. Their stares, giving him to himself, filled something long empty within him, and were like green blades sprouting in his consciousness. There was fullness, and strength and peace about it all. He saw himself, cloudy, but real. He saw the faces of the people at the tables round him. White lights, or as now, the pink lights of the Crimson Gardens gave a glow and immediacy to white faces. The pleasure of it, equal to that of love or dream, of seeing this. Art and Bona and Helen? He'd look. They were wonderfully flushed and beautiful. Not for himself; because they were. Distantly. Who were they, anyway? God, if he knew them. He'd come in with them. Of that he was sure. Come where? Into life? Yes. No. Into the Crimson Gardens. A part of life. A carbon bubble. Would it look purple if he went out into the night and looked at it? His sudden starting to rise almost upset the table.

"What in hell—pardon—whats the matter, Paul?"

"I forgot my cigarettes—"

"Youre smoking one."

"So I am. Pardon me."

The waiter straightens them out. Takes their order.

Art: What in hell's eating Paul? Moony aint the word for it. From bad to worse. And those godam people staring so. Paul's a queer fish. Doesnt seem to mind. . . He's my pal, let me tell you, you horn-rimmed owl-eyed hyena at that table, and a lot better than you who-ever you are. . . Queer about him. I could stick up for him if he'd only come out, one way or the other, and tell a feller. Besides, a room-mate has a right to know. Thinks I wont understand. Said so. He's got a swell head when it comes to brains, all right. God, he's a good straight feller, though. Only, moony. Nut. Nuttish. Nuttery. Nutmeg. . . "What'd you say, Helen?"

"I was talking to Bona, thank you."

"Well, its nothing to get spiffy about."

"What? Oh, of course not. Please lets dont start some silly argument all over again."

"Well."

"Well."

"Now thats enough. Say, waiter, whats the matter with our order? Make it snappy, will you?"

Crimson Gardens. Hurrah! So one feels. The drinks come. Four highballs. Art passes cigarettes. A girl dressed like a bare-back rider in flaming pink, makes her way through tables to the dance floor. All lights are dimmed till they seem a lush afterglow of crimson. Spotlights the girl. She sings. "Liza, Little Liza Jane."

Paul is rosy before his window.

He moves, slightly, towards Bona.

With his own glow, he seeks to penetrate a dark pane.

Paul: From the South. What does that mean, precisely, except that you'll love or hate a nigger? Thats a lot. What does it mean except that in Chicago you'll have the courage to neither love or hate. A priori. But it would seem that you have. Queer words, arent these, for a man who wears blue pants on a gym floor in the daytime. Well, never matter. You matter. I'd like to know you whom I look at. Know, not love. Not that knowing is a greater pleasure; but that I have just found the joy of it. You came just a month too late. Even this afternoon I dreamed. To-night, along the Boulevard, you found me cold. Paul Johnson, cold! Thats a good one, eh, Art, you fine old stupid fellow, you! But I feel good! The color and the music and the song. . . A Negress chants a lullaby beneath the mate-eyes of a southern planter. O song! . . And those flushed faces. Eager brilliant eyes. Hard to imagine them as unawakened. Your own. Oh, they're awake all right. "And you know it too, dont you Bona?"

"What, Paul?"

"The truth of what I was thinking."

"I'd like to know I know—something of you."

"You will—before the evening's over. I promise it."

Crimson Gardens. Hurrah! So one feels. The bare-back rider balances agilely on the applause which is the tail of her song. Orchestral instruments warm up for jazz. The flute is a cat that ripples its fur against the deep-purring saxophone. The drum throws sticks. The cat jumps on the piano keyboard. Hi diddle, hi diddle, the cat and the fiddle. Crimson Gardens . . hurrah! . . jumps over the moon. Crimson Gardens! Helen . . . O Eliza . . . rabbit-eyes sparkling, plays up to, and tries to placate what she considers to be Paul's contempt. She always does that . . . Little Liza Jane . . . Once home, she burns with the thought of what she's done. She says all manner of snidy things about him, and swears that she'll never go out again when he is along. She tries to get Art to break with him, saying, that if Paul, whom the whole dormitory calls a nigger, is more to him than she is, well, she's through. She does not break with Art. She goes out as often as she can with Art and Paul. She explains this to herself by a piece of information which a friend of hers had given her: men like him (Paul) can fascinate. One is not responsible for fascination. Not one girl had really loved Paul; he fascinated them. Bona didn't; only thought she did. Time would tell. And of course, *she* didn't. Liza. . . She plays up to, and tries to placate, Paul.

"Paul is so deep these days, and I'm so glad he's found some one to interest him."

"I dont believe I do."

The thought escapes from Bona just a moment before her anger at having said it.

Bona: You little puffy cat, I do. I do!

Dont I, Paul? her eyes ask.

Her answer is a crash of jazz from the palm-hidden orchestra. Crimson Gardens is a body whose blood flows to a clot upon the dance floor. Art and Helen clot. Soon, Bona and Paul. Paul finds her a little stiff, and his mind, wandering to Helen (silly little kid who wants every highball spoon her hands touch, for a souvenir), supple, perfect little dancer, wishes for the next dance when he and Art will exchange.

Bona knows that she must win him to herself.

"Since when have men like you grown cold?"

"The first philosopher."

"I thought you were a poet—or a gym director."

"Hence, your failure to make love."

Bona's eyes flare. Water. Grow red about the rims. She would like to tear away from him and dash across the clotted floor.

"What do you mean?"

"Mental concepts rule you. If they were flush with mine—good. I dont believe they are."

"How do you know, Mr. Philosopher?"

"Mostly a priori."

"You talk well for a gym director."

"And you—"

"I hate you. Ou!"

She presses away. Paul, conscious of the convention in it, pulls her to him. Her body close. Her head still strains away. He nearly crushes her. She tries to pinch him. Then sees people staring, and lets her arms fall. Their eyes meet. Both, contemptuous. The dance takes blood from their minds and packs it, tingling, in the torsos of their swaying bodies. Passionate blood leaps back into their eyes. They are a dizzy blood clot on a gyrating floor. They know that the pink-faced people have no part in what they feel. Their instinct leads them away from Art and Helen, and towards the big uniformed black man who opens and closes the gilded exit door. The cloak-room girl is tolerant of their impatience over such trivial things as wraps. And slightly superior. As the black man swings the door for them, his eyes are knowing. Too many couples have passed out, flushed and fidgety, for him not to know. The chill air is a shock to Paul. A strange thing happens. He sees the Gardens purple, as if he were way off. And a spot is in the purple. The spot comes furiously towards him. Face of the black man. It leers. It smiles sweetly like a child's. Paul leaves Bona and darts back so quickly that he doesnt give the door-man a chance to open. He swings in. Stops. Before the huge bulk of the Negro.

"Youre wrong."

"Yassur."

"Brother, youre wrong.

"I came back to tell you, to shake your hand, and tell you that you are wrong. That something beautiful is going to happen. That the Gardens are purple like a bed of roses would be at dusk. That I came into the Gardens, into life in the Gardens with one whom I did not know. That I danced with her, and did not know her. That I felt passion, contempt and passion for her whom I did not know. That I thought of her. That my thoughts were matches thrown into a dark window. And all the while the Gardens were purple like a bed of roses would be at dusk. I came back to tell you, brother, that white faces are petals of roses. That dark faces are petals of dusk. That I am going out and gather petals. That I am going out and know her whom I brought here with me to these Gardens which are purple like a bed of roses would be at dusk."

Paul and the black man shook hands.

When he reached the spot where they had been standing, Bona was gone.

KABNIS

⌞ ── ⌟

1

Ralph Kabnis, propped in his bed, tries to read. To read himself to sleep. An oil lamp on a chair near his elbow burns unsteadily. The cabin room is spaced fantastically about it. Whitewashed hearth and chimney, black with sooty saw-teeth. Ceiling, patterned by the fringed globe of the lamp. The walls, unpainted, are seasoned a rosin yellow. And cracks between the boards are black. These cracks are the lips the night winds use for whispering. Night winds in Georgia are vagrant poets, whispering. Kabnis, against his will, lets his book slip down, and listens to them. The warm whiteness of his bed, the lamp-light, do not protect him from the weird chill of their song:

> White-man's land.
> Niggers, sing.
> Burn, bear black children
> Till poor rivers bring
> Rest, and sweet glory
> In Camp Ground.

Kabnis' thin hair is streaked on the pillow. His hand strokes the slim silk of his mustache. His thumb, pressed under his chin, seems to be trying to give squareness and projection to it. Brown eyes stare from a lemon face. Moisture gathers beneath his arm-pits. He slides down beneath the cover, seeking release.

Kabnis: Near me. Now. Whoever you are, my warm glowing sweetheart, do not think that the face that rests beside you is the real Kabnis. Ralph Kabnis is a dream. And dreams are faces with large eyes and weak chins and broad brows that get smashed by the fists of square faces. The body of the world is bull-necked. A dream is a soft face that fits uncertainly upon it. . . . God, if I could develop that in words. Give what I know a bull-neck and a heaving body, all would go well with me, wouldnt it, sweetheart? If I could feel that I came to the South to face it. If I, the dream (not what is weak and afraid in me) could become the face of the South. How my lips would sing for it, my songs being the lips of its soul. Soul. Soul hell. There aint no such thing. What in hell was that?

A rat had run across the thin boards of the ceiling. Kabnis thrusts his head out from the covers. Through the cracks, a powdery faded red dust sprays down on him. Dust of slavefields, dried, scattered. . . No use to read. Christ, if he only could drink himself to sleep. Something as sure as fate was going to happen. He couldnt stand this thing much longer. A hen, perched on a shelf in the adjoining room begins to tread. Her nails scrape the soft wood. Her feathers ruffle.

"Get out of that, you egg-laying bitch."

Kabnis hurls a slipper against the wall. The hen flies from her perch and cackles as if a skunk were after her.

"Now cut out that racket or I'll wring your neck for you."

Answering cackles arise in the chicken yard.

"Why in Christ's hell cant you leave me alone? Damn it, I wish your cackle would choke you. Choke every mother's son of them in this God-forsaken hole. Go away. By God I'll wring your neck for you if you dont. Hell of a mess I've got in: even the poultry is hostile. Go way. Go way. By God, I'll . . ."

Kabnis jumps from his bed. His eyes are wild. He makes for the door. Bursts through it. The hen, driving blindly at the window-pane, screams. Then flies and flops around trying to elude him. Kabnis catches her.

"Got you now, you she-bitch."

With his fingers about her neck, he thrusts open the outside door and steps out into the serene loveliness of Georgian autumn moonlight. Some distance off, down in the valley, a band of pine-smoke, silvered gauze, drifts steadily. The half-moon is a white child that sleeps upon the tree-tops of the forest. White winds croon its sleep-song:

> rock a-by baby . . .
> Black mother sways, holding a white child on her bosom.
> when the bough bends . . .
> Her breath hums through pine-cones.
> cradle will fall. . .
> Teat moon-children at your breasts,
> down will come baby. . .
> Black mother.

Kabnis whirls the chicken by its neck, and throws the head away. Picks up the hopping body, warm, sticky, and hides it in a clump of bushes. He wipes blood from his hands onto the coarse scant grass.

Kabnis: Thats done. Old Chromo in the big house there will wonder whats become of her pet hen. Well, it'll teach her a lesson: not to make a hen-coop of my quarters. Quarters. Hell of a fine quarters, I've got. Five years ago; look at me now. Earth's child. The earth my mother. God is a profligate red-nosed man about town. Bastardy; me. A bastard son has got a right to curse his maker. God. . .

Kabnis is about to shake his fists heavenward. He looks up, and the night's beauty strikes him dumb. He falls to his knees. Sharp stones cut through his thin pajamas. The shock sends a shiver over him. He quivers. Tears mist his eyes. He writhes.

"God Almighty, dear God, dear Jesus, do not torture me with beauty. Take it away. Give me an ugly world. Ha, ugly. Stinking like unwashed niggers. Dear Jesus, do not chain me to myself and set these hills and valleys, heaving with folk-songs, so close to me that I cannot reach them. There is a radiant beauty in the night that touches and . . . tortures me. Ugh. Hell. Get up, you damn fool. Look around. Whats beautiful there? Hog pens and chicken yards. Dirty red mud. Stinking outhouse. Whats beauty anyway but ugliness if it hurts you? God, he doesnt exist, but nevertheless He is ugly. Hence, what comes from Him is ugly. Lynchers and business men, and that cockroach Hanby, especially. How come that he gets to be principal of a school? Of the school I'm driven to teach in? God's handiwork, doubtless. God and Hanby, they belong together. Two godam moral-spouters. Oh, no, I wont let that emotion come up in me. Stay down. Stay down, I tell you. O Jesus, Thou art beautiful. . . Come, Ralph, pull yourself together. Curses and adoration dont come from what is sane. This loneliness, dumbness, awful, intangible oppression is enough to drive a man insane. Miles from nowhere. A speck on a Georgia hillside. Jesus, can you imagine it—an atom of dust in agony on a hillside? Thats a spectacle for you. Come, Ralph, old man, pull yourself together."

Kabnis has stiffened. He is conscious now of the night wind, and of how it chills him. He rises. He totters as a man would who for the first time uses artificial limbs. As a completely artificial man would. The large frame house, squatting on brick pillars, where the principal of the school, his wife, and the boarding girls sleep, seems a curious shadow of his mind. He tries, but cannot convince himself of its reality. His gaze drifts down into the vale, across the swamp, up over the solid dusk bank of pines, and rests, bewildered-like, on the courthouse tower. It is dull silver in the moonlight. White child that sleeps upon the top of pines. Kabnis' mind clears. He sees himself yanked beneath that tower. He sees white minds, with indolent assumption, juggle justice and a nigger. . . Somewhere, far off in the straight line of his sight, is Augusta. Christ, how cut off from everything he is. And hours, hours north, why not say a lifetime north? Washington sleeps. Its still, peaceful streets, how desirable they are. Its people whom he had always half-way despised. New York? Impossible. It was a fiction. He had dreamed it. An impotent nostalgia grips him. It becomes intolerable. He forces himself to narrow to a cabin silhouetted on a knoll about a mile away. Peace. Negroes within it are content. They farm. They sing. They love. They sleep. Kabnis wonders if perhaps they can feel him. If perhaps he gives them bad dreams. Things are so immediate in Georgia.

Thinking that now he can go to sleep, he re-enters his room. He builds a fire in the open hearth. The room dances to the tongues of flames, and sings to the crackling and spurting of the logs. Wind comes up between the floor boards, through the black cracks of the walls.

Kabnis: Cant sleep. Light a cigarette. If that old bastard comes over here and smells smoke, I'm done for. Hell of a note, cant even smoke. The stillness of it: where they burn and hang men, you cant smoke. Cant take a swig of licker. What do they think this is, anyway, some sort of temperance school? How did I ever land in such a hole? Ugh. One might just as well be in his grave. Still as a grave. Jesus, how still everything is. Does the world know how still it is? People make noise. They are afraid of silence. Of what lives, and God, of what dies in silence. There must be many dead things moving in silence. They come here to touch me. I swear I feel their fingers. . . Come, Ralph, pull yourself together. What in hell was that? Only the rustle of leaves, I guess. You know, Ralph, old man, it wouldnt surprise me at all to see a ghost. People dont think there are such things. They rationalize their fear, and call their cowardice science. Fine bunch, they are. Damit, that was a noise. And not the wind either. A chicken maybe. Hell, chickens dont wander around this time of night. What in hell is it?

A scraping sound, like a piece of wood dragging over the ground, is coming near.

"Ha, ha. The ghosts down this way havent got any chains to rattle, so they drag trees along with them. Thats a good one. But no joke, something is outside this house, as sure as hell. Whatever it is, it can get a good look at me and I cant see it. Jesus Christ!"

Kabnis pours water on the flames and blows his lamp out. He picks up a poker and stealthily approaches the outside door. Swings it open, and lurches into the night. A calf, carrying a yoke of wood, bolts away from him and scampers down the road.

"Well, I'm damned. This godam place is sure getting the best of me. Come, Ralph, old man, pull yourself together. Nights cant last forever. Thank God for that. Its Sunday already. First time in my life I've ever wanted Sunday to come. Hell of a day. And down here there's no such thing as ducking church. Well, I'll see Halsey and Layman, and get a good square meal. Thats something. And Halsey's a damn good feller. Cant talk to him, though. Who in Christ's world can I talk to? A hen. God. Myself. . . I'm going bats, no doubt of that. Come now, Ralph, go in and make yourself go to sleep. Come now . . . in the door . . . thats right. Put the poker down. There. All right. Slip under the sheets. Close your eyes. Think nothing . . . a long time . . . nothing, nothing. Dont even think nothing. Blank. Not even blank. Count. No, mustnt count. Nothing . . . blank . . . nothing . . . blank . . . space without stars in it. No, nothing . . . nothing. . ."

Kabnis sleeps. The winds, like soft-voiced vagrant poets sing:

> White-man's land.
> Niggers, sing.
> Burn, bear black children
> Till poor rivers bring
> Rest, and sweet glory
> In Camp Ground.

2

The parlor of Fred Halsey's home. There is a seediness about it. It seems as though the fittings have given a frugal service to at least seven generations of middle-class shop-owners. An open grate burns cheerily in contrast to the gray cold changed autumn weather. An old-fashioned mantelpiece supports a family clock (not running), a figure or two in imitation bronze, and two small group pictures. Directly above it, in a heavy oak frame, the portrait of a bearded man. Black hair, thick and curly, intensifies the pallor of the high forehead. The eyes are daring. The nose, sharp and regular. The poise suggests a tendency to adventure checked by the necessities of absolute command. The portrait is that of an English gentleman who has retained much of his culture, in that money has enabled him to escape being drawn through a land-grubbing pioneer life. His nature and features, modified by marriage and circumstances, have been transmitted to his great-grandson, Fred. To the left of this picture, spaced on the wall, is a smaller portrait of the great-grandmother. That here there is a Negro strain, no one would doubt. But it is difficult to say in precisely what feature it lies. On close inspection, her mouth is seen to be wistfully twisted. The expression of her face seems to shift before one's gaze—now ugly, repulsive; now sad, and somehow beautiful in its pain. A tin wood-box rests on the floor below. To the right of the great-grandfather's portrait hangs a family group: the father, mother, two brothers, and one sister of Fred. It includes himself some thirty years ago when his face was an olive white, and his hair luxuriant and dark and wavy. The father is a rich brown. The mother, practically white. Of the children, the girl, quite young, is like Fred; the two brothers, darker. The walls of the room are plastered and painted green. An old upright piano is tucked into the corner near the window. The window looks out on a forlorn, box-like, whitewashed frame church. Negroes are gathering, on foot, driving questionable gray and brown mules, and in an occasional Ford, for afternoon service. Beyond, Georgia hills roll off into the distance, their dreary aspect heightened by the gray spots of unpainted one- and two-room shanties. Clumps of pine trees here and there are the dark points the whole landscape is approaching. The church bell tolls. Above its squat tower, a great spiral of buzzards reaches far into the heavens. An ironic comment upon the path that leads into the Christian land. . . Three rocking chairs are grouped around the grate. Sunday papers scattered on the floor indicate a recent usage. Halsey, a well-built, stocky fellow, hair cropped close, enters the room. His Sunday clothes smell of wood and glue, for it is his habit to potter around his wagon-shop even on the Lord's day. He is followed by Professor Layman, tall, heavy, loose-jointed Georgia Negro, by turns teacher and preacher, who has traveled in almost every nook and corner of the state and hence knows more than would be good for anyone other than a silent man. Kabnis, trying to force through a gathering heaviness, trails in behind them. They slip into chairs before the fire.

Layman: Sholy fine, Mr. Halsey, sholy fine. This town's right good at feedin folks, better'n most towns in th state, even for preachers, but I ken say this beats um all. Yassur. Now aint that right, Professor Kabnis?

Kabnis: Yes sir, this beats them all, all right—best I've had, and thats a fact, though my comparison doesnt carry far, y'know.

Layman: Hows that, Professor?

Kabnis: Well, this is my first time out—

Layman: For a fact. Aint seed you round so much. Whats th trouble? Dont like our folks down this away?

Halsey: Aint that, Layman. He aint like most northern niggers that way. Aint a thing stuck-up about him. He likes us, you an me, maybe all—its that red mud over yonder—gets stuck in it an cant get out. (Laughs.) An then he loves th fire so, warm as its been. Coldest Yankee I've ever seen. But I'm goin t get him out now in a jiffy, eh, Kabnis?

Kabnis: Sure, I should say so, sure. Dont think its because I dont like folks down this way. Just the opposite, in fact. Theres more hospitality and everything. Its diff—that is, theres lots of northern exaggeration about the South. Its not half the terror they picture it. Things are not half bad, as one could easily figure out for himself without ever crossing the Mason and Dixie line: all these people wouldnt stay down here, especially the rich, the ones that could easily leave, if conditions were so mighty bad. And then too, sometime back, my family were southerners y'know. From Georgia, in fact—

Layman: Nothin t feel proud about, Professor. Neither your folks nor mine.

Halsey (in a mock religious tone): Amen t that, brother Layman. Amen (turning to Kabnis, half playful, yet somehow dead in earnest). An Mr. Kabnis, kindly remember youre in th land of cotton—hell of a land. Th white folks get th boll; th niggers get th stalk. An dont you dare touch th boll, or even look at it. They'll swing y sho. (Laughs.)

Kabnis: But they wouldnt touch a gentleman—fellows, men like us three here—

Layman: Nigger's a nigger down this away, Professor. An only two dividins: good an bad. An even they aint permanent categories. They sometimes mixes um up when it comes t lynchin. I've seen um do it.

Halsey: Dont let th fear int y, though, Kabnis. This county's a good un. Aint been a stringin up I can remember. (Laughs.)

Layman: This is a good town an a good county. But theres some that makes up fer it.

Kabnis: Things are better now though since that stir about those peonage cases, arent they?

Layman: Ever hear tell of a single shot killin moren one rabbit, Professor?

Kabnis: No, of course not, that is, but then—

Halsey: Now I know you werent born yesterday, sprung up so rapid like you aint heard of th brick thrown in th hornets' nest. (Laughs.)

Kabnis: Hardly, hardly, I know—

Halsey: Course y do. (To Layman) See, northern niggers aint as dumb as they make out t be.

Kabnis (overlooking the remark): Just stirs them up to sting.

Halsey: T perfection. An put just like a professor should put it.

Kabnis: Thats what actually did happen?

Layman: Well, if it aint sos only because th stingers already movin jes as fast as they ken go. An been goin ever since I ken remember, an then some mo. Though I dont usually make mention of it.

Halsey: Damn sight better not. Say, Layman, you come from where theyre always swarmin, dont y?

Layman: Yassur. I do that, sho. Dont want t mention it, but its a fact. I've seed th time when there werent no use t even stretch out flat upon th ground. Seen um shoot an cut a man t pieces who had died th night befo. Yassur. An they didnt stop when they found out he was dead—jes went on ahackin at him anyway.

Kabnis: What did you do? What did you say to them, Professor?

Layman: Thems th things you neither does a thing or talks about if y want t stay around this away, Professor.

Halsey: Listen t what he's tellin y, Kabnis. May come in handy some day.

Kabnis: Cant something be done? But of course not. This preacher-ridden race. Pray and shout. Theyre in the preacher's hands. Thats what it is. And the preacher's hands are in the white man's pockets.

Halsey: Present company always excepted.

Kabnis: The Professor knows I wasnt referring to him.

Layman: Preacher's a preacher anywheres you turn. No use exceptin.

Kabnis: Well, of course, if you look at it that way. I didnt mean— But cant something be done?

Layman: Sho. Yassur. An done first rate an well. Jes like Sam Raymon done it.

Kabnis: Hows that? What did he do?

Layman: Th white folks (reckon I oughtnt tell it) had jes knocked two others like you kill a cow—brained um with an ax, when they caught Sam Raymon by a stream. They was about t do fer him when he up and says, "White folks, I gotter die, I knows that. But wont y let me die in my own way?" Some was fer gettin after him, but th boss held um back and says, "Jes so longs th nigger dies—" An Sam fell down ont his knees an prayed, "O Lord, Ise comin to y," and he up an jumps int th stream.

Singing from the church becomes audible. Above it, rising and falling in a plaintive moan, a woman's voice swells to shouting. Kabnis hears it. His face gives way to an expression of mingled fear, contempt, and pity. Layman takes no notice of it. Halsey grins at Kabnis. He feels like having a little sport with him.

Halsey: Lets go t church, eh, Kabnis?

Kabnis (seeking control): All right—no sir, not by a damn sight. Once a days enough for me. Christ, but that stuff gets to me. Meaning no reflection on you, Professor.

Halsey: Course not. Say, Kabnis, noticed y this morning. What'd y get up for an go out?

Kabnis: Couldnt stand the shouting, and thats a fact. We dont have that sort of thing up North. We do, but, that is, some one should see to it that they are stopped or put out when they get so bad the preacher has to stop his sermon for them.

Halsey: Is that th way youall sit on sisters up North?

Kabnis: In the church I used to go to no one ever shouted—

Halsey: Lungs weak?

Kabnis: Hardly, that is—

Halsey: Yankees are right up t th minute in tellin folk how t turn a trick. They always were good at talkin.

Kabnis: Well, anyway, they should be stopped.

Layman: Thats right. Thats true. An its th worst ones in th community that comes int th church t shout. I've sort a made a study of it. You take a man what drinks, th biggest licker-head around will come int th church an yell th loudest. An th sister whats done wrong, an is always doin wrong, will sit down in th Amen corner an swing her arms an shout her head off. Seems as if they cant control themselves out in th world; they cant control themselves in church. Now dont that sound logical, Professor?

Halsey: Reckon its as good as any. But I heard that queer cuss over yonder—y know him, dont y, Kabnis? Well, y ought t. He had a run-in with your boss th other day—same as you'll have if you dont walk th chalk-line. An th quicker th better. I hate that Hanby. Ornery bastard. I'll mash his mouth in one of these days. Well, as I was sayin, that feller, Lewis's name, I heard him sayin somethin about a stream whats dammed has got t cut loose somewheres. An that sounds good. I know th feelin myself. He strikes me as knowin a bucketful bout most things, that feller does. Seems like he doesnt want t talk, an does, sometimes, like Layman here. Damn queer feller, him.

Layman: Cant make heads or tails of him, an I've seen lots o queer possums in my day. Everybody's wonderin about him. White folks too. He'll have t leave here soon, thats sho. Always askin questions. An I aint seed his lips move once. Pokin round an notin somethin. Noted what I said th other day, an that werent fer notin down.

Kabnis: What was that?

Layman: Oh, a lynchin that took place bout a year ago. Th worst I know of round these parts.

Halsey: Bill Burnam?

Layman: Na. Mame Lamkins.

Halsey grunts, but says nothing.

The preacher's voice rolls from the church in an insistent chanting monotone. At regular intervals it rises to a crescendo note. The sister begins to shout. Her voice, high-pitched and hysterical, is almost perfectly attuned to the nervous key of Kabnis. Halsey notices his distress, and is amused by it. Layman's face is expressionless. Kabnis wants to hear the story of Mame Lamkins. He does not want to hear it. It can be no worse than the shouting.

Kabnis (his chair rocking faster): What about Mame Lamkins?

Halsey: Tell him, Layman.

The preacher momentarily stops. The choir, together with the entire congregation, sings an old spiritual. The music seems to quiet the shouter. Her heavy breathing has the sound of evening winds that blow through pinecones. Layman's voice is uniformly low and soothing. A canebrake, murmuring the tale to its neighbor-road would be more passionate.

Layman: White folks know that niggers talk, an they dont mind jes so long as nothing comes of it, so here goes. She was in th family-way, Mame Lamkins was. They killed her in th street, an some white man seein th risin in her stomach as she lay there soppy in her blood like any cow, took an ripped her belly open, an th kid fell out. It was living; but a nigger baby aint supposed t live. So he jabbed his knife in it an stuck it t a tree. An then they all went away.

Kabnis: Christ no! What had she done?

Layman: Tried t hide her husband when they was after him.

A shriek pierces the room. The bronze pieces on the mantel hum. The sister cries frantically: "Jesus, Jesus, I've found Jesus. O Lord, glory t God, one mo sinner is acomin home." At the height of this, a stone, wrapped round with paper, crashes through the window. Kabnis springs to his feet, terror-stricken. Layman is worried. Halsey picks up the stone. Takes off the wrapper, smooths it out, and reads: "You northern nigger, its time fer y t leave. Git along now." Kabnis knows that the command is meant for him. Fear squeezes him. Caves him in. As a violent external pressure would. Fear flows inside him. It fills him up. He bloats. He saves himself from bursting by dashing wildly from the room. Halsey and Layman stare stupidly at each other. The stone, the crumpled paper are things, huge things that weight them. Their thoughts are vaguely concerned with the texture of the stone, with the color of the paper. Then they remember the words, and begin to shift them about in sentences. Layman even construes them grammatically. Suddenly the sense of them comes back to Halsey. He grips Layman by the arm and they both follow after Kabnis.

A false dusk has come early. The countryside is ashen, chill. Cabins and roads and canebrakes whisper. The church choir, dipping into a long silence, sings:

> My Lord, what a mourning,
> My Lord, what a mourning,
> My Lord, what a mourning,
> When the stars begin to fall.

Softly luminous over the hills and valleys, the faint spray of a scattered star. . .

3

A splotchy figure drives forward along the cane- and corn-stalk hemmed-in road. A scarecrow replica of Kabnis, awkwardly animate. Fantastically plastered with red Georgia mud. It skirts the big house whose windows shine like mellow lanterns in the dusk. Its shoulder jogs against a sweet-gum tree. The figure caroms off against the cabin door, and lunges in. It slams the door as if to prevent some one entering after it.

"God Almighty, theyre here. After me. On me. All along the road I saw their eyes flaring from the cane. Hounds. Shouts. What in God's name did I run here for? A mud-hole trap. I stumbled on a rope. O God, a rope. Their clammy hands were like the love of death playing up and down my spine. Trying to trip my legs. To trip my spine. Up and down my spine. My spine. . . My legs. . . Why in hell didnt they catch me?"

Kabnis wheels around, half defiant, half numbed with a more immediate fear.

"Wanted to trap me here. Get out o there. I see you."

He grabs a broom from beside the chimney and violently pokes it under the bed. The broom strikes a tin wash-tub. The noise bewilders. He recovers.

"Not there. In the closet."

He throws the broom aside and grips the poker. Starts towards the closet door, towards somewhere in the perfect blackness behind the chimney.

"I'll brain you."

He stops short. The barks of hounds, evidently in pursuit, reach him. A voice, liquid in distance, yells, "Hi! Hi!"

"O God, theyre after me. Holy Father, Mother of Christ—hell, this aint no time for prayer—"

Voices, just outside the door:

"Reckon he's here."

"Dont see no light though."

The door is flung open.

Kabnis: Get back or I'll kill you.

He braces himself, brandishing the poker.

Halsey (coming in): Aint as bad as all that. Put that thing down.

Layman: Its only us, Professor. Nobody else after y.

Kabnis: Halsey. Layman. Close that door. Dont light that light. For godsake get away from there.

Halsey: Nobody's after y, Kabnis, I'm tellin y. Put that thing down an get yourself together.

Kabnis: I tell you they are. I saw them. I heard the hounds.

Halsey: These aint th days of hounds an Uncle Tom's Cabin, feller. White folks aint in fer all them theatrics these days. Theys more direct than that. If what they wanted was t get y, theyd have just marched right in an took y where y sat. Somebodys down by th branch chasin rabbits an atreein possums.

A shot is heard.

Halsey: Got him, I reckon. Saw Tom goin out with his gun. Tom's pretty lucky most times.

He goes to the bureau and lights the lamp. The circular fringe is patterned on the ceiling. The moving shadows of the men are huge against the bare wall boards. Halsey walks up to Kabnis, takes the poker from his grip, and without more ado pushes him into a chair before the dark hearth.

Halsey: Youre a mess. Here, Layman. Get some trash an start a fire.

Layman fumbles around, finds some newspapers and old bags, puts them in the hearth, arranges the wood, and kindles the fire. Halsey sets a black iron kettle where it soon will be boiling. Then takes from his hip-pocket a bottle of corn licker which he passes to Kabnis.

Halsey: Here. This'll straighten y out a bit.

Kabnis nervously draws the cork and gulps the licker down.

Kabnis: Ha. Good stuff. Thanks. Thank y, Halsey.

Halsey: Good stuff! Youre damn right. Hanby there dont think so. Wonder he doesnt come over t find out whos burnin his oil. Miserly bastard, him. Th boys what made this stuff—are y listenin t me,

Kabnis? th boys what made this stuff have got th art down like I heard you say youd like t be with words. Eh? Have some, Layman?

Layman: Dont think I care for none, thank y jes th same, Mr. Halsey.

Halsey: Care hell. Course y care. Everybody cares around these parts. Preachers an school teachers an everybody. Here. Here, take it. Dont try that line on me.

Layman limbers up a little, but he cannot quite forget that he is on school ground.

Layman: Thats right. Thats true, sho. Shinin is th only business what pays in these hard times.

He takes a nip, and passes the bottle to Kabnis. Kabnis is in the middle of a long swig when a rap sounds on the door. He almost spills the bottle, but manages to pass it to Halsey just as the door swings open and Hanby enters. He is a well-dressed, smooth, rich, black-skinned Negro who thinks there is no one quite so suave and polished as himself. To members of his own race, he affects the manners of a wealthy white planter. Or, when he is up North, he lets it be known that his ideas are those of the best New England tradition. To white men he bows, without ever completely humbling himself. Tradesmen in the town tolerate him because he spends his money with them. He delivers his words with a full consciousness of his moral superiority.

Hanby: Hum. Erer, Professor Kabnis, to come straight to the point: the progress of the Negro race is jeopardized whenever the personal habits and examples set by its guides and mentors fall below the acknowledged and hard-won standard of its average member. This institution, of which I am the humble president, was founded, and has been maintained at a cost of great labor and untold sacrifice. Its purpose is to teach our youth to live better, cleaner, more noble lives. To prove to the world that the Negro race can be just like any other race. It hopes to attain this aim partly by the salutary examples set by its instructors. I cannot hinder the progress of a race simply to indulge a single member. I have thought the matter out beforehand, I can assure you. Therefore, if I find your resignation on my desk by to-morrow morning, Mr. Kabnis, I shall not feel obliged to call in the sheriff. Otherwise. . ."

Kabnis: A fellow can take a drink in his own room if he wants to, in the privacy of his own room.

Hanby: His room, but not the institution's room, Mr. Kabnis.

Kabnis: This is my room while I'm in it.

Hanby: Mr. Clayborn (the sheriff) can inform you as to that.

Kabnis: Oh, well, what do I care—glad to get out of this mud-hole.

Hanby: I should think so from your looks.

Kabnis: You neednt get sarcastic about it.

Hanby: No, that is true. And I neednt wait for your resignation either, Mr. Kabnis.

Kabnis: Oh, you'll get that all right. Dont worry.

Hanby: And I should like to have the room thoroughly aired and cleaned and ready for your successor by to-morrow noon, Professor.

Kabnis (trying to rise): You can have your godam room right away. I dont want it.

Hanby: But I wont have your cursing.

Halsey pushes Kabnis back into his chair.

Halsey: Sit down, Kabnis, till I wash y.

Hanby (to Halsey): I would rather not have drinking men on the premises, Mr. Halsey. You will oblige me—

Halsey: I'll oblige you by stayin right on this spot, this spot, get me? till I get damned ready t leave.

He approaches Hanby. Hanby retreats, but manages to hold his dignity.

Halsey: Let me get you told right now, Mr. Samuel Hanby. Now listen t me. I aint no slick an span slave youve hired, an dont y think it for a minute. Youve bullied enough about this town. An besides, wheres that bill youve been owin me? Listen t me. If I dont get it paid in by tmorrer noon, Mr. Hanby (he mockingly assumes Hanby's tone and manner), I shall feel obliged t call th sheriff. An that sheriff'll be myself who'll catch y in th road an pull y out your buggy an rightly attend t y. You heard me. Now leave him alone. I'm takin him home with me. I got it fixed. Before you came in. He's goin t work with me. Shapin shafts and buildin wagons'll make a man of him what nobody, y get me? what nobody can take advantage of. Thats all. . .

Halsey burrs off into vague and incoherent comment.

Pause. Disagreeable.

Layman's eyes are glazed on the spurting fire.

Kabnis wants to rise and put both Halsey and Hanby in their places. He vaguely knows that he must do this, else the power of direction will completely slip from him to those outside. The conviction is just strong enough to torture him. To bring a feverish, quick-passing flare into his eyes. To mutter words soggy in hot saliva. To jerk his arms upward in futile protest. Halsey, noticing his gestures, thinks it is water that he desires. He brings a glass to him. Kabnis slings it to the floor. Heat of the conviction dies. His arms crumple. His upper lip, his mustache, quiver. Rap! rap, on the door. The sounds slap Kabnis. They bring a hectic color to his cheeks. Like huge cold finger tips they touch his skin and goose-flesh it. Hanby strikes a commanding pose. He moves toward Layman. Layman's face is innocently immobile.

Halsey: Whos there?

Voice: Lewis.

Halsey: Come in, Lewis. Come on in.

Lewis enters. He is the queer fellow who has been referred to. A tall wiry copper-colored man, thirty perhaps. His mouth and eyes suggest purpose guided by an adequate intelligence. He is what a stronger Kabnis might have been, and in an odd faint way resembles him. As he steps towards the others, he seems to be issuing sharply from a vivid dream. Lewis shakes hands with Halsey. Nods perfunctorily to Hanby, who has stiffened to meet him. Smiles rapidly at Layman, and settles with real interest on Kabnis.

Lewis: Kabnis passed me on the road. Had a piece of business of my own, and couldnt get here any sooner. Thought I might be able to help in some way or other.

Halsey: A good baths bout all he needs now. An somethin t put his mind t rest.

Lewis: I think I can give him that. That note was meant for me. Some Negroes have grown uncomfortable at my being here—

Kabnis: You mean, Mr. Lewis, some colored folks threw it? Christ Almighty!

Halsey: Thats what he means. An just as I told y. White folks more direct than that.

Kabnis: What are they after you for?

Lewis: Its a long story, Kabnis. Too long for now. And it might involve present company. (He laughs pleasantly and gestures vaguely in the direction of Hanby.) Tell you about it later on perhaps.

Kabnis: Youre not going?

Lewis: Not till my month's up.

Halsey: Hows that?

Lewis: I'm on a sort of contract with myself. (Is about to leave.) Well, glad its nothing serious—

Halsey: Come round t th shop sometime why dont y, Lewis? I've asked y enough. I'd like t have a talk with y. I aint as dumb as I look. Kabnis an me'll be in most any time. Not much work these days. Wish t hell there was. This burg gets to me when there aint. (In answer to Lewis' question.) He's goin t work with me. Ya. Night air this side th branch aint good fer him. (Looks at Hanby. Laughs.)

Lewis: I see. . .

His eyes turn to Kabnis. In the instant of their shifting, a vision of the life they are to meet. Kabnis, a promise of a soil-soaked beauty;

uprooted, thinning out. Suspended a few feet above the soil whose touch would resurrect him. Arm's length removed from him whose will to help. . . There is a swift intuitive interchange of consciousness. Kabnis has a sudden need to rush into the arms of this man. His eyes call, "Brother." And then a savage, cynical twist-about within him mocks his impulse and strengthens him to repulse Lewis. His lips curl cruelly. His eyes laugh. They are glittering needles, stitching. With a throbbing ache they draw Lewis to. Lewis brusquely wheels on Hanby.

Lewis: I'd like to see you, sir, a moment, if you don't mind.

Hanby's tight collar and vest effectively preserve him.

Hanby: Yes, erer, Mr. Lewis. Right away.

Lewis: See you later, Halsey.

Halsey: So long—thanks—sho hope so, Lewis.

As he opens the door and Hanby passes out, a woman, miles down the valley, begins to sing. Her song is a spark that travels swiftly to the near-by cabins. Like purple tallow flames, songs jet up. They spread a ruddy haze over the heavens. The haze swings low. Now the whole countryside is a soft chorus. Lord. O Lord. . . Lewis closes the door behind him. A flame jets out. . .

The kettle is boiling. Halsey notices it. He pulls the wash-tub from beneath the bed. He arranges for the bath before the fire.

Halsey: Told y them theatrics didnt fit a white man. Th niggers, just like I told y. An after him. Aint surprisin though. He aint bowed t none of them. Nassur. T nairy a one of them nairy an inch nairy a time. An only mixed when he was good an ready—

Kabnis: That song, Halsey, do you hear it?

Halsey: Thats a man. Hear me, Kabnis? A man—

Kabnis: Jesus, do you hear it.

Halsey: Hear it? Hear what? Course I hear it. Listen t what I'm tellin y. A man, get me? They'll get him yet if he dont watch out.

Kabnis is jolted into his fear.

Kabnis: Get him? What do you mean? How? Not lynch him?

Halsey: Na. Take a shotgun an shoot his eyes clear out. Well, anyway, it wasnt fer you, just like I told y. You'll stay over at th house an work with me, eh, boy? Good t get away from his nobs, eh? Damn big stiff though, him. An youre not th first an I can tell y. (Laughs.)

He bustles and fusses about Kabnis as if he were a child. Kabnis submits, wearily. He has no will to resist him.

Layman (his voice is like a deep hollow echo): Thats right. Thats true, sho. Everybody's been expectin that th bust up was comin. Surprised um all y held on as long as y did. Teachin in th South aint th

thing fer y. Nassur. You ought t be way back up North where sometimes I wish I was. But I've hung on down this away so long—

Halsey: An therc'll never be no leavin time fer y.

4

A month has passed.

Halsey's work-shop. It is an old building just off the main street of
Sempter. The walls to within a few feet of the ground are of an age-
worn cement mixture. On the outside they are considerably crumbled
and peppered with what looks like musket-shot. Inside, the plaster has
fallen away in great chunks, leaving the laths, grayed and cobwebbed,
exposed. A sort of loft above the shop proper serves as a break-water
for the rain and sunshine which otherwise would have free entry to
the main floor. The shop is filled with old wheels and parts of wheels,
broken shafts, and wooden litter. A double door, midway the street
wall. To the left of this, a work-bench that holds a vise and a variety
of wood-work tools. A window with as many panes broken as whole,
throws light on the bench. Opposite, in the rear wall, a second window looks out upon the back yard. In the left wall, a rickety smoke-
blackened chimney, and hearth with fire blazing. Smooth-worn
chairs grouped about the hearth suggest the village meeting-place.
Several large wooden blocks, chipped and cut and sawed on their
upper surfaces are in the middle of the floor. They are the supports
used in almost any sort of wagon-work. Their idleness means that
Halsey has no worth-while job on foot. To the right of the central
door is a junk heap, and directly behind this, stairs that lead down
into the cellar. The cellar is known as "The Hole." Besides being the
home of a very old man, it is used by Halsey on those occasions when
he spices up the life of the small town.

Halsey, wonderfully himself in his work overalls, stands in the
doorway and gazes up the street, expectantly. Then his eyes grow
listless. He slouches against the smooth-rubbed frame. He lights a
cigarette. Shifts his position. Braces an arm against the door. Kabnis
passes the window and stoops to get in under Halsey's arm. He is
awkward and ludicrous, like a schoolboy in his big brother's ncw
overalls. He skirts the large blocks on the floor, and drops into a chair
before the fire. Halsey saunters towards him.

Kabnis: Time f lunch.

Halsey: Ya.

He stands by the hearth, rocking backward and forward. He
stretches his hands out to the fire. He washes them in the warm glow
of the flames. They never get cold, but he warms them.

Kabnis: Saw Lewis up th street. Said he'd be down.

Halsey's eyes brighten. He looks at Kabnis. Turns away. Says nothing. Kabnis fidgets. Twists his thin blue cloth-covered limbs. Pulls closer to the fire till the heat stings his shins. Pushes back. Pokes the burned logs. Puts on several fresh ones. Fidgets. The town bell strikes twelve.

Kabnis: Fix it up f tnight?

Halsey: Leave it t me.

Kabnis: Get Lewis in?

Halsey: Tryin t.

The air is heavy with the smell of pine and resin. Green logs spurt and sizzle. Sap trickles from an old pine-knot into the flames. Layman enters. He carries a lunch-pail. Kabnis, for the moment, thinks that he is a day laborer.

Layman: Evenin, gen'lemun.

Both: Whats say, Layman.

Layman squares a chair to the fire and droops into it. Several town fellows, silent unfathomable men for the most part, saunter in. Overalls. Thick tan shoes. Felt hats marvelously shaped and twisted. One asks Halsey for a cigarette. He gets it. The blacksmith, a tremendous black man, comes in from the forge. Not even a nod from him. He picks up an axle and goes out. Lewis enters. The town men look curiously at him. Suspicion and an open liking contest for possession of their faces. They are uncomfortable. One by one they drift into the street.

Layman: Heard y was leavin, Mr. Lewis.

Kabnis: Months up, eh? Hell of a month I've got.

Halsey: Sorry y goin, Lewis. Just gettin acquainted like.

Lewis: Sorry myself, Halsey, in a way—

Layman: Gettin t like our town, Mr. Lewis?

Lewis: I'm afraid its on a different basis, Professor.

Halsey: An I've yet t hear about that basis. Been waitin long enough, God knows. Seems t me like youd take pity on a feller if nothin more.

Kabnis: Somethin that old black cockroach over yonder doesnt like, whatever it is.

Layman: Thats right. Thats right, sho.

Halsey: A feller dropped in here tother day an said he knew what you was about. Said you had queer opinions. Well, I could have told him you was a queer one, myself. But not th way he was driftin. Didnt mean anything by it, but just let drop he thought you was a little wrong up here—crazy, y'know. (Laughs.)

Kabnis: Y mean old Blodson? Hell, he's bats himself.

Lewis: I remember him. We had a talk. But what he found queer, I think, was not my opinions, but my lack of them. In half an hour he had settled everything: boll weevils, God, the World War. Weevils and wars are the pests that God sends against the sinful. People are too weak to correct themselves: the Redeemer is coming back. Get ready, ye sinners, for the advent of Our Lord. Interesting, eh, Kabnis? but not exactly what we want.

Halsey: Y could have come t me. I've sho been after y enough. Most every time I've seen y.

Kabnis (sarcastically): Hows it y never came t us professors?

Lewis: I did—to one.

Kabnis: Y mean t say y got somethin from that celluloid-collar-eraser-cleaned old codger over in th mud hole?

Halsey: Rough on th old boy, aint he? (Laughs.)

Lewis: Something, yes. Layman here could have given me quite a deal, but the incentive to his keeping quiet is so much greater than anything I could have offered him to open up, that I crossed him off my mind. And you—

Kabnis: What about me?

Halsey: Tell him, Lewis, for godsake tell him. I've told him. But its somethin else he wants so bad I've heard him downstairs mumblin with th old man.

Lewis: The old man?

Kabnis: What about me? Come on now, you know so much.

Halsey: Tell him, Lewis. Tell it t him.

Lewis: Life has already told him more than he is capable of knowing. It has given him in excess of what he can receive. I have been offered. Stuff in his stomach curdled, and he vomited me.

Kabnis' face twitches. His body writhes.

Kabnis: You know a lot, you do. How about Halsey?

Lewis: Yes . . . Halsey? Fits here. Belongs here. An artist in your way, arent you, Halsey?

Halsey: Reckon I am, Lewis. Give me th work and fair pay an I aint askin nothin better. Went over-seas an saw France; an I come back. Been up North; an I come back. Went t school; but there aint no books whats got th feel t them of them there tools. Nassur. An I'm atellin y.

A shriveled, bony white man passes the window and enters the shop. He carries a broken hatchet-handle and the severed head. He speaks with a flat, drawn voice to Halsey, who comes forward to meet him.

Mr. Ramsay: Can y fix this fer me, Halsey?

Halsey (looking it over): Reckon so, Mr. Ramsay. Here, Kabnis. A little practice fer y.

Halsey directs Kabnis, showing him how to place the handle in the vise, and cut it down. The knife hangs. Kabnis thinks that it must be dull. He jerks it hard. The tool goes deep and shaves too much off. Mr. Ramsay smiles brokenly at him.

Mr. Ramsay (to Halsey): Still breakin in the new hand, eh, Halsey? Seems like a likely enough faller once he gets th hang of it.

He gives a tight laugh at his own good humor. Kabnis burns red. The back of his neck stings him beneath his collar. He feels stifled. Through Ramsay, the whole white South weighs down upon him. The pressure is terrific. He sweats under the arms. Chill beads run down his body. His brows concentrate upon the handle as though his own life was staked upon the perfect shaving of it. He begins to out and out botch the job. Halsey smiles.

Halsey: He'll make a good un some of these days, Mr. Ramsay.

Mr. Ramsay: Y ought t know. Yer daddy was a good un before y. Runs in th family, seems like t me.

Halsey: Thats right, Mr. Ramsay.

Kabnis is hopeless. Halsey takes the handle from him. With a few deft strokes he shaves it. Fits it. Gives it to Ramsay.

Mr. Ramsay: How much on this?

Halsey: No charge, Mr. Ramsay.

Mr. Ramsay (going out): All right, Halsey. Come down an take it out in trade. Shoe-strings or something.

Halsey: Yassur, Mr. Ramsay.

Halsey rejoins Lewis and Layman. Kabnis, hangdog-fashion, follows him.

Halsey: They like y if y work fer them.

Layman: Thats right, Mr. Halsey. Thats right, sho.

The group is about to resume its talk when Hanby enters. He is all energy, bustle, and business. He goes direct to Kabnis.

Hanby: An axle is out in the buggy which I would like to have shaped into a crow-bar. You will see that it is fixed for me.

Without waiting for an answer, and knowing that Kabnis will follow, he passes out. Kabnis, scowling, silent, trudges after him.

Hanby (from the outside): Have that ready for me by three o'clock, young man. I shall call for it.

Kabnis (under his breath as he comes in): Th hell you say, you old black swamp-gut.

He slings the axle on the floor.

Halsey: Wheeee!

Layman, lunch finished long ago, rises, heavily. He shakes hands with Lewis.

Layman: Might not see y again befo y leave, Mr. Lewis. I enjoys t hear y talk. Y might have been a preacher. Maybe a bishop some day. Sho do hope t see y back this away again sometime, Mr. Lewis.

Lewis: Thanks, Professor. Hope I'll see you.

Layman waves a long arm loosely to the others, and leaves. Kabnis goes to the door. His eyes, sullen, gaze up the street.

Kabnis: Carrie K.'s comin with th lunch. Bout time.

She passes the window. Her red girl's-cap, catching the sun, flashes vividly. With a stiff, awkward little movement she crosses the doorsill and gives Kabnis one of the two baskets which she is carrying. There is a slight stoop to her shoulders. The curves of her body blend with this to a soft rounded charm. Her gestures are stiffly variant. Black bangs curl over the forehead of her oval-olive face. Her expression is dazed, but on provocation it can melt into a wistful smile. Adolescent. She is easily the sister of Fred Halsey.

Carrie K.: Mother says excuse her, brother Fred an Ralph, fer bein late.

Kabnis: Everythings all right an O.K., Carrie Kate. O.K. an all right.

The two men settle on their lunch. Carrie, with hardly a glance in the direction of the hearth, as is her habit, is about to take the second basket down to the old man, when Lewis rises. In doing so he draws her unwitting attention. Their meeting is a swift sun-burst. Lewis impulsively moves towards her. His mind flashes images of her life in the southern town. He sees the nascent woman, her flesh already stiffening to cartilage, drying to bone. Her spirit-bloom, even now touched sullen, bitter. Her rich beauty fading. . . He wants to—He stretches forth his hands to hers. He takes them. They feel like warm cheeks against his palms. The sun-burst from her eyes floods up and haloes him. Christ-eyes, his eyes look to her. Fearlessly she loves into them. And then something happens. Her face blanches. Awkwardly she draws away. The sin-bogies of respectable southern colored folks clamor at her: "Look out! Be a *good* girl. A *good* girl. Look out!" She gropes for her basket that has fallen to the floor. Finds it, and marches with a rigid gravity to her task of feeding the old man. Like the glowing white ash of burned paper, Lewis' eyelids, wavering, settle down. He stirs in the direction of the rear window. From the back yard, mules tethered to odd trees and posts blink dumbly at him. They too seem burdened with an impotent pain. Kabnis and Halsey are still busy with their lunch. They havent noticed him. After a while he turns to them.

Lewis: Your sister, Halsey, whats to become of her? What are you going to do for her?

Halsey: Who? What? What am I goin t do? . . .

Lewis: What I mean is, what does she do down there?

Halsey: Oh. Feeds th old man. Had lunch, Lewis?

Lewis: Thanks, yes. You have never felt her, have you, Halsey? Well, no, I guess not. I dont suppose you can. Nor can she. . . Old man? Halsey, some one lives down there? I've never heard of him. Tell me—

Kabnis takes time from his meal to answer with some emphasis:

Kabnis: Theres lots of things you aint heard of.

Lewis: Dare say. I'd like to see him.

Kabnis: You'll get all th chance you want tnight.

Halsey: Fixin a little somethin up fer tnight, Lewis. Th three of us an some girls. Come round bout ten-thirty.

Lewis: Glad to. But what under the sun does he do down there?

Halsey: Ask Kabnis. He blows off t him every chance he gets.

Kabnis gives a grunting laugh. His mouth twists. Carrie returns from the cellar. Avoiding Lewis, she speaks to her brother.

Carrie K.: Brother Fred, father hasnt eaten now goin on th second week, but mumbles an talks funny, or tries t talk when I put his hands ont th food. He frightens me, an I dunno what t do. An oh, I came near fergettin, brother, but Mr. Marmon—he was eatin lunch when I saw him—told me t tell y that th lumber wagon busted down an he wanted y t fix it fer him. Said he reckoned he could get it t y after he ate.

Halsey chucks a half-eaten sandwich in the fire. Gets up. Arranges his blocks. Goes to the door and looks anxiously up the street. The wind whirls a small spiral in the gray dust road.

Halsey: Why didnt y tell me sooner, little sister?

Carrie K.: I fergot t, an just remembered it now, brother.

Her soft rolled words are fresh pain to Lewis. He wants to take her North with him What for? He wonders what Kabnis could do for her. What she could do for him. Mother him. Carrie gathers the lunch things, silently, and in her pinched manner, curtsies, and departs. Kabnis lights his after-lunch cigarette. Lewis, who has sensed a change, becomes aware that he is not included in it. He starts to ask again about the old man. Decides not to. Rises to go.

Lewis: Think I'll run along, Halsey.

Halsey: Sure. Glad t see y any time.

Kabnis: Dont forget tnight.

Lewis: Dont worry. I wont. So long.

Kabnis: So long. We'll be expectin y.

Lewis passes Halsey at the door. Halsey's cheeks form a vacant smile. His eyes are wide awake, watching for the wagon to turn from Broad Street into his road.

Halsey: So long.

His words reach Lewis halfway to the corner.

5

Night, soft belly of a pregnant Negress, throbs evenly against the torso of the South. Night throbs a womb-song to the South. Cane- and cotton-fields, pine forests, cypress swamps, sawmills, and factories are fecund at her touch. Night's womb-song sets them singing. Night winds are the breathing of the unborn child whose calm throbbing in the belly of a Negress sets them somnolently singing. Hear their song.

> White-man's land.
> Niggers, sing.
> Burn, bear black children
> Till poor rivers bring
> Rest, and sweet glory
> In Camp Ground.

Sempter's streets are vacant and still. White paint on the wealthier houses has the chill blue glitter of distant stars. Negro cabins are a purple blur. Broad Street is deserted. Winds stir beneath the corrugated iron canopies and dangle odd bits of rope tied to horse- and mule-gnawed hitching-posts. One store window has a light in it. Chesterfield cigarette and Chero-Cola cardboard advertisements are stacked in it. From a side door two men come out. Pause, for a last word and then say good night. Soon they melt in shadows thicker than they. Way off down the street four figures sway beneath iron awnings which form a sort of corridor that imperfectly echoes and jumbles what they say. A fifth form joins them. They turn into the road that leads to Halsey's workshop. The old building is phosphorescent above deep shade. The figures pass through the double door. Night winds whisper in the eaves. Sing weirdly in the ceiling cracks. Stir curls of shavings on the floor. Halsey lights a candle. A good-sized lumber wagon, wheels off, rests upon the blocks. Kabnis makes a face at it. An unearthly hush is upon the place. No one seems to want to talk. To move, lest the scraping of their feet. . .

Halsey: Come on down this way, folks.

He leads the way. Stella follows. And close after her, Cora, Lewis, and Kabnis. They descend into the Hole. It seems huge, limitless in the candle light. The walls are of stone, wonderfully fitted. They have no openings save a small iron-barred window toward the top of each. They are dry and warm. The ground slopes away to the rear of the building and thus leaves the south wall exposed to the sun. The blacksmith's shop is plumb against the right wall. The floor is clay. Shavings have at odd times been matted into it. In the right-hand corner, under the stairs, two good-sized pine mattresses, resting on cardboard, are on either side of a wooden table. On this are several half-burned candles and an oil lamp. Behind the table, an irregular piece of mirror hangs on the wall. A loose something that looks to be a gaudy ball costume dangles from a near-by hook. To the front, a second table holds a lamp and several whiskey glasses. Six rickety chairs are near this table. Two old wagon wheels rest on the floor. To the left, sitting in a high-backed chair which stands upon a low platform, the old man. He is like a bust in black walnut. Gray-bearded. Gray-haired. Prophetic. Immobile. Lewis' eyes are sunk in him. The others, unconcerned, are about to pass on to the front table when Lewis grips Halsey and so turns him that the candle flame shines obliquely on the old man's features.

Lewis: And he rules over—

Kabnis: Th smoke an fire of th forge.

Lewis: Black Vulcan? I wouldnt say so. That forehead. Great woolly beard. Those eyes. A mute John the Baptist of a new religion—or a tongue-tied shadow of an old.

Kabnis: His tongue is tied all right, an I can vouch f that.

Lewis: Has he never talked to you?

Halsey: Kabnis wont give him a chance.

He laughs. The girls laugh. Kabnis winces.

Lewis: What do you call him?

Halsey: Father.

Lewis: Good. Father what?

Kabnis: Father of hell.

Halsey: Father's th only name we have fer him. Come on. Lets sit down an get t th pleasure of the evenin.

Lewis: Father John it is from now on. . .

Slave boy whom some Christian mistress taught to read the Bible. Black man who saw Jesus in the ricefields, and began preaching to his people. Moses- and Christ-words used for songs. Dead blind father of a muted folk who feel their way upward to a life that crushes or absorbs them. (Speak, Father!) Suppose your eyes could see, old man. (The years hold hands. O Sing!) Suppose your lips. . .

Halsey, does he never talk?

Halsey: Na. But sometimes. Only seldom. Mumbles. Sis says he talks—

Kabnis: I've heard him talk.

Halsey: First I've ever heard of it. You dont give him a chance. Sis says she's made out several words, mostly one—an like as not cause it was "sin."

Cora laughs in a loose sort of way. She is a tall, thin, mulatto woman. Her eyes arc deep-set behind a pointed nose. Her hair is coarse and bushy. Seeing that Stella also is restless, she takes her arm and the two women move towards the table. They slip into chairs. Halsey follows and lights the lamp. He lays out a pack of cards. Stella sorts them as if telling fortunes. She is a beautifully proportioned, large-eyed, brown-skin girl. Except for the twisted line of her mouth when she smiles or laughs, there is about her no suggestion of the life she's been through. Kabnis, with great mock-solemnity, goes to the corner, takes down the robe, and dons it. He is a curious spectacle, acting a part, yet very real. He joins the others at the table. They are used to him. Lewis is surprised. He laughs. Kabnis shrinks and then glares at him with a furtive hatred. Halsey, bringing out a bottle of corn licker, pours drinks.

Halsey: Come on, Lewis. Come on, you fellers. Heres lookin at y.

Then, as if suddenly recalling something, he jerks away from the table and starts towards the steps.

Kabnis: Where y goin, Halsey?

Halsey: Where? Where y think? That oak beam in th wagon—

Kabnis: Come ere. Come ere. Sit down. What in hell's wrong with you fellers? You with your wagon. Lewis with his Father John. This aint th time fer foolin with wagons. Daytime's bad enough f that. Ere, sit down. Ere, Lewis, you too sit down. Have a drink. Thats right. Drink corn licker, love th girls, an listen t th old man mumblin sin.

There seems to be no good-time spirit to the party. Something in the air is too tense and deep for that. Lewis, seated now so that his eyes rest upon the old man, merges with his source and lets the pain and beauty of the South meet him there. White faces, pain-pollen, settle downward through a cane-sweet mist and touch the ovaries of yellow flowers. Cotton-bolls bloom, droop. Black roots twist in a parched red soil beneath a blazing sky. Magnolias, fragrant, a trifle futile, lovely, far off. . . His eyelids close. A force begins to heave and rise. . . Stella is serious, reminiscent.

Stella: Usall is brought up t hate sin worse than death—

Kabnis: An then before you have y eyes half open, youre made t love it if y want t live.

Stella: Us never—

Kabnis: Oh, I know your story: that old prim bastard over yonder, an then old Calvert's office—

Stella: It wasnt them—

Kabnis: I know. They put y out of church, an then I guess th preacher came around an asked f some. But thats your body. Now me—

Halsey (passing him the bottle): All right, kid, we believe y. Here, take another. Wheres Clover, Stel?

Stella: You know how Jim is when he's just out th swamp. Done up in shine an wouldnt let her come. Said he'd bust her head open if she went out.

Kabnis: Dont see why he doesnt stay over with Laura, where he belongs.

Stella: Ask him, an I reckon he'll tell y. More than you want.

Halsey: Th nigger hates th sight of a black woman worse than death. Sorry t mix y up this way, Lewis. But y see how tis.

Lewis' skin is tight and glowing over the fine bones of his face. His lips tremble. His nostrils quiver. The others notice this and smile knowingly at each other. Drinks and smokes are passed around. They pay no neverminds to him. A real party is being worked up. Then Lewis opens his eyes and looks at them. Their smiles disperse in hot-cold tremors. Kabnis chokes his laugh. It sputters, gurgles. His eyes flicker and turn away. He tries to pass the thing off by taking a long drink which he makes considerable fuss over. He is drawn back to Lewis. Seeing Lewis' gaze still upon him, he scowls.

Kabnis: Whatsha lookin at me for? Y want t know who I am? Well, I'm Ralph Kabnis—lot of good its goin t do y. Well? Whatsha keep lookin for? I'm Ralph Kabnis. Aint that enough f y? Want th whole family history? Its none of your godam business, anyway. Keep off me. Do y hear? Keep off me. Look at Cora. Aint she pretty enough t look at? Look at Halsey, or Stella. Clover ought t be here an you could look at her. An love her. Thats what you need. I know—

Lewis: Ralph Kabnis gets satisfied that way?

Kabnis: Satisfied? Say, quit your kiddin. Here, look at that old man there. See him? He's satisfied. Do I look like him? When I'm dead I dont expect t be satisfied. Is that enough f y, with your godam nosin, or do you want more? Well, y wont get it, understand?

Lewis: The old man as symbol, flesh, and spirit of the past, what do you think he would say if he could see you? You look at him, Kabnis.

Kabnis: Just like any done-up preacher is what he looks t me. Jam some false teeth in his mouth and crank him, an youd have God Almighty spit in torrents all around th floor. Oh, hell, an he reminds me of that black cockroach over yonder. An besides, he aint my past. My ancestors were Southern blue-bloods—

Lewis: And black.

Kabnis: Aint much difference between blue an black.

Lewis: Enough to draw a denial from you. Cant hold them, can you? Master; slave. Soil; and the overarching heavens. Dusk; dawn. They fight and bastardize you. The sun tint of your cheeks, flame of the great season's multi-colored leaves, tarnished, burned. Split, shredded: easily burned. No use. . .

His gaze shifts to Stella. Stella's face draws back, her breasts come towards him.

Stella: I aint got nothin f y, mister. Taint no use t look at me.

Halsey: Youre a queer feller, Lewis, I swear y are. Told y so, didnt I, girls? Just take him easy though, an he'll be ridin just th same as any Georgia mule, eh, Lewis? (Laughs.)

Stella: I'm goin t tell y somethin, mister. It aint t you, t th Mister Lewis what noses about. Its t somethin different, I dunno what. That old man there—maybe its him—is like m father used t look. He used t sing. An when he could sing no mo, they'd allus come f him an carry him t church an there he'd sit, befo th pulpit, aswayin an alcadin every song. A white man took m mother an it broke th old man's heart. He died; an then I didnt care what become of me, an I dont now. I dont care now. Dont get it in y head I'm some sentimental Susie askin for yo sop. Nassur. But theres somethin t yo th others aint got. Boars an kids an fools—thats all I've known. Boars when their fever's up. When their fever's up they come t me. Halsey asks me over when he's off th job. Kabnis—it ud be a sin t play with him. He takes it out in talk.

Halsey knows that he has trifled with her. At odd things he has been inwardly penitent before her tasking him. But now he wants to hurt her. He turns to Lewis.

Halsey: Lewis, I got a little licker in me, an thats true. True's what I said. True. But th stuff just seems t wake me up an make my mind a man of me. Listen. You know a lot, queer as hell as y are, an I want t ask y some questions. Theyre too high fer them, Stella an Cora an Kabnis, so we'll just excuse em. A chat between ourselves. (Turns to the others.) You-all cant listen in on this. Twont interest y. So just leave th table t this gen'lemun an myself. Go long now.

Kabnis gets up, pompous in his robe, grotesquely so, and makes as if to go through a grand march with Stella. She shoves him off, roughly, and in a mood swings her body to the steps. Kabnis grabs Cora and parades around, passing the old man, to whom he bows in mock-curtsy. He sweeps by the table, snatches the licker bottle, and then he and Cora sprawl on the mattresses. She meets his weak approaches after the manner she thinks Stella would use.

Halsey contemptuously watches them until he is sure that they are settled.

Halsey: This aint th sort o thing f me, Lewis, when I got work upstairs. Nassur. You an me has got things t do. Wastin time on common low-down women—say, Lewis, look at her now—Stella— aint she a picture? Common wench—na she aint, Lewis. You know she aint. I'm only tryin t fool y. I used t love that girl. Yassur. An sometimes when th moon is thick an I hear dogs up th valley barkin an some old woman fetches out her song, an th winds seem like th Lord made them fer t fetch an carry th smell o pine an cane, an there aint no big job on foot, I sometimes get t thinkin that I still do. But I want t talk t y, Lewis, queer as y are. Y know, Lewis, I went t school once. Ya. In Augusta. But it wasnt a regular school. Na. It was a pussy Sunday-school masqueradin under a regular name. Some goody-goody teachers from th North had come down t teach th niggers. If you was nearly white, they liked y. If you was black, they didnt. But it wasnt that—I was all right, y see. I couldnt stand em messin an pawin over m business like I was a child. So I cussed em out an left. Kabnis there ought t have cussed out th old duck over yonder an left. He'd a been a better man tday. But as I was sayin, I couldnt stand their ways. So I left an came here an worked with my father. An been here ever since. He died. I set in f myself. An its always been; give me a good job an sure pay an I aint far from being satisfied, so far as satisfaction goes. Prejudice is everywheres about this country. An a nigger aint in much standin anywheres. But when it comes t pottin round an doin nothin, with nothin bigger'n an ax- handle t hold a feller down, like it was a while back befo I got this job—that beam ought t be—but tmorrow mornin early's time enough f that. As I was sayin, I gets t thinkin. Play dumb naturally t white folks. I gets t thinkin. I used to subscribe t th *Literary Digest* an that helped along a bit. But there werent nothing I could sink m teeth int. Theres lots I want t ask y, Lewis. Been askin y t come around. Couldnt get y. Cant get in much tnight. (He glances at the others. His mind fastens on Kabnis.) Say, tell me this, whats on your mind t say on that feller there? Kabnis' name. One queer bird ought t know another, seems like t me.

Licker has released conflicts in Kabnis and set them flowing. He pricks his ears, intuitively feels that the talk is about him, leaves Cora, and approaches the table. His eyes are watery, heavy with passion. He stoops. He is a ridiculous pathetic figure in his showy robe.

Kabnis: Talkin bout me. I know. I'm th topic of conversation everywhere theres talk about this town. Girls an fellers. White folks as well. An if its me youre talkin bout, guess I got a right t listen in. Whats sayin? Whats sayin bout his royal guts, the Duke? Whats sayin, eh?

Halsey (to Lewis): We'll take it up another time.

Kabnis: No nother time bout it. Now. I'm here now an talkin's just begun. I was born an bred in a family of orators, thats what I was.

Halsey: Preachers.

Kabnis: Na. Preachers hell. I didnt say wind-busters. Y misapprehended me. Y understand what that means, dont y? All right then, y misapprehended me. I didnt say preachers. I said orators. O R A - T O R S. Born one an I'll die one. You understand me, Lewis. (He turns to Halsey and begins shaking his finger in his face.) An as f you, youre all right f choppin things from blocks of wood. I was good at that th day I ducked th cradle. An since then, I've been shapin words after a design that branded here. Know whats here? M soul. Ever heard o that? Th hell y have. Been shapin words t fit m soul. Never told y that before, did I? Thought I couldnt talk. I'll tell y. I've been shapin words; ah, but sometimes theyre beautiful an golden an have a taste that makes them fine t roll over with y tongue. Your tongue aint fit f nothin but t roll an lick hog-meat.

Stella and Cora come up to the table.

Halsey: Give him a shove there, will y, Stel?

Stella jams Kabnis in a chair. Kabnis springs up.

Kabnis: Cant keep a good man down. Those words I was tellin y about, they wont fit int th mold thats branded on m soul. Rhyme, y see? Poet, too. Bad rhyme. Bad poet. Somethin else youve learned tnight. Lewis dont know it all, an I'm atellin y. Ugh. Th form thats burned int my soul is some twisted awful thing that crept in from a dream, a godam nightmare, an wont stay still unless I feed it. An it lives on words. Not beautiful words. God Almighty no. Misshapen, split-gut, tortured, twisted words. Layman was feedin it back there that day you thought I ran out fearin things. White folks feed it cause their looks are words. Niggers, black niggers feed it cause theyre evil an their looks are words. Yallar niggers feed it. This whole damn bloated purple country feeds it cause its goin down t hell in a holy avalanche of words. I want t feed th soul—I know what that is; th preachers dont—but I've got t feed it. I wish t God some lynchin white man ud stick his knife through it an pin it to a tree. An pin it to a tree. You hear me? Thats a wish f y, you little snot-nosed pups who've been makin fun of me, an fakin that I'm weak. Me, Ralph Kabnis weak. Ha.

Halsey: Thats right, old man. There, there. Here, so much exertion merits a fittin reward. Help him t be seated, Cora.

Halsey gives him a swig of shine. Cora glides up, seats him, and then plumps herself down on his lap, squeezing his head into her breasts. Kabnis mutters. Tries to break loose. Curses. Cora almost stifles him. He goes limp and gives up. Cora toys with him. Ruffles his hair. Braids it. Parts it in the middle. Stella smiles contemptuously. And then a sudden anger sweeps her. She would like to lash Cora from the place. She'd like to take Kabnis to some distant pine grove and nurse and mother him. Her eyes flash. A quick tensioning throws her breasts and neck into a poised strain. She starts towards them. Halsey grabs her arm and pulls her to him. She struggles. Halsey pins her arms and kisses her. She settles, spurting like a pine-knot afire.

Lewis finds himself completely cut out. The glowing within him subsides. It is followed by a dead chill. Kabnis, Carrie, Stella, Halsey, Cora, the old man, the cellar, and the work-shop, the southern town descend upon him. Their pain is too intense. He cannot stand it. He bolts from the table. Leaps up the stairs. Plunges through the work-shop and out into the night.

6

The cellar swims in a pale phosphorescence. The table, the chairs, the figure of the old man are amœba-like shadows which move about and float in it. In the corner under the steps, close to the floor, a solid blackness. A sound comes from it. A forcible yawn. Part of the blackness detaches itself so that it may be seen against the grayness of the wall. It moves forward and then seems to be clothing itself in odd dangling bits of shadow. The voice of Halsey, vibrant and deepened, calls.

Halsey: Kabnis. Cora. Stella.

He gets no response. He wants to get them up, to get on the job. He is intolerant of their sleepiness.

Halsey: Kabnis! Stella! Cora!

Gutturals, jerky and impeded, tell that he is shaking them.

Halsey: Come now, up with you.

Kabnis (sleepily and still more or less intoxicated): Whats th big idea? What in hell—

Halsey: Work. But never you mind about that. Up with you.

Cora: Oooooo! Look here, mister, I aint used t bein thrown int th street befo day.

Stella: Any bunk whats worked is worth in wages moren this. But come on. Taint no use t arger.

Kabnis: I'll arger. Its preposterous—

The girls interrupt him with none too pleasant laughs.

Kabnis: Thats what I said. Know what it means, dont y? All right, then. I said its preposterous t root an artist out o bed at this ungodly hour, when there aint no use t it. You can start your damned old work. Nobody's stoppin y. But what we got t get up for? Fraid somebody'll see th girls leavin? Some sport, you are. I hand it t y.

Halsey: Up you get, all th same.

Kabnis: Oh, th hell you say.

Halsey: Well, son, seeing that I'm th kindhearted father, I'll give y chance t open your eyes. But up y get when I come down.

He mounts the steps to the work-shop and starts a fire in the hearth. In the yard he finds some chunks of coal which he brings in and throws on the fire. He puts a kettle on to boil. The wagon draws him. He lifts an oak-beam, fingers it, and becomes abstracted. Then comes to himself and places the beam upon the work-bench. He looks over some newly cut wooden spokes. He goes to the fire and pokes it. The coals are red-hot. With a pair of long prongs he picks them up and places them in a thick iron bucket. This he carries downstairs. Outside, darkness has given way to the impalpable grayness of dawn. This early morning light, seeping through the four barred cellar windows, is the color of the stony walls. It seems to be an emanation from them. Halsey's coals throw out a rich warm glow. He sets them on the floor, a safe distance from the beds.

Halsey: No foolin now. Come. Up with you.

Other than a soft rustling, there is no sound as the girls slip into their clothes. Kabnis still lies in bed.

Stella (to Halsey): Reckon y could spare us a light?

Halsey strikes a match, lights a cigarette, and then bends over and touches flame to the two candles on the table between the beds. Kabnis asks for a cigarette. Halsey hands him his and takes a fresh one for himself. The girls, before the mirror, are doing up their hair. It is bushy hair that has gone through some straightening process. Character, however, has not all been ironed out. As they kneel there, heavy-eyed and dusky, and throwing grotesque moving shadows on the wall, they are two princesses in Africa going through the early-morning ablutions of their pagan prayers. Finished, they come forward to stretch their hands and warm them over the glowing coals.

Red dusk of a Georgia sunset, their heavy, coal-lit faces. . . Kabnis suddenly recalls something.

Kabnis: Th old man talked last night.

Stella: And so did you.

Halscy: In your dreams.

Kabnis: I tell y, he did. I know what I'm talkin about. I'll tell y what he said. Wait now, lemme see.

Halsey: Look out, brother, th old man'll be getting int you by way o dreams. Come, Stel, ready? Cora? Coffee an eggs f both of you.

Halsey goes upstairs.

Stella: Gettin generous, aint he?

She blows the candles out. Says nothing to Kabnis. Then she and Cora follow after Halsey. Kabnis, left to himself, tries to rise. He has slept in his robe. His robe trips him. Finally, he manages to stand up. He starts across the floor. Half-way to the old man, he falls and lies quite still. Perhaps an hour passes. Light of a new sun is about to filter through the windows. Kabnis slowly rises to support upon his elbows. He looks hard, and internally gathers himself together. The side face of Father John is in the direct line of his eyes. He scowls at him. No one is around. Words gush from Kabnis.

Kabnis: You sit there like a black hound spiked to an ivory pedestal. An all night long I heard you murmurin that devilish word. They thought I didnt hear y, but I did. Mumblin, feedin that ornery thing thats livin on my insides. Father John. Father of Satan, more likely. What does it mean t you? Youre dead already. Death. What does it mean t you? To you who died way back there in th 'sixties. What are y throwin it in my throat for? Whats it goin t get y? A good smashin in th mouth, thats what. My fist'll sink int y black mush face clear t y guts—if y got any. Dont believe y have. Never seen signs of none. Death. Death. Sin an Death. All night long y mumbled death. (He forgets the old man as his mind begins to play with the word and its associations.) Death . . . these clammy floors . . . just like th place they used t stow away th worn-out, no-count niggers in th days of slavery . . . that was long ago; not so long ago . . . no windows (he rises higher on his elbows to verify this assertion. He looks around, and, seeing no one but the old man, calls.) Halsey! Halsey! Gone an left me. Just like a nigger. I thought he was a nigger all th time. Now I know it. Ditch y when it comes right down t it. Damn him anyway. Godam him. (He looks and re-sees the old man.) Eh, you? T hell with you too. What do I care whether you can see or hear? You know what hell is cause youve been there. Its a feelin an its ragin in my soul in a way that'll pop out of me an run you through, an scorch y, an burn an rip your soul. Your soul. Ha. Nigger soul. A gin soul that gets drunk on a preacher's words. An screams. An shouts. God Almighty, how I hate that shoutin. Where's th beauty in that? Gives a buzzard a windpipe an I'll bet a dollar t a dime th buzzard ud beat y to it. Aint surprisin th white folks hate y so. When you had eyes, did you ever see th beauty of th world? Tell me that. Th hell y did. Now dont tell me. I know y didnt. You couldnt have. Oh, I'm drunk an just as good as dead, but no eyes that have seen beauty ever lose their sight. You aint got no sight. If you had, drunk as I am, I hope Christ will kill me if I couldnt see it. Your eyes are dull and watery, like fish eyes. Fish eyes are dead eyes. Youre an old man, a dead fish man, an black at that. Theyve put y here t die, damn fool y are not t know it. Do y know how many feet youre under ground? I'll tell y. Twenty. An do y think you'll ever see th light of day again, even if you wasnt blind? Do y think youre out of slavery? Huh? Youre where they used t throw th worked-out, no-count slaves. On a damp clammy floor of a dark scum-hole. An they called that an infirmary. Th sons-a. . . Why I can already see you toppled off that stool an stretched out on th floor beside me—not beside me, damn you, by yourself, with th flies buzzin an lickin God knows what they'd find on a dirty, black, foul-breathed mouth like yours. . .

Some one is coming down the stairs. Carrie, bringing food for the old man. She is lovely in her fresh energy of the morning, in the calm untested confidence and nascent maternity which rise from the purpose of her present mission. She walks to within a few paces of Kabnis.

Carrie K.: Brother says come up now, brother Ralph.

Kabnis: Brother doesnt know what he's talkin bout.

Carrie K.: Yes he does, Ralph. He needs you on th wagon.

Kabnis: He wants me on th wagon, eh? Does he think some wooden thing can lift me up? Ask him that.

Carrie K.: He told me t help y.

Kabnis: An how would you help me, child, dear sweet little sister? She moves forward as if to aid him.

Carrie K.: I'm not a child, as I've more than once told you, brother Ralph, an as I'll show you now.

Kabnis: Wait, Carrie. No, thats right. Youre not a child. But twont do t lift me bodily. You dont understand. But its th soul of me that needs th risin.

Carrie K.: Youre a bad brother an just wont listen t me when I'm tellin y t go t church.

Kabnis doesnt hear her. He breaks down and talks to himself.

Kabnis: Great God Almighty, a soul like mine cant pin itself onto a wagon wheel an satisfy itself in spinnin round. Iron prongs an hickory sticks, an God knows what all . . . all right for Halsey . . . use him. Me? I get my life down in this scum-hole. Th old man an me—

Carrie K.: Has he been talkin?

Kabnis: Huh? Who? Him? No. Dont need to. I talk. An when I really talk, it pays th best of them t listen. Th old man is a good listener. He's deaf; but he's a good listener. An I can talk t him. Tell him anything.

Carrie K.: He's deaf an blind, but I reckon he hears, an sees too, from th things I've heard.

Kabnis: No. Cant. Cant I tell you. How's he do it?

Carrie K.: Dunno, except I've heard that th souls of old folks have a way of seein things.

Kabnis: An I've heard them call that superstition.

The old man begins to shake his head slowly. Carrie and Kabnis watch him, anxiously. He mumbles. With a grave motion his head nods up and down. And then, on one of the down-swings—

Father John (remarkably clear and with great conviction): Sin.

He repeats this word several times, always on the downward nodding. Surprised, indignant, Kabnis forgets that Carrie is with him.

Kabnis: Sin! Shut up. What do you know about sin, you old black bastard. Shut up, an stop that swayin an noddin your head.

Father John: Sin.

Kabnis tries to get up.

Kabnis: Didnt I tell y t shut up?

Carrie steps forward to help him. Kabnis is violently shocked at her touch. He springs back.

Kabnis: Carrie! What . . . how . . . Baby, you shouldnt be down here. Ralph says things. Doesnt mean to. But Carrie, he doesnt know what he's talkin about. Couldnt know. It was only a preacher's sin they knew in those old days, an that wasnt sin at all. Mind me, th only sin is whats done against th soul. Th whole world is a conspiracy t sin, especially in America, an against me. I'm th victim of their sin. I'm what sin is. Does he look like me? Have you ever heard him say th things youve heard me say? He couldnt if he had th Holy Ghost t help him. Dont look shocked, little sweetheart, you hurt me.

Father John: Sin.

Kabnis: Aw, shut up, old man.

Carrie K.: Leave him be. He wants t say somethin. (She turns to the old man.) What is it, Father?

Kabnis: Whatsha talkin t that old deaf man for? Come away from him.

Carrie K.: What is it, Father?

The old man's lips begin to work. Words are formed incoherently. Finally, he manages to articulate—

Father John: Th sin whats fixed . . . (Hesitates.)

Carrie K. (restraining a comment from Kabnis): Go on, Father.

Father John: . . . upon th white folks—

Kabnis: Suppose youre talkin about that bastard race thats roamin round th country. It looks like sin, if thats what y mean. Give us somethin new an up t date.

Father John: —f tellin Jesus—lies. O th sin th white folks 'mitted when they made th Bible lie.

Boom. Boom. BOOM! Thuds on the floor above. The old man sinks back into his stony silence. Carrie is wet-eyed. Kabnis, contemptuous.

Kabnis: So thats your sin. All these years t tell us that th white folks made th Bible lie. Well, I'll be damned. Lewis ought t have been here. You old black fakir—

Carrie K.: Brother Ralph, is that your best Amen?

She turns him to her and takes his hot cheeks in her firm cool hands. Her palms draw the fever out. With its passing, Kabnis crumples. He sinks to his knees before her, ashamed, exhausted. His eyes squeeze tight. Carrie presses his face tenderly against her. The suffocation of her fresh starched dress feels good to him. Carrie is about to lift her hands in prayer, when Halsey, at the head of the stairs, calls down.

Halsey: Well, well. Whats up? Aint you ever comin? Come on. Whats up down there? Take you all mornin t sleep off a pint? Youre weakenin, man, youre weakenin. Th axle an th beam's all ready waitin f y. Come on.

Kabnis rises and is going doggedly towards the steps. Carrie notices his robe. She catches up to him, points to it, and helps him take it off. He hangs it, with an exaggerated ceremony, on its nail in the corner. He looks down on the tousled beds. His lips curl bitterly. Turning, he stumbles over the bucket of dead coals. He savagely jerks it from the floor. And then, seeing Carrie's eyes upon him, he swings the pail carelessly and with eyes downcast and swollen, trudges upstairs to the work-shop. Carrie's gaze follows him till he is gone. Then she goes to the old man and slips to her knees before him. Her lips murmur, "Jesus, come."

Light streaks through the iron-barred cellar window. Within its soft circle, the figures of Carrie and Father John.

Outside, the sun arises from its cradle in the tree-tops of the forest. Shadows of pines are dreams the sun shakes from its eyes. The sun arises. Gold-glowing child, it steps into the sky and sends a birth-song slanting down gray dust streets and sleepy windows of the southern town.

THE END

ZORA NEALE HURSTON
Photograph by Carl Van Vechten.
By permission of the Estate of Carl Van Vechten.
Joseph Solomon, Executor.

ZORA NEALE HURSTON

1891 TO 1960

Z ora Neale Hurston arrived in New York City in January 1925, one of the earliest recruits of the nascent Harlem Renaissance. As a student writer at Howard University in Washington, D.C., Hurston had impressed both Alain Locke, who taught philosophy at Howard, and Charles S. Johnson, editor of *Opportunity*, the organ of the New York-based National Urban League. Dedicated to publishing the work of promising young writers, Johnson urged Hurston to come to New York. After she did so, Johnson helped her find employment and introduced her to influential literary people. Most important, *Opportunity* published Hurston's first significant short story, "Spunk," which was reprinted later that year in Locke's landmark anthology *The New Negro*. By the summer of 1926, Hurston had joined Langston Hughes, Wallace Thurman, and Bruce Nugent (the most bohemian and outspoken of the younger Harlem writers) to edit *Fire!!*, a quarterly of arts and letters whose iconoclasm, especially toward the standards upheld by the likes of Johnson and Locke, ensured its demise after only one issue. To *Fire!!* Hurston contributed, "Sweat," a story many believe to be the best work of short fiction Hurston wrote during the Harlem Renaissance.

The setting, characters, and ethos of "Sweat" draw on Hurston's memories of the rugged all-black town of Eatonville, Florida, her home and the center of her fictional universe. From her father, John Hurston, a Baptist minister who also served as Eatonville's mayor, Zora learned the power that came from quick wits and well-aimed words tested in the verbal combats and the "lying [i.e., storytelling] sessions" that distinguished the oral culture of blacks in the South. In her autobiography, *Dust Tracks on a Road* (1942), Zora thanked her mother Lucy for encouraging her childhood independence and ambitions, in direct opposition to John Hurston's warning that "white folks were not going to stand for" a black woman with "my sassy tongue." The talents and temperament Zora derived from both parents, along with a healthy respect for herself, gave her the impetus to leave Eatonville in 1904 after her mother's death and pursue schooling in Jacksonville, Florida, and eventually at Morgan Academy in Baltimore and Howard University. Thus by the time Hurston was ready to launch her literary career in the mid-1920s in New York, she was well prepared to ride the high tide of surging self-confidence that put Harlem's flashiest literary denizens on the shores of unexpected celebrity. It did not take long for Zora Hurston—gifted mimic, side-splitting comic, and captivating storyteller in the "down-home" southern mode—to build a reputation as one of those New Negroes most in demand on Harlem's fashionable party and night-club circuit. As her writing proved, however, Hurston was much more than the female minstrel and artist-hustler that some, like Langston Hughes, judged her to be. For it was Hurston, more than perhaps anyone else among the writers of the Harlem Renaissance, who possessed a first-hand, bone-deep affinity with black folk, their lore, and their forms of expression, which her formal education and individual genius enabled her to represent in ways unique to the renaissance and unprecedented in the history of African American fiction.

"Sweat" bears many of the earmarks of Hurston's distinctiveness as a writer. The story refuses to represent southern blacks in accordance with traditional white racist stereotypes of blacks as comically low-class, nor does it abide by the credo well established in African American literature that writers of the race should specialize in enviable high-class Negroes. Instead Hurston identifies her protagonist as plainly and unashamedly working-class, a self-supporting laundry-woman, the virtual antitype of the dependent "mammy" image of black southern women so prevalent in the popular media of the time. Anticipating many of the realistically portrayed southern black women of Hurton's later novels, Delia Jones has the physical toughness and the spiritual resources not just to survive the oppressive conditions of her life but to triumph over the worst of them. Observing her struggle to maintain her dignity against her husband's abuse, the black men who serve as a kind of Greek chorus in the story provide a strong sense of the judgment of the African American community and of the values on which that community is based. Ultimately it is Hurston's determination to represent the sustaining character of African American community in a working-class black woman, in her dialect speech, her beliefs and values, and her heroic reclamation of herself, that makes "Sweat" such a breakthrough for black women's fiction in the Harlem Renaissance.

Two and a half years after coming to New York to pursue a literary career, Zora Hurston left Harlem to undertake serious social science fieldwork in Florida in an effort to satisfy the requirements of a degree program in anthropology from Barnard College of Columbia University. During the next decade Hurston did extensive original research in African American folk cultures in the American South and in the Caribbean. She did some college teaching, won two fellowships for advanced study and fieldwork in anthropology, and worked in the Federal Theater Project in New York and the Federal Writers' Project in Florida. During these years Hurston melded her creativity and her anthropological research in several successful ventures, producing a series of concerts and folk dramas in the early 1930s, a well-received first novel, *Jonah's Gourd Vine* (1934), and the first book of folklore by a black American, *Mules and Men* (1935). The stimulus for undertaking *Jonah's Gourd Vine* came from a publisher's positive response to Hurston's 1933 short story, "The Gilded Six-Bits," which, like her first novel, deals with marriage and infidelity in a southern African American setting. Despite severe financial constraints in the late 1930s, Hurston saw through to publication the novel on which her literary fame now rests—*Their Eyes Were Watching God* (1937)—as well as the experimental fiction, *Moses, Man of the Mountain* (1939), a fusion of biblical narrative and African American myth.

After World War II, the increasingly conservative cast of her writing, which was invested much more in journalism than in fiction, led to Hurston's almost total eclipse as a literary figure in the 1950s. Her death in a welfare home in Fort Pierce, Florida, in 1960 went unnoticed. In the concluding chapter to *Dust Tracks on a Road*, Hurston reckons in an inimitable, signature metaphor the price she paid for who she was determined to be: "I have been in Sorrow's kitchen and licked out all the pots." Yet, as she maintained in another autobiographical statement written during the Harlem Renaissance, "I am not tragically colored. There is no great sorrow dammed up in my soul, nor lurking behind my eyes. . . . No one on earth ever had a greater chance for glory." It is now amply clear that few African American writers made as much of that chance as Zora Neale Hurston.

SUGGESTIONS FOR FURTHER READING

Awkward, Michael. *Inspiriting Influences: Tradition, Revision, and Afro-American Women's Novels.* New York: Columbia University Press, 1989.
Gates, Henry Louis, Jr. *The Signifying Monkey.* New York: Oxford University Press, 1988.

Hemenway, Robert E. *Zora Neale Hurston*. Urbana: University of Illinois Press, 1977.

Holloway, Karla. *The Character of the Word: The Texts of Zora Neale Hurston*. Westport, CT: Greenwood Press, 1987.

Howard, Lillie P. *Zora Neale Hurston*. Boston: Twayne, 1980.

Hurston, Zora Neale. *Dust Tracks on a Road*. Ed. Robert E. Hemenway. 2nd ed. Urbana: University of Illinois Press, 1984.

————. *I Love Myself When I Am Laughing . . . And Then Again When I Am Looking Mean and Impressive: A Zora Neale Hurston Reader*. Ed. Alice Walker. Introd. Mary Helen Washington. Old Westbury, NY: Feminist Press, 1979.

Jones, Gayl. *Liberating Voices: Oral Tradition in African American Literature*. Cambridge, MA: Harvard University Press, 1991.

Newson, Adele S. *Zora Neale Hurston: A Reference Guide*. Boston: G. K. Hall, 1987.

SWEAT

It was eleven o'clock of a Spring night in Florida. It was Sunday. Any other night, Delia Jones would have been in bed for two hours by this time. But she was a washwoman, and Monday morning meant a great deal to her. So she collected the soiled clothes on Saturday when she returned the clean things. Sunday night after church, she sorted them and put the white things to soak. It saved her almost a half day's start. A great hamper in the bedroom held the clothes that she brought home. It was so much neater than a number of bundles lying around.

She squatted in the kitchen floor beside the great pile of clothes, sorting them into small heaps according to color, and humming a song in a mournful key, but wondering through it all where Sykes, her husband, had gone with her horse and buckboard.

Just then something long, round, limp and black fell upon her shoulders and slithered to the floor beside her. A great terror took hold of her. It softened her knees and dried her mouth so that it was a full minute before she could cry out or move. Then she saw that it was the big bull whip her husband liked to carry when he drove.

She lifted her eyes to the door and saw him standing there bent over with laughter at her fright. She screamed at him.

"Sykes, what you throw dat whip on me like dat? You know it would skeer me—looks just like a snake, an' you knows how skeered Ah is of snakes."

"Course Ah knowed it! That's how come Ah done it." He slapped his leg with his hand and almost rolled on the ground in his mirth. "If you such a big fool dat you got to have a fit over a earth worm or a string, Ah don't keer how bad Ah skeer you."

"You aint got no business doing it. Gawd knows it's a sin. Some day Ah'm gointuh drop dead from some of yo' foolishness. 'Nother thing, where you been wid mah rig? Ah feeds dat pony. He aint fuh you to be drivin' wid no bull whip."

"You sho is one aggravatin' nigger woman!" he declared and stepped into the room. She resumed her work and did not answer him at once. "Ah done tole you time and again to keep them white folks' clothes outa dis house."

He picked up the whip and glared down at her. Delia went on with her work. She went out into the yard and returned with a galvanized tub and sit it on the washbench. She saw that Sykes had kicked all of the clothes together again, and now stood in her way truculently, his whole manner hoping, *praying*, for an argument. But she walked calmly around him and commenced to re-sort the things.

"Next time, Ah'm gointer kick 'em outdoors," he threatened as he struck a match along the leg of his corduroy breeches.

Delia never looked up from her work, and her thin, stooped shoulders sagged further.

"Ah aint for no fuss t'night Sykes. Ah just come from taking sacrament at the church house."

He snorted scornfully. "Yeah, you just come from de church house on a Sunday night, but heah you is gone to work on them clothes. You ain't nothing but a hypocrite. One of them amen-corner Christians—sing, whoop, and shout, then come home and wash white folks clothes on the Sabbath."

He stepped roughly upon the whitest pile of things, kicking them helter-skelter as he crossed the room. His wife gave a little scream of dismay, and quickly gathered them together again.

"Sykes, you quit grindin' dirt into these clothes! How can Ah git through by Sat'day if Ah don't start on Sunday?"

"Ah don't keer if you never git through. Anyhow, Ah done promised Gawd and a couple of other men, Ah aint gointer have it in mah house. Don't gimme no lip neither, else Ah'll throw 'em out and put mah fist up side yo' head to boot."

Delia's habitual meekness seemed to slip from her shoulders like a blown scarf. She was on her feet; her poor little body, her bare knuckly hands bravely defying the strapping hulk before her.

"Looka heah, Sykes, you done gone too fur. Ah been married to you fur fifteen years, and Ah been takin' in washin' fur fifteen years. Sweat, sweat, sweat! Work and sweat, cry and sweat, pray and sweat!"

"What's that got to do with me?" he asked brutally.

"What's it got to do with you, Sykes? Mah tub of suds is filled yo' belly with vittles more times than yo' hands is filled it. Mah sweat is done paid for this house and Ah reckon Ah kin keep on sweatin' in it."

She seized the iron skillet from the stove and struck a defensive pose, which act surprised him greatly, coming from her. It cowed him and he did not strike her as he usually did.

"Naw you won't," she panted, "that ole snaggle-toothed black woman you runnin' with aint comin' heah to pile up on *mah* sweat and blood. You aint paid for nothin' on this place, and Ah'm gointer stay right heah till Ah'm toted out foot foremost."

"Well, you better quit gittin' me riled up, else thcy'll be totin' you out sooner than you expect. Ah'm so tired of you Ah don't know whut to do. Gawd! how Ah hates skinny wimmen!"

A little awed by this new Delia, he sidled out of the door and slammed the back gate after him. He did not say where he had gone, but she knew too well. She knew very well that he would not return until nearly daybreak also. Her work over, she went on to bed but not to sleep at once. Things had come to a pretty pass!

She lay awake, gazing upon the debris that cluttered their matrimonial trail. Not an image left standing along the way. Anything like flowers had long ago been drowned in the salty stream that had been pressed from her heart. Her tears, her sweat, her blood. She had brought love to the union and he had brought a longing after the flesh. Two months after the wedding, he had given her the first brutal beating. She had the memory of his numerous trips to Orlando with all of his wages when he had returned to her penniless, even before the first year had passed. She was young and soft then, but now she thought of her knotty, muscled limbs, her harsh knuckly hands, and drew herself up into an unhappy little ball in the middle of the big feather bed. Too late now to hope for love, even if it were not Bertha it would be someone else. This case differed from the others only in that she was bolder than the others. Too late for everything except her little home. She had built it for her old days, and planted one by one the trees and flowers there. It was lovely to her, lovely.

Somehow, before sleep came, she found herself saying aloud: "Oh well, whatever goes over the Devil's back, is got to come under his belly. Sometime or ruther, Sykes, like everybody else, is gointer reap his sowing." After that she was able to build a spiritual earthworks against her husband. His shells could no longer reach her. *Amen.* She went to sleep and slept until he announced his presence in bed by kicking her feet and rudely snatching the cover away.

"Gimme some kivah heah, an' git yo' damn foots over on yo' own side! Ah oughter mash you in yo' mouf fuh drawing dat skillet on me."

Delia went clear to the rail without answering him. A triumphant indifference to all that he was or did.

The week was as full of work for Delia as all other weeks, and Saturday found her behind her little pony, collecting and delivering clothes.

It was a hot, hot day near the end of July. The village men on Joe Clarke's porch even chewed cane listlessly. They did not hurl the cane-knots as usual. They let them dribble over the edge of the porch. Even conversation had collapsed under the heat.

"Heah come Delia Jones," Jim Merchant said, as the shaggy pony came 'round the bend of the road toward them. The rusty buckboard was heaped with baskets of crisp, clean laundry.

"Yep," Joe Lindsay agreed. "Hot or col', rain or shine, jes ez reg'lar ez de weeks roll roun' Delia carries 'em an' fetches 'em on Sat'day."

"She better if she wanter eat," said Moss. "Syke Jones aint wuth de shot an' powder hit would tek tuh kill 'em. Not to *huh* he aint."

"He sho' aint," Walter Thomas chimed in. "It's too bad, too, cause she wuz a right pritty lil trick when he got huh. Ah'd uh mah'ied huh mahseff if he hadnter beat me to it."

Delia nodded briefly at the men as she drove past.

"Too much knockin' will ruin *any* 'oman. He done beat huh 'nough tuh kill three women, let 'lone change they looks," said Elijah Mosely. "How Syke kin stommuck dat big black greasy Mogul he's layin' roun' wid, gits me. Ah swear dat eight-rock couldn't kiss a sardine can Ah done thowed out de back do' 'way las' yeah."

"Aw, she's fat, thass how come. He's allus been crazy 'bout fat women," put in Merchant. "He'd a' been tied up wid one long time ago if he could a' found one tuh have him. Did Ah tell yuh 'bout him come sidlin' roun' *mah* wife—bringin' her a basket uh pce cans outa his yard fuh a present? Yes-sir, mah wife! She tol' him tuh take 'em right straight back home, cause Delia works so hard ovah dat washtub she reckon everything on de place taste lak sweat an' soap-suds. Ah jus' wisht Ah'd a' caught 'im 'roun' dere! Ah'd a' made his hips ketch on fiah down dat shell road."

"Ah know he done it, too. Ah sees 'im grinnin' at every 'oman dat passes," Walter Thomas said. "But even so, he useter eat some mighty big hunks uh humble pie tuh git dat lil' 'oman he got. She wuz ez pritty ez a speckled pup! Dat wuz fifteen yeahs ago. He useter be so skeered uh losin' huh, she could make him do some parts of a husband's duty. Dey never wuz de same in de mind."

"There oughter be a law about him," said Lindsay. He aint fit tuh carry guts tuh a bear."

Clarke spoke for the first time. "Taint no law on earth dat kin make a man be decent if it aint in 'im. There's plenty men dat takes a wife lak dey do a joint uh sugar-cane. It's round, juicy an' sweet when dey gits it. But dey squeeze an' grind, squeeze an' grind an' wring tell dey wring every drop uh pleasure dat's in 'em out. When dey's satisfied dat dey is wrung dry, dey treats 'em jes lak dey do a cane-chew. Dey thows 'em away. Dey knows whut dey is doin' while dey is at it, an' hates theirselves fuh it but they keeps on hangin' after huh tell she's empty. Den dey hates huh fuh bein' a cane-chew an' in de way."

"We oughter take Syke an' dat stray 'oman uh his'n down in Lake Howell swamp an' lay on de rawhide till they cain't say 'Lawd a' mussy.' He allus wuz uh ovahbearin' niggah, but since dat white 'oman from up north done teached 'im how to run a automobile, he done got to biggety to live—an' we oughter kill 'im." Old Man Anderson advised.

A grunt of approval went around the porch. But the heat was melting their civic virtue and Elijah Moseley began to bait Joe Clarke.

"Come on, Joe, git a melon outa dere an' slice it up for yo' customers. We'se all sufferin' wid de heat. De bear's done got *me!*"

"Thass right, Joe, a watermelon is jes' whut Ah needs tuh cure de eppizudicks," Walter Thomas joined forces with Moseley. "Come on dere, Joe. We all is steady customers an' you aint set us up in a long time. Ah chooses dat long, bowlegged Floridy favorite."

"A god, an' be dough You all gimme twenty cents and slice away," Clarke retorted. "Ah needs a col' slice m'self. Heah, everybody chip in. Ah'll lend y'll mah meat knife."

The money was quickly subscribed and the huge melon brought forth. At that moment, Sykes and Bertha arrived. A determined silence fell on the porch and the melon was put away again.

Merchant snapped down the blade of his jackknife and moved toward the store door.

"Come on in, Joe, an' gimme a slab uh sow belly an' uh pound uh coffee—almost fuhgot 'twas Sat'day. Got to git on home." Most of the men left also.

Just then Delia drove past on her way home, as Sykes was ordering magnificently for Bertha. It pleased him for Delia to see.

"Git whutsoever yo' heart desires, Honey. Wait a minute, Joe. Give huh two botles uh strawberry soda-water, uh quart uh parched ground-peas, an' a block uh chewin' gum."

With all this they left the store, with Sykes reminding Bertha that this was his town and she could have it if she wanted it.

The men returned soon after they left, and held their watermelon feast.

"Where did Syke Jones git dat 'oman from nohow?" Lindsay asked.

"Ovah Apopka. Guess dey musta been cleanin' out de town when she lef'. She don't look lak a thing but a hunk uh liver wid hair on it."

"Well, she sho' kin squall," Dave Carter contributed. "When she gits ready tuh laff, she jes' opens huh mouf an' latches it back tuh de las' notch. No ole grandpa alligator down in Lake Bell ain't got nothin' on huh."

Bertha had been in town three months now. Sykes was still paying her room rent at Della Lewis'—the only house in town that would have taken her in. Sykes took her frequently to Winter Park to "stomps." He still assured her that he was the swellest man in the state.

"Sho' you kin have dat lil' ole house soon's Ah kin git dat 'oman outa dere. Everything b'longs tuh me an' you sho' kin have it. Ah sho' 'bominates uh skinny 'oman. Lawdy, you sho' is got one portly shape on you! You kin git *anything* you wants. Dis is *mah* town an' you sho' kin have it."

Delia's work-worn knees crawled over the earth in Gethsemane and up the rocks of Calvary many, many times during these months. She avoided the villagers and meeting places in her efforts to be blind and deaf. But Bertha nullified this to a degree, by coming to Delia's house to call Sykes out to her at the gate.

Delia and Sykes fought all the time now with no peaceful interludes. They slept and ate in silence. Two or three times Delia had attempted a timid friendliness, but she was repulsed each time. It was plain that the breaches must remain agape.

The sun had burned July to August. The heat streamed down like a million hot arrows, smiting all things living upon the earth. Grass withered, leaves browned, snakes went blind in shedding and men and dogs went mad. Dog days!

Delia came home one day and found Sykes there before her. She wondered, but started to go on into the house without speaking, even though he was standing in the kitchen door and she must either stoop under his arm or ask him to move. He made no room for her. She noticed a soap box beside the steps, but paid no particular attention to it, knowing that he must have brought it there. As she was stooping to pass under his outstretched arm, he suddenly pushed her backward, laughingly.

"Look in de box dere Delia, Ah done brung yuh somethin'!"

She nearly fell upon the box in her stumbling, and when she saw what it held, she all but fainted outright.

"Syke! Syke, mah Gawd! You take dat rattlesnake 'way from heah! You *gottuh*. Oh, Jesus, have mussy!"

"Ah aint gut tuh do nuthin' uh de kin'—fact is Ah aint got tuh do nothin' but die. Taint no use uh you puttin' on airs makin' out lak you skeered uh dat snake—he's gointer stay right heah tell he die. He wouldn't bite me cause Ah knows how tuh handle 'im. Nohow he wouldn't risk breakin' out his fangs 'gin *yo'* skinny laigs."

"Naw, now Syke, don't keep dat thing 'roun' heah tuh skeer me tuh death. You knows Ah'm even feared uh earth worms. Thass de biggest snake Ah evah did see. Kill 'im Syke, please."

"Doan ast me tuh do nothin' fuh yuh. Goin' 'roun' tryin' tuh be so damn asterperious. Naw, Ah aint gonna kill it. Ah think uh damn sight mo' uh him dan you! Dat's a nice snake an' anybody doan lak 'im kin jes' hit de grit."

The village soon heard that Sykes had the snake, and came to see and ask questions.

"How de hen-fire did you ketch dat six-foot rattler, Syke?" Thomas asked.

"He's full uh frogs so he caint hardly move, thass how Ah eased up on 'm. But Ah'm a snake charmer an' knows how tuh handle 'em. Shux, dat aint nothin'. Ah could ketch one eve'y day if Ah so wanted tuh."

"Whut he needs is a heavy hick'ry club leaned real heavy on his head. Dat's de bes 'way tuh charm a rattlesnake."

"Naw, Walt, y'll jes' don't understand dese diamon' backs lak Ah do," said Sykes in a superior tone of voice.

The village agreed with Walter, but the snake stayed on. His box remained by the kitchen door with its screen wire covering. Two or three days later it had digested its meal of frogs and literally came to life. It rattled at every movement in the kitchen or the yard. One day as Delia came down the kitchen steps she saw his chalky-white fangs curved like scimitars hung in the wire meshes. This time she did not run away with averted eyes as usual. She stood for a long time in the doorway in a red fury that grew bloodier for every second that she regarded the creature that was her torment.

That night she broached the subject as soon as Sykes sat down to the table.

"Syke, Ah wants you tuh take dat snake 'way fum heah. You done starved me an' Ah put up widcher, you done beat me and Ah took dat, but you done kilt all mah insides bringin' dat varmint heah."

Sykes poured out a saucer full of coffee and drank it deliberately before he answered her.

"A whole lot Ah keer 'bout how you feels inside uh out. Dat snake aint goin' no damn wheah till Ah gits ready fuh 'im tuh go. So fur as beatin' is concerned, yuh aint took near all dat you gointer take ef yuh stay 'roun' *me*."

Delia pushed back her plate and got up from the table. "Ah hates you, Sykes," she said calmly. "Ah hates you tuh de same degree dat Ah useter love yuh. Ah done took an' took till mah belly is full up tuh mah neck. Dat's de reason Ah got mah letter fum de church an' moved mah membership tuh Woodbridge—so Ah don't haftuh take no sacrament wid yuh. Ah don't wantuh see yuh 'roun' me atall. Lay 'roun' wid dat 'oman all yuh wants tuh, but gwan 'way fum me an' mah house. At hates yuh lak uh suck-egg dog."

Sykes almost let the huge wad of corn bread and collard greens he was chewing fall out of his mouth in amazement. He had a hard time whipping himself up to the proper fury to try to answer Delia.

"Well, Ah'm glad you does hate me. Ah'm sho' tiahed uh you hangin' ontuh me. Ah don't want yuh. Look at yuh stringey ole neck! Yo' rawbony laigs an' arms is enough tuh cut uh man tuh death. You looks jes' lak de devvul's doll-baby tuh *me*. You cain't hate me no worse dan Ah hates you. Ah been hatin' *you* fuh years.

"Yo' ole black hide don't look lak nothin' tuh me, but uh passle uh wrinkled up rubber, wid yo' big ole yeahs flappin' on each side lak up paih uh buzzard wings. Don't think Ah'm gointuh be run 'way fum mah house neither. Ah'm goin' tuh de white folks bout *you*, mah young man, de very nex' time you lay yo' han's on me. Mah cup is done run ovah." Delia said this with no signs of fear and Sykes departed from the house, threatening her, but made not the slightest move to carry out any of them.

That night he did not return at all, and the next day being Sunday, Delia was glad that she did not have to quarrel before she hitched up her pony and drove the four miles to Woodbridge.

She stayed to the night service—"love feast"—which was very warm and full of spirit. In the emotional winds her domestic trials were borne far and wide so that she sang as she drove homeward,

> "Jurden water, black an' col'
> Chills de body, not de soul
> An' Ah wantah cross Jurden in uh calm time."

She came from the barn to the kitchen door and stopped.

"Whut's de mattah, ol' satan, you aint kickin' up yo' racket?" She addressed the snake's box. Complete silence. She went on into the house with a new hope in its birth struggles. Perhaps her threat to go to the white folks had frightened Sykes! Perhaps he was sorry! Fifteen years of misery and suppression had brought Delia to the place where she would hope *anything* that looked towards a way over or through her wall of inhibitions.

She felt in the match safe behind the stove at once for a match. There was only one there.

"Dat niggah wouldn't fetch nothin' heah tuh save his rotten neck, but he kin run thew whut Ah brings quick enough. Now he done toted off nigh on tuh haff uh box uh matches. He done had dat 'oman heah in mah house, too."

Nobody but a woman could tell how she knew this even before she struck the match. But she did and it put her into a new fury.

Presently she brought in the tubs to put the white things to soak. This time she decided she need not bring the hamper out of the bedroom; she would go in there and do the sorting. She picked up the pot-bellied lamp and went in. The room was small and the hamper stood hard by the foot of the white iron bed. She could sit and reach through the bedposts—resting as she worked.

"Ah wantah cross Jurden in uh calm time." She was singing again. The mood of the "love feast" had returned. She threw back the lid of the basket almost gaily. Then, moved by both horror and terror, he spring back toward the door. *There lay the snake in the basket!* He moved sluggishly at first, but even as she turned round and round, jumped up and down in an insanity of fear, he began to stir vigorously. She saw him pouring his awful beauty from the basket upon the bed, then she seized the lamp and ran as fast as she could to the kitchen. The wind from the open door blew out the light and the darkness added to her terror. She sped to the darkness of the yard, slamming the door after her before she thought to set down the lamp. She did not feel safe even on the ground, so she climbed up in the hay barn.

There for an hour or more she lay sprawled upon the hay a gibbering wreck.

Finally she grew quiet, and after that, coherent thought. With this, stalked through her a cold, bloody rage. Hours of this. A period of introspection, a space of retrospection, then a mixture of both. Out of this an awful calm.

"Well, Ah done de bes' Ah could. If things aint right, Gawd knows taint mah fault."

She went to sleep—a twitchy sleep—and woke up to a faint gray sky. There was a loud hollow sound below. She peered out. Sykes was at the wood-pile, demolishing a wire-covered box.

He hurried to the kitchen door, but hung outside there some minutes before he entered, and stood some minutes more inside before he closed it after him.

The gray in the sky was spreading. Delia descended without fear now, and crouched beneath the low bedroom window. The drawn shade shut out the dawn, shut in the night. But the thin walls held back no sound.

"Dat ol' scratch is woke up now!" She mused at the tremendous whirr inside, which every woodsman knows, is one of the sound illusions. The rattler is a ventriloquist. His whirr sounds to the right, to the left, straight ahead, behind, close under foot—everywhere but where it is. Woe to him who guesses wrong unless he is prepared to hold up his end of the argument! Sometimes he strikes without rattling at all.

Inside, Sykes heard nothing until he knocked a pot lid off the stove while trying to reach the match safe in the dark. He had emptied his pockets at Bertha's.

The snake seemed to wake up under the stove and Sykes made a quick leap into the bedroom. In spite of the gin he had had, his head was clearing now.

"Mah Gawd!" he chattered, "ef Ah could on'y strack uh light!"

The rattling ceased for a moment as he stood paralyzed. He waited. It seemed that the snake waited also.

"Oh, fuh de light! Ah thought he'd be too sick"—Sykes was muttering to himself when the whirr began again, closer, right underfoot this time. Long before this, Sykes' ability to think had been flattened down to primitive instinct and he leaped—onto the bed.

Outside Delia heard a cry that might have come from a maddened chimpanzee, a stricken gorilla. All the terror, all the horror, all the rage that man possibly could express, without a recognizable human sound.

A tremendous stir inside there, another series of animal screams, the intermittent whirr of the reptile. The shade torn violently down from the window, letting in the red dawn, a huge brown hand seizing the window stick, great dull blows upon the wooden floor punctuating the gibberish of sound long after the rattle of the snake had abruptly subsided. All this Delia could see and hear from her place beneath the window, and it made her ill. She crept over to the four-o'clocks and stretched herself on the cool earth to recover.

She lay there. "Delia, Delia!" She could hear Sykes calling in a most despairing tone as one who expected no answer. The sun crept on up, and he called. Delia could not move—her legs were gone flabby. She never moved, he called, and the sun kept rising.

"Mah Gawd!" She heard him moan, "Mah Gawd fum Heben!" She heard him stumbling about and got up from her flower-bed. The sun was growing warm. As she approached the door she heard him call out hopefully, "Delia, is dat you Ah heah?"

She saw him on his hands and knees as soon as she reached the door. He crept an inch or two toward her—all that he was able, and she saw his horribly swollen neck and his one open eye shining with hope. A surge of pity too strong to support bore her away from that eye that must, could not, fail to see the tubs. He would see the lamp. Orlando with its doctors was too far. She could scarcely reach the Chinaberry tree, where she waited in the growing heat while inside she knew the cold river was creeping up and up to extinguish that eye which must know by now that she knew.

THE GILDED SIX-BITS

It was a Negro yard around a Negro house in a Negro settlement that looked to the payroll of the G and G Fertilizer works for its support.

But there was something happy about the place. The front yard was parted in the middle by a sidewalk from gate to door-step, a sidewalk edged on either side by quart bottles driven neck down into the ground on a slant. A mess of homey flowers planted without a plan but blooming cheerily from their helter-skelter places. The fence and house were whitewashed. The porch and steps scrubbed white.

The front door stood open to the sunshine so that the floor of the front room could finish drying after its weekly scouring. It was Saturday. Everything clean from the front gate to the privy house. Yard raked so that the strokes of the rake would make a pattern. Fresh newspaper cut in fancy edge on the kitchen shelves.

Missie May was bathing herself in the galvanized washtub in the bedroom. Her dark-brown skin glistened under the soapsuds that skittered down from her wash rag. Her stiff young breasts thrust forward aggressively like broad-based cones with the tips lacquered in black.

She heard men's voices in the distance and glanced at the dollar clock on the dresser.

"Humph! Ah'm way behind time t'day! Joe gointer be heah 'fore Ah git mah clothes on if Ah don't make haste."

She grabbed the clean meal sack at hand and dried herself hurriedly and began to dress. But before she could tie her slippers, there came the ring of singing metal on wood. Nine times.

Missie May grinned with delight. She had not seen the big tall man come stealing in the gate and creep up the walk grinning happily at the joyful mischief he was about to commit. But she knew that it was her husband throwing silver dollars in the door for her to pick up and pile beside her plate at dinner. It was this way every Saturday afternoon. The nine dollars hurled into the open door, he scurried to a hiding place behind the cape jasmine bush and waited.

Missie May promptly appeared at the door in mock alarm.

"Who dat chunkin' money in mah do'way?" she demanded. No answer from the yard. She leaped off the porch and began to search the shrubbery. She peeped under the porch and hung over the gate to look up and down the road. While she did this, the man behind the jasmine darted to the china berry tree. She spied him and gave chase.

"Nobody ain't gointer be chunkin' money at me and Ah not do 'em nothin'," she shouted in mock anger. He ran around the house with Missie May at his heels. She overtook him at the kitchen door. He ran inside but could not close it after him before she crowded in and locked with him in a rough and tumble. For several minutes the two were a furious mass of male and female energy. Shouting, laughing, twisting, turning, tussling, tickling each other in the ribs; Missie May clutching onto Joe and Joe trying, but not too hard, to get away.

"Missie May, take yo' hand out mah pocket!" Joe shouted out between laughs.

"Ah ain't, Joe, not lessen you gwine gimme whateve' it is good you got in yo' pocket. Turn it go, Joe, do Ah'll tear yo' clothes."

"Go on tear 'em. You de one dat pushes de needles round heah. Move yo' hand Missie May."

"Lemme git dat paper sack out yo' pocket. Ah bet its candy kisses."

"Tain't. Move yo' hand. Woman ain't got no business in a man's clothes nohow. Go way."

Missie May gouged way down and gave an upward jerk and triumphed.

"Unhhunh! Ah got it. It 'tis so candy kisses. Ah knowed you had somethin' for me in yo' clothes. Now Ah got to see whut's in every pocket you got."

Joe smiled indulgently and let his wife go through all of his pockets and take out the things that he had hidden there for her to find. She bore off the chewing gum, the cake of sweet soap, the pocket handkerchief as if she had wrested them from him, as if they had not been bought for the sake of this friendly battle.

"Whew! dat play-fight done got me all warmed up." Joe exclaimed. "Got me some water in de kittle?"

"Yo' water is on de fire and yo' clean things is cross de bed. Hurry up and wash yo'self and git changed so we kin eat. Ah'm hongry." As Missie said this, she bore the steaming kettle into the bedroom.

"You ain't hongry, sugar," Joe contradicted her. "Youse jes' a little empty. Ah'm de one whut's hongry. Ah could eat up camp meetin', back off 'ssociation, and drink Jurdan dry. Have it on de table when Ah git out de tub."

"Don't you mess wid mah business, man. You git in yo' clothes. Ah'm a real wife, not no dress and breath. Ah might not look lak one, but if you burn me, you won't git a thing but wife ashes."

Joe splashed in the bedroom and Missie May fanned around in the kitchen. A fresh red and white checked cloth on the table. Big pitcher of buttermilk beaded with pale drops of butter from the churn. Hot fried mullet, crackling bread, ham hock atop a mound of string beans and new potatoes, and perched on the window-sill a pone of spicy potato pudding.

Very little talk during the meal but that little consisted of banter that pretended to deny affection but in reality flaunted it. Like when Missie May reached for a second helping of the tater pone. Joe snatched it out of her reach.

After Missie May had made two or three unsuccessful grabs at the pan, she begged, "Aw, Joe gimme some mo' dat tater pone."

"Nope, sweetenin' is for us men-folks. Y'all pritty lil frail eels don't need nothin' lak dis. You too sweet already."

"Please, Joe."

"Naw, naw. Ah don't want you to git no sweeter than whut you is already. We goin' down de road a lil piece t'night so you go put on yo' Sunday-go-to-meetin' things."

Missie May looked at her husband to see if he was playing some prank. "Sho nuff, Joe?"

"Yeah. We goin' to de ice cream parlor."

"Where de ice cream parlor at, Joe?"

"A new man done come heah from Chicago and he done got a place and took and opened it up for a ice cream parlor, and bein' as it's real swell, Ah wants you to be one de first ladies to walk in dere and have some set down."

"Do Jesus, Ah ain't knowed nothin' 'bout it. Who de man done it?"

"Mister Otis D. Slemmons, of spots and places—Memphis, Chicago, Jacksonville, Philadelphia and so on."

"Dat heavy-set man wid his mouth full of gold teethes?"

"Yeah. Where did you see 'im at?"

"Ah went down to de sto' tuh git a box of lye and Ah seen 'im standin' on de corner talkin' to some of de mens, and Ah come on back and went to scrubbin' de floor, and he passed and tipped his hat whilst Ah was scourin' de steps. Ah thought Ah never seen *him* befo'."

Joe smiled pleasantly. "Yeah, he's up to date. He got de finest clothes Ah ever seen on a colored man's back."

"Aw, he don't look no better in his clothes than you do in yourn. He got a puzzlegut on 'im and he so chuckle-headed, he got a pone behind his neck."

Joe looked down at his own abdomen and said wistfully, "Wisht Ah had a build on me lak he got. He ain't puzzle-gutted, honey. He jes' got a corperation. Dat make 'm look lak a rich white man. All rich mens is got some belly on 'em."

"Ah seen de pitchers of Henry Ford and he's a spare-built man and Rockefeller look lak he ain't got but one gut. But Ford and Rockefeller and dis Slemmons and all de rest kin be as many-gutted as dey please, Ah'm satisfied wid you jes' lak you is, baby. God took pattern after a pine tree and built you noble. Youse a pritty man, and if Ah knowed any way to make you mo' pritty still Ah'd take and do it."

Joe reached over gently and toyed with Missie May's ear. "You jes' say dat cause you love me, but Ah know Ah can't hold no light to Otis D. Slemmons. Ah ain't never been nowhere and Ah ain't got nothin' but you."

Missie May got on his lap and kissed him and he kissed back in kind. Then he went on. "All de womens is crazy 'bout 'im everywhere he go."

"How you know dat, Joe?"

"He tole us so hisself."

"Dat don't make it so. His mouf is cut cross-ways, ain't it? Well, he kin lie jes' lak anybody else."

"Good Lawd, Missie! You womens sho is hard to sense into things. He's got a five-dollar gold piece for a stick-pin and he got a ten-dollar gold piece on his watch chain and his mouf is jes' crammed full of gold teethes. Sho wisht it wuz mine. And whut make it so cool, he got money 'cumulated. And womens give it all to 'im."

"Ah don't see whut de womens see on 'im. Ah wouldn't give 'im a wink if de sheriff wuz after 'im."

"Well, he tole us how de white womens in Chicago give 'im all dat gold money. So he don't 'low nobody to touch it at all. Not even put dey finger on it. Dey tole 'im not to. You kin make 'miration at it, but don't tetch it."

"Whyn't he stay up dere where dey so crazy 'bout 'im?"

"Ah reckon dey done made 'im vast-rich and he wants to travel some. He say dey wouldn't leave 'im hit a lick of work. He got mo' lady people crazy 'bout him than he kin shake a stick at."

"Joe, Ah hates to see you so dumb. Dat stray nigger jes' tell y'all anything and y'all b'lieve it."

"Go 'head on now, honey and put on yo' clothes. He talkin' 'bout his pritty womens—Ah want 'im to see *mine*."

Missie May went off to dress and Joe spent the time trying to make his stomach punch out like Slemmons' middle. He tried the rolling swagger of the stranger, but found that his tall bone-and-muscle stride fitted ill with it. He just had time to drop back into his seat before Missie May came in dressed to go.

On the way home that night Joe was exultant. "Didn't Ah say ole Otis was swell? Can't he talk Chicago talk? Wuzn't dat funny whut he said when great big fat ole Ida Armstrong come in? He asted me, 'Who is dat broad wid de forte shake?' Dat's a new word. Us always thought forty was a set of figgers but he showed us where it means a whole heap of things. Sometimes he don't say forty, he jes' say thirty-eight and two and dat mean de same thing. Know whut he tole me when Ah wuz payin' for our ice cream? He say, 'Ah have to hand it to you, Joe. Dat wife of yours is jes' thirty-eight and two. Yessuh, she's forte!' Ain't he killin'?"

"He'll do in case of a rush. But he sho is got uh heap uh gold on 'im. Dat's de first time Ah ever seed gold money. It lookted good on him sho nuff, but it'd look a whole heap better on you."

"Who, me? Missie May youse crazy! Where would a po' man lak me git gold money from?"

Missie May was silent for a minute, then she said, "Us might find some goin' long de road some time. Us could."

"Who would be losin' gold money round heah? We ain't even seen none dese white folks wearin' no gold money on dey watch chain. You must be figgerin' Mister Packard or Mister Cadillac goin' pass through heah."

"You don't know whut been lost 'round heah. Maybe somebody way back in memorial times lost they gold money and went on off and it ain't never been found. And then if we wuz to find it, you could wear some 'thout havin' no gang of womens lak dat Slemmons say he got."

Joe laughed and hugged her. "Don't be so wishful 'bout me. Ah'm satisfied de way Ah is. So long as Ah be yo' husband, Ah don't keer 'bout nothin' else. Ah'd ruther all de other womens in de world to be dead than for you to have de toothache. Less we go to bed and git our night rest."

It was Saturday night once more before Joe could parade his wife in Slemmons' ice cream parlor again. He worked the night shift and Saturday was his only night off. Every other evening around six o'clock he left home, and dying dawn saw him hustling home around the lake where the challenging sun flung a flaming sword from east to west across the trembling water.

That was the best part of life—going home to Missie May. Their white-washed house, the mock battle on Saturday, the dinner and ice cream parlor afterwards, church on Sunday nights when Missie out-dressed any woman in town—all, everything was right.

One night around eleven the acid ran out at the G. and G. The foreman knocked off the crew and let the steam die down. As Joe rounded the lake on his way home, a lean moon rode the lake in a silver boat. If anybody had asked Joe about the moon on the lake, he would have said he hadn't paid it any attention. But he saw it with his feelings. It made him yearn painfully for Missie. Creation obsessed him. He thought about children. They had been married more than a year now. They had money put away. They ought to be making little feet for shoes. A little boy child would be about right.

He saw a dim light in the bedroom and decided to come in through the kitchen door. He could wash the fertilizer dust off himself before presenting himself to Missie May. It would be nice for her not to know that he was there until he slipped into his place in bed and hugged her back. She always liked that.

He eased the kitchen door open slowly and silently, but when he went to set his dinner bucket on the table he bumped it into a pile of dishes, and something crashed to the floor. He heard his wife gasp in fright and hurried to reassure her.

"Iss me, honey. Don't git skeered."

There was a quick, large movement in the bedroom. A rustle, a thud, and a stealthy silence. The light went out.

What? Robbers? Murderers? Some varmint attacking his helpless wife, perhaps. He struck a match, threw himself on guard and stepped over the door-sill into the bedroom.

The great belt on the wheel of Time slipped and eternity stood still. By the match light he could see the man's legs fighting with his breeches in his frantic desire to get them on. He had both chance and time to kill the intruder in his helpless condition—half in and half out of his pants—but he was too weak to take action. The shapeless enemies of humanity that live in the hours of Time had waylaid Joe. He was assaulted in his weakness. Like Samson awakening after his haircut. So he just opened his mouth and laughed.

The match went out and he struck another and lit the lamp. A howling wind raced across his heart, but underneath its fury he heard his wife sobbing and Slemmons pleading for his life. Offering to buy it with all that he had. "Please, suh, don't kill me. Sixty-two dollars at de sto'. Gold money."

Joe just stood. Slemmons looked at the window, but it was screened. Joe stood out like a rough-backed mountain between him and the door. Barring him from escape, from sunrise, from life.

He considered a surprise attack upon the big clown that stood there laughing like a chessy cat. But before his fist could travel an inch, Joe's own rushed out to crush him like a battering ram. Then Joe stood over him.

"Git into yo' damn rags, Slemmons, and dat quick."

Slemmons scrambled to his feet and into his vest and coat. As he grabbed his hat, Joe's fury overrode his intentions and he grabbed at Slemmons with his left hand and struck at him with his right. The right landed. The left grazed the front of his vest. Slemmons was knocked a somersault into the kitchen and fled through the open door. Joe found himself alone with Missie May, with the golden watch charm clutched in his left fist. A short bit of broken chain dangled between his fingers.

Missie May was sobbing. Wails of weeping without words. Joe stood, and after awhile he found out that he had something in his hand. And then he stood and felt without thinking and without seeing with his natural eyes. Missie May kept on crying and Joe kept on feeling so much and not knowing what to do with all his feelings, he put Slemmons' watch charm in his pants pocket and took a good laugh and went to bed.

"Missie May, whut you cryin' for?"

"Cause Ah love you so hard and Ah know you don't love *me* no mo'."

Joe sank his face into the pillow for a spell then he said huskily, "You don't know de feelings of dat yet, Missie May."

"Oh Joe, honey, he said he wuz gointer give me dat gold money and he jes' kept on after me—"

Joe was very still and silent for a long time. Then he said, "Well, don't cry no mo', Missie May. Ah got yo' gold piece for you."

The hours went past on their rusty ankles. Joe still and quiet on one bed-rail and Missie May wrung dry of sobs on the other. Finally the sun's tide crept upon the shore of night and drowned all its hours. Missie May with her face stiff and streaked towards the window saw the dawn come into her yard. It was day. Nothing more. Joe wouldn't be coming home as usual. No need to fling open the front door and sweep off the porch, making it nice for Joe. Never no more breakfast to cook; no more washing and starching of Joe's jumper-jackets and pants. No more nothing. So why get up?

With this strange man in her bed, she felt embarrassed to get up and dress. She decided to wait till he had dressed and gone. Then she would get up, dress quickly and be gone forever beyond reach of Joe's looks and laughs. But he never moved. Red light turned to yellow, then white.

From beyond the no-man's land between them came a voice. A strange voice that yesterday had been Joe's.

"Missie May, ain't you gonna fix me no breakfus'?"

She sprang out of bed. "Yeah, Joe. Ah didn't reckon you wuz hongry."

No need to die today. Joe needed her for a few more minutes anyhow.

Soon there was a roaring fire in the cook stove. Water bucket full and two chickens killed. Joe loved fried chicken and rice. She didn't deserve a thing and good Joe was letting her cook him some breakfast. She rushed hot biscuits to the table as Joe took his seat.

He ate with his eyes in his plate. No laughter, no banter.

"Missie May, you ain't eatin' yo' breakfus'."

"Ah don't choose none, Ah thank yuh."

His coffee cup was empty. She sprang to refill it. When she turned from the stove and bent to set the cup beside Joe's plate, she saw the yellow coin on the table between them.

She slumped into her seat and wept into her arms.

Presently Joe said calmly, "Missie May, you cry too much. Don't look back lak Lot's wife and turn to salt."

The sun, the hero of every day, the impersonal old man that beams as brightly on death as on birth, came up every morning and raced across the blue dome and dipped into the sea of fire every evening. Water ran down hill and birds nested.

Missie knew why she didn't leave Joe. She couldn't. She loved him too much, but she could not understand why Joe didn't leave her. He was polite, even kind at times, but aloof.

There were no more Saturday romps. No ringing silver dollars to stack beside her plate. No pockets to rifle. In fact the yellow coin in his trousers was like a monster hiding in the cave of his pockets to destroy her.

She often wondered if he still had it, but nothing could have induced her to ask nor yet to explore his pockets to see for herself. Its shadow was in the house whether or no.

One night Joe came home around midnight and complained of pains in the back. He asked Missie to rub him down with liniment. It had been three months since Missie had touched his body and it all seemed strange. But she rubbed him. Grateful for the chance. Before morning, youth triumphed and Missie exulted. But the next day, as she joyfully made up their bed, beneath her pillow she found the piece of money with the bit of chain attached.

Alone to herself, she looked at the thing with loathing, but look she must. She took it into her hands with trembling and saw first thing that it was no gold piece. It was a gilded half dollar. Then she knew why Slemmons had forbidden anyone to touch his gold. He trusted village eyes at a distance not to recognize his stick-pin as a gilded quarter, and his watch charm as a four-bit piece.

She was glad at first that Joe had left it there. Perhaps he was through with her punishment. They were man and wife again. Then another thought came clawing at her. He had come home to buy from her as if she were any woman in the long house. Fifty cents for her love. As if to say that he could pay as well as Slemmons. She slid the coin into his Sunday pants pocket and dressed herself and left his house.

Half way between her house and the quarters she met her husband's mother, and after a short talk she turned and went back home. Never would she admit defeat to that woman who prayed for it nightly. If she had not the substance of marriage she had the outside show. Joe must leave *her*. She let him see she didn't want his old gold four-bits too.

She saw no more of the coin for some time though she knew that Joe could not help finding it in his pocket. But his health kept poor, and he came home at least every ten days to be rubbed.

The sun swept around the horizon, trailing its robes of weeks and days. One morning as Joe came in from work, he found Missie May chopping wood. Without a word he took the ax and chopped a huge pile before he stopped.

"You ain't got no business choppin' wood, and you know it."

"How come? Ah been choppin' it for de last longest."

"Ah ain't blind. You makin' feet for shoes."

"Won't you be glad to have a lil baby chile, Joe?"

"You know dat 'thout astin' me."

"Iss gointer be a boy chile and de very spit of you."

"You reckon, Missie May?"

"Who else could it look lak?"

Joe said nothing, but he thrust his hand deep into his pocket and fingered something there.

It was almost six months later Missie May took to bed and Joe went and got his mother to come wait on the house.

Missie May was delivered of a fine boy. Her travail was over when Joe came in from work one morning. His mother and the old women were drinking great bowls of coffee around the fire in the kitchen.

The minute Joe came into the room his mother called him aside.

"How did Missie May make out?" he asked quickly.

"Who, dat gal? She strong as a ox. She gointer have plenty mo'. We done fixed her wid de sugar and lard to sweeten her for de nex' one."

Joe stood silent awhile.

"You ain't ast 'bout de baby, Joe. You oughter be mighty proud cause he sho is de spittin' image of yuh, son. Dat's yourn all right, if you never git another one, dat un is yourn. And you know Ah'm mighty proud too, son, cause Ah never thought well of you marryin' Missie May cause her ma used tuh fan her foot round right smart and Ah been mighty skeered dat Missie May wuz gointer git misput on her road."

Joe said nothing. He fooled around the house till late in the day then just before he went to work, he went and stood at the foot of the bed and asked his wife how she felt. He did this every day during the week.

On Saturday he went to Orlando to make his market. It had been a long time since he had done that.

Meat and lard, meal and flour, soap and starch. Cans of corn and tomatoes. All the staples. He fooled around town for awhile and bought bananas and apples. Way after while he went around to the candy store.

"Hello, Joe," the clerk greeted him. "Ain't seen you in a long time."

"Nope, Ah ain't been heah. Been round in spots and places."

"Want some of them molasses kisses you always buy?"

"Yessuh." He threw the gilded half dollar on the counter. "Will dat spend?"

"Whut is it, Joe? Well, I'll be doggone! A gold-plated four-bit piece. Where'd you git it, Joe?"

"Offen a stray nigger dat come through Eatonville. He had it on his watch chain for a charm—goin' round making out iss gold money. Ha ha! He had a quarter on his tie pin and it wuz all golded up too. Tryin' to fool people. Makin' out he so rich and everything. Ha! Ha! Tryin' to tole off folkses wives from home."

"How did you git it, Joe? Did he fool you, too?"

"Who, me? Naw suh! He ain't fooled me none. Know whut Ah done? He come round me wid his smart talk. Ah hauled off and knocked 'im down and took his old four-bits way from 'im. Gointer buy my wife some good ole lasses kisses wid it. Gimme fifty cents worth of dem candy kisses."

"Fifty cents buys a mighty lot of candy kisses, Joe. Why don't you split it up and take some chocolate bars, too. They eat good, too."

"Yessuh, dey do, but Ah wants all dat in kisses. Ah got a lil boy chile home now. Tain't a week old yet, but he kin suck a sugar tit and maybe eat one them kisses hisself."

Joe got his candy and left the store. The clerk turned to the next customer. "Wisht I could be like these darkies. Laughin' all the time. Nothin' worries 'em."

Back in Eatonville, Joe reached his own front door. There was the ring of singing metal on wood. Fifteen times. Missie May couldn't run to the door, but she crept there as quickly as she could.

"Joe Banks, Ah hear you chunkin' money in mah do'way. You wait till Ah got mah strength back and Ah'm gointer fix you for dat."

CLAUDE McKAY
Photograph by Carl Van Vechten.
By permission of the Estate of Carl Van Vechten.
Joseph Solomon, Executor.

CLAUDE McKAY

1890 TO 1948

Claude McKay was known notoriously to many as "the *enfant terrible* of the Harlem Renaissance." Deserved or not, McKay's reputation as the most racially militant and politically radical of the literary leaders of the renaissance emerged after the publication of his most famous poem, "If We Must Die," in the summer of 1919. A defiant answer to the bloody race riots engineered by whites to maintain the racial status quo in the United States after World War I, "If We Must Die" urged African Americans to fight to the death against any attempts to cow them into old patterns of submission. "If We Must Die" and subsequent poems of revolutionary outrage against racist and capitalist oppression identified McKay well before the onset of the Harlem Renaissance as a new kind of Negro poet, one who used poetry as a weapon to advance black liberation and international anticolonialism. Yet in McKay's most widely read collection of poetry, *Harlem Shadows* (1922), another side of this complex man's temperament—his delight in the sensuous, his romantic affinities with nature, his nostalgia for a pastoral life and values—came to light, complementing his satiric stance toward white civilization and his embittered resistance to all that it seemed to stand for. The characters in McKay's novels articulate the tensions he lived with and strived to reconcile as an artist who strongly identified with both the pastoral realm and the urban scene, with traditional folk values and individualistic rejection of those values, with the quest for belonging and the acceptance of alienation—in sum, with all that being a modern black man entailed in the early twentieth century.

Festus Claudius McKay was born and grew up on a farm in Jamaica. The youngest of eleven children, he was raised to respect the traditions of his parents, members of the independent black peasantry that had settled on the land after slavery had been abolished in the 1830s. As a young poet McKay wrote in the dialect of the black country folk, whom he admired and defended against the economic exploitation of whites. Seeking advanced training in agronomy because he doubted that he could support himself as a poet, McKay migrated to the United States. He studied briefly at Tuskegee Institute in Alabama and later at Kansas State University, but he never completed work for a degree. Instead he moved to New York City in 1914, where he wrote for avant garde and radical journals such as *Seven Arts* and the *Liberator*. His poetic models—Elizabethan and Romantic lyrics as well as the sonnet—were conservative, but his message was often anything but. Renouncing an American social, political, and economic system that seemed to him hopelessly corrupted by a racism and greed, McKay moved on to England in 1919 to work on a Communist weekly. The verse he published during his two-year stay in England, collected in 1920 in a slim volume entitled *Spring in New Hampshire*, brought McKay favorable comparisons to such acclaimed post-World War I poets as Siegfried Sassoon and Rupert Brooke.

Early in 1921 Claude McKay returned to New York. He worked as an editor of the *Liberator*, joining other prominent black West Indians and left-wing white writers in radical literary ventures. McKay's contacts within the leadership of the National Association for the Advancement of Colored People (NAACP) helped him place *Harlem Shadows* with a prominent New York publisher. The many glowing reviews of *Harlem Shadows* made McKay the most celebrated African American poet in the United States, the pacesetter for the black artistic renaissance that was beginning to stir in Harlem. Yet instead of staying on to write and promote his own work and that of other young black writers who were starting to surface in Harlem, McKay left the United States six months after *Harlem Shadows* was published. His characteristic restlessness and search for a community congenial to his ideals impelled him to visit the new Soviet Union.

Lionized and feted in Moscow and Leningrad, McKay enjoyed a personal triumph as a black literary cause célèbre. But Western Europe and America offered more freedom and support for his literary ambitions, a major reason for McKay's decision to move to Berlin in the spring of 1923. For the next eleven years he lived and worked in Germany, France, Spain, and North Africa while combating ill health and financial dependency. His friends helped him secure a contract with Harper & Brothers, a well-established New York publisher, that obliged the poet to produce three novels and a collection of short stories. In 1928 the first and most popular of McKay's novels appeared under the title *Home to Harlem*.

The first African American novel to reach the best-seller lists, *Home to Harlem* is the story of a free-wheeling, high-living black soldier's return to a Harlem that had become by the mid-1920s synonymous with hedonism and the flouting of accepted standards of sexual morality and respectable behavior. The renaissance in Harlem was in full swing when McKay's perfectly timed novel came out. Both the author and the book received considerable publicity because of *Home to Harlem*'s evocation of the myth of the black metropolis: "Chocolate Harlem! Sweet Harlem! . . . The sugared laughter. The honey-talk on its streets. . . . Oh, the contagious fever of Harlem. Burning everywhere in dark-eyed Harlem." Jake Brown, the hero of *Home to Harlem*, was controversial, however, especially in the eyes of African American reviewers. Some condemned him as merely a retooled stereotype of the thoughtless, oversexed black vagrant of countless white jokes and scurrilous newspaper reports. Other blacks welcomed Jake's freedom from pretense, his healthy assertion of his own manhood, and his almost instinctive recognition of the speciousness of white "civilization."

McKay articulated his long-standing critique of "the illness of this age" not only through Jake Brown's episodic story of self-indulgence but also through the unresolved ruminations of Ray, an alienated Haitian intellectual who is both attracted to and disquieted by the example of Jake. Ray's impatience with what he calls "the contented hogs in the pigpen of Harlem" betrays McKay's doubts about the liberating potential of the much-ballyhooed "primitivism" of Harlem's fast life. What seemed gloriously therapeutic to many whites afflicted with what they considered the inhibitions and hypocrisies of American "puritanism" takes on a more divided significance at the end of *Home to Harlem* when Ray decides to leave Harlem and all it represents. Somewhere between the majority of the hard-living blacks in *Home to Harlem*, who feel very much at home there, and the minority represented by Ray, who feels marginal both to Jake's Harlem and to the white world, stands Claude McKay reflecting on his own unfulfilled search for an intellectual and spiritual home.

In *Banjo* (1929), McKay's second picaresque novel, Jake and Ray turn up in the French port of Marseilles, where they are absorbed into a loose fraternity of black sailors from all over the world intent on having a rollicking good time. A collection of short stories, *Gingertown* (1932), revealed the attraction that Jamaica was exerting once again on McKay's imagination. *Banana Bottom* (1933), the most carefully thought out of McKay's novels, is set in the novelist's island homeland and focuses on the choices facing Bita Plant, a sensitive and cultured black woman who, unlike McKay's previous female characters, wants something more in life than pleasing a virile black man in bed. Through her marriage decision Bita is able to reconcile the conflicts previewed in Ray's tortured ambivalence toward knowledge and instinct, self-fulfillment and community.

McKay's fictional career ended in generally favorable reviews but poor sales for *Banana Bottom*. Through the remainder of the Depression decade, McKay struggled to support himself as a journalist and a member of the New York Federal Writers' Project. In 1937 he published an autobiography *A Long Way from Home*. In 1940 he organized his research on grass-roots movements and working-class life in Harlem into a sociological study *Harlem, Negro Metropolis*. By this time McKay had become a vociferous critic of Communism, whose ideology, he was convinced, offered little serious redress for the grievances of people of color against the evils of racial exploitation in the United States. As an alternative he recommended heightened solidarity within the African American community and attacked black political and civil rights leaders for failing to build social, economic, and religious institutions by and for the black masses. Increasingly isolated by what many perceived as an unprogressive political program, McKay converted to Roman Catholicism, moved to Chicago, and during the last four years of his life devoted himself to teaching in a Catholic school. In 1946 he completed a brief memoir, *My Green Hills of Jamaica* (1979), which took him home, finally, in a lyrical mood of wonder and love to the pastoral world of his childhood.

SUGGESTIONS FOR FURTHER READING

Cooper, Wayne F. *Claude McKay: Rebel Sojourner in the Harlem Renaissance*. Baton Rouge: Louisiana State University Press, 1987.

Gayle, Addison. *Claude McKay: The Black Poet at War*. Detroit: Broadside, 1972.

Giles, James. *Claude McKay*. Boston: Twayne, 1976.

McKay, Claude. *A Long Way from Home*. New York: Lee Furnam, 1937.

Ramchand, Kenneth. *The West Indian Novel and Its Background*. New York: Barnes and Noble, 1970.

HOME TO HARLEM

Going Back Home

I

All that Jake knew about the freighter on which he stoked was that it stank between sea and sky. He was working with a dirty Arab crew. The captain signed him on at Cardiff because one of the Arabs had quit the ship. Jake was used to all sorts of rough jobs, but he had never before worked in such a filthy dinghy.

The white sailors who washed the ship would not wash the stokers' water-closet, because they despised the Arabs. And the Arabs themselves made no effort to keep the place clean, although it adjoined their sleeping berth.

The cooks hated the Arabs because they did not eat pork. Whenever there was pork for dinner, something else had to be prepared for the Arabs. The cooks put the stokers' meat, cut in unappetizing chunks, in a broad pan, and the two kinds of vegetables in two other pans. The stoker who carried the food back to the bunks always put one pan inside of the other, and sometimes the bottoms were dirty and bits of potato peelings or egg shells were mixed in with the meat and the vegetables.

The Arabs took up a chunk of meat with their coal-powdered fingers, bit or tore off a piece, and tossed the chunk back into the pan. It was strange to Jake that these Arabs washed themselves after eating and not before. They ate with their clothes stiff-starched to their bodies with coal and sweat. And when they were finished, they stripped and washed and went to sleep in the stinking-dirty bunks. Jake was used to the lowest and hardest sort of life, but even his leather-lined stomach could not endure the Arabs' way of eating. Jake also began to despise the Arabs. He complained to the cooks about the food. He gave the chef a ten-shilling note, and the chef gave him his eats separately.

One of the sailors flattered Jake. "You're the same like us chaps. You ain't like them dirty jabbering coolies."

But Jake smiled and shook his head in a non-committal way. He knew that if he was just like the white sailors, he might have signed on as a deckhand and not as a stoker. He didn't care about the dirty old boat, anyhow. It was taking him back home—that was all he cared about. He made his shift all right, stoking four hours and resting eight. He didn't sleep well. The stokers' bunks were lousy, and fetid with the mingled smell of stale food and water-closet. Jake had attempted to keep the place clean, but to do that was impossible. Apparently the Arabs thought that a sleeping quarters could also serve as a garbage can.

"Nip me all you wanta, Mister Louse," said Jake. "Roll on, Mister Ship, and stinks all the way as you rolls. Jest take me 'long to Harlem is all I pray. I'm crazy to see again the brown-skin chippies 'long Lenox Avenue. Oh boy!"

Jake was tall, brawny, and black. When America declared war upon Germany in 1917 he was a longshoreman. He was working on a Brooklyn pier, with a score of men under him. He was a little boss and a very good friend of his big boss, who was Irish. Jake thought he would like to have a crack at the Germans. . . . And he enlisted.

In the winter he sailed for Brest with a happy chocolate company. Jake had his own daydreams of going over the top. But his company was held at Brest. Jake toted lumber—boards, planks, posts, rafters— for the hundreds of huts that were built around the walls of Brest and along the coast between Brest and Saint-Pierre, to house the United States soldiers.

Jake was disappointed. He had enlisted to fight. For what else had he been sticking a bayonet into the guts of a stuffed man and aiming bullets straight into a bull's-eye? Toting planks and getting into rows with his white comrades at the Bal Musette were not adventure.

Jake obtained leave. He put on civilian clothes and lit out for Havre. He liquored himself up and hung round a low-down café in Havre for a week.

One day an English sailor from a Channel sloop made up to Jake. "Darky," he said, "you 'arvin' a good time 'round 'ere."

Jake thought how strange it was to hear the Englishman say "darky" without being offended. Back home he would have been spoiling for a fight. There he would rather hear "nigger" than "darky," for he knew that when a Yankee said "nigger" he meant hatred for Negroes, whereas when he said "darky" he meant friendly contempt. He preferred white folks' hatred to their friendly contempt. To feel their hatred made him strong and aggressive, while their friendly contempt made him ridiculously angry, even against his own will.

"Sure Ise having a good time, all right," said Jake. He was making a cigarette and growling cusses at French tobacco. "But Ise got to get a move on 'fore very long."

"Where to?" his new companion asked.

"Any place, Buddy. I'm always ready for something new," announced Jake.

"Been in Havre a long time?"

"Week or two," said Jake. "I tooks care of some mules over heah. Twenty, God damn them, days across the pond. And then the boat plows round and run off and leaves me behind. Kain you beat that, Buddy?"

"It wasn't the best o' luck," replied the other. "Ever been to London?"

"Nope, Buddy," said Jake. "France is the only country I've struck yet this side the water."

The Englishman told Jake that there was a sailor wanted on his tug.

"We never 'ave a full crew—since the war," he said.

Jake crossed over to London. He found plenty of work there as a docker. He liked the West India Docks. He liked Limehouse. In the pubs men gave him their friendly paws and called him "darky." He liked how they called him "darky." He made friends. He found a woman. He was happy in the East End.

The Armistice found him there. On New-Year's Eve, 1919, Jake went to a monster dance with his woman, and his docker friends and their women, in the Mile End Road.

The Armistice had brought many more black men to the East End of London. Hundreds of them. Some of them found work. Some did not. Many were getting a little pension from the government. The price of sex went up in the East End, and the dignity of it also. And that summer Jake saw a big battle staged between the colored and white men of London's East End. Fisticuffs, razor and knife and gun play. For three days his woman would not let him out-of-doors. And when it was all over he was seized with the awful fever of lonesomeness. He felt all alone in the world. He wanted to run away from the kind-heartedness of his lady of the East End.

"Why did I ever enlist and come over here?" he asked himself. "Why did I want to mix mahself up in a white folks' war? It ain't ever was any of black folks' affair. Niggers am evah always such fools, anyhow. Always thinking they've got something to do with white folks' business."

Jake's woman could do nothing to please him now. She tried hard to get down into his thoughts and share them with him. But for Jake this woman was now only a creature of another race—of another world. He brooded day and night.

It was two years since he had left Harlem. Fifth Avenue, Lenox Avenue, and One Hundred and Thirty-fifth Street, with their chocolate-brown and walnut-brown girls, were calling him.

"Oh, them legs!" Jake thought. "Them tantalizing brown legs! . . . Barron's Cabaret! . . . Leroy's Cabaret! . . . Oh, boy!"

Brown girls rouged and painted like dark pansies. Brown flesh draped in soft colorful clothes. Brown lips full and pouted for sweet kissing. Brown breasts throbbing with love.

"Harlem for mine!" cried Jake. "I was crazy thinkin' I was happy over heah. I wasn't mahself. I was like a man charged up with dope every day. That's what it was. Oh, boy! Harlem for mine!

"Take me home to Harlem, Mister Ship! Take me home to the brown gals waiting for the brown boys that done show their mettle over there. Take me home, Mister Ship. Put your beak right into that water and jest move along." . . .

Arrival

II

Jake was paid off. He changed a pound note he had brought with him. He had fifty-nine dollars. From South Ferry he took an express subway train for Harlem.

Jake drank three Martini cocktails with cherries in them. The price, he noticed, had gone up from ten to twenty-five cents. He went to Bank's and had a Maryland fried-chicken feed—a big one with candied sweet potatoes.

He left his suitcase behind the counter of a saloon on Lenox Avenue. He went for a promenade on Seventh Avenue between One Hundred and Thirty-fifth and One Hundred and Fortieth Streets. He thrilled to Harlem. His blood was hot. His eyes were alert as he sniffed the street like a hound. Seventh Avenue was nice, a little too nice that night.

Jake turned off on Lenox Avenue. He stopped before an ice-cream parlor to admire girls sipping ice-cream soda through straws. He went into a cabaret. . . .

A little brown girl aimed the arrow of her eye at him as he entered. Jake was wearing a steel-gray English suit. It fitted him loosely and well, perfectly suited his presence. She knew at once that Jake must have just landed. She rested her chin on the back of her hands and smiled at him. There was something in his attitude, in his hungry wolf's eyes, that went warmly to her. She was brown, but she had tinted her leaf-like face to a ravishing chestnut. She had on an orange scarf over a green frock, which was way above her knees, giving an adequate view of legs lovely in fine champagne-colored stockings. . . .

Her shaft hit home. . . . Jake crossed over to her table. He ordered Scotch and soda.

"Scotch is better with soda or even water," he said. "English folks don't take whisky straight, as we do."

But she preferred ginger ale in place of soda. The cabaret singer, seeing that they were making up to each other, came expressly over to their table and sang. Jake gave the singer fifty cents. . . .

Her left hand was on the table. Jake covered it with his right.

"Is it clear sailing between us, sweetie?" he asked.

"Sure thing. . . . You just landed from over there?"

"Just today!"

"But there wasn't no boat in with soldiers today, daddy."

"I made it in a special one."

"Why, you lucky baby! . . . I'd like to go to another place, though. What about you?"

"Anything you say, I'm game," responded Jake.

They walked along Lenox Avenue. He held her arm. His flesh tingled. He felt as if his whole body was a flaming wave. She was intoxicated, blinded under the overwhelming force.

But nevertheless she did not forget her business.

"How much is it going to be, daddy?" she demanded.

"How much? *How* much? Five?"

"Aw no, daddy. . . ."

"Ten?"

She shook her head.

"Twenty, sweetie!" he said, gallantly.

"Daddy," she answered, "I wants fifty."

"Good," he agreed. He was satisfied. She was responsive. She was beautiful. He loved the curious color on her cheek.

They went to a buffet flat on One Hundred and Thirty-seventh Street. The proprietress opened the door without removing the chain and peeked out. She was a matronly mulatto woman. She recognized the girl, who had put herself in front of Jake, and she slid back the chain and said, "Come right in."

The windows were heavily and carefully shaded. There was beer and wine, and there was plenty of hard liquor. Black and brown men sat at two tables in one room, playing poker. In the other room a phonograph was grinding out a "blues," and some couples were dancing, thick as maggots in a vat of sweet liquor, and as wriggling.

Jake danced with the girl. They shuffled warmly, gloriously about the room. He encircled her waist with both hands, and she put both of hers up to his shoulders and laid her head against his breast. And they shuffled around.

"Harlem! Harlem!" thought Jake. "Where else could I have all this life but Harlem? Good old Harlem! Chocolate Harlem! Sweet Harlem! Harlem, I've got you' number down. Lenox Avenue, you're a bear, I know it. And, baby honey, sure enough youse a pippin for your pappy. Oh, boy!" . . .

After Jake had paid for his drinks, that fifty-dollar note was all he had left in the world. He gave it to the girl. . . .

"Is we going now, honey?" he asked her.

"Sure, daddy. Let's beat it." . . .

Oh, to be in Harlem again after two years away. The deep-dyed color, the thickness, the closeness of it. The noises of Harlem. The sugared laughter. The honey-talk on its streets. And all night long, ragtime and "blues" playing somewhere, . . . singing somewhere, dancing somewhere! Oh, the contagious fever of Harlem. Burning everywhere in dark-eyed Harlem. . . . Burning now in Jake's sweet blood. . . .

He woke up in the morning in a state of perfect peace. She brought him hot coffee and cream and doughnuts. He yawned. He sighed. He was satisfied. He breakfasted. He washed. He dressed. The sun was shining. He sniffed the fine dry air. Happy, familiar Harlem.

"I ain't got a cent to my name," mused Jake, "but ahm as happy as a prince, all the same. Yes, I is."

He loitered down Lenox Avenue. He shoved his hand in his pocket—pulled out the fifty-dollar note. A piece of paper was pinned to it on which was scrawled in pencil:

"Just a little gift from a baby girl to a honey boy!"

Zeddy

III

"Great balls of fire! Looka here! See mah luck!" Jake stopped in his tracks . . . went on . . . stopped again . . . retraced his steps . . . checked himself. "Guess I won't go back right now. Never let a woman think you're too crazy about her. But she's a particularly sweet piece a business. . . . Me and her again tonight. . . . Handful o' luck shot straight outa heaven. Oh, boy! Harlem is mine!"

Jake went rolling along Fifth Avenue. He crossed over to Lenox Avenue and went into Uncle Doc's saloon, where he had left his bag. Called for a glass of Scotch. "Gimme the siphon, Doc. I'm off the straight stuff."

"Iszh you? Counta what?"

"Hits the belly better this way. I l'arned it over the other side."

A slap on the shoulder brought him sharply round. "Zeddy Plummer! What grave is you arisen from?" he cried.

"Buddy, you looks so good to me, I could kish you," Zeddy said.

"Where?"

"Everywhere. . . . French style."

"One on one cheek and one on the other."

"Savee-vous?"

"Parlee-vous?"

Uncle Doc set another glass on the counter and poured out pure Bourbon. Zeddy reached a little above Jake's shoulders. He was stocky, thick-shouldered, flat-footed, and walked like a bear. Some more customers came in and the buddies eased round to the short side of the bar.

"What part of the earth done belch you out?" demanded Zeddy. "Nevah heared no God's tidings a you sence we missed you from Brest."

"And how about you?" Jake countered. "Didn't them Germans git you scrambling over the top?"

"Nevah see'd them, buddy. None a them showed the goose-step around Brest. Have a shot on me. . . . Well, dawg bite me, but— say, Jake, we've got some more stuff to booze over."

Zeddy slapped Jake on his breast and looked him over again. "Tha's some stuff you're strutting in, boh. 'Tain't 'Merican and it ain't French." . . .

"English." Jake showed his clean white teeth.

"Mah granny an' me! You been in that theah white folks' country, too?"

"And don't I look as if Ise been? Where else could a fellow git such good and cheap man clothes to cover his skin?"

"Buddy, I know it's the trute. What you doing today?"

"No, when you make me think ovit, particular thing. And you?"

"I'm alongshore but—I ain't agwine to work thisaday."

"I guess I've got to be heaving along right back to it, too, in pretty short time. I got to get me a room but—"

Uncle Doc reminded Jake that his suit-case was there.

"I ain't nevah fohgitting all mah worldly goods," responded Jake.

Zeddy took Jake to a pool-room where they played. Jake was the better man. From the pool-room they went to Aunt Hattie's chitterling joint in One Hundred and Thirty-second Street, where they fed. Fricassee chicken and rice. Green peas. Stewed corn.

Aunt Hattie's was renowned among the lowly of Harlem's Black Belt. It was a little basement joint, smoke-colored. And Aunt Hattie was weather-beaten dark-brown, cheery-faced, with two rusty-red front teeth sticking together conspicuously out of her twisted, spread-away mouth. She cooked delicious food—home-cooked food they called it. None of the boys loafing round that section of Fifth Avenue would dream of going to any other place for their "poke chops."

Aunt Hattie admired her new customer from the kitchen door and he quite filled her sight. And when she went with the dish rag to wipe the oil-cloth before setting down the cocoanut pie, she rubbed her breast against Jake's shoulder and a sensual light gleamed in her aged smoke-red eyes.

The buddies talked about the days of Brest. Zeddy recalled the everlasting unloading and unloading of ships and the toting of lumber. The house of the Young Men's Christian Association, overlooking the harbor, where colored soldiers were not wanted. . . . The central Rue de Siam and the point near the Prefecture of Marine, from which you could look down on the red lights of the Quartier Réservé. The fatal fights between black men and white in the *maisons closes*. The encounters between apaches and white Americans. The French sailors that couldn't get the Yankee idea of amour and men. And the cemetery, just beyond the old mediæval gate of the town, where he left his second-best buddy.

"Poor boh. Was always belly-aching for a chance over the top. Nevah got it nor nothing. Not even a baid in the hospital. Strong like a bull, yet just knocked off in the dark through raw cracker cussedness. . . . Some life it was, buddy, in them days. We was always on the defensive as if the boches, as the froggies called them, was right down on us."

"Yet you stuck t'rough it toting lumber. Got back to Harlem all right, though."

"You bet I did, boh. You kain trust Zeddy Plummer to look out for his own black hide. . . . But you, buddy. How come you just vanished thataway like a spook? How did you take your tail out ovit?"

Jake told Zeddy how he walked out of it straight to the station in Brest. Le Havre. London. The West India Docks. And back home to Harlem.

"But you must keep it dark, buddy," Zeddy cautioned. "Don't go shooting off your mouth too free. Gov'mant still smoking out deserters and draft dodgers."

"I ain't told no nigger but you, boh. Nor ofay, neither. Ahm in your confidence, chappie."

"That's all right, buddy." Zeddy put his hand on Jake's knee. "It's better to keep your business close all the time. But I'll tell you this for your perticular information. Niggers am awful close-mouthed in some things. There is fellows here in Harlem that just telled the draft to mount upstairs. Pohlice and soldiers were hunting ev'where foh them. And they was right here in Harlem. Fifty dollars apiece foh them. All their friends knowed it and not a one gived them in. I tell you, niggers am amazing sometimes. Yet other times, without any natural reason, they will just go vomiting out their guts to the ofays about one another."

"God; but it's good to get back home again!" said Jake.

"I should think you was hungry foh a li'l' brown honey. I tell you trute, buddy. I made mine ovah there, spitin' ov ev'thing. I l'arned her a little z'inglise and she l'arned me beaucoup plus the French stuff. . . . The real stuff, buddy. But I was tearin' mad and glad to get back all the same. Take it from me, buddy, there ain't no honey lak to that theah comes out of our own belonging-to-us honeycomb."

"Man, what you telling me?" cried Jake. "Don't I knows it? What else you think made me leave over the other side? And dog mah doggone ef I didn't find it just as I landed."

"K-hhhhhhh! K-hhhhhhhh!" Zeddy laughed. "Dog mah cats! You done tasted the real life a'ready?"

"Last night was the end of the world, buddy, and tonight ahm going back there," chanted Jake as he rose and began kicking up his heels round the joint.

Zeddy also got up and put on his gray cap. They went back to the pool-room. Jake met two more fellows that he knew and got into a ring of Zeddy's pals. . . . Most of them were longshoremen. There was plenty of work, Jake learned. Before he left the pool-room he and Zeddy agreed to meet the next evening at Uncle Doc's.

"Got to work tomorrow, boh," Zeddy informed Jake.

. . . .

"Good old New York! The same old wench of a city. Elevated racketing over you' head. Subway bellowing under you' feet. Me foh wrastling round them piers again. Scratching down to the bottom of them ships and scrambling out. All alongshore for me now. No more fooling with the sea. Same old New York. Everybody dashing round like crazy. . . . Same old New York. But the ofay faces am different from those ovah across the pond. Sure they is. Stiffer. Tighter. Yes, they is that. . . . But the sun does better here than over there. And the sky's so high and dry and blue. And the air it—O Gawd it works in you' flesh and blood like Scotch. O Lawdy, Lawdy! I wants to live to a hundred and finish mah days in New York."

Jake threw himself up as if to catch the air pouring down from the blue sky. . . .

"Harlem! Harlem! Little thicker, little darker and noisier and smellier, but Harlem just the same. The niggers done plowed through Hundred and Thirtieth Street. Heading straight foh One Hundred and Twenty-fifth. Spades beyond Eighth Avenue. Going, going, going Harlem! Going up! Nevah befoh I seed so many dickty shines in sich swell motor-cars. Plenty moh nigger shops. Seventh Avenue done gone high-brown. O Lawdy! Harlem bigger, Harlem better . . . and sweeter."

. . . .

"Street and streets! One Hundred and Thirty-second, Thirty-third, Thirty-fourth. It wasn't One Hundred and Thirty-fifth and it wasn't beyond theah. . . . O Lawd! how did I fohgit to remember the street and number. I reeled outa there like a drunken man. I been so happy. . . .

"Thirty-fourth, Thirty-second, Thirty-third. . . . Only difference in the name. All the streets am just the same and all the houses 'like as peas. I could try this one heah or that one there but— Rabbit foot! I didn't even git her name. Oh, Jakie, Jake! What a big Ah-Ah you is.

"I was a fool not to go back right then when I feeled like it. What did I want to tighten up mahself and crow and strut like a crazy cat for? A grand Ah-Ah I is. Feet in mah hands! Take me back to the Baltimore tonight. I ain't gwine to know no peace till I lay these here hands on mah tantalizing brown again."

Congo Rose

IV

All the old cabarets were going still. Connor's was losing ground. The bed of red roses that used to glow in the ceiling was almost dim now. The big handsome black girl that always sang in a red frock was no longer there. What a place Connor's was from 1914 to 1916 when that girl was singing and kicking and showing her bright green panties there! And the little ebony drummer, beloved of every cabaret lover in Harlem, was a fiend for rattling the drum!

Barron's was still Barron's, depending on its downtown white trade. Leroy's, the big common rendezvous shop for everybody. Edmond's still in the running. A fine new place that was opened in Brooklyn was freezing to death. Brooklyn never could support anything.

Goldgraben's on Lenox Avenue was leading all the Negro cabarets a cruel dance. The big-spirited Jew had brought his cabaret up from the basement and established it in a hall blazing with lights, overlooking Lenox Avenue. He made a popular Harlem Negro manager. There the joy-loving ladies and gentlemen of the Belt collected to show their striking clothes and beautiful skin. Oh, it was some wonderful sight to watch them from the pavement! No wonder the lights of Connor's were dim. And Barron's had plunged deeper for the ofay trade. Goldgraben was grabbing all the golden-browns that had any spendable dough.

But the Congo remained in spite of formidable opposition and foreign exploitation. The Congo was a real throbbing little Africa in New York. It was an amusement place entirely for the unwashed of the Black Belt. Or, if they were washed, smells lingered telling the nature of their occupation. Pot-wrestlers, third cooks, W. C. attendants, scrub maids, dish-washers, stevedores.

Girls coming from the South to try their future in New York always reached the Congo first. The Congo was African in spirit and color. No white persons were admitted there. The proprietor knew his market. He did not cater to the fast trade. "High yallers" were scarce there. Except for such sweetmen that lived off the low-down dark trade.

When you were fed up with the veneer of Seventh Avenue, and Goldgraben's Afro-Oriental garishness, you would go to the Congo and turn rioting loose in all the tenacious odors of service and the warm indigenous smells of Harlem, fooping or jig-jagging the night away. You would if you were a black kid hunting for joy in New York.

Jake went down to the Baltimore. No sign of his honey girl anywhere. He drank Scotch after Scotch. His disappointment mounted to anger against himself—turned to anger against his honey girl. His eyes roved round the room, but saw nobody.

"Oh what a big Ah-Ah I was!"

All round the den, luxuriating under the little colored lights, the dark dandies were loving up their pansies. Feet tickling feet under tables, tantalizing liquor-rich giggling, hands busy above.

"Honey gal! Honey gal! What other sweet boy is loving you now? Don't you know your last night's daddy am waiting for you?"

The cabaret singer, a shiny coffee-colored girl in a green frock and

Indian-waved hair, went singing from table to table in a man's bass
voice.

> "You wanta know how I do it,
>   How I look so good, how I am so happy,
>   All night on the blessed job—
>   How I slide along making things go snappy?
>   It is easy to tell,
>   I ain't got no plan—
>   But I'm crazy, plumb crazy
>   About a man, mah man.

> "It ain't no secret as you think,
>   The glad heart is a state o' mind—
>   Throw a stone in the river and it will sink;
>   But a feather goes whirling on the wind.
>   It is easy to tell. . . ."

She stopped more than usual at Jake's table. He gave her a half dollar. She danced a jagging jig before him that made the giggles rise
like a wave in the room. The pansies stared and tightened their grip
on their dandies. The dandies tightened their hold on themselves.
They looked the favored Jake up and down. All those perfection struts
for him. Yet he didn't seem aroused at all.

> "I'm crazy, plumb crazy
> About a man, mah man. . . ."

The girl went humming back to her seat. She had poured every
drop of her feeling into the song.

> "Crazy, plumb crazy about a man, mah man. . . ."

Dandies and pansies, chocolate, chestnut, coffee, ebony, cream,
yellow, everybody was teased up to the high point of excitement. . . .

> "Crazy, plumb crazy about a man, mah man. . . ."

The saxophone was moaning it. And feet and hands and mouths
were acting it. Dancing. Some jigged, some shuffled, some walked,
and some were glued together swaying on the dance floor.

Jake was going crazy. A hot fever was burning him up. . . .

Where was the singing gal that had danced to him? That dancing was for him all right. . . .

A crash cut through the music. A table went jazzing into the drum. The cabaret singer lay sprawling on the floor. A raging putty-skinned mulattress stamped on her ribs and spat in her face! "That'll teach you to leave mah man be every time." A black waiter rushed the mulattress. "Git off'n her. 'Causen she's down."

A potato-yellow man and a dull-black were locked. The proprietor, a heavy brown man, worked his elbow like a hatchet between them.

The antagonists glowered at each other.

"What you want to knock the gal down like that for, I acks you?"

"Better acks her why she done spits on mah woman."

"*Woman!* White man's wench, you mean. You low-down tripe. . . ."

The black man heaved toward the yellow, but the waiters hooked and hustled him off. . . . Sitting at a table, the cabaret singer was soothing her eye.

"Git out on the sidewalk, all you troublemakers," cried the proprietor. "And you, Bess," he cried to the cabaret singer, "nevah you show your face in mah place again."

The cabaret was closed for the rest of the night. Like dogs flicked apart by a whip-cord, the jazzers stood and talked resentfully in the street.

"Hi, Jake"—Zeddy, rocking into the group with a nosy air, spotted his buddy—"was you in on the li'l' fun?"

"Yes, buddy, but I wasn't mixed up in it. Sometimes they turn mah stomach, the womens. The same in France, the same in England, the same in Harlem. White against white and black against white and yellow against black and brown. We's all just crazy-dog mad. Ain't no peace on earth with the womens and there ain't no life anywhere without them."

"You said it, boh. It's a be-be itching life"—Zeddy scratched his flank—"and we're all sons of it. . . . But what is you hitting round this joint? I thought you would be feeding off milk and honey tonight?"

"Hard luck, buddy. Done lose out counta mah own indilgence. I fohgit the street and the house. Thought I'd find her heah but. . . ."

"What you thinking 'bout, boh?"

"That gal got beat up in the Baltimore. She done sings me into a tantalizing mood. Ahm feeling like."

"Let's take a look in on the Congo, boh. It's the best pick-me-up place in Harlem."

"I'm with you, buddy."

"Always packed with the best pickings. When the chippies come up from down home, tha's where they hangs out first. You kain always find something that New York ain't done made a fool of yet. Theah's a high-yaller entertainer there that I'se got a crush on, but she ain't nevah gived me a encouraging eye."

"I ain't much for the high-yallers after having been so much fed-up on the ofays," said Jake. "They's so doggone much alike."

"Ah no, boh. A sweet-lovin' high-yaller queen's got something different. K-hhhhhh, K-hhhhhh. Something nigger."

The Congo was thick, dark-colorful, and fascinating. Drum and saxophone were fighting out the wonderful drag "blues" that was the favorite of all the low-down dance halls. In all the better places it was banned. Rumor said it was a police ban. It was an old tune, so far as popular tunes go. But at the Congo it lived fresh and green as grass. Everybody there was giggling and wriggling to it.

> And it is ashes to ashes and dust to dust,
> Can you show me a woman that a man can trust?
>
> > Oh, baby, how are you?
> > Oh, baby, what are you?
> > Oh, can I have you now,
> > Or have I got to wait?
> > Oh, let me have a date,
> > Why do you hesitate?
>
> And there is two things in Harlem I don't understan'
> It is a bulldycking woman and a faggotty man.
>
> > Oh, baby how are you?
> > Oh, baby, what are you? . . .

Jake and Zeddy picked two girls from a green bench and waded into the hot soup. The saxophone and drum fought over the punctuated notes. The cymbals clashed. The excitement mounted. Couples breasted each other in rhythmical abandon, grinned back at their friends and chanted:

> > "Oh, baby, how are you?
> > Oh, baby, what are you? . . ."

Clash! The cymbal snuffed out saxophone and drum, the dancers fell apart,—reeled, strutted, drifted back to their green places. . . .

Zeddy tossed down the third glass of Gordon gin and became aware of Rose, the Congo entertainer, singing at the table. Happy for the moment, he gave her fifty cents. She sang some more, but Zeddy saw that it was all for Jake. Finished, she sat down, uninvited, at their table.

How many nights, hungry nights, Zeddy had wished that Rose would sit down voluntarily at his table. He had asked her sometimes. She would sit, take a drink and leave. Nothing doing. If he was a "big nigger," perhaps—but she was too high-priced for him. Now she was falling for Jake. Perhaps it was Jake's nifty suit. . . .

"Gin for mine," Rose said. Jake ordered two gins and a Scotch. "Scotch! That's an ofay drink," Rose remarked. "And I've seen the monkey-chasers order it when they want to put on style."

"It's good," Jake said. "Taste it."

She shook her head. "I have befoh. I don't like the taste. Gimme gin every time or good old red Kentucky."

"I got used to it over the other side," Jake said.

"Oh! You're an over-yonder baby! Sure enough!" She fondled his suit in admiration.

Zeddy, like a good understanding buddy, had slipped away. Another Scotch and Gordon Dry. The glasses kissed. Like a lean lazy leopard the mulattress reclined against Jake.

The milk cans were sounding on the pavements and a few pale stars were still visible in the sky when Rose left the Congo with both hands entwined in Jake's arm.

"You gwina stay with me, mah brown?"

"I ain't got me a room yet," he said.

"Come stay with me always. Got any stuff to bring along?"

"Mah suitcase at Uncle Doc's."

They went to her room in One Hundred and Thirty-third street. Locking the door, she said: "You remember the song they used to sing before you all went over there, mah brown?"

Softly she chanted:

"If I had some one like you at home
    I wouldn't wanta go out, I wouldn't wanta go out. . . .
    If I had some one like you at home,
    I'd put a padlock on the door. . . ."

She hugged him to her.

"I love you. I ain't got no man."

"Gwan, tell that to the marines," he panted.

"Honest to God. Lemme kiss you nice."

It was now eating-time in Harlem. They were hungry. They washed and dressed.

"If you'll be mah man always, you won't have to work," she said.

"Me?" responded Jake. "I've never been a sweetman yet. Never lived off no womens and never will. I always works."

"I don't care what you do whilst you is mah man. But hard work's no good for a sweet-loving papa."

On the Job Again

V

Jake stayed on in Rose's room. He could not feel about her as he did for his little lost maroon-brown of the Baltimore. He went frequently to the Baltimore, but he never saw her again. Then he grew to hate that cabaret and stopped going there.

The mulattress was charged with tireless activity and Jake was her big, good slave. But her spirit lacked the charm and verve, the infectious joy, of his little lost brown. He sometimes felt that she had no spirit at all—that strange, elusive something that he felt in himself, sometimes here, sometimes there, roaming away from him, going back to London, to Brest, Le Havre, wandering to some unknown new port, caught a moment by some romantic rhythm, color, face, passing through cabarets, saloons, speakeasies, and returning to him. . . . The little brown had something of that in her, too. That night he had felt a reaching out and marriage of spirits. . . . But the mulattress was all a wonderful tissue of throbbing flesh. He had never once felt in her any tenderness or timidity or aloofness. . . .

Jake was working longshore. Hooking barrels and boxes, wrestling with chains and cranes. He didn't have a little-boss job this time. But that didn't worry him. He was one blackamoor that nourished a perfect contempt for place. There were times when he divided his days between Rose and Uncle Doc's saloon and Dixie Red's pool-room.

He never took money from her. If he gambled away his own and was short, he borrowed from Nije Gridley, the longshoreman broker. Nije Gridley was a tall, thin, shiny black man. His long eyelashes gave his sharp eyes a sleepy appearance, but he was always wide awake. Before Jake was shipped to France, Nije had a rooming-house in Harlem's Fifth Avenue, worked a little at longshoring himself, and lent money on the checks of the hard-gambling boys. Now he had three rooming-houses, one of which, free of mortgage, he owned. His lean belly bore a heavy gold chain and he strutted Fifth and

Lenox in a ministerial crow-black suit. With the war boom of wages, the boys had gambled heavily and borrowed recklessly.

Ordinarily, Nije lent money at the rate of a dollar on four and two on eight per week. He complained bitterly of losses. Twenty-five dollars loaned on a check which, presented, brought only a day's pay. There were tough fellows that played him that game sometimes. They went and never returned to borrow again. But Nije's interest covered up such gaps. And sometimes he gave ten dollars on a forty-dollar check, drew the wages, and never saw his customer again, who had vanished entirely out of that phase of Harlem life.

One week when they were not working, Zeddy came to Jake with wonderful news. Men were wanted at a certain pier to unload pine-apples at eight dollars a day. Eight dollars was exceptional wages, but the fruit was spoiling.

Jake went with Zeddy and worked the first day with a group of Negroes and a few white men. The white men were not regular dock workers. The only thing that seemed strange to Jake was that all the men ate inside and were not allowed outside the gates for lunch. But, on the second day, his primitive passion for going against regulation urged him to go out in the street after lunch.

Heaving casually along West Street, he was hailed by a white man. "Hello, fellow-worker!"

"Hello, there! What's up?" Jake asked.

"You working in there?"

"Sure I is. Since yestidday."

The man told Jake that there was a strike on and he was scabbing. Jake asked him why there were no pickets if there was a strike. The man replied that there were no pickets because the union leaders were against the strike, and had connived with the police to beat up and jail the pickets.

"Well, pardner," Jake said, "I've done worked through a tur'ble assortaments o' jobs in mah lifetime, but I ain't nevah yet scabbed it on any man. I done work in this heah country, and I works good and hard over there in France. I works in London and I nevah was a blackleg, although I been the only black man in mah gang."

"Fine, fellow-worker; that's a real man's talk," said the white man. He took a little red book out of his pocket and asked Jake to let him sign him up in his union.

"It's the only one in the country for a red-blooded worker, no matter what race or nation he belongs to."

"Nope, I won't scab, but I ain't a joiner kind of a fellah," said Jake. "I ain't no white folks' nigger and I ain't no poah white's fool. When I longshored in Philly I was a good union man. But when I made

New York I done finds out that they gived the colored mens the worser piers and holds the bes'n a' them foh the Irishmen. No, pardner, keep you' card. I take the best I k'n get as I goes mah way. But I tells you, things ain't none at all lovely between white and black in this heah Gawd's own country."

"We take all men in our union regardless—" But Jake was haunching along out of hearing down West Street. . . . Suddenly he heard sharp, deep, distressful grunts, and saw behind some barrels a black man down and being kicked perilously in the rear end by two white men. Jake drew his hook from his belt and, waving it in the air, he rushed them. The white men shot like rats to cover. The down man scrambled to his feet. One of Zeddy's pals, Jake recognized him.

"What's the matter, buddy, the peckawoods them was doing you in?"

"Becaz they said there was a strike in theah. And I said I didn't give a doughnut, I was going to work foh mah money all the same. I got one o' them bif! in the eye, though. . . ."

"Don't go back, buddy. Let the boss-men stick them jobs up. They are a bunch of rotten aigs. Just using us to do their dirty work. Come on, let's haul bottom away from here to Harlem."

At Dixie Red's pool-room that evening there were some fellows with bandaged arms and heads. One iron-heavy, blue-black lad (he was called Liver-lip behind his back, because of the plankiness of his lips) carried his arm in a sling, and told Jake how he happened to be like that.

"They done jumped on me soon as I turned mah black moon on that li'l saloon tha's catering to us niggers. Heabenly God! But if the stars them didn't twinkle way down in mah eyes. But easy, easy, old man, I got out mah shaving steel and draws it down the goosey flesh o' one o' them, and, buddy, you shoulda heah him squeal. . . . The pohlice?" His massive mouth molded the words to its own form. "They tooks me, yes, but tunned me loose by'n'by. They's with us this time, boh, but, Lawdy! if they hadn't did entervention I woulda gutted gizzard and kidney outa that white tripe."

Jake was angry with Zeddy and asked him, when he came in, why he had not told him at first that the job was a scab job.

"I won't scab on nobody, not even the orneriest crackers," he said.

"Bull Durham!" cried Zeddy. "What was I going to let on about anything for? The boss-man done paid me to git him mens, and I got them. Ain't I working there mahself? I'll take any job in this heah Gawd's country that the white boss make it worf mah while to work at."

"But it ain't decent to scab," said Jake.

"Decent mah black moon!" shouted Zeddy. "I'll scab through hell to make mah living. Scab job or open shop or union am all the same jobs to me. White mens don't want niggers in them unions, nohow. Ain't you a good carpenter? And ain't I a good blacksmith? But kain we get a look-in on our trade heah in this white man's city? Ain't white mens done scabbed niggers outa all the jobs they useter hold down heah in this city? Waiter, bootblack, and barber shop?"

"With all a that scabbing is a low-down deal," Jake maintained.

"Me eye! Seems lak youse gittin' religion, boh. Youse talking death, tha's what you sure is. One thing I know is niggers am made foh life. And I want to live, boh, and feel plenty o' the juice o' life in mah blood. I wanta live and I wanta love. And niggers am got to work hard foh that. Buddy, I'll tell you this and I'll tell it to the wo'l'—all the crackers, all them poah white trash, all the nigger-hitting and nigger-breaking white folks—I loves life and I got to live and I'll scab through hell to live."

Jake did not work again that week. By Saturday morning he didn't have a nickel, so he went to Nije Gridley to borrow money. Nije asked him if he was going that evening to Billy Biasse's railroad flat, the longshoremen gaming rendezvous. Jake said no, he was going with Zeddy to a buffet flat in One Hundred and Fortieth Street. The buffet flat was the rendezvous of a group of railroad porters and club waiters who gambled for big stakes. Jake did not go there often because he had to dress up as if he were going to a cabaret. Also, he was not a big-stake gambler. . . . He preferred Billy Biasse's, where he could go whenever he liked with hook and overalls.

"Oh, that's whar Zeddy's hanging out now," Nije commented, casually.

For some time before Jake's return from Europe Zeddy had stopped going to Billy Biasse's. He told Jake he was fed up with it. Jake did not know that Zeddy owed Nije money and that he did not go to Billy Biasse's because Nije often went there. . . .

Later in the evening Nije went to Billy Biasse's and found a longshoreman who was known at the buffet flat, to take him there.

Gambling was a bigger game than sex at this buffet flat. The copper-hued lady who owned it was herself a very good poker-player. There were only two cocoa-brown girls there. Not young or attractive. They made a show of doing something, serving drinks and trying hard to make jokes. In dining- and sitting-room, five tables were occupied by card-players. Railroad porters, longshoremen, waiters; tight-faced, anxious-eyed. Zeddy sat at the same table with the lady of the flat. He had just eliminated two cards and asked for two when Nije and his escort were let into the flat. Zeddy smelled his man and knew it was Nije without looking up.

Nije swaggered past Zeddy and joined a group at another table. The gaming went on with intermittent calls for drinks. Nije sat where he could watch Zeddy's face. Zeddy also, although apparently intent on the cards, kept a wary eye on Nije. Sometimes their eyes met. No one was aware of the challenge that was developing between the two men.

There was a little slackening in the games, a general call for drinks, and a shifting of chairs. Nije got nearer to Zeddy. . . . Half-smiling and careless-like, he planted his boot-heel upon Zeddy's toes.

"Git off mah feets," Zeddy barked. The answer was a hard blow in the face. Zeddy tasted blood in his mouth. He threw his muscular gorilla body upon the tall Nije and hugged him down to the floor.

"You blasted black Jew, say you' prayers!" cried Zeddy.

"Ain't scared o' none o' you barefaced robber niggers." Nije was breathing hard under Zeddy and trying to get the better of him by the help of the wall.

"Black man," growled Zeddy, "I'se gwineta cut your throat just so sure as God is white."

With his knee upon Nije's chest and his left hand on his windpipe, Zeddy flashed the deadly-gleaming blade out of his back pocket. The proprietress let loose a blood-curdling scream, but before Zeddy's hand could achieve its purpose, Jake aimed a swift kick at his elbow. The razor flew spinning upward and fell chopping through a glass of gin on the pianola.

The proprietress fell upon Zeddy and clawed at him. "Wha's the matter all you bums trying to ruin mah place?" she cried. "Ain't I been a good spoht with you all, making everything here nice and respectable?"

Jake took charge of Zeddy. Two men hustled Nije off away out of the flat.

"Who was it put the krimp on me?" asked Zeddy.

"You ought to praise the Lawd you was saved from Sing Sing and don't ask no questions," the woman replied.

Everybody was talking.

"How did that long, tall, blood-suckin' nigger get in heah?"

"Soon as this heah kind a business stahts, the dicks will sartain sure git on to us."

"It ain't no moh than last week they done raided Madame Jerkin's, the niftiest buffet flat in Harlem. O Lawdy!"

"That ole black cock," growled Zeddy, "he wouldn'a' crowed

round Harlem no moh after I'd done made that theah fine blade talk in his throat."

"Shut up you," the proprietress said, "or I'll throw you out." And Zeddy, the ape, who was scared of no man in the place, became humble before the woman. She began setting the room to order, helped by the two cocoa-brown girls. A man shuffling a pack of cards called to Zeddy and Jake.

But the woman held up her hand. "No more card-playing tonight. I feel too nervous."

"Let's dance, then," suggested the smaller cocoa-brown girl.

A "blues" came trotting out of the pianola. The proprietress bounced into Jake's arms. The men sprang at the two girls. The unlucky ones paired off with each other.

Oh, "blues," "blues," "blues." Black-framed white grinning. Finger-snapping. Undertone singing. The three men with women teasing the stags. Zeddy's gorilla feet dancing down the dark death lurking in his heart. Zeddy dancing with a pal. "Blues," "blues," "blues." Red moods, black moods, golden moods. Curious, syncopated slipping-over into one mood, back-sliding back to the first mood. Humming in harmony, barbaric harmony, joy-drunk, chasing out the shadow of the moment before.

Myrtle Avenue

VI

Zeddy was excited over Jake's success in love. He thought how often he had tried to make up to Rose, without succeeding. He was crazy about finding a woman to love him for himself.

He had been married when he was quite a lad to a crust-yellow girl in Petersburg. Zeddy's wife, after deceiving him with white men, had run away from him to live an easier life. That was before Zeddy came North. Since then he had had many other alliances. But none had been successful.

It was true that no Black Belt beauty would ever call Zeddy "mah han'some brown." But there were sweetmen of the Belt more repulsive than he, that women would fight and murder each other for. Zeddy did not seem to possess any of that magic that charms and holds women for a long time. All his attempts at home-making had failed. The women left him when he could not furnish the cash to meet the bills. They never saw his wages. For it was gobbled up by his voracious passion for poker and crap games. Zeddy gambled in

Harlem. He gambled with white men down by the piers. And he was always losing.

"If only I could get those kinda gals that falls foh Jake," Zeddy mused. "And Jake is such a fool spade. Don't know how to handle the womens."

Zeddy's chance came at last. One Saturday a yellow-skinned youth, whose days and nights were wholly spent between pool-rooms and Negro speakeasies, invited Zeddy to a sociable at a grass-widow's who lived in Brooklyn and worked as a cook downtown in New York. She was called Gin-head Susy. She had a little apartment in Myrtle Avenue near Prince Street.

Susy was wonderfully created. She was of the complexion known among Negroes as spade or chocolate-to-the-bone. Her eyes shone like big white stars. Her chest was majestic and the general effect like a mountain. And that mountain was overgrand because Susy never wore any other but extremely French-heeled shoes. Even over the range she always stood poised in them and blazing in bright-hued clothes.

The burning passion of Susy's life was the yellow youth of her race. Susy came from South Carolina. A yellow youngster married her when she was fifteen and left her before she was eighteen. Since then she had lived with a yellow complex at the core of her heart.

Civilization had brought strikingly exotic types into Susy's race. And like many, many Negroes, she was a victim to that. . . . Ancient black life rooted upon its base with all its fascinating new layers of brown, low-brown, high-brown, nut-brown, lemon, maroon, olive, mauve, gold. Yellow balancing between black and white. Black reaching out beyond yellow. Almost-white on the brink of a change. Sucked back down into the current of black by the terribly sweet rhythm of black blood. . . .

Susy's life of yellow complexity was surcharged with gin. There were whisky and beer also at her sociable evenings, but gin was the drink of drinks. Except for herself, her parties were all-male. Like so many of her sex, she had a congenital contempt for women. All-male were her parties and as yellow as she could make them. A lemon-colored or paper-brown pool-room youngster from Harlem's Fifth Avenue or from Prince Street. A bellboy or railroad waiter or porter. Sometimes a chocolate who was a quick, nondiscriminating lover and not remote of attitude like the pampered high-browns. But chocolates were always a rarity among Susy's front-roomful of gin-lovers.

Yet for all of her wages drowned in gin, Susy carried a hive of discontents in her majestic breast. She desired a lover, something like her undutiful husband, but she desired in vain. Her guests consumed her gin and listened to the phonograph, exchanged rakish stories, and when they felt fruit-ripe to dropping, left her place in pursuit of pleasures elsewhere.

Sometimes Susy managed to lay hold of a yellow one for some time. Something all a piece of dirty rags and stench picked up in the street. Cleansed, clothed, and booted it. But so soon as he got his curly hair straightened by the process of Harlem's Ambrozine Palace of Beauty, and started in strutting the pavement of Lenox Avenue, feeling smart as a moving-picture dandy, he would leave Susy.

Apart from Susy's repellent person, no youthful sweetman attempting to love her could hold out under the ridicule of his pals. Over their games of pool and craps the boys had their cracks at Susy.

"What about Gin-head Susy tonight?"

"Sure, let's go and look the crazy old broad over."

"I'll go anywhere foh selling of good booze."

"She's sho one ugly spade, but she's right there with her Gordon Dry."

"She ain't got 'em from creeps to crown and her trotters is B flat, but her gin is regal."

But now, after all the years of gin sociables and unsatisfactory lemons, Susy was changing just a little. She was changing under the influence of her newly-acquired friend, Lavinia Curdy, the only woman whom she tolerated at her parties. That was not so difficult, as Miss Curdy was less attractive than Susy. Miss Curdy was a putty-skinned mulattress with purple streaks on her face. Two of her upper front teeth had been knocked out and her lower lip slanted pathetically leftward. She was skinny and when she laughed she resembled an old braying jenny.

When Susy came to know Miss Curdy, she unloaded a quantity of the stuff of her breast upon her. Her drab childhood in a South Carolina town. Her early marriage. No girlhood. Her husband leaving her. And all the yellow men that had beaten her, stolen from her, and pawned her things.

Miss Curdy had been very emphatic to Susy about "yaller men." "I know them from long experience. They never want to work. They're a lazy and shiftless lot. Want to be kept like women. I found that out a long, long time ago. And that's why when I wanted a man foh keeps I took me a black plug-ugly one, mah dear."

It wouldn't have supported the plausibility of Miss Curdy's advice if she had mentioned that more than one black plug-ugly had ruthlessly cut loose from her. As the black woman had had her entanglements in yellow, so had the mulattress hers of black. But, perhaps, Miss Curdy did not realize that she could not help desiring black. In her salad days as a business girl her purse was controlled by many a black man. Now, however, her old problems did not arise in exactly the same way,—her purse was old and worn and flat and attracted no attention.

"A black man is as good to me as a yaller when I finds a real one." Susy lied a little to Miss Curdy from a feeling that she ought to show some pride in her own complexion.

"But all these sociables—and you spend so much coin on gin," Miss Curdy had said.

"Well, that's the trute, but we all of us drinks it. And I loves to have company in mah house, plenty of company."

But when Susy came home from work one evening and found that her latest "yaller" sweetie had stolen her suitcase and best dresses and pawned even her gas range, she resolved never to keep another of his kind as a "steady." At least she made that resolve to Miss Curdy. But the sociables went on and the same types came to drink the Saturday evenings away, leaving the two women at the finish to their empty bottles and glasses. Once Susy did make a show of a black lover. He was the house man at the boarding-house where she cooked. But the arrangement did not hold any time, for Susy demanded of the chocolate extremely more than she ever got from her yellows.

"Well, boh, we's Brooklyn bound tonight," said Zeddy to Jake.

"You got to show me that Brooklyn's got any life to it," replied Jake.

"Theah's life anywheres theah's booze and jazz, and theah's cases o' gin and a gramophone whar we's going."

"Has we got to pay foh it, buddy?"

"No, boh, eve'ything is f. o. c. ef the lady likes you."

"Blimey!" A cockney phrase stole Jake's tongue. "Don't bull me."

"I ain't. Honest-to-Gawd Gordon Dry, and moh—ef you're the goods, all f. o. c."

"Well, I'll be browned!" exclaimed Jake.

Zeddy also took along Strawberry Lips, a new pal, burnt-cork black, who was thus nicknamed from the peculiar stage-red color of his mouth. Strawberry Lips was typically the stage Negro. He was proof that a generalization has some foundation in truth. . . . You might live your life in many black belts and arrive at the conclusion that there is no such thing as a typical Negro—no minstrel coon off the stage, no Thomas Nelson Page's nigger, no Octavus Roy Cohen's porter, no lineal descendant of Uncle Tom. Then one day your theory may be upset through meeting with a type by far more perfect than any created counterpart.

"Myrtle Avenue used to be a be-be itching of a place," said Strawberry Lips, "when Doc Giles had his gambling house on there and Elijah Bowers was running his cabaret. H'm. But Bowers was some big guy. He knew swell white folks in politics, and had a grand automobile and a high-yaller wife that hadn't no need of painting to pass. His cabaret was running neck and neck with Marshall's in Fifty-third Street. Then one night he killed a man in his cabaret, and that finished him. The lawyers got him off. But they cleaned him out dry. Done broke him, that case did. And today he's plumb down and out."

Jake, Zeddy, and Strawberry Lips had left the subway train at Borough Hall and were walking down Myrtle Avenue.

"Bowers' cabaret was some place for the teasing-brown pick-me-up then, brother—and the snow. The stuff was cheap then. You sniff, boh?" Strawberry Lips asked Jake and Zeddy.

"I wouldn't know befoh I sees it," Jake laughed.

"I ain't no habitual prisoner," said Zeddy, "but I does any little thing for a change. Keep going and active with anything, says I."

The phonograph was discharging its brassy jazz notes when they entered the apartment. Susy was jerking herself from one side to the other with a potato-skinned boy. Miss Curdy was half-hopping up and down with the only chocolate that was there. Five lads, ranging from brown to yellow in complexion, sat drinking with jaded sneering expressions on their faces. The one that had invited Zeddy was among them. He waved to him to come over with his friends.

"Sit down and try some gin," he said. . . .

Zeddy dipped his hand in his pocket and sent two bones rolling on the table.

"Ise with you, chappie," his yellow friend said. The others crowded around. The gramophone stopped and Susy, hugging a bottle, came jerking on her French heels over to the group. She filled the glasses and everybody guzzled gin.

Miss Curdy looked the newcomers over, paying particular attention to Jake. A sure-enough eye-filling chocolate, she thought. I would like to make a steady thing of him.

Over by the door two light-brown lads began arguing about an actress of the leading theater of the Black Belt.

"I tell you I knows Gertie Kendall. I know her more'n I know you."

"Know her mah granny. You knows her just like I do, from the balcony of the Lafayette. Don't hand me none o' that fairy stuff, for I ain't gwine to swallow it."

"Youse an aching pain. I knows her, I tell you. I even danced with her at Madame Mulberry's apartment. You thinks I only hangs out with low-down trash becassin Ise in a place like this, eh? I done met mos'n all our big niggers: Jack Johnson, James Reese Europe, Adah Walker, Buddy, who used to play that theah drum for them Castle Walkers, and Madame Walker."

"Yaller, it 'pears to me that youse jest a nacherally-born story-teller. You really spec's me to believe youse been associating with the mucty-mucks of the race? Gwan with you. You'll be telling me next you done speaks with Charlie Chaplin and John D. Rockefeller—"

Miss Curdy had tuned her ears to the conversation and broke in: "Why, what is that to make so much fuss about? Sure he can dance with Gertie Kendall and know the dickty niggers. In my sporting days I knew Bert Williams and Walker and Adah Overton and Editor Tuk-slack and all that upstage race gang that wouldn't touch Jack Johnson with a ten-foot pole. I lived in Washington and had Congressmen for my friends—foop! Why you can get in with the top-crust crowd at any swell ball in Harlem. All you need is clothes and the coin. I know them all, yet I don't feel a bit haughty mixing here with Susy and you all."

"I guess you don't now," somebody said.

Gin went round . . . and round . . . and round. . . . Desultory dancing. . . . Dice. . . . Blackjack. . . . Poker. . . . The room became a close, live, intense place. Tight-faced, the men seemed interested only in drinking and gaming, while Susy and Miss Curdy, guzzling hard, grew uglier. A jungle atmosphere pervaded the room, and, like shameless wild animals hungry for raw meat, the females savagely searched the eyes of the males. Susy's eyes always came back to settle upon the lad that had invited Zeddy. He was her real object. And Miss Curdy was ginned up with high hopes of Jake.

Jake threw up the dice and Miss Curdy seized her chance to get him alone for a little while.

"The cards do get so tiresome," she said. "I wonder how you men can go on and on all night long poking around with poker."

"Better than worser things," retorted Jake. Disgusted by the purple streaks, he averted his eyes from the face of the mulattress.

"I don't know about that," Miss Curdy bridled. "There's many nice ways of spending a sociable evening between ladies and gentlemen."

"Got to show me," said Jake, simply because the popular phrase intrigued his tongue.

"*And that I can.*"

Irritated, Jake turned to move away.

"Where you going? Scared of a lady?"

Jake recoiled from the challenge, and shuffled away from the hideous mulattress. From experience in seaport towns in America, in France, in England, he had concluded that a woman could always go farther than a man in coarseness, depravity, and sheer cupidity. Men were ugly and brutal. But beside women they were merely vicious children. Ignorant about the aim and meaning and fulfillment of life; uncertain and indeterminate; weak. Rude children who loved excelling in spectacular acts to win the applause of women.

But women were so realistic and straight-going. *They* were the real controlling force of life. Jake remembered the bal-musette fights between colored and white soldiers in France. Blacks, browns, yellows, whites. . . . He remembered the interracial sex skirmishes in England. Men fought, hurt, wounded, killed each other. Women, like blazing torches, egged them on or denounced them. Victims of sex, the men seemed foolish, ape-like blunderers in their pools of blood. Didn't know what they were fighting for, except it was to gratify some vague feeling about women. . . .

Jake's thoughts went roaming after his little lost brown of the Baltimore. The difference! She, in one night, had revealed a fine different world to him. Mystery again. A little stray girl. Finer than the finest!

Some of the fellows were going. In a vexed spirit, Susy had turned away from her unresponsive mulatto toward Zeddy. Relieved, the mulatto yawned, threw his hands backwards and said: "I guess mah broad is home from Broadway by now. Got to final on home to her. Harlem, lemme see you."

Miss Curdy was sitting against the mantelpiece, charming Strawberry Lips. Marvelous lips. Salmon-pink and planky. She had hoisted herself upon his knees, her arm around his thick neck.

Jake went over to the mantelpiece to pour a large chaser of beer and Miss Curdy leered at him. She disgusted him. His life was a free coarse thing, but he detested nastiness and ugliness. Guess I'll haul bottom to Harlem, he thought. Congo Rose was a rearing wild animal, all right, but these women, these boys. . . . Skunks, tame skunks, all of them!

He was just going out when a chocolate lad pointed at a light-brown and said: "The pot calls foh four bits, chappie. Come across or stay out."

"Lemme a quarter!"

"Ain't got it. Staying out?"

Biff! Square on the mouth. The chocolate leaped up like a tiger-cat at his assailant, carrying over card table, little pile of money, and half-filled gin glasses with a crash. Like an enraged ram goat, he held and butted the light-brown boy twice, straight on the forehead. The victim crumpled with a thud to the floor. Susy jerked over to the felled boy and hauled him, his body leaving a liquid trail, to the door. She flung him out in the corridor and slammed the door.

"Sarves him right, pulling off that crap in mah place. And you, Mis'er Jack Johnson," she said to the chocolate youth, "lemme miss you quick."

"He done hits me first," the chocolate said.

"I knows it, but I ain't gwina stand foh no rough-house in mah place. Ise got a dawg heah wif me all ready foh bawking."

"K-hhhhh, K-hhhhh," laughed Strawberry Lips. "Oh, boh, I know it's the trute, but—"

The chocolate lad slunk out of the flat.

"Lavinia," said Susy to Miss Curdy, "put on that theah 'Tickling Blues' on the victroly."

The phonograph began its scraping and Miss Curdy started jig-jagging with Strawberry Lips. Jake gloomed with disgust against the door.

"Getting outa this, buddy?" he asked Zeddy.

"Nobody's chasing *us*, boh." Zeddy commenced stepping with Susy to the "Tickling Blues."

Outside, Jake found the light-brown boy still half-stunned against the wall.

"Ain't you gwine at home?" Jake asked him.

"I can't find a nickel foh car fare," said the boy.

Jake took him into a saloon and bought him a lemon squash. "Drink that to clear you' haid," he said. "And heah's car fare." He gave the boy a dollar. "Whar you living at?"

"San Juan Hill."

"Come on, le's git the subway, then."

The Myrtle Avenue Elevated train passed with a high raucous rumble over their heads.

"Myrtle Avenue," murmured Jake. "Pretty name, all right, but it stinks like a sewer. Legs and feets! Come take me outa it back home to Harlem."

Zeddy's Rise and Fall
VII

Zeddy was scarce in Harlem. And Strawberry Lips was also scarce. It was fully a week after the Myrtle Avenue gin-fest before Jake saw Zeddy again. They met on the pavement in front of Uncle Doc's saloon.

"Why, where in the sweet name of niggers in Harlem, buddy, you been keeping you'-self?"

"Whar you think?"

"Think? I been very much thinking that Nije Cridley done git you."

"How come you git thataway, boh? Nije Cridley him ain't got a chawnst on the carve or the draw ag'inst Zeddy Plummer so long as Ise got me a black moon."

"Well, what's it done git you, then?"

"Myrtle Avenue."

"Come outa that; you ain't talking. . . ."

"The trute as I knows it, buddy."

"Crazy dog bite mah laig!" cried Jake. "You ain't telling me that you done gone. . . ."

"Transfer mah suitcase and all mah pohsitions to Susy."

"Gin-head Susy!"

"Egsactly; that crechur is mah ma-ma now. I done express mahself ovah theah on that very mahv'lously hang-ovah afternoon of that gin-nity mawnin' that you left me theah. And Ise been right theah evah since."

"Well, Ise got to wish you good luck, buddy, although youse been keeping it so dark."

"It's the darkness of new loving, boh. But the honeymoon is good and well ovah, and I'll be li'l moh in Harlem as usual, looking the chippies and chappies ovah. I ain't none at all stuck on Brooklyn."

"It's a swah hole all right," said Jake.

"But theah's sweet stuff in it." Zeddy tongue-wiped his fleshy lips with a salacious laugh.

"It's all right, believe me, boh," he informed Jake. "Susy ain't nothing to look at like you' fair-brown queen, but she's tur'bly sweet loving. You know when a ma-ma ain't the goods in looks and figure, she's got to make up foh it some. And that Susy does. And she treats me right. Gimme all I wants to drink and brings home the goodest poke chops and fried chicken foh me to put away under mah shirt. . . . Youse got to come and feed with us all one o' these heah evenings."

It was a party of five when Jake went again to Myrtle Avenue for the magnificent free-love feast that Susy had prepared. It was Susy's free Sunday. Miss Curdy and Strawberry Lips were also celebrating. Susy had concocted a pitcherful of knock-out gin cocktails. And such food! Susy could cook. Perhaps it was her splendid style that made her sink all her wages in gin and sweetmen. For she belonged to the ancient aristocracy of black cooks, and knew that she was always sure of a good place, so long as the palates of rich Southerners retained their discriminating taste.

Cream tomato soup. Ragout of chicken giblets. Southern fried chicken. Candied sweet potatoes. Stewed corn. Rum-flavored fruit salad waiting in the ice-box. . . . The stars rolling in Susy's shining face showed how pleased she was with her art.

She may be fat and ugly as a turkey, thought Jake, but her eats am sure beautiful.

"Heah! Pass me you' plate," Susy gave Jake a leg. Zeddy held out his plate again and got a wing. Strawberry Lips received a bit of breast. . . .

"No more chicken for me, Susy," Miss Curdy mumbled, "but I *will* have another helping of that there stewed corn. I don't know what ingredients yo-all puts in it, but, Lawdy! I never tasted anything near so good."

Susy beamed and dipped up three spoonfuls of corn. "Plenty, thank you," Miss Curdy stopped her from filling up her saucer. . . . Susy drank off a tumbler of cocktail at a draught, and wiped her lips with the white serviette that was stuck into the low neck of her vermillion crepe-de-chine blouse. . . .

When Jake was ready to leave, Zeddy announced that he would take a little jaunt with him to Harlem.

"You ain'ta gwine to do no sich thing as that," Susy said.

"Yes I is," responded Zeddy. "Wha' there is to stop me?"

"I is," said Susy.

"And what foh?"

" 'Causen I don't wanchu to go to Harlem. What makes you niggers love Harlem so much? Because it's a bloody ungodly place where niggers nevah go to bed. All night running around speakeasies and cabarets, where bad, hell-bent nigger womens am giving up themselves to open sin."

Susy stood broad and aggressive against the window overlooking Myrtle Avenue.

"Harlem is all right," said Zeddy. "I ain't knocking round no cabarets and speakeasies. Ahm just gwine ovah wif Jake to see somathem boys."

"Can that boy business!" cried Susy. "I've had anuff hell scrapping wif the women ovah mah mens. I ain't agwine to have no Harlem boys seducin' mah man away fwom me. The boy business is a fine excuse indeedy foh sich womens as ain't wise. I always heah the boss say to the missus, 'I gwine out foh a little time wif the boys, dearie.' when him wants an excuse foh a night off. I ain't born yestiday, honey. If you wants the boys foh a li'l' game o' poky, you bring 'em ovah heah. I ain't got the teeeniest bit of objection, and Ise got plenty o' good Gordon Dry foh eve'body."

"Ise got to go scares them up to bring them heah," said Zeddy.

"But not tonight or no night," declared Susy. "You kain do that in the daytime, foh you ain't got nothing to do."

Zeddy moved toward the mantelpiece to get his cap, but Susy blocked his way and held the cap behind her.

Zeddy looked savagely in her eyes and growled: "Come outa that, sistah, and gimme mah cap. It ain't no use stahting trouble."

Susy looked steadily in his eyes and chucked the cap at him. "Theah's you cap, but ef you stahts leaving me nights you . . ."

"What will you do?" asked Zeddy.

"I'll put you' block in the street."

Zeddy's countenance fell flat from its high aggressiveness.

"Well s'long, eve'body," said Jake.

Zeddy put on his cap and rocked out of the apartment after him. In the street he asked Jake, "Think I ought to take a crack at Harlem with you tonight, boh?"

"Not ef you loves you' new home, buddy," Jake replied.

"Bull! That plug-ugly black woman is ornery like hell. I ain't gwineta let her bridle and ride me. . . . You ain't in no pickle like that with Rose, is you?"

"Lawd, no! I do as I wanta. But I'm one independent cuss, buddy. We ain't sitchuate the same. I works."

"Black womens when theyse ugly am all sistahs of Satan," declared Zeddy.

"It ain't the black ones only," said Jake.

"I wish I could hit things off like you, boh," said Zeddy. . . . "Well, I'll see you all some night at Billy Biasse's joint. . . . S'long. Don't pick up no bad change."

From that evening Zeddy began to discover that it wasn't all fine and lovely to live sweet. Formerly he had always been envious when any of his pals pointed out an extravagantly-dressed dark dandy and remarked, "He was living sweet." There was something so romantic about the sweet life. To be the adored of a Negro lady of means, or of a pseudo grass-widow whose husband worked on the railroad, or of a hard-working laundress or cook. It was much more respectable and enviable to be sweet—to belong to the exotic aristocracy of sweetmen than to be just a common tout.

But there were strings to Susy's largesse. The enjoyment of Harlem's low night life was prohibited to Zeddy. Susy was jealous of him in the proprietary sense. She believed in free love all right, but not for the man she possessed and supported. She warned him against the ornery hussies of her race.

"Nigger hussies nevah wanta git next to a man 'cep'n' when he's a-looking good to another woman," Susy declared. "I done gived you fair warning to jest keep away from the buffet-flat widdahs and thim Harlem street floaters; foh ef I ketch you making a fool woman of me, I'll throw you' pants in the street."

"Hi, but youse talking sistah. Why don't you wait till you see something before you staht in chewing the rag?"

"I done give you the straight stuff in time so you kain watch you'self when I kain't watch you. I ain't bohding and lodging no black man foh'm to be any other nigger woman's daddy."

So, in a few pointed phrases, Susy let Zeddy understand precisely what she would stand for. Zeddy was well kept like a prince of his type. He could not complain about food . . . and bed. Susy was splendid in her matriarchal way, rolling her eyes with love or disapproval at him, according to the exigencies of the moment.

The Saturday-night gin parties went on as usual. The brown and high-brown boys came and swilled. Miss Curdy was a constant visitor, frequently toting Strawberry Lips along. About her general way of handling things Susy brooked no criticism from Zeddy. She had bargained with him in the interest of necessity and of rivalry and she paid and paid fully, but grimly. She was proud to have a man to boss about in an intimate, casual way.

"Git out another bottle of gin, Zeddy. . . ."

"Bring along that packet o' saltines. . . ."

"Put on that theah 'Tickling Blues' that we's all just crazy about."

To have an aggressive type like Zeddy at her beck and call considerably increased Susy's prestige and clucking pride. She noticed, with carefully-concealed delight, that the interest of the yellow gin-swillers was piqued. She became flirtatious and coy by turns. And she was rewarded by fresh attentions. Even Miss Curdy was now meeting with new adventures, and she was prompted to expatiate upon men and love to Susy.

"Men's got a whole lot of women in their nature, I tell you. Just as women never really see a man until he's looking good to another woman and the hussies want to steal him, it's the same thing with men, mah dear. So soon as a woman is all sugar and candy for another man, you find a lot of them heart-breakers all trying to get next to her. Like a set of strutting game cocks all priming themselves to crow over a li'l' piece o' nothing."

"That's the gospel trute indeed," agreed Susy. "I done have a mess of knowledge 'bout men tucked away heah." Susy tapped her head of tight-rolled kinks knotted with scraps of ribbon of different colors. "I pays foh what I know and I've nevah been sorry, either. Yes, mam, I done larned about mah own self fust. Had no allusions about mahself. I knowed that I was black and ugly and no-class and unejucated. And I knowed that I was bohn foh love. . . . Mah mammy did useter warn me about love. All what the white folks call white slavery theseadays. I dunno ef theah's another name foh the nigger-an'-white side ovit down home in Dixie. Well, I soon found out it wasn't womens alone in the business, sposing thimselves like vigitables foh sale in the market. No, mam! I done soon l'arned that the mens was most buyable thimselves. Mah heart-breaking high-yaller done left me sence—how miny wintahs I been counting this heah Nothan snow? All thim and some moh—dawggone ef I remimber. But evah since I been paying sistah, paying good and hard foh mah loving feelings."

"Life ain't no country picnic with sweet flute and fiddle," Miss Curdy sighed.

"Indeed not," Susy was emphatic. "It ain't got nothing to do with the rubbish we l'arn at Sunday school and the sweet snooziness I used to lap up in thim blue-cover story books. My God! the things I've seen! Working with white folks, so dickty and high-and-mighty, you think theyse nevah oncet naked and thim feets nevah touch ground. Yet all the silks and furs and shining diamonds can't hide the misery a them lives. . . . Servants and heart-breakers from outside stealing the husband's stuff. And all the men them that can't find no sweet-loving life at home. Lavinia, I done seen life."

"Me, too, I have seen the real life, mixing as I used to in *real* society," said Miss Curdy.

"I know society, too, honey, even though I only knows it watching from the servant window. And I know it ain't no different from *us*. It's the same life even ef they drink champagne and we drink gin."

"You said it and said it right," responded Miss Curdy.

Zeddy discovered that in his own circles in Harlem he had become something of a joke. It was known that he was living sweet. But his buddies talked about his lady riding him with a cruel bit.

"He was kept, all right," they said, "kept under 'Gin-head' Susy's skirt."

He had had to fight a fellow in Dixie Red's pool-room, for calling him a "skirt-man."

He was even teased by Billy Biasse or Billy, the Wolf, as he was nicknamed. Billy boasted frankly that he had no time for women.

Black women, or the whole diversified world of the sex were all the same to him.

"So Harlem, after the sun done set, has no fun at all foh you, eh, boh?" Billy asked Zeddy.

Zeddy growled something indistinct.

"Sweet with the bit in you' mouf. Black woman riding her nigger. Great life, boh, ef you don't weaken."

"Bull! Wha's the matter with you niggers, anyhow?" Zeddy said in a sort of general way. "Ain't it better than being a wolf?"

"Ise a wolf, all right, but I ain't a lone one," Billy grinned. "I guess Ise the happiest, well-feddest wolf in Harlem. Oh, boy!"

Zeddy spent that evening in Harlem drinking with Jake and two more longshoremen at Uncle Doc's saloon. Late in the night they went to the Congo. Zeddy returned to Myrtle Avenue, an hour before it was time for Susy to rise, fully ginned up.

To Susy's "Whar you been?" he answered, "Shut up or I'll choke you," staggered, swayed, and swept from the dresser a vase of chrysanthemums that broke on the floor.

"Goddam fool flowers," he growled. "Why in hell didn't you put them out of the way, hey, you Suze?"

"Oh, keep quiet and come along to bed," said Susy.

A week later he repeated the performance, coming home with alarming symptoms of gin hiccough. Susy said nothing. After that Zeddy began to prance, as much as a short, heavy-made human could, with the bit out of his mouth. . . .

One Saturday night Susy's gin party was a sad failure. Nobody came beside Miss Curdy with Strawberry Lips. (Zeddy had left for Harlem in the afternoon.) They drank to themselves and played coon-can. Near midnight, when Miss Curdy was going, she said offhandedly, "I wouldn't mind sampling one of those Harlem cabarets now." Susy at once seized upon the idea.

"Sure. Let's go to Harlem for a change."

They caught the subway train for Harlem. Arrived there they gravitated to the Congo.

Before Susy left Myrtle Avenue, Zeddy was already at the Congo with a sweet, timid, satin-faced brown just from down home, that he had found at Aunt Hattie's and induced to go with him to the cabaret. Jake sat at Zeddy's table. Zeddy was determined to go the limit of independence, to show the boys that he was a cocky sweetman and no skirt-man. Plenty of money. He was treating. He wore an elegant nigger-brown sports suit and patent-leather shoes with cream-light spats such as all the sweet swells love to strut in. If Zeddy had only been taller, trimmer, and well-arched he would have been one of Harlem's dandiest sports.

His new-found brown had a glass of Virginia Dare before her; he was drinking gin. Jake, Scotch-and-soda; and Rose, who sat with them when she was not entertaining, had ordered White Rock. The night before, or rather the early morning after her job was done, she had gone on a champagne party and now she was sobering up.

Billy Biasse was there at a neighboring table with a longshoreman and a straw-colored boy who was a striking advertisement of the Ambrozine Palace of Beauty. The boy was made up with high-brown powder, his eyebrows were elongated and blackened up, his lips streaked with the dark rouge so popular in Harlem, and his carefully-straightened hair lay plastered and glossy under Madame Walker's absinthe-colored salve "for milady of fashion and color."

"Who's the doll baby at the Wolf's table?" Zeddy asked.

"Tha's mah dancing pardner," Rose answered.

"Another entertainer? The Congo is gwine along fast enough."

"You bet you," said Jake. "And the ofays will soon be nosing it out. Then we'll have to take a back seat."

"Who's the Wolf?" Timidly Zeddy's girl asked.

Zeddy pointed out Billy.

"But why Wolf?"

"Khhhhhhh—Khhhhhhhh . . ." Zeddy laughed. " 'Causen he eats his own kind."

It was time for Rose to dance. Her partner had preceded her to the open space and was standing, arm akimbo against the piano, talking to the pianist. The pianist was a slight-built, long-headed fellow. His face shone like anthracite, his eyes were arresting, intense, deep-yellow slits. He seemed in a continual state of swaying excitement, whether or not he was playing.

They were ready, Rose and the dancer-boy. The pianist began, his eyes toward the ceiling in a sort of savage ecstatic dream. Fiddler, saxophonist, drummer, and cymbalist seemed to catch their inspiration from him. . . .

When Luty dances, everything
  Is dancing in the cabaret.
The second fiddle asks the first:
  What makes you sound that funny way?
The drum talks in so sweet a voice,
  The cymbal answers in surprise,

The lights put on a brighter glow
    To match the shine of Luty's eyes.

For he's a foot-manipulating fool
    When he hears that crazy moan
    Come rolling, rolling outa that saxophone. . . .
Watch that strut; there's no keeping him cool
    When he's a-rearing with that saxophone. . . .
    Oh, the tearing, tantalizing tone!
    Of that moaning saxophone. . . .
        That saxophone. . . .
        That saxophone. . . .

They danced, Rose and the boy. Oh, they danced! An exercise of rhythmical exactness for two. There was no motion she made that he did not imitate. They reared and pranced together, smacking palm against palm, working knee between knee, grinning with real joy. They shimmied, breast to breast, bent themselves far back and shimmied again. Lifting high her short skirt and showing her green bloomers, Rose kicked. And in his tight nigger-brown suit, the boy kicked even with her. They were right there together, neither going beyond the other. . . .

And the pianist! At intervals his yellow eyes, almost bloodshot, swept the cabaret with a triumphant glow, gave the dancers a caressing look, and returned to the ceiling. Lean, smart fingers beating barbaric beauty out of a white frame. Brown bodies, caught up in the wild rhythm, wiggling and swaying in their seats.

For he's a foot-manipulating fool
    When he hears that crazy moan
    Come rolling, rolling outa that saxophone. . . .
        That saxophone. . . .
        That saxophone. . . .

Rose was sipping her White Rock. Her partner, at Billy's table, sucked his iced creme-de-menthe through a straw. The high wave of joyful excitement had subsided and the customers sat casually drinking and gossiping as if they had not been soaring a minute before in a realm of pure joy.

From his place, giving a good view of the staircase, Zeddy saw two apparently familiar long legs swinging down the steps. Sure enough, he knew those big, thick-soled red boots.

"Them feets look jest laka Strawberry Lips' own," he said to Jake.

Jake looked and saw first Strawberry Lips enter the cabaret, with Susy behind balancing upon her French heels, and Miss Curdy. Susy was gorgeous in a fur coat of rich shiny black, like her complexion. Opened, it showed a cérise blouse and a yellow-and-mauve check skirt. Her head of thoroughly-straightened hair flaunted a green hat with a decoration of red ostrich plumes.

"Great balls of fire! Here's you doom, buddy," said Jake.

"Doom, mah granny," retorted Zeddy. "Ef that theah black ole cow come fooling near me tonight, I'll show her who's wearing the pants."

Susy did not see Zeddy until her party was seated. It was Miss Curdy who saw him first. She dug into Susy's side with her elbow and cried:

"For the love of Gawd, looka there!"

Susy's star eyes followed Miss Curdy's. She glared at Zeddy and fixed her eyes on the girl with him for a moment. Then she looked away and grunted: "He thinks he's acting smart, eh? Him and I will wrastle that out to a salution, but I ain't agwine to raise no stink in heah."

"He's got some more nerve pulling off that low-down stuff, and on your money, too," said Miss Curdy.

"Who that?" asked Strawberry Lips.

"Ain't you seen your best friends over there?" retorted Miss Curdy.

Strawberry Lips waved at Zeddy and Jake, but they were deliberately keeping their eyes away from Susy's table. He got up to go to them.

"Where you going?" Miss Curdy asked.

"To chin wif—"

A yell startled the cabaret. A girl had slapped another's face and replied to her victim's cry of pain with, "If you no like it you can lump it!"

"You low an' dutty bobbin-bitch!"

"Bitch is bobbin in you' sistah's coffin."

They were West Indian girls.

"I'll mek mah breddah beat you' bottom foh you."

"Gash it and stop you' jawing."

They were interrupted by another West Indian girl, who wore a pink-flowered muslin frock and a wide jippi-jappa hat from which charmingly hung two long ends of broad peagreen ribbon.

"It's a shame. Can't you act like decent English people?" she said. Gently she began pushing away the assaulted girl, who burst into tears.

"She come boxing me up ovah a dutty-black 'Merican coon."

"Mek a quick move or I'll box you bumbole ovah de moon," her assailant cried after her. . . .

"The monkey-chasers am scrapping," Zeddy commented.

"In a language all their own," said Jake.

"They are wild womens, buddy, and it's a wild language they're using, too," remarked a young West Indian behind Jake.

"Hmm! but theyse got the excitement fever," a lemon-colored girl at a near table made her contribution and rocked and twisted herself coquettishly at Jake. . . .

Susy had already reached the pavement with Miss Curdy and Strawberry Lips. Susy breathed heavily.

"Lesh git furthest away from this low-down vice hole," she said. "Leave that plug-ugly nigger theah. I ain't got no more use foh him nohow."

"I never did have any time for Harlem," said Miss Curdy. "When I was high up in society all respectable colored people lived in Washington. There was no Harlem full a niggers then. I declare—"

"I should think the nigger heaven of a theater downtown is better than anything in this heah Harlem," said Susy. "When we feels like going out, it's better we enjoy ourse'f in the li'l' corner the white folks 'low us, and then shuffle along back home. It's good and quiet ovah in Brooklyn."

"And we can have all the inside fun we need," said Miss Curdy.

"Brooklyn ain't no better than Harlem," said Strawberry Lips, running the words rolling off his tongue. "Theah's as much shooting-up and cut-up in Prince Street and—"

"There ain't no compahrison atall," stoutly maintained Susy. "This here Harlem is a stinking sink of iniquity. Nigger hell! That's what it is. Looka that theah ugly black nigger loving up a scrimpy brown gal right befoh mah eyes. Jest daring me to turn raw and loose lak them monkey-chasing womens thisanight. But that I wouldn't do. I ain't a woman abandoned to sich publicity stunts. Not even though mah craw was full to bursting. Lemme see'm tonight. . . . Yessam, this heah Harlem is sure nigger hell. Take me way away from it."

When Zeddy at last said good night to his new-found brown, he went straight to an all-night barrel-house and bought a half a pint of whisky. He guzzled the liquor and smashed the flask on the pavement. Drew up his pants, tightened his belt and growled, "Now I'm ready for Susy."

He caught the subway train for Brooklyn. Only local trains were running and it was quite an hour and a half before he got home. He staggered down Myrtle Avenue well primed with the powerful stimulation of gin-and-whisky.

At the door of Susy's apartment he was met by his suitcase. He recoiled as from a blow struck at his face. Immediately he became sober. His eyes caught a little white tag attached to the handle. Examining it by the faint gaslight he read, in Susy's handwriting: "Kip owt that meen you."

Susy had put all Zeddy's belongings into the suitcase, keeping back what she had given him: two fancy-colored silk shirts, silk handkerchiefs, a mauve dressing-gown, and a box of silk socks.

"What he's got on that black back of his'n he can have," she had said while throwing the things in the bag.

Zeddy beat on the door with his fists.

"Wha moh you want?" Susy's voice bawled from within. "Ain'tchu got all you stuff theah? Gwan back where youse coming from."

"Lemme in and quit you joking," cried Zeddy.

"You ugly flat-footed zigaboo," shouted Susy, "may I ketch the 'lectric chair without conversion ef I 'low you dirty black pusson in mah place again. And you better git quick foh I staht mah dawg bawking at you."

Zeddy picked up his suitcase. "Come on, Mistah Bag. Le's tail along back to Harlem. Leave black woman 'lone wif her gin and ugly mug. Black woman is hard luck."

The Raid of the Baltimore

VIII

The blazing lights of the Baltimore were put out and the entrance was padlocked. Fifth Avenue and Lenox talked about nothing else. Buddy meeting buddy and chippie greeting chippie, asked: "Did you hear the news?" . . . "Well, what do you know about that?"

Yet nothing sensational had happened in the Baltimore. The police had not, on a certain night, swept into it and closed it up because of indecent doings. No. It was an indirect raid. Oh, and that made the gossip toothier! For the Baltimore was not just an ordinary cabaret. It had mortgages and policies in the best of the speakeasy places of the Belt. And the mass of Harlem held the Baltimore in high respect because (it was rumored and believed) it was protected by Tammany Hall.

Jake, since he had given up hoping about his lost brown, had stopped haunting the Baltimore, yet he had happened to be very much in on the affair that cost the Baltimore its license. Jake's living with Rose had, in spite of himself, projected him into a more elegant atmosphere of worldliness. Through Rose and her associates he had gained access to buffet flats and private rendezvous apartments that were called "nifty."

And Jake was a high favorite wherever he went. There was something so naturally beautiful about his presence that everybody liked and desired him. Buddies, on the slightest provocation, were ready to fight for him, and the girls liked to make an argument around him.

Jake had gained admission to Madame Adeline Suarez's buffet flat, which was indeed a great feat. He was the first longshoreman, colored or white, to tread that magnificent red carpet. Madame Suarez catered to sporty colored persons of consequence only and certain groups of downtown whites that used to frequent Harlem in the good old pre-prohibition days.

"Ain't got no time for cheap-no-'count niggers," Madame Suarez often said. "Gimme their room to their company any time, even if they've got money to spend." Madame Suarez came from Florida and she claimed Cuban descent through her father. By her claim to that exotic blood she moved like a queen among the blue-veins of the colored sporting world.

But Jake's rough charm could conquer anything.

"Ofay's mixing in!" he exclaimed to himself the first night he penetrated into Madame Suarez's. "But ofay or ofay not, this here is the real stuff," he reflected. And so many nights he absented himself from the Congo (he had no interest in Rose's art of flirting money out of hypnotized newcomers) to luxuriate with charmingly painted pansies among the colored cushions and under the soft, shaded lights of Madame Suarez's speakeasy. It was a new world for Jake and he took it easily. That was his natural way, wherever he went, whatever new people he met. It had helped him over many a bad crossing at Brest at Havre and in London. . . . Take it easy . . . take life easy. Sometimes he was disgusted with life, but he was never frightened of it.

Jake had never seen colored women so carefully elegant as these rich-browns and yellow-creams at Madame Suarez's. They were fascinating in soft bright draperies and pretty pumps and they drank liquor with a fetching graceful abandon. Gin and whisky seemed to lose their barbaric punch in that atmosphere and take on a romantic color. The women's coiffure was arranged in different striking styles and their arms and necks and breasts tinted to emphasize the peculiar richness of each skin. One girl, who was the favorite of Madame Suarez, and the darkest in the group, looked like a breathing statue of burnished bronze. With their arresting poses and gestures, their deep shining painted eyes, they resembled the wonderfully beautiful pictures of women of ancient Egypt.

Here Jake brushed against big men of the colored sporting world and their white friends. That strange un-American world where colored meets and mingles freely and naturally with white in amusement basements, buffet flats, poker establishments. Sometimes there were two or three white women, who attracted attention because they were white and strange to Harlem, but they appeared like faded carnations among those burning orchids of a tropical race.

One night Jake noticed three young white men, clean-shaven, flashily-dressed, who paid for champagne for everybody in the flat. They were introduced by a perfectly groomed dark-brown man, a close friend of the boss of the Baltimore. Money seemed worthless to them except as a means of getting fun out of it. Madame Suarez made special efforts to please them. Showed them all of the buffet flat, even her own bedroom. One of them, very freckled and red-haired, sat down to the piano and jazzed out popular songs. The trio radiated friendliness all around them. Danced with the colored beauties and made lively conversation with the men. They were gay and recklessly spendthrift. . . .

They returned on a Saturday night, between midnight and morning, when the atmosphere of Madame Suarez's was fairly bacchic and jazz music was snake-wriggling in and out and around everything and forcing everybody into amatory states and attitudes. The three young white men had two others with them. At the piano a girl curiously made up in mauve was rendering the greatest ragtime song of the day. Broadway was wild about it and Harlem was crazy. All America jazzed to it, and it was already world-famous. Already being jazzed perhaps in Paris and Cairo, Shanghai, Honolulu, and Java. It was a song about cocktails and cherries. Like this in some ways:

> Take a juicy cocktail cherry,
> Take a dainty little bite,
> And we'll all be very merry
> On a cherry drunk tonight.

> We'll all be merry when you have a cherry,
> And we'll twine and twine like a fruitful vine,
> Grape vine, red wine, babe mine, bite a berry,
> You taste a cherry and twine, rose vine, sweet wine.
>   Cherry-ee-ee-ee-ee, cherry-ee-ee-ee-ee-ee, ee-ee-ee
>   Cherry-ee-ee-ee-ee, cherry-ee-ee-ee-ee-ee, ee-ee-ee
>   Grape vine, rose vine, sweet wine. . . .

> Love is like a cocktail cherry,
> Just a fruity little bit,

And you've never yet been merry,
  If you've not been drunk on it.

We'll all be merry when you have. . . .

The women, carried away by the sheer rhythm of delight, had risen above their commercial instincts (a common trait of Negroes in emotional states) and abandoned themselves to pure voluptuous jazzing. They were gorgeous animals swaying there through the dance, punctuating it with marks of warm physical excitement. The atmosphere was charged with intensity and over-charged with currents of personal reaction. . . .

Then the five young white men unmasked as the Vice Squad and killed the thing.

Dicks! They had wooed and lured and solicited for their trade. For two weeks they had spilled money like water at the Baltimore. Sometimes they were accompanied by white girls who swilled enormous quantities of champagne and outshrieked the little ginned-up Negresses and mulattresses of the cabaret. They had posed as good fellows, regular guys, looking for a good time only in the Black Belt. They were wearied of the pleasures of the big white world, wanted something new—the primitive joy of Harlem.

So at last, with their spendthrift and charming ways, they had convinced the wary boss of the Baltimore that they were fine fellows. The boss was a fine fellow himself, who loved life and various forms of fun and had no morals about them. And so one night when the trio had left their hired white ladies behind, he was persuaded to give his youthful white guests an introduction to Madame Adeline Suarez's buffet flat. . . .

The uniformed police were summoned. Madame Suarez and her clients were ordered to get ready to go down to the Night Court. The women asked permission to veil themselves. Many windows were raked up in the block and heads craned forth to watch the prisoners bundled into waiting taxicabs. The women were afraid. Some of them were false grass-widows whose husbands were working somewhere. Some of them were church members. Perhaps one could claim a place in local society!

They were all fined. But Madame Suarez, besides being fined, was sent to Blackwell's Island for six months.

To the two white girls that were also taken in the raid the judge remarked that it was a pity he had no power to order them whipped. For whipping was the only punishment he considered suitable for white women who dishonored their race by associating with colored persons.

The high point of the case was the indictment of the boss of the Baltimore as accessory to the speakeasy crime. The boss was not convicted, but the Baltimore was ordered to be padlocked. That decision was appealed. But the cabaret remained padlocked. A black member of Tammany had no chances against the Moral Arm of the city.

The Belt's cabaret sets licked their lips over the sensation for weeks. For a long time Negro proprietors would not admit white customers into their cabarets and near-white members of the black race, whose features were unfamiliar in Harlem, had a difficult time proving their identity.

Jake Makes a Move

IX

Coming home from work one afternoon, Jake remarked a taxicab just driving away from his house. He was quite a block off, but he thought it was his number. When he entered Rose's room he immediately detected an unfamiliar smell. He had an uncanny sharp nose for strange smells. Rose always had visitors, of course. Girls, and fellows, too, of her circle. But Jake had a feeling that his nose had scented something foreign to Harlem. The room was close with tobacco smoke; there were many Melachrino butts in a tray, and a half-used box of the same cigarettes on a little table drawn up against the scarlet-covered couch. Also, there was a half-filled bottle of Jake's Scotch whisky on the table and glasses for two. Rose was standing before the dresser, arranging her hair.

"Been having company?" Jake asked, carelessly.

"Yep. It was only Gertie Blake."

Jake knew that Rose was lying. Her visitor had not been Gertie Blake. It had been a man, a strange man, doubtless a white man. Yet he hadn't the slightest feeling of jealousy or anger, whatever the visitor was. Rose had her friends of both sexes and was quite free in her ways. At the Congo she sat and drank and flirted with many fellows. That was a part of her business. She got more tips that way, and the extra personal bargains that gave her the means to maintain her style of living. All her lovers had always accepted her living entirely free. For that made it possible for her to keep them living carefree and sweet.

Rose was disappointed in Jake. She had wanted him to live in the usual sweet way, to be brutal and beat her up a little, and take away her money from her. Once she had a rough leather-brown man who used to beat her up regularly. Sometimes she was beaten so badly she had to stay indoors for days, and to her visiting girl pals she exhibited her bruises and blackened eyes with pride.

As Jake was not brutally domineering, she cooled off from him perceptibly. But she could not make him change. She confided to her friends that he was "good loving but" (making use of a contraction that common people employ) "a big Ah-Ah all the same." She felt no thrill about the business when her lover was not interested in her earnings.

Jake did not care. He did not love her, had never felt any deep desire for her. He had gone to live with her simply because she had asked him when he was in a fever mood for a steady mate. There was nothing about Rose that touched and roused him as his vivid recollection of his charming little brown-skin of the Baltimore. Rose's room to him was like any ordinary lodging in Harlem. While the room of his little lost brown lived in his mind a highly magnified affair: a bed of gold, fresh, white linen, a magic carpet, all bathed in the rarest perfume. . . . Rose's perfume made his nose itch. It was rank.

He came home another afternoon and found her with a bright batik kimono carelessly wrapped around her and stretched full-length on the couch. There were Melachrino stubs lying about and his bottle of Scotch was on the mantelpiece. Evidently the strange visitor of the week before had been there again.

"Hello!" She yawned and flicked off her cigarette ash and continued smoking. A chic veneer over a hard, restless, insensitive body. Fascinating, nevertheless. . . . For the moment, just as she was, she was desirable and provoked responses in him. He shuffled up to the couch and caressed her.

"Leave me alone, I'm tired," she snarled.

The rebuff hurt Jake. "You slut!" he cried. He went over to the mantelpiece and added, "Youse just everybody's teaser."

"You got a nearve talking to me that way," said Rose. "Since when you staht riding the high horse?"

"It don't take no nearve foh me to tell you what you is. Fact is I'm right now sure tiahd to death of living with you."

"You poor black stiff!" Rose cried. And she leaped over at Jake and scratched at his face.

Jake gave her two savage slaps full in her face and she dropped moaning at his feet.

"There! You done begged foh it," he said. He stepped over her and went out.

Walking down the street, he looked at his palms. "Ahm shame o' you, hands," he murmured. "Mah mother useter tell me, 'Nevah hit no woman,' but that hussy jest made me do it . . . jest *made* me. . . . Well, I'd better pull outa that there mud-hole. . . . It wasn't what I come back to Gawd's own country foh. No, sirree! You bet it wasn't. . . ."

When he returned to the house he heard laughter in the room. Gertie Blake was there and Rose was telling a happy tale. He stood by the closed door and listened for a while.

"Have another drink, Gertie. Don't ever get a wee bit delicate when youse with me. . . . My, mah dear, but he did slap the daylights outa me. When I comed to I wanted to kiss his feet, but he was gone."

"Rose! You're the limit. But didn't it hurt awful?"

"Didn't hurt enough. Honey, it's the first time I ever felt his real strength. A hefty-looking one like him, always acting so nice and proper. I almost thought he was getting sissy. But he's a *ma-an* all right. . . ."

A nasty smile stole into Jake's features. He could not face those women. He left the house again. He strolled down to Dixie Red's pool-room and played awhile. From there he went with Zeddy to Uncle Doc's saloon.

He went home again and found Rose stunning in a new cloth-of-gold frock shining with brilliants. She was refixing a large artificial yellow rose to the side of a pearl-beaded green turban. Jake, without saying a word, went to the closet and took down his suitcase. Then he began tossing shirts, underwear, collars, and ties on to the couch.

"What the devil you're doing?" Rose wheeled round and stared at him in amazement, both hands gripping the dresser behind her.

"Kain't you see?" Jake replied.

She moved down on him like a panther, swinging her hips in a wonderful, rhythmical motion. She sprang upon his neck and brought him down.

"Oh, honey, you ain't mad at me 'counta the little fuss tonight?"

"I don't like hitting no womens," returned Jake's hard-breathing muffled voice.

"Daddy! I love you the more for that."

"You'll spile you' new clothes," Jake said, desperately.

"Hell with them! I love mah daddy moh'n anything. And mah daddy loves me, don't he? Daddy!"

Rose switched on the light and looked at her watch.

"My stars, daddy! We been honey-dreaming some! I am two hours late."

She jumped up and jig-stepped. "I should worry if the Congo . . . I should worry mumbo-jumbo."

She smoothed out her frock, arranged her hair, and put the turban on. "Come along to the Congo a little later," she said to Jake. "Let's celebrate on champagne."

The door closed on him. . . .

"O Lawdy!" he yawned, stretched himself, and got up. He took the rest of his clothes out of the closet, picked up the crumpled things from the couch, packed, and walked out with his suitcase.

SECOND PART

The Railroad

X

Over the heart of the vast gray Pennsylvania country the huge black animal snorted and roared, with sounding rods and couplings, pulling a long chain of dull-brown boxes packed with people and things, trailing on the blue-cold air its white masses of breath.

Hell was playing in the hot square hole of a pantry and the coffin-shaped kitchen of the dining-car. The short, stout, hard-and-horny chef was terrible as a rhinoceros. Against the second, third, and fourth cooks he bellied his way up to the little serving door and glared at the waiters. His tough, aproned front was a challenge to them. In his oily, shining face his big white eyes danced with meanness. All the waiters had squeezed into the pantry at once, excitedly snatching, dropping and breaking things.

"Hey, you there! You mule!"[1] The chef shouted at the fourth waiter. "Who told you to snitch that theah lamb chops outa the hole?"

"I done think they was the one I ordered—"

"Done think some hell, you down-home black fool. Ain't no thinking to be done on here—"

"Chef, ain't them chops ready yet?" a waiter asked.

"Don't rush me, nigger," the chef bellowed back. "Wha' yu'all trying to do? Run me up a tree? Kain't run this here chef up no tree. Jump off ef you kain't ride him." His eyes gleamed with grim humor. "Jump off or lay down. This heah white man's train service ain't no nigger picnic."

The second cook passed up a platter of chops. The chef rushed it through the hole and licked his fingers.

"There you is, yaller. Take it away. Why ain't you gone yet? Show me some service, yaller, show me some service." He rocked his thick,

[1] The fourth waiter on the railroad is nick-named "mule" because he works under the orders of the pantry-man.

tough body sideways in a sort of dance, licked the sweat from his brow with his forefinger and grunted with aggressive self-satisfaction. Then he bellied his way back to the range and sent the third cook up to the serving window.

"Tha's the stuff to hand them niggers," he told the third cook. "Keep 'em up a tree all the time, but don't let 'em get you up there."

Jake, for he was the third cook, took his place by the window and handed out the orders. It was his first job on the railroad, but from the first day he managed his part perfectly. He rubbed smoothly along with the waiters by remaining himself and not trying to imitate the chef nor taking his malicious advice.

Jake had taken the job on the railroad just to break the hold that Harlem had upon him. When he quitted Rose he felt that he ought to get right out of the atmosphere of Harlem. If I don't git away from it for a while, it'll sure git me, he mused. But not ship-and-port-town life again. I done had enough a that here and ovah there. . . . So he had picked the railroad. One or two nights a week in Harlem. And all the days on the road. He would go on like that until he grew tired of that rhythm. . . .

The rush was over. Everything was quiet. The corridors of the dining-car were emptied of their jam of hungry, impatient guests. The "mule" had scrubbed the slats of the pantry and set them up to dry. The other waiters had put away silver and glasses and soiled linen. The steward at his end of the car was going over the checks. Even the kitchen work was finished and the four cooks had left their coffin for the good air of the dining-room. They sat apart from the dining-room boys. The two grades, cooks and waiters, never chummed together, except for gambling. Some of the waiters were very haughty. There were certain light-skinned ones who went walking with pals of their complexion only in the stop-over cities. Others, among the older men, were always dignified. They were fathers of families, their wives moved in some sphere of Harlem society, and their movements were sometimes chronicled in the local Negro newspapers.

Sitting at one of the large tables, four of the waiters were playing poker. Jake wanted to join them, but he had no money. One waiter sat alone at a small table. He was reading. He was of average size, slim, a smooth pure ebony with straight features and a suggestion of whiskers. Jake shuffled up to him and asked him for the loan of two dollars. He got it and went to play. . . .

Jake finished playing with five dollars. He repaid the waiter and said: "Youse a good sport. I'll always look out for you in that theah hole."

The waiter smiled. He was very friendly. Jake half-sprawled over the table. "Wha's this here stuff you reading? Looks lak Greek to me." He spelled the title, "s-a-p-h-o, Sapho."

"What's it all about?" Jake demanded, flattening down the book on the table with his friendly paw. The waiter was reading the scene between Fanny and Jean when the lover discovers the letters of his mistress's former woman friend and exclaims: "Ah *Oui* . . . *Sapho* . . . *toute la lyre*. . . ."

"It's a story," he told Jake, "by a French writer named Alphonse Daudet. It's about a sporting woman who was beautiful like a rose and had the soul of a wandering cat. Her lovers called her Sapho. I like the story, but I hate the use of Sapho for its title."

"Why does you?" Jake asked.

"Because Sappho was a real person. A wonderful woman, a great Greek poet—"

"So theah *is* some Greek in the book!" said Jake.

The waiter smiled. "In a sense, yes."

And he told Jake the story of Sappho, of her poetry, of her loves and her passion for the beautiful boy, Phaon. And of her leaping into the sea from the Leucadian cliff because of her love for him.

"Her story gave two lovely words to modern language," said the waiter.

"Which one them?" asked Jake.

"Sapphic and Lesbian . . . beautiful words."

"What is that there Leshbian?"

". . . Lovely word, eh?"

"Tha's what we calls bulldyker in Harlem," drawled Jake. "Them's all ugly womens."

"Not *all*. And that's a damned ugly name," the waiter said. "Harlem is too savage about some things. *Bulldyker*," the waiter stressed with a sneer.

Jake grinned. "But tha's what they is, ain't it?"

He began humming:

> "And there is two things in Harlem I don't understan'
> It is a bulldyking woman and a faggoty man. . . ."

Charmingly, like a child that does not know its letters, Jake turned the pages of the novel. . . .

"Bumbole! This heah language is most different from how they talk it."

"Bumbole" was now a popular expletive for Jake, replacing such expressions as "Bull," "bawls," "walnuts," and "blimey." Ever since the night at the Congo when he heard the fighting West Indian girl cry, "I'll slap you bumbole," he had always used the word. When his friends asked him what it meant, he grinned and said, "Ask the monks."

"You know French?" the waiter asked.

"Parlee-vous? Mademoiselle, un baiser, s'il vous plait. Voilà! I larned that much offn the froggies."

"So you were over there?"

"Au oui, camarade," Jake beamed. "I was way, way ovah there after Democracy and them boches, and when I couldn't find one or the other, I jest turned mah black moon from the A. E. F. . . . . But you! How come you jest plowing through this here stuff lak that? I could nevah see no light at all in them print, chappie. *Eh bien. Mais vous compris beaucoup.*"

"C'est ma langue maternelle."

"Hm!" Jake made a face and scratched his head. *"Comprendre pas,* chappie. Tell me in straight United States."

"French is my native language. I—"

"Don't crap me," Jake interrupted. "Ain'tchu—ain'tchu one of us, too?"

"Of course I'm Negro," the waiter said, "but I was born in Hayti and the language down there is French."

"Hayti . . . Hayti," repeated Jake. "Tha's where now? Tha's—"

"An island in the Caribbean—near the Panama Canal."

Jake sat like a big eager boy and learned many facts about Hayti before the train reached Pittsburgh. He learned that the universal spirit of the French Revolution had reached and lifted up the slaves far away in that remote island; that Black Hayti's independence was more dramatic and picturesque than the United States' independence and that it was a strange, almost unimaginable eruption of the beautiful ideas of the "Liberté, Egalité, Fraternité" of Mankind, that shook the foundations of that romantic era.

For the first time he heard the name Toussaint L'Ouverture, the black slave and leader of the Haytian slaves. Heard how he fought and conquered the slave-owners and then protected them; decreed laws for Hayti that held more of human wisdom and nobility than the Code Napoleon; defended his baby revolution against the Spanish and the English vultures; defeated Napoleon's punitive expedition; and how tragically he was captured by a civilized trick, taken to France, and sent by Napoleon to die broken-hearted in a cold dungeon.

"A black man! A black man! Oh, I wish I'd been a soldier under sich a man!" Jake said, simply.

He plied his instructor with questions. Heard of Dessalines, who carried on the fight begun by Toussaint L'Ouverture and kept Hayti independent. But it was incredible to Jake that a little island of freed slaves had withstood the three leading European powers. The waiter told him that Europe was in a complex state of transition then, and that that wonderful age had been electrified with universal ideas— ideas so big that they had lifted up ignorant people, even black, to the stature of gods.

"The world doesn't know," he continued, "how great Toussaint L'Ouverture really was. He was not merely great. He was lofty. He was good. The history of Hayti today might have been different if he had been allowed to finish his work. He was honored by a great enigmatic poet of that period. And I honor both Toussaint and the poet by keeping in my memory the wonderful, passionate lines."

He quoted Wordsworth's sonnet.

"Toussaint, the most unhappy Man of Men!
 Whether the whistling Rustic tend his plough
 Within thy hearing, or thy head be now
Pillowed in some deep dungeon's earless den;—
Oh miserable Chieftain! Where and when
 Wilt thou find patience? Yet die not; do thou
 Wear rather in thy bonds a cheerful brow:
Though fallen Thyself never to rise again,
Live, and take comfort. Thou hast left behind
 Powers that will work for thee, air, earth, and skies;
There's not a breathing of the common wind
 That will forget thee; thou hast great allies;
 Thy friends are exultations, agonies,
And love, and Man's unconquerable Mind."

Jake felt like one passing through a dream, vivid in rich, varied colors. It was revelation beautiful in his mind. That brief account of an island of savage black people, who fought for collective liberty and was struggling to create a culture of their own. A romance of his race, just down there by Panama. How strange!

Jake was very American in spirit and shared a little of that comfortable Yankee contempt for poor foreigners. And as an American Negro he looked askew at foreign niggers. Africa was jungle, and Africans bush niggers, cannibals. And West Indians were monkey-chasers. But now he felt like a boy who stands with the map of the world in colors before him, and feels the wonder of the world.

The waiter told him that Africa was not jungle as he dreamed of it, nor slavery the peculiar role of black folk. The Jews were the slaves of the Egyptians, the Greeks made slaves of their conquered, the Gauls and Saxons were slaves of the Romans. He told Jake of the old destroyed cultures of West Africa and of their vestiges, of black kings who struggled stoutly for the independence of their kingdoms: Prempreh of Ashanti, Tofa of Dahomey, Gbehanzin of Benin, Cetawayo of Zulu-Land, Menelik of Abyssinia. . . .

Had Jake ever heard of the little Republic of Liberia, founded by American Negroes? And Abyssinia, deep-set in the shoulder of Africa, besieged by the hungry wolves of Europe? The only nation that has existed free and independent from the earliest records of history until today! Abyssinia, oldest unconquered nation, ancient-strange as Egypt, persistent as Palestine, legendary as Greece, magical as Persia.

There was the lovely legend of her queen who visited the court of the Royal Rake of Jerusalem, and how he fell in love with her. And her beautiful black body made the Sage so lyrical, he immortalized her in those wonderful pagan verses that are sacred to the hearts of all lovers—even the heart of the Church. . . . The catty ladies of the court of Jerusalem were jealous of her. And Sheba reminded them that she was black but beautiful. . . . And after a happy period she left Jerusalem and returned to her country with the son that came of the royal affair. And that son subsequently became King of Abyssinia. And to this day the rulers of Abyssinia carry the title, Lion of Judah, and trace their descent direct from the liaison of the Queen of Sheba with King Solomon.

First of Christian nations also is the claim of this little kingdom! Christian since the time when Philip, the disciple of Jesus, met and baptized the minister of the Queen of Abyssinia and he returned to his country and converted the court and people to Christianity.

Jake listened, rapt, without a word of interruption.

"All the ancient countries have been yielding up the buried secrets of their civilizations," the waiter said. "I wonder what Abyssinia will yield in her time? Next to the romance of Hayti, because it is my native country, I should love to write the romance of Abyssinia . . . Ethiopia."

"Is that theah country the same Ethiopia that we done l'arned about in the Bible?" asked Jake.

"The same. The Latin peoples still call it Ethiopia."

"Is you a professor?"

"No, I'm a student."

"Whereat? Where did you l'arn English?"

"Well, I learned English home in Port-au-Prince. And I was at

Howard. You know the Negro university at Washington. Haven't even finished there yet."

"Then what in the name of mah holy rabbit foot youse doing on this heah white man's chuh-chuh? It ain't no place foh no student. It seems to me you' place down there sounds a whole lot better."

"Uncle Sam put me here."

"Whadye mean Uncle Sam?" cried Jake. "Don't hand me that bull."

"Let me tell you about it," the waiter said. "Maybe you don't know that during the World War Uncle Sam grabbed Hayti. My father was an official down there. He didn't want Uncle Sam in Hayti and he said so and said it loud. They told him to shut up and he wouldn't, so they shut him up in jail. My brother also made a noise and American marines killed him in the street. I had nobody to pay for me at the university, so I had to get out and work. *Voilà!*"

"And you ain't gwine to study no moh?"

"Never going to stop. I study now all the same when I get a little time. Every free day I have in New York I spend at the library downtown. I read there and I write."

Jake shook his head. "This heah work is all right for me, but for a chappie like you. . . . Do you like waiting on them ofays? 'Sall right working longshore or in a kitchen as I does it, but to be rubbing up against them and bowing so nice and all a that. . . ."

"It isn't so bad," the waiter said. "Most of them are pretty nice. Last trip I waited on a big Southern Senator. He was perfectly gentlemanly and tipped me half a dollar. When I have the blues I read Dr. Frank Crane."

Jake didn't understand, but he spat and said a stinking word. The chef called him to do something in the kitchen.

"Leave that theah professor and his nonsense," the chef said. . . .

The great black animal whistled sharply and puff-puffed slowly into the station of Pittsburgh.

Snowstorm in Pittsburgh

XI

In the middle of the little bridge built over the railroad crossing he was suddenly enveloped in a thick mass of smoke spouted out by an in-rushing train. That was Jake's first impression of Pittsburgh. He stepped off the bridge into a saloon. From there along a dull-gray street of grocery and fruit shops and piddling South-European children. Then he was on Wiley Avenue, the long, gray, uphill street.

Brawny bronze men in coal-blackened and oil-spotted blue overalls shadowed the doorways of saloons, pool-rooms, and little basement restaurants. The street was animated with dark figures going up, going down. Houses and men, women, and squinting cats and slinking dogs, everything seemed touched with soot and steel dust.

"So this heah is the niggers' run," said Jake. "I don't like its 'pearance, nohow." He walked down the street and remarked a bouncing little chestnut-brown standing smartly in the entrance of a basement eating-joint. She wore a knee-length yellow-patterned muslin frock and a white-dotted blue apron. The apron was a little longer than the frock. Her sleeves were rolled up. Her arms were beautiful, like smooth burnished bars of copper.

Jake stopped and said, "Howdy!"

"Howdy again!" the girl flashed a row of perfect teeth at him.

"Got a bite of anything good?"

"I should say so, Mister Ma-an."

She rolled her eyes and worked her hips into delightful free-and-easy motions. Jake went in. He was not hungry for food. He looked at a large dish half filled with tapioca pudding. He turned to the pie-case on the counter.

"The peach pie is the best," said the girl, her bare elbow on the counter; "it's fresh." She looked straight in his eyes. "All right, I'll try peach," he said, and, magnetically, his long, shining fingers touched her hand. . . .

In the evening he found the Haytian waiter at the big Wiley Avenue pool-room. Quite different from the pool-rooms in Harlem, it was a sort of social center for the railroad men and the more intelligent black workmen of the quarter. Tobacco, stationery, and odds and ends were sold in the front part of the store. There was a table where customers sat and wrote letters. And there were pretty chocolate dolls and pictures of Negroid types on sale. Curious, pathetic pictures; black Madonna and child; a kinky-haired mulatto angel with African lips and Nordic nose, soaring on a white cloud up to heaven; Jesus blessing a black child and a white one; a black shepherd carrying a white lamb—all queerly reminiscent of the crude prints of the great Christian paintings that are so common in poor religious homes.

"Here he is!" Jake greeted the waiter. "What's the new?"

"Nothing new in Soot-hill; always the same."

The railroad men hated the Pittsburgh run. They hated the town, they hated Wiley Avenue and their wretched free quarters that were in it. . . .

"What're you going to do?"

"Ahm gwine to the colored show with a li'l' brown piece," said Jake.

"You find something already? My me! You're a fast-working one."

"Always the same whenever I hits a new town. Always in cock-tail luck, chappie."

"Which one? Manhattan or Bronx?"

"It's Harlem-Pittsburgh thisanight," Jake grinned. "Wachyu gwine make?"

"Don't know. There's nothing ever in Pittsburgh for me. I'm in no mood for the leg-show tonight, and the colored show is bum. Guess I'll go sleep if I can."

"Awright, I'll see you li'l' later, chappie." Jake gripped his hand. "Say—whyn't you tell a fellow you' name? Youse sure more'n second waiter as Ise more'n third cook. Ev'body calls me Jake. And you?"

"Raymond, but everybody calls me Ray."

Jake heaved off. Ray bought some weekly Negro newspapers: *The Pittsburgh Courier, The Baltimore American, The Negro World, The Chicago Defender.* Here he found a big assortment of all the Negro publications that he never could find in Harlem. In a next-door saloon he drank a glass of sherry and started off for the waiters' and cooks' quarters.

It was long after midnight when Jake returned to quarters. He had to pass through the Western men's section to get to the Eastern crews. Nobody was asleep in the Western men's section. No early-morning train was chalked up on their board. The men were grouped off in poker and dice games. Jake hesitated a little by one group, fascinated by a wiry little long-headed finger-snapping black, who with strenuous h'h, h'h, h'h, h'h, was zestfully throwing the bones. Jake almost joined the game but he admonished himself: "You winned five dollars thisaday and you made a nice li'l brown piece. Wha'more you want?" . . .

He found the beds assigned to the members of his crew. They were double beds, like Pullman berths. Three of the waiters had not come in yet. The second and the fourth cooks were snoring, each a deep frothy bass and a high tenor, and scratching themselves in their sleep. The chef sprawled like the carcass of a rhinoceros, half-naked, mouth wide open. Tormented by bedbugs, he had scratched and tossed in his sleep and hoofed the covers off the bed. Ray was sitting on a lower berth on his Negro newspapers spread out to form a sheet. He had thrown the sheets on the floor, they were so filthy from other men's sleeping. By the thin flame of gaslight he was killing bugs.

"Where is I gwine to sleep?" asked Jake.

"Over me, if you can. I saved the bunk for you," said Ray.

"Some music the niggers am making," remarked Jake, nodding in the direction of the snoring cooks. "But whasmat, chappie, you ain't sleeping?"

"Can't you see?"

"Bugs. Bumbole! This is a hell of a dump for a man to sleep in."

"The place is rocking crazy with them," said Ray. "I hauled the cot away from the wall, but the mattress is just swarming."

Hungry and bold, the bugs crept out of their chinks and hunted for food. They stopped dead-still when disturbed by the slightest shadow, and flattened their bellies against the wall.

"Le's get outa this stinking dump and chase a drink, chappie."

Ray jumped out of his berth, shoved himself into his clothes and went with Jake. The saloon near by the pool-room was still open. They went there. Ray asked for sherry.

"You had better sample some hard liquor if youse gwine back to wrastle with them bugs tonight," Jake suggested.

Ray took his advice. A light-yellow fellow chummed up with the boys and invited them to drink with him. He was as tall as Jake and very thin. There was a vacant, wandering look in his kindly-weak eyes. He was a waiter on another dining-car of the New York-Pittsburgh run. Ray mentioned that he had to quit his bed because he couldn't sleep.

"This here town is the rottenest lay-over in the whole railroad field," declared the light-yellow. "I don't never sleep in the quarters here."

"Where do you sleep, then?" asked Ray.

"Oh, I got a sweet baby way up yonder the other side of the hill."

"Oh, ma-ma!" Jake licked his lips. "So youse all fixed up in this heah town?"

"Not going there tonight, though," the light-yellow said in a careless, almost bored tone. "Too far for mine."

He asked Jake and Ray if they would like to go to a little open-all-night place. They were glad to hear of that.

"Any old thing, boh," Jake said, "to get away from that theah Pennsy bug house."

The little place was something of a barrel-house speak-easy, crowded with black steel-workers in overalls and railroad men, and foggy with smoke. They were all drinking hard liquor and playing cards. The boss was a stocky, genial brown man. He knew the light-yellow waiter and shook hands with him and his friends. He moved away some boxes in a corner and squeezed a little table in it, specially for them. They sat down, jammed into the corner, and drank whisky.

"Better here than the Pennsy pigpen," said the light-yellow.

He was slapped on the back by a short, compact young black.

"Hello, you! What you think youse doing theah?"

"Ain't figuring," retorted the light-yellow, "is you?"

"On the red moon gwine around mah haid, yes. How about a li'l' good snow?"

"Now you got mah number down, Happy."

The black lad vanished again through a mysterious back door.

The light-yellow said: "He's the biggest hophead I ever seen. Nobody can sniff like him. Yet he's always the same happy nigger, stout and strong like a bull."

He took another whisky and went like a lean hound after Happy. Jake looked mischievously at the little brown door, remarking: "It's a great life ef youse in on it." . . .

The light-yellow came back with a cold gleam in his eyes, like arsenic shining in the dark. His features were accentuated by a rigid, disturbing tone and he resembled a smiling wax figure.

"Have a li'l stuff with the bunch?" he asked Jake.

"I ain't got the habit, boh, but I'll try anything once again."

"And you?" The light-yellow turned to Ray.

"No, chief, thank you, but I don't want to."

The waiter went out again with Jake on his heels. Beyond the door, five fellows, kneeling in the sawdust, were rolling the square bones. Others sat together around two tables with a bottle of red liquor and thimble-like glasses before them.

"Oh, boy!" one said. "When I get home tonight it will be some more royal stuff. I ain'ta gwine to work none 'tall tomorrow."

"Shucks!" Another spread away his big mouth. "This heah ain't nothing foh a fellow to turn royal loose on. I remimber when I was gwine with a money gang that hed no use foh nothing but the pipe. That theah time was life, buddy."

"Wha' sorta pipe was that there?" asked Jake.

"The Chinese stuff, old boy."

Instead of deliberately fisting his, like the others, Jake took it up carelessly between his thumb and forefinger and inhaled.

"Say what you wanta about Chinee or any other stuff," said Happy, "but theah ain't nothing can work wicked like snow and whisky. It'll flip you up from hell into heaven befoh you knows it."

Ray looked into the room.

"Who's you li'l' mascot?" Happy asked the light-yellow.

"Tha's mah best pal," Jake answered. "He's got some moh stuff up here," Jake tapped his head.

"Better let's go on back to quarters," said Ray.

"To them bugs?" demanded Jake.

"Yes, I think we'd better."

"Awright, anything you say, chappie. I kain sleep through worser things." Jake took a few of the little white packets from Happy and gave him some money. "Guess I might need them some day. You never know."

Jake fell asleep as soon as his head touched the dirty pillow. Below him, Ray lay in his bunk, tormented by bugs and the snoring cooks. The low-burning gaslight flickered and flared upon the shadows. The young man lay under the untellable horror of a dead-tired man who wills to sleep and cannot.

In other sections of the big barn building the faint chink of coins touched his ears. Those men gambling the hopeless Pittsburgh night away did not disturb him. They were so quiet. It would have been better, perhaps, if they were noisy. He closed his eyes and tried to hynotize himself to sleep. Sleep . . . sleep . . . sleep . . . sleep . . . sleep. . . . He began counting slowly. His vigil might break and vanish somnolently upon some magic number. He counted a million. Perhaps love would appease this unwavering angel of wakefulness. Oh, but he could not pick up love easily on the street as Jake. . . .

He flung himself, across void and water, back home. Home thoughts, if you can make them soft and sweet and misty-beautiful enough, can sometimes snare sleep. There was the quiet, chalky-dusty street and, jutting out over it, the front of the house that he had lived in. The high staircase built on the outside, and pots of begonias and ferns on the landing. . . .

All the flowering things he loved, red and white and pink hibiscus, mimosas, rhododendrons, a thousand glowing creepers, climbing and spilling their vivid petals everywhere, and bright-buzzing humming-birds and butterflies. All the tropic-warm lilies and roses. Giddy-high erect thatch palms, slender, tall, fur-fronded ferns, majestic cotton trees, stately bamboos creating a green grandeur in the heart of space. . . .

Sleep remained cold and distant. Intermittently the cooks broke their snoring with masticating noises of their fat lips, like animals eating. Ray fixed his eyes on the offensive bug-bitten bulk of the chef. These men claimed kinship with him. They were black like him. Man and nature had put them in the same race. He ought to love them and feel them (if they felt anything). He ought to if he had a shred of social morality in him. They were all chain-ganged together and he was counted as one link. Yet he loathed every soul in that great barrack-room, except Jake. Race. . . . Why should he have and love a race?

Races and nations were things like skunks, whose smells poisoned the air of life. Yet civilized mankind reposed its faith and future in their ancient, silted channels. Great races and big nations! There must be something mighty inspiriting in being the citizen of a great strong nation. To be the white citizen of a nation that can say bold, challenging things like a strong man. Something very different from the keen ecstatic joy a man feels in the romance of being black. Something the black man could never feel nor quite understand.

Ray felt that as he was conscious of being black and impotent, so, correspondingly, each marine down in Hayti must be conscious of being white and powerful. What a unique feeling of confidence about life the typical white youth of his age must have! Knowing that his skin-color was a passport to glory, making him one with ten thousands like himself. All perfect Occidentals and investors in that grand business called civilization. That grand business in whose pits sweated and snored, like the cooks, all the black and brown hybrids and mongrels, simple earth-loving animals, without aspirations toward national unity and racial arrogance.

He remembered when little Hayti was floundering uncontrolled, how proud he was to be the son of a free nation. He used to feel condescendingly sorry for those poor African natives; superior to ten millions of suppressed Yankee "coons." Now he was just one of them and he hated them for being one of them. . . .

But he was not entirely of them, he reflected. He possessed another language and literature that they knew not of. And some day Uncle Sam might let go of his island and he would escape from the clutches of that magnificent monster of civilization and retire behind the natural defenses of his island, where the steam-roller of progress could not reach him. Escape he would. He had faith. He had hope. But, oh, what would become of that great mass of black swine, hunted and cornered by slavering white canaille! Sleep! oh, sleep! Down Thought!

But all his senses were burning wide awake. Thought was not a beautiful and reassuring angel, a thing of soothing music and light laughter and winged images glowing with the rare colors of life. No. It was suffering, horribly real. It seized and worried him from every angle. Pushed him toward the sheer precipice of imagination. It was awful. He was afraid. For thought was a terrible tiger clawing at his small portion of gray substance, throttling, tearing, and tormenting him with pitiless ferocity. Oh, a thousand ideas of life were shrieking at him in a wild orgy of mockery! . . .

He was in the middle of a world suspended in space. A familiar line lit up, like a flame, the vast, crowded, immensity of his vision.

Et l'âme du monde est dans l'air.

A moment's respite. . . .

A loud snore from the half-naked chef brought him back to the filthy fact of the quarters that the richest railroad in the world had provided for its black servitors. Ray looked up at Jake, stretched at full length on his side, his cheek in his right hand, sleeping peacefully, like a tired boy after hard playing, so happy and sweet and handsome. He remembered the neatly-folded white papers in Jake's pocket. Maybe that was the cause of his sleeping so soundly. He reached his hand up to the coat hanging on the nail above his head. It was such an innocent little thing—like a headache powder the paper of which you wipe with your tongue, so that none should be wasted. Apparently the first one had no effect and Ray took the rest.

Sleep capitulated.

Immediately he was back home again. His father's house was a vast forest full of blooming hibiscus and mimosas and giant evergreen trees. And he was a gay humming-bird, fluttering and darting his long needle beak into the heart of a bell-flower. Suddenly he changed into an owl flying by day. . . . Howard University was a prison with white warders. . . . Now he was a young shining chief in a marble palace; slim, naked negresses dancing for his pleasure; courtiers reclining on cushions soft like passionate kisses; gleaming-skinned black boys bearing goblets of wine and obedient eunuchs waiting in the offing. . . .

And the world was a blue paradise. Everything was in gorgeous blue of heaven. Woods and streams were blue, and men and women and animals, and beautiful to see and love. And he was a blue bird in flight and a blue lizard in love. And life was all blue happiness. Taboos and terrors and penalties were transformed into new pagan delights, orgies of Orient-blue carnival, of rare flowers and red fruits, cherubs and seraphs and fetishes and phalli and all the most-high gods. . .

A thousand pins were pricking Ray's flesh and he was shouting for Jake, but his voice was so faint he could not hear himself. Jake had him in his arms and tried to stand him upon his feet. He crumpled up against the bunk. All his muscles were loose, his cells were cold, and the rhythm of being arrested.

It was high morning and time to go to the train. Jake had picked up the empty little folds of paper from the floor and restored them to his pocket. He knew what had happened to them, and guessed why. He went and called the first and fourth waiters.

The chef bulked big in the room, dressed and ready to go to the railroad yards. He gave a contemptuous glance at Jake looking after Ray and said: "Better leave that theah nigger professor alone and come on 'long to the dining-car with us. That theah nigger is dopey from them books o' hisn. I done told befoh them books would git him yet."

The chef went off with the second and fourth cooks. Jake stayed with Ray. They got his shoes and coat on. The first waiter telephoned the steward, and Ray was taken to the hospital.

"We may all be niggers aw'right, but we ain't nonetall all the same," Jake said as he hurried along to the dining-car, thinking of Ray.

The Treeing of the Chef
XII

Perhaps the chef of Jake's dining-car was the most hated chef in the service. He was repulsive in every aspect. From the elevated bulk of his gross person to the matted burrs of his head and the fat cigar, the constant companion of his sloppy mouth, that he chewed and smoked at the same time. The chef deliberately increased his repulsiveness of form by the meannesses of his spirit.

"I know Ise a mean black nigger," he often said, "and I'll let you all know it on this heah white man's car, too."

The chef was a great black bundle of consciously suppressed desires. That was doubtless why he was so ornery. He was one of the model chefs of the service. His kitchen was well-ordered. The checking up of his provisions always showed a praiseworthy balance. He always had his food ready on time, feeding the heaviest rush of customers as rapidly as the lightest. He fed the steward excellently. He fed the crew well. In a word, he did his duty as only a martinet can.

A chef who is "right-there" at every call is the first asset of importance on an *à la carte* restaurant-car. The chef lived rigidly up to that fact and above it. He was also painfully honest. He had a mulatto wife and a brown boy-child in New York and he never slipped away any of the company's goods to them. Other dining-car men had devised a system of getting by the company's detectives with choice brands of the company's foodstuffs. The chef kept away from that. It was long since the yard detectives had stopped searching any parcel that *he* carried off with him.

"I don't want none o' the white-boss stuff foh mine," he declared. "Ise making enough o' mah own to suppoht mah wife and kid."

And more, the chef had a violent distaste for all the stock things that "coons" are supposed to like to the point of stealing them. He would not eat watermelon, because white people called it "the niggers' ice-cream." Pork chops he fancied not. Nor corn pone. And the idea of eating chicken gave him a spasm. Of the odds and ends of chicken gizzard, feet, head, rump, heart, wing points, and liver—the chef would make the most delicious stew for the crew, which he never touched himself. The Irish steward never missed his share of it. But for his meal the chef would grill a steak or mutton chop or fry a fish. Oh, chef was big and haughty about not being "no regular darky"! And although he came from the Alabama country, he pretended not to know a coon tail from a rabbit foot.

"All this heah talk about chicken-loving niggers," he growled chuckingly to the second cook. "The way them white passengers clean up on mah fried chicken I wouldn't trust one o' them anywheres near mah hen-coop."

Broiling tender corn-fed chicken without biting a leg. Thus, grimly, the chef existed. Humored and tolerated by the steward and hated by the waiters and undercooks. Jake found himself on the side of the waiters. He did not hate the chef (Jake could not hate anybody). But he could not be obscenely sycophantic to him as the second cook, who was just waiting for the chance to get the chef's job. Jake stood his corner in the coffin, doing his bit in diplomatic silence. Let the chef bawl the waiters out. He would not, like the second cook, join him in that game.

Ray, perhaps, was the chief cause of Jake's silent indignation. Jake had said to him: "I don't know how all you fellows can stand that theah God-damn black bull. I feels like falling down mahself." But Ray had begged Jake to stay on, telling him that he was the only decent man in the kitchen. Jake stayed because he liked Ray. A big friendship had sprung up between them and Jake hated to hear the chef abusing his friend along with the other waiters. The other cooks and waiters called Ray "Professor." Jake had never called him that. Nor did he call him "buddy," as he did Zeddy and his longshoremen friends. He called him "chappie" in a genial, semi-paternal way.

Jake's life had never before touched any of the educated of the ten dark millions. He had, however, a vague idea of who they were. He knew that the "big niggers" that were gossiped about in the saloons and the types he had met at Madame Adelina Suarez's were not *the* educated ones. The educated "dick-tees," in Jake's circles were often subjects for raw and funny sallies. He had once heard Miss Curdy putting them in their place while Susy's star eyes gleamed warm approval.

"Honey, I lived in Washington and I knowed inside and naked out the stuck-up bush-whackers of the race. They all talks and act as if loving was a sin, but I tell you straight, I wouldn't trust any of them after dark with a preacher. . . . Don't ask me, honey. I seen and I knows them all."

"I guess you does, sistah," Susy had agreed. "Nobody kaint hand *me* no fairy tales about niggers. Wese all much of a muchness when you git down to the real stuff."

Difficulties on the dining-car were worsened by a feud between the pantry and the kitchen. The first waiter, who was pantryman by regulation, had a grievance against the chef and was just waiting to "get" him. But, the chef being such a paragon, the "getting" was not easy.

Nothing can be worse on a dining-car than trouble between the pantry and the kitchen, for one is as necessary to the other as oil is to salad. But the war was covertly on and the chef was prepared to throw his whole rhinoceros weight against the pantry. The first waiter had to fight cautiously. He was quite aware that a first-class chef was of greater value than a first-class pantryman.

The trouble had begun through the "mule." The fourth man—a coffee-skinned Georgia village boy, timid like a country girl just come to town—hated the nickname, but the chef would call him nothing else.

"Call him 'Rhinoceros' when he calls you 'Mule,' " Ray told the fourth waiter, but he was too timid to do it. . . .

The dining-car was resting on the tracks in the Altoona yards, waiting for a Western train. The first, third, and fifth waiters were playing poker. Ray was reading Dostoievski's *Crime and Punishment*. The fourth waiter was working in the pantry. Suddenly the restaurant-car was shocked by a terrible roar.

"Gwan I say! Take that theah ice and beat it, you black sissy." . . .

"This ice ain't good for the pantry. You ought to gimme the cleaner one," the timid fourth man stood his ground.

The cigar of the chef stood up like a tusk. Fury was dancing in his enraged face and he would have stamped the guts out of the poor, timid boy if he was not restrained by the fear of losing his job. For on the dining-car, he who strikes the first blow catches the punishment.

"Quit jawing with me, nigger waiter, or I'll jab this heah ice-pick in you' mouf."

"Come and do it," the fourth waiter said, quietly.

"God dam' you' soul!" the chef bellowed. "Ef you don't quit chewing the rag—ef you git fresh with me, I'll throw you off this bloody car. S'elp mah Gawd, I will. You disnificant down-home mule."

The fourth waiter glanced behind him down the corridor and saw Ray, book in hand, and the other waiters, who had left their cards to see the cause of the tumult. Ray winked at the fourth waiter. He screwed up his courage and said to the chef: "I ain't no mule, and youse a dirty rhinoceros."

The chef seemed paralyzed with surprise. "Wha's that name you done call me? Wha's rhinasras?"

All the waiters laughed. The chef looked ridiculous and Ray said: "Why, chef, don't you know? That's the ugliest animal in all Africa."

The chef looked apoplectic. . . . "I don't care a dime foh all you nigger waiters and I ain't joking wif any of you. Cause you manicuring you' finger nails and rubbing up you' stinking black hide against white folks in that theah diner, you all think youse something. But lemme tell you straight, you ain't nothing atall."

"But, chef," cried the pantryman, "why don't you stop riding the fourth man? Youse always riding him."

"Riding who? I nevah rode a man in all mah life. I jest tell that black skunk what to do and him stahts jawing with me. I don't care about any of you niggers, nohow."

"Wese all tiahd of you cussin' and bawking," said the pantryman. "Why didn't you give the boy a clean piece of ice and finish? You know we need it for the water."

"Yaller nigger, you'd better gwan away from here."

"Don't call me no yaller nigger, you black and ugly cotton-field coon."

"Who dat? You bastard-begotten dime-snatcher, you'd better gwan back to you' dining-room or I'll throw this heah garbage in you' crap-yaller face. . . . I'd better git long far away from you all 'foh I lose mah haid." The chef bounced into the kitchen and slammed the door.

That "bastard-begotten dime-snatcher" grew a cancer in the heart of the pantryman. It rooted deep because he *was* an "illegitimate" and he bitterly hated the whites he served ("crackers," he called them all) and the tips he picked up. He knew that his father was some red-necked white man who had despised his mother's race and had done nothing for him.

The sight of the chef grew more and more unbearable each day to the pantryman. He thought of knifing or plugging him with a gun some night. He had nursed his resentment to the point of madness and was capable of any act. But getting the chef in the dark would not have been revenge enough. The pantryman wanted the paragon to live, so that he might invent a way of bringing him down humiliatingly from his perch.

But the chef was hard to "get." He had made and kept his place by being a perfect brutal machine, with that advantage that all mechanical creatures have over sensitive human beings. One day the pantryman thought he almost had his man. The chef had fed the steward, but kept the boys waiting for their luncheon. The waiters thought that he had one of his ornery spells on and was intentionally punishing them. They were all standing in the pantry, except Ray.

The fifth said to the first: "Ask him why he don't put the grub in the hole, partner. I'm horse-ways hungry."

"Ask him you'self. I ain't got nothing to do with that black hog moh'n giving him what b'longs to him in this heah pantry."

"Mah belly's making a most beautiful commotion. Jest lak a bleating lamb," drawled the third.

The fifth waiter pushed up the little glass door and stuck his head in the kitchen: "Chef, when are we gwine to go away from here?"

"Keep you' shirt on, nigger," flashed back from the kitchen. "You-all'll soon be stuffing you'self full o' the white man's poke chops. Better than you evah smell in Harlem."

"Wese werking foh't same like you is," the fifth man retorted.

"I don't eat no poke chops, nigger. I cooks the stuff, but I don't eat it, nevah."

"P'raps youse chewing a worser kind o' meat."

"Don't gimme no back talk, nigger waiter. Looka heah—"

The steward came into the pantry and said: "Chef, it's time to feed the boys. They're hungry. We had a hard day, today."

The chef's cigar drooped upon his slavering lip and almost fell. He turned to the steward with an injured air. "Ain't I doing mah best? Ain't I been working most hard mahself? I done get yourn lunch ready and am getting the crew's own and fixing foh dinner at the same time. I ain't tuk a mouful mahse'f—"

The steward had turned his heels on the pantry. The chef was enraged that he had intervened on behalf of the waiters.

"Ef you dime-chasing niggers keep fooling with me on this car," he said, "I'll make you eat mah spittle. I done do it a'ready and I'll do it again. I'll spit in you' eats—"

"Wha's that? The boss sure gwine to settle this." The pantryman dashed out of the pantry and called the steward. . . . "Ain't any of us waiters gwine to stay on heah Mis'r Farrel, with a chef like this."

"What's that, now?" The steward was in the pantry again. "What's this fine story, chef?"

"Nothing at all, Sah Farrel. I done pull a good bull on them fellars, tha's all. Cause theyse all trying to get mah goat. L'em quit fooling with the kitchen, Sah Farrel. I done pull a good bull on them fellars, tha's all. Cause theyse all trying to get mah goat. L'em quit fooling with the kitchen, Sah Farrel. I does mah wuk and I don't want no fooling fwom them nigger waiters, nohow."

"I guess you spit in it as you said, all right," cried the pantryman. . . . "Yes, you! You'd wallow in a pigpen and eat the filth, youse so doggone low-down."

"Now cut all o' that out," said the steward. "How could he do anything like that, when he eats the food, and I do meself?"

"In the hole!" shouted Jake.

The third and fifth waiters hurried into the pantry and brought out the waiters' food. . . . First a great platter of fish and tomatoes, then pork chops and mashed potatoes, steaming Java and best Borden's cream. The chef had made home-made bread baked in the form of little round caps. Nice and hot, they quickly melted the butter that the boys sandwiched between them. He was a splendid cook, an artist in creating palatable stuff. He came out of the kitchen himself, to eat in the dining-room and, diplomatically, he helped himself from the waiters' platter of fish. . . . Delicious food. The waiters fell to it with keen relish. Obliterated from their memory the sewer-incident of the moment before. . . . Feeding, feeding, feeding.

But Ray remembered and visualized, and his stomach turned. He left the food and went outside, where he found Jake taking the air. He told Jake how he felt.

"Oh, the food is all right," said Jake. "I watch him close anough in that there kitchen, and he knows I ain't standing in with him in no low-down stuff."

"But do you think he would ever do such a thing?" asked Ray.

Jake laughed. "What won't a bad nigger do when he's good and mean way down in his heart? I ain't 'lowing mahself careless with none o' that kind, chappie."

Two Pullman porters came into the dining-car in the middle of the waiters' meal.

"Here is the chambermaids," grinned the second cook.

"H'm, but how you all loves to call people names, though," commented the fourth waiter.

The waiters invited the porters to eat with them. The pantryman went to get them coffee and cream. The chef offered to scramble some eggs. He went back to the kitchen and, after a few minutes, the fourth cook brought out a platter of scrambled eggs for the two porters. The chef came rocking importantly behind the fourth cook. A clean white cap was poised on his head and fondly he chewed his cigar. A perfect menial of the great railroad company. He felt a wave of goodness sweeping over him, as if he had been patted on the head by the Angel Gabriel for his good works. He asked the porters if they had enough to eat and they thanked him and said they had more than enough and that the food was wonderful. The chef smiled broadly. He beamed upon steward, waiters, and porters, and his eyes said: See what a really fine fellow I am in spite of all the worries that go with the duties of a chef?

One day Ray saw the chef and the pantryman jesting while the pantryman was lighting his cigarette from the chef's stump of cigar. When Ray found the pantryman alone, he laughingly asked him if he and the chef had smoked the tobacco of peace.

"Fat chance!" retorted the first waiter. "I gotta talk to him, for we get the stores together and check up together with the steward, and I gotta hand him the stuff tha's coming to him outa the pantry, but I ain't settle mah debt with him yet. I ain't got no time for no nigger that done calls me 'bastard-begotten' and means it."

"Oh, forget it!" said Ray. "Christ was one, too, and we all worship him."

"Wha' you mean?" the pantryman demanded.

"What I said," Ray replied. . . .

"Oh! . . . Ain't you got no religion in you none 'tall?"

"My parents were Catholic, but I ain't nothing. God is white and has no more time for niggers than you've got for the chef."

"Well, I'll be browned but once!" cried the pantryman. "Is that theah what youse l'arning in them books? Don't you believe in getting religion?"

Ray laughed.

"You kain laugh, all right, but watch you' step Gawd don't get you yet. Youse sure trifling."

The coldness between the kitchen and the pantry continued, unpleasantly nasty, like the wearing of wet clothes, after the fall of a heavy shower, when the sun is shining again. The chef was uncomfortable. A waiter had never yet opposed open hostility to his personality like that. He was accustomed to the crew's surrendering to his ways with even a little sycophancy. It was always his policy to be amicable with the pantryman, playing him against the other waiters, for it was very disagreeable to keep up a feud when the kitchen and the pantry had so many unavoidable close contacts.

So the chef made overtures to the pantryman with special toothsome tidbits, such as he always prepared only for the steward and himself. But the pantryman refused to have any specially-prepared-for-his-Irishness-the-Steward's stuff that the other waiters could not share. Thereupon the chef gave up trying to placate him and started in hating back with profound African hate. African hate is deep down and hard to stir up, but there is no hate more realistic when it is stirred up.

One morning in Washington the iceman forgot to supply ice to the dining-car. One of the men had brought a little brass top on the diner and the waiters were excited over an easy new game called "put-and-take." The pantryman forgot his business. The chef went to another dining-car and obtained ice for the kitchen. The pantryman did not remember anything about ice until the train was well on its way to New York. He remembered it because the ice-cream was turning soft. He put his head through the hole and asked Jake for a piece of ice. The chef said no, he had enough for the kitchen only.

With a terrible contented expression the chef looked with malicious hate into the pantryman's yellow face. The pantryman glared back at the villainous black face and jerked his head in rage. The ice-cream turned softer. . . .

Luncheon was over, all the work was done, everything in order, and the entire crew was ready to go home when the train reached New York. The steward wanted to go directly home. But he had to wait and go over to the yards with the keys, so that the pantryman could ice up. And the pantryman was severely reprimanded for his laxity in Washington. . . .

The pantryman bided his time, waiting on the chef. He was cordial. He even laughed at the jokes the chef made at the other waiters' expense. The chef swelled bigger in his hide, feeling that everything had bent to his will. The pantryman waited, ignoring little moments for the big moment. It came.

One morning both the second and the fourth cook "fell down on the job," neither of them reporting for duty. The steward placed an order with the commissary superintendent for two cooks. Jake stayed in the kitchen, working, while the chef and the pantryman went to the store for the stock. . . .

The chef and the pantryman returned together with the large baskets of provisions for the trip. The eggs were carried by the chef himself in a neat box. Remembering that he had forgotten coffee, he sent Jake back to the store for it. Then he began putting away the kitchen stuff. The pantryman was putting away the pantry stuff. . . .

A yellow girl passed by and waved a smile at the chef. He grinned, his teeth champing his cigar. The chef hated yellow men with "cracker" hatred, but he loved yellow women with "cracker" love. His other love was gin. But he never carried a liquor flask on the diner, because it was against regulations. And he never drank with any of the crew. He drank alone. And he did other things alone. In Philadelphia or Washington he never went to a buffet flat with any of the men.

The girls working in the yards were always flirting with him. He fascinated them, perhaps because he was so Congo mask-like in aspect and so duty-strict. They could often wheedle something nice out of other chefs, but nothing out of *the* chef. He would rather give them his money than a piece of the company's raw meat. The chef was generous in his way; Richmond Pete, who owned the saloon near the yards in Queensborough, could attest to that. He had often gossiped about the chef. How he "blowed them gals that he had a crush on in the family room and danced an elephant jig while the gals were pulling his leg."

The yellow girl that waved at the chef through the window was pretty. Her gesture transformed his face into a foolish broad-smiling thing. He stepped outside the kitchen for a moment to have a tickling word with her.

In that moment the pantryman made a lightning-bolt move; and shut down the little glass door between the pantry and the kitchen. . . .

The train was speeding its way west. The first call for dinner had been made and the dining-room was already full. Over half a dozen calls for eggs of different kinds had been bawled out before the chef discovered that the basket of eggs was missing. The chef asked the pantryman to call the steward. The pantryman, curiously preoccupied, forgot. Pandemonium was loose in the pantry and kitchen when the steward, radish-red, stuck his head in.

The chef's lower lip had flopped low down, dripping, and the cigar had fallen somewhere. "Cut them aiggs off o' the bill, Sah Farrel. O Lawd!" he moaned, "Ise sartain sure I brought them aiggs on the car mahself, and now I don't know where they is."

"What kind o' blah is that?" cried the steward. "The eggs must be there in the kitchen. I saw them with the stock meself."

"And I brought them here hugging them, Boss, ef I ain't been made fool of by something." The rhinoceros had changed into a meek black lamb. "O Lawd! and I ain't been outa the kitchen sence. Ain't no mortal hand could tuk them. Some evil hand. O Lawd!—"

"Hell!" The steward dashed out of the pantry to cut all the egg dishes off the bill. The passengers were getting clamorous. The waiters were asking those who had ordered eggs to change to something else. . . .

The steward suggested searching the pantry. The pantry was ransacked. "Them ain't there, cep'n' they had feets to walk. O Lawd of Heaben!" the chef groaned. "It's something deep and evil, I knows, for I ain't been outa this heah kitchen." His little flirtation with the yellow girl was completely wiped off his memory.

Only Jake was keeping his head in the kitchen. He was acting second cook, for the steward had not succeeded in getting one. The fourth cook he had gotten was new to the service and he was standing, conspicuously long-headed, with gaping mouth.

"Why'n the debbil's name don't you do some'n, nigger?" bellowed the chef, frothy at the corners of his mouth.

"The chef is up a tree, all right," said Ray to the pantryman.

"And he'll break his black hide getting down," the pantryman replied, bitterly.

"Chef!" The yellow pantryman's face carried a royal African grin. "What's the matter with you and them aiggs?"

"I done gived them to you mammy."

"And fohget you wife, ole timer? Ef you ain't a chicken-roost nigger, as you boast, you surely loves the nest."

Gash! The chef, at last losing control of himself, shied a huge ham bone at the pantryman. The pantryman sprang back as the ham bone flew through the aperture and smashed a bottle of milk in the pantry.

"What's all this bloody business today?" cried the steward, who was just entering the pantry. . . . "What nonsense is this, chef? You've made a mess of things already and now you start fighting with the waiters. You can't do like that. You losing your head?"

"Lookahere, Sah Farrel, I jes' want ev'body to leave me 'lone."

"But we must all team together on the dining-car. That's the only way. You can't start fighting the waiters because you've lost the eggs."

"Sah Farrel, leave me alone, I say," half roared, half moaned the chef, "or I'll jump off right now and let you run you' kitchen you'self."

"What's that?" The steward started.

"I say I'll jump off, and I mean it as Gawd's mah maker."

The steward slipped out of the pantry without another word.

The steward obtained a supply of eggs in Harrisburg the next morning. The rest of the trip was made with the most dignified formalities between him and the chef. Between the pantry and the chef the atmosphere was tenser, but there were no more explosions.

The dining-car went out on its next trip with a new chef. And the old chef, after standing a little of the superintendent's notoriously sharp tongue, was sent to another car as second cook.

"Hit those fellahs in the pocket-book is the only way," the pantryman overheard the steward talking to one of his colleagues. "Imagine an old experienced chef threatening to jump off when I was short of a second cook."

They were getting the stock for the next trip in the commissary. Jake turned to the pantryman: "But it was sure peculiar, though, how them aiggs just fly outa that kitchen lak that way."

"Maybe they all hatched and growed wings when ole black bull was playing with that sweet yaller piece," the pantryman laughed.

"Honest, though, how do you think it happened?" persisted Jake. "Did you hoodoo them aiggs, or what did you do?"

"I wouldn't know atall. Better ask them rats in the yards ef they sucked the shells dry. What you' right hand does don't tell it to the left, says I."

"You done said a mou'ful, but how did you get away with it so quiet?"

"I ain't said nothing discrimination and I ain't nevah."

"Don't figure against me. Ise with you, buddy," said Jake, "and now that wese good and rid of him, I hope all we niggers will pull together like civilization folks."

"Sure we will. There ain't another down-home nigger like him in this white man's service. He was riding too high and fly, brother. I knew he would tumble and bust something nasty. But I ain't said I knowed a thing about it, all the same."

One Night in Philly
XIII

One night in Philadelphia Jake breezed into the waiters' quarters in Market Street, looking for Ray. It was late. Ray was in bed. Jake pulled him up.

"Come on outa that, you slacker. Let's go over to North Philly."

"What for?"

"A li'l' fun. I knows a swell outfit I wanta show you."

"Anything new?"

"Don't know about anything *new*, chappie, but I know there's something *good* right there in Fifteenth Street."

"Oh, I know all about that. I don't want to go."

"Come on. Don't be so particular about you' person. You gotta go with me."

"I have a girl in New York."

"Tha's awright. This is Philly."

"I tell you, Jake, there's no fun in those kinds for me. They'll bore me just like that night in Baltimore."

"Oh, these here am different chippies, I tell you. Come on, le's spend the night away from this damn dump. Wese laying ovah all day tomorrow."

"And some of them will say such rotten things. Pretty enough, all right, but their mouths are loaded with filth, and that's what gets me."

"Them's different ovah there, chappie. I'll kiss the Bible on it. Come on, now. It's no fun me going alone."

They went to a house in Fifteenth Street. As they entered Jake was greeted by a mulatto woman in the full vigor of middle life.

"Why, *you* heart-breaker! It's ages and ages since I saw you. You and me sure going to have a bust-up tonight."

Jake grinned, prancing a little, as if he were going to do the old cake-walk.

"Here, Laura, this is mah friend," he introduced Ray casually.

"Bring him over here and sit down," Madame Laura commanded.

She was a big-boned woman, but very agile. A long, irregular, rich-brown face, roving black eyes, deep-set, and shiny black hair heaped upon her head. She wore black velvet, a square-cut blouse low down on her breasts, and a string of large coral beads. The young girls of that house envied her finely-preserved form and her carriage and wondered if they would be anything like that when they reached her age.

The interior of this house gave Ray a shock. It looked so much like a comfortable boarding-house where everybody was cheerful and nice coquettish girls in colorful frocks were doing the waiting. . . . There were a few flirting couples, two groups of men playing cards, and girls hovering around. An attractive black woman was serving sandwiches, gin and bottled beer. At the piano, a slim yellow youth was playing a "blues." . . . A pleasant house party, similar to any other among colored people of that class in Baltimore, New Orleans, Charleston, Richmond, or even Washington, D. C. Different, naturally, from New York, which molds all peoples into a hectic rhythm of its own. Yet even New York, passing its strange thousands through its great metropolitan mill, cannot rob Negroes of their native color and laughter.

"Mah friend's just keeping me company," Jake said to the woman. "He ain't regular—you get me? And I want him treated right."

"He'll be treated better here than he would in church." She laughed and touched Ray's calf with the point of her slipper.

"What kind o' bust-up youse gwine to have with me?" demanded Jake.

"I'll show you just what I'm going to do with you for forgetting me so long."

She got up and went into an adjoining room. When she returned an attractively made-up brown girl followed her carrying a tray with glasses and a bottle of champagne. . . . The cork hit the ceiling, bang! And deftly the woman herself poured the foaming liquor without a wasted drop.

"There! That's our bust-up," she said. "Me and you and your friend. Even if he's a virgin he's all right. I know you ain't never going around with no sap-head."

"Give me some, too," a boy of dull-gold complexion materialized by the side of Madame Laura and demanded a drink. He was about eleven years old.

Affectionately she put her arm around him and poured out a small glass of champagne. The frailness of the boy was pathetic; his eyes were sleepy-sad. He resembled a reed fading in a morass.

"Who is he?" Ray asked.

"He's my son," responded Madame Laura. "Clever kid, too. He loves books."

"Ray will like him, then," said Jake. "Books is his middle name."

Ray suddenly felt a violent dislike for the atmosphere. At first he had liked the general friendliness and warmth and naturalness of it. All so different from what he had expected. But something about the presence of the little boy there and his being the woman's son disgusted him. He could not analyse his aversion. It was just an instinctive, intolerant feeling that the boy did not belong to that environment and should not be there.

He went from Madame Laura and Jake over to the piano and conversed with the pianist. When he glanced again at the table he had left, Madame Laura had her arm around Jake's neck and his eyes were strangely shining.

Madame Laura had set the pace. There were four other couples making love. At one table a big-built, very black man was amusing himself with two attractive girls, one brown-skinned and the other yellow. The girls' complexion was heightened by High-Brown Talc powder and rouge. A bottle of Muscatel stood on the table. The man was well dressed in nigger-brown and he wore an expensive diamond ring on his little finger.

The stags were still playing cards, with girls hovering over them. The happy-faced black woman was doing the managing, as Madame Laura was otherwise engaged. The pianist began banging another blues.

Ray felt alone and a little sorry for himself. Now that he was there, he would like to be touched by the spirit of that atmosphere and, like Jake, fall naturally into its rhythm. He also envied Jake. Just for this night only he would like to be like him. . . .

They were dancing. The little yellow girl, her legs kicked out at oblique angles, appeared as if she were going to fall through the big-built black man.

> We'll all be merry when you taste a cherry,
> And we'll twine and twine like a fruitful vine.

In the middle of the floor, a young railroad porter had his hand flattened straight down the slim, cérise-chiffoned back of a brown girl. Her head was thrown back and her eyes held his gleaming eyes. Her lips were parted with pleasure and they stood and rocked in an ecstasy. Their feet were not moving. Only their bodies rocked, rocked to the "blues.". . .

Ray remarked that Jake was not in the room, nor was Madame Laura in evidence. A girl came to him. "Why is you so all by you'self, baby? Don't you wanta dance some? That there is some more temptation 'blues.' "

Tickling, enticing syncopation. Ray felt that he ought to dance to it. But some strange thing seemed to hold him back from taking the girl in his arms.

"Will you drink something, instead?" he found a way out.

"Awwww-right," disappointed, she drawled.

She beckoned to the happy-faced woman.

"Virginia Dare."

"I'll have some, too," Ray said.

Another brown girl joined them.

"Buy mah pal a drink, too?" the first girl asked.

"Why, certainly," he answered.

The woman brought two glasses of Virginia Dare and Ray ordered a third.

Such a striking exotic appearance the rouge gave these brown girls. Rouge that is so cheap in its general use had here an uncommon quality. Rare as the red flower of the hibiscus would be in a florist's window on Fifth Avenue. Rouge on brown, a warm, insidious chestnut color. But so much more subtle than chestnut. The round face of the first girl, the carnal sympathy of her full, tinted mouth, touched Ray. But something was between them. . . .

The piano-player had wandered off into some dim, far-away, ancestral source of music. Far, far away from music-hall syncopation and jazz, he was lost in some sensual dream of his own. No tortures, banal shrieks and agonies. Tum-tum . . . tum-tum . . . tum-tum . . . tum-tum. . . . The notes were naked acute alert. Like black youth burning naked in the bush. Love in the deep heart of the jungle. . . . The sharp spring of a leopard from a leafy limb, the snarl of a jackal, green lizards in amorous play, the flight of a plumed bird, and the sudden laughter of mischievous monkeys in their green homes. Tum-tum . . . tum-tum . . . tum-tum . . . tum-tum. . . . Simple-clear and quivering. Like a primitive dance of war or of love . . . the marshaling of spears or the sacred frenzy of a phallic celebration.

Black lovers of life caught up in their own free native rhythm, threaded to a remote scarce-remembered past, celebrating the midnight hours in themselves, for themselves, of themselves, in a house in Fifteenth Street, Philadelphia. . . .

"Raided!" A voice screamed. Standing in the rear door, a policeman, white, in full uniform, smilingly contemplated the spectacle. There was a wild scramble for hats and wraps. The old-timers giggled, shrugged, and kept their seats. Madame Laura pushed aside the policeman.

"Keep you' pants on, all of you and carry on with you' fun. What's matter? Scared of a uniform? Pat"—she turned to the policeman—"what you want to throw a scare in the company for? Come on here with you."

The policeman, twirling his baton, marched to a table and sat down with Madame Laura.

"Geewizard!" Jake sat down, too. "Tell 'em next time not to ring the fire alarm so loud."

"You said it, honey-stick. There are no cops in Philly going to mess with this girl. Ain't it the truth, Pat?" Madame Laura twisted the policeman's ear and bridled.

"I know it's the Bible trute," the happy-faced black lady chanted in a sugary voice, setting a bottle of champagne and glasses upon the table and seating herself familiarly beside the policeman.

The champagne foamed in the four glasses.

"Whar's mah li'l' chappie?" Jake asked.

"Gone, maybe. Don't worry," said Madame Laura. "Drink!"

Four brown hands and one white. Chink!

"Here's to you, Pat," cried Madame Laura. "There's Irish in me from the male line." She toasted:

"Flixy, flaxy, fleasy,
Make it good and easy,
Flix for start and flax for snappy,
Niggers and Irish will always be happy."

The policeman swallowed his champagne at a gulp and got up. "Gotta go now. Time for duty."

"You treat him nice. Is it for love or protection?" asked Jake.

"He's loving *her*"—Madame Laura indicated the now coy lady who helped her manage—"but he's protecting *me*. It's a long time since I ain't got no loving inclination for any skin but chocolate. Get me?"

When Jake returned to the quarters he found Ray sleeping quietly. He did not disturb him. The next morning they walked together to the yards.

"Did the policeman scare you, too, last night?" asked Jake.

"What policeman?"

"Oh, didn't you see him? There was a policeman theah and somebody hollered 'Raid!' scaring everybody. I thought you'd done tuk you'self away from there in quick time becasn a that."

"No, I left before that, I guess. Didn't even smell one walking all the way to the quarters in Market Street."

"Why'd you beat it? One o' the li'l' chippies had a crush on you. Oh, boy! and she was some piece to look at."

"I know it. She was kind of nice. But she had some nasty perfume on her that turned mah stomach."

"Youse awful queer, chappie," Jake commented.

"Why, don't you ever feel those sensations that just turn you back in on yourself and make you isolated and helpless?"

"Wha'd y'u mean?"

"I mean if sometimes you don't feel as I felt last night?"

"Lawdy no. Young and pretty is all I feel."

They stopped in a saloon. Jake had a small whisky and Ray an egg-nogg.

"But Madame Laura isn't young," resumed Ray.

"Ain't she?" Jake showed his teeth. "I'd back her against some of the youngest. She's a wonder, chappie. Her blood's like good liquor. She gave me a present, too. Looka here." Jake took from his pocket a lovely slate-colored necktie sprinkled with red dots. Ray felt the fineness of it.

"Ef I had the sweetman disinclination I wouldn't have to work, chappie," Jake rocked proudly in his walk. "But tha's the life of a pee-wee cutter, says I. Kain't see it for mine."

"She was certainly nice to you last night. And the girls were nice, too. It was just like a jolly parlor social."

"Oh, sure! Them gals not all in the straight business, you know. Some o' them works and just go there for a good time, a li'l' extra stuff. . . . It ain't like that nonetall ovah in Europe, chappie. They wouldn't 'a' treated you so nice. Them places I sampled ovah there was all straight raw business and no camoflage."

"Did you prefer them?"

"Hell, no! I prefer the niggers' way every time. They does it better. . . ."

"Wish I could feel the difference as you do, Jakie. I lump all those ladies together, without difference of race."

"Youse crazy, chappie. You ain't got no experience about it. There's all kinds a difference in that theah life. Sometimes it's the people make the difference and sometimes it's the place. And as foh them sweet marchants, there's as much difference between them as you find in any other class a people. There is them slap-up private-apartmant ones, and there is them of the dickty buffet flats; then the low-down speakeasy customers; the cabaret babies, the family-entrance clients, and the street fliers."

They stopped on a board-walk. The dining-car stood before them, resting on one of the hundred tracks of the great Philadelphia yards.

"I got a free permit to a nifty apartment in New York, chappie, and the next Saturday night we lay over together in the big city Ise gwine to show you some real queens. It's like everything else in life. Depends on you' luck."

"And you are one lucky dog," Ray laughed.

Jake grinned: "I'd tell you about a li'l' piece o' sweetness I picked up in a cabaret the first day I landed from ovah the other side. But it's too late now. We gotta start work."

"Next time, then," said Ray.

Jake swung himself up by the rear platform and entered the kitchen. Ray passed round by the other side into the dining-room.

Interlude

XIV

Dusk gathered in blue patches over the Black Belt. Lenox Avenue was vivid. The saloons were bright, crowded with drinking men jammed tight around the bars, treating one another and telling the incidents of the day. Longshoremen in overalls with hooks, Pullman porters holding their bags, waiters, elevator boys. Liquor-rich laughter, banana-ripe laughter. . . .

The pavement was a dim warm bustle. Women hurrying home from day's work to get dinner ready for husbands who worked at night. On their arms brown bags and black containing a bit of meat, a head of lettuce, butter. Young men who were stagging through life, passing along with brown-paper packages, containing a small steak, a pork chop, to do their own frying.

From out of saloons came the savory smell of corned beef and cabbage, spare-ribs, Hamburger steaks. Out of little cook-joints wedged in side streets, tripe, pigs' feet, hogs' ears and snouts. Out of apartments, steak smothered with onions, liver and bacon, fried chicken.

The composite smell of cooked stuff assaulted Jake's nostrils. He was hungry. His landlady was late bringing his food. Maybe she was out on Lenox Avenue chewing the rag with some other Ebenezer soul, thought Jake.

Jake was ill. The doctor told him that he would get well very quickly if he remained quietly in bed for a few days.

"And you mustn't drink till you are better. It's bad for you," the doctor warned him.

But Jake had his landlady bring him from two to four pails of beer every day. "I must drink some'n," he reasoned, "and beer can't make me no harm. It's light."

When Ray went to see him, Jake laughed at his serious mien.

"Tha's life, chappie. I goes way ovah yonder and wander and fools around and I hed no mind about nothing. Then I come back to mah own home town and, oh, you snake-bite! When I was in the army, chappie, they useter give us all sorts o' lechers about canshankerous nights and prophet-lactic days, but I nevah pay them no mind. Them things foh edjucated guys like you who lives in you' head."

"They are for you, too," Ray said. "This is a new age with new methods of living. You can't just go on like a crazy ram goat as if you were living in the Middle Ages."

"Middle Ages! I ain't seen them yet and don't nevah wanta. All them things you talk about am kill-joy things, chappie. The trute is they make me feel shame."

Ray laughed until tears trickled down his cheeks. . . . . He visualized Jake being ashamed and laughed again.

"Sure," said Jake. "I'd feel ashame' ef a chippie—No, chappie, them stuff is foh you book fellahs. I runs around all right, but Ise lak a sailor that don't know nothing about using a compass, but him always hits a safe port."

"You didn't this time, though, Jakie. Those devices that you despise are really for you rather than for me or people like me, who don't live your kind of free life. If you, and the whole strong race of workingman who live freely like you, don't pay some attention to them, then you'll all wither away and rot like weeds."

"Let us pray!" said Jake.

"*That* I don't believe in."

"Awright, then, chappie."

On the next trip, the dining-car was shifted off its scheduled run and returned to New York on the second day, late at night. It was ordered out again early the next day. Ray could not get round to see Jake, so he telephoned his girl and asked her to go.

Agatha had heard much of Ray's best friend, but she had never met him. Men working on a train have something of the spirit of men working on a ship. They are, perforce, bound together in comradeship of a sort in that close atmosphere. In the stop-over cities they go about in pairs or groups. But the camaraderie breaks up on the platform in New York as soon as the dining-car returns there. Every man goes his own way unknown to his comrades. Wife or sweetheart or some other magnet of the great magic city draws each off separately.

Agatha was a rich-brown girl, with soft amorous eyes. She worked as assistant in a beauty parlor of the Belt. She was a Baltimore girl and had been living in New York for two years. Ray had met her the year before at a basket-ball match and dance.

She went to see Jake in the afternoon. He was sitting in a Morris chair, reading the Negro newspaper, *The Amsterdam News*, with a pail of beer beside him, when Agatha rapped on the door.

Jake thought it was the landlady. He was thrown off his balance by the straight, beautiful girl who entered the room and quietly closed the door behind her.

"Oh, keep your seat, please," she begged him. "I'll sit there," she indicated a brown chair by the cherrywood chiffonier.

"Ray asked me to come. He was doubled out this morning and couldn't get around to see you. I brought these for you."

She put a paper bag of oranges on the table. "Where shall I put these?" She showed him a charming little bouquet of violets. Jake's drinking-glass was on the floor, half full, beside the pail of beer.

"It's all right, here!" On the chipped, mildew-white wash-stand there was another glass with a tooth-brush. She took the tooth-brush out, poured some water in the glass, put the violets in, and set it on the chiffonier.

"There!" she said.

Jake thanked her. He was diffident. She was so different a girl from the many he had known. She was certainly one of those that Miss Curdy would have sneered at. She was so full of simple self-assurance and charm. Mah little sister down home in Petersburg, he thought, might have turned out something lak this ef she'd 'a' had a chance to talk English like in books and wear class-top clothes. Nine years sence I quit home. She must be quite a li'l woman now herself.

Jake loved women's pretty clothes. The plain nigger-brown coat Agatha wore, unbuttoned, showed a fresh peach-colored frock. He asked after Ray.

"I didn't see him myself this trip," she said. "He telephoned me about you."

Jake praised Ray as his best pal.

"He's a good boy," she agreed. She asked Jake about the railroad. "It must be lots of fun to ride from one town to the other like that. I'd love it, for I love to travel. But Ray hates it."

"It ain't so much fun when youse working," replied Jake.

"I guess you're right. But there's something marvelous about meeting people for a little while and serving them and never seeing them again. It's romantic. You don't have that awful personal everyday contact that domestic workers have to get along with. If I was a man and had to be in service, I wouldn't want better than the railroad."

"Some'n to that, yes," agreed Jake. . . . "But it ain't all peaches, neither, when all them passengers rush you like a herd of hungry swine."

Agatha stayed twenty minutes.

"I wish you better soon," she said, bidding Jake good-by. "It was nice to know you. Ray will surely come to see you when he gets back this time."

Jake drank a glass of beer and eased his back, full length on the little bed.

"She is sure some wonderful brown," he mused. "Now I sure does understand why Ray is so scornful of them easy ones." He gazed at the gray door. It seemed a shining panel of gold through which a radiant vision had passed.

"She sure does like that theah Ray an unconscionable lot. I could see the love stuff shining in them mahvelous eyes of hers when I talked about him. I s'pose it's killing sweet to have some'n loving you up thataway. Some'n real fond o' you for you own self lak, lak—jest lak how mah mammy useter love pa and do everything foh him bafore he done took and died off without giving no notice. . . ."

His thoughts wandered away back to his mysterious little brown of the Baltimore. She was not elegant and educated, but she was nice. Maybe if he found her again—it would be better than just running wild around like that! Thinking honestly about it, after all, he was never satisfied, flopping here and sleeping there. It gave him a little cocky pleasure to brag of his conquests to the fellows around the bar. But after all the swilling and boasting, it would be a thousand times nicer to have a little brown woman of his own to whom he could go home and be his simple self with. Lay his curly head between her brown breasts and be fondled and be the spoiled child that every man loves sometimes to be when he is all alone with a woman. *That* he could never be with the Madame Lauras. They expected him always to be the prancing he-man. Maybe it was the lack of a steady girl that kept him running crazy around. Boozing and poking and rooting around, jolly enough all right, but not altogether contented.

The landlady did not appear with Jake's dinner.

"Guess she is somewhere rocking soft with gin," he thought. "Ise feeling all right enough to go out, anyhow. Guess I'll drop in at Uncle Doc's and have a good feed of spare-ribs. Hm! but the stuff coming out of these heah Harlem kitchens is enough to knock me down. They smell so good."

He dressed and went out. "Oh, Lenox Avenue, but you look good to me, now. Lawdy! though, how the brown-skin babies am humping it along! Strutting the joy-stuff! Invitation for a shimmy. O Lawdy! Pills and pisen, you gotta turn me loose, quick."

Billy Biasse was drinking at the bar of Uncle Doc's when Jake entered.

"Come on, you, and have a drink," Billy cried. "Which hole in Harlem youse been burying you'self in all this time?"

"Which you figure? There is holes outside of Harlem too, boh." Jake ordered a beer.

"Beer!" exclaimed Billy. "Quit you fooling and take some real liquor, nigger. Ise paying foh it. Order that theah ovah-water liquor you useter be so dippy about. That theah Scotch."

"I ain't quite all right, Billy. Gotta go slow on the booze."

"Whasmat? . . . Oh, foh Gawd's sake! Don't let the li'l' beauty break you' heart. Fix her up with gin."

"Might as well, and then a royal feed o' spare-ribs," agreed Jake.

He asked for Zeddy.

"Missing sence all the new moon done bless mah luck that you is, too. Last news I heard 'bout him, the gen'man was Yonkers anchored."

"And Strawberry Lips?"

"That nigger's back home in Harlem where he belongs. He done long ago quit that ugly yaller razor-back. And you, boh. Who's providing foh you' wants sence you done turn Congo Rose down?"

"Been running wild in the paddock of the Pennsy."

"Oh, boh, you sure did breaks the sweet-loving haht of Congo Rose. One night she stahted to sing 'You broke mah haht and went away' and she jest bust out crying theah in the cabaret and couldn't sing no moh. She hauled harself whimpering out there, and she laid off o' the Congo foh moh than a week. That li'l' goosey boy had to do the strutting all by himse'f."

"She was hot stuff all right." Jake laughed richly. "But I had to quit her or she would have made me either a no-'count or a bad nigger."

Warmed up by meeting an old pal and hearing all the intimate news of the dives, Jake tossed off he knew not how many gins. He told Billy Biasse of the places he had nosed out in Baltimore and Philadelphia. The gossip was good. Jake changed to Scotch and asked for the siphon.

He had finished the first Scotch and asked for another, when a pain gripped his belly with a wrench that almost tore him apart. Jake groaned and doubled over, staggered into a corner, and crumpled up on the floor. Perspiration stood in beads on his forehead, trickled down his rigid, chiseled features. He heard the word "ambulance" repeated several times. He thought first of his mother. His sister. The little frame house in Petersburg. The backyard of bleached clothes on the line, the large lilac tree and the little forked lot that yielded red tomatoes and green peas in spring.

"No hospital foh me," he muttered. "Mah room is jest next doh. Take me theah."

Uncle Doc told his bar man to help Billy Biasse lift Jake.

"Kain you move you' laigs any at all, boh?" Billy asked.

Jake groaned: "I kain try."

The men took him home. . . .

Jake's landlady had been invited to a fried-chicken feed in the basement lodging of an Ebenezer sister and friend on Fifth Avenue. The sister friend had rented the basement of the old-fashioned house and appropriated the large backyard for her laundry work. She went out and collected soiled linen every Monday. Her wealthiest patrons sent their chauffeurs round with their linen. And the laundress was very proud of white chauffeurs standing their automobiles in front of her humble basement. She noticed with heaving chest that the female residents of the block rubber-necked. Her vocation was very profitable. And it was her pleasure sometimes to invite a sister of her church to dinner. . . .

The fried chicken, with sweet potatoes, was excellent. Over it the sisters chinned and grinned, recounting all the contemporary scandals of the Negro churches. . . .

At last Jake's landlady remembered him and staggered home to prepare his beef broth. But when she took it up to him she found that Jake was out. Returning to the kitchen, she stumbled and broke the white bowl, made a sign with her rabbit foot, and murmured, foggily: "Theah's sure a cross coming to thisa house. I wonder it's foh who?"

The bell rang and rang again and again in spite of the notice: Ring once. And when the landlady opened the door and saw Jake supported between two men, she knew that the broken white bowl was for him and that his time was come.

Relapse

XV

Billy Biasse telephoned to the doctor, a young chocolate-complexioned man. He was graduate of a Negro medical college in Tennessee and of Columbia University. He was struggling to overcome the prejudices of the black populace against Negro doctors and wedge himself in among the Jewish doctors that prescribed for the Harlem clientele. A clever man, he was trying, through Democratic influence, to get an appointment in one of the New York hospitals. Such an achievement would put him all over the Negro press and get him all the practice and more than he could handle in the Belt.

Ray had sent Jake to him. . . .

The landlady brought Jake a rum punch. He shook his head. With a premonition of tragedy, she waited for the doctor, standing against the chiffonier, a blue cloth carelessly knotted round her head. . . .

In the corridor she questioned Billy Biasse about Jake's seizure.

"All you younger generation in Harlem don't know no God," she accused Billy and indicted Young Harlem. "All you know is cabarets and movies and the young gals them exposing them legs a theirs in them jumper frocks."

"I wouldn't know 'bout that," said Billy.

"You all ought to know, though, and think of God Almighty before the trumpet sound and it's too late foh black sinners. I nevah seen so many trifling and ungodly niggers as there is in this heah Harlem." She thought of the broken white bowl. "And I done had a warning from heaben."

The doctor arrived. Ordered a hot-water bottle for Jake's belly and a hot lemon drink. There was no other remedy to help him but what he had been taking.

"You've been drinking," the doctor said.

"Jest a li'l' beer," Jake murmured.

"O Lawdy! though, listen at him!" cried the landlady. "Mister, if he done had a glass, he had a barrel a day. Ain't I been getting it foh him?"

"Beer is the worst form of alcohol you could ever take in your state," said the doctor. "Couldn't be anything worse. Better you had taken wine."

Jake growled that he didn't like wine.

"It's up to you to get well," said the doctor. "You have been ill like that before. It's a simple affair if you will be careful and quiet for a little while. But it's very dangerous if you are foolish. I know you chaps take those things lightly. But you shouldn't, for the consequences are very dangerous."

Two days later Ray's diner returned to New York. It was early afternoon and the crew went over to the yards to get the stock for the next trip. And after stocking up Ray went directly to see Jake.

Jake was getting along all right again. But Ray was alarmed when he heard of his relapse. Indeed, Ray was too easily moved for the world he lived in. The delicate-fibered mechanism of his being responded to sensations that were entirely beyond Jake's comprehension.

"The doctor done hand me his. The landlady stahted warning me against sin with her mouth stinking with gin. And now mah chappie's gwina join the gang." Jake laughed heartily.

"But you must be careful, Jake. You're too sensible not to know good advice from bad."

"Oh, sure, chappie, I'll take care. I don't wanta be crippled up as the doctor says I might. Mah laigs got many moh miles to run yet, chasing after the sweet stuff o' life, chappie."

"Good oh Jake! I know you love life too much to make a fool of yourself like so many of those other fellows. I've never knew that this thing was so common until I started working on the railroad. You know the fourth had to lay off this trip."

"You don't say!"

"Yes, he's got a mean one. And the second cook on Bowman's diner he's been in a chronic way for about three months."

"But how does he get by the doctor? All them crews is examined every week."

"Hm! . . ." Ray glanced carelessly through *The Amsterdam News.*

"I saw Madame Laura in Fairmount Park and I told her you were sick. I gave her your address, too."

"Bumbole! What for?"

"Because she asked me for it. She was sympathetic."

"I never give mah address to them womens, chappie. Bad system that."

"Why?"

"Because you nevah know when they might bust in on you and staht a rough-house. Them's all right, them womens . . . in their own parlors."

"I guess you ought to know. I don't," said Ray. "Say, why don't you move out of this dump up to the Forties? There's a room in the same house I stay in. Cheap. Two flights up, right on the court. Steam heat and everything."

"I guess I could stand a new place to lay mah carcass in, all right," Jake drawled. "Steam heats you say? I'm sure sick o' this here praying-ma-ma hot air. And the trute is it ain't nevah much hotter than mah breath."

"All right. When do you want me to speak to the landlady about the room?"

"This heah very beautiful night, chappie. Mah rent is up tomorrow and I moves. But you got to do me a li'l' favor. Go by Billy Biasse this night and tell him to come and git his ole buddy's suitcase and see him into his new home tomorrow morning."

Jake was as happy as a kid. He would be frisking if he could. But Ray was not happy. The sudden upset of affairs in his home country had landed him into the quivering heart of a naked world whose reality was hitherto unimaginable. It was what they called in print and polite conversation "the underworld." The compound word baffled him, as some English words did sometimes. Why *under*world he could never understand. It was very much upon the surface as were the other divisions of human life. Having its heights and middle and depths and secret places even as they. And the people of this world, waiters, cooks, chauffeurs, sailors, porters, guides, ushers, hod-carriers, factory hands—all touched in a thousand ways the people of the other divisions. They worked over there and slept over here, divided by a street.

Ray had always dreamed of writing words some day. Weaving words to make romance, ah! There were the great books that dominated the bright dreaming and dark brooding days when he was a boy. *Les Misérables, Nana, Uncle Tom's Cabin, David Copperfield, Nicholas Nickleby, Oliver Twist.*

From them, by way of free-thought pamphlets, it was only a stride to the great scintillating satirists of the age—Bernard Shaw, Ibsen, Anatole France, and the popular problemist, H. G. Wells. He had lived on that brilliant manna that fell like a flame-fall from those burning stars. Then came the great mass carnage in Europe and the great mass revolution in Russia.

Ray was not prophetic-minded enough to define the total evil that the one had wrought nor the ultimate splendor of the other. But, in spite of the general tumults and threats, the perfectly-organized national rages, the ineffectual patching of broken, and hectic rebuilding of shattered, things, he had perception enough to realize that he had lived over the end of an era.

And also he realized that his spiritual masters had not crossed with him into the new. He felt alone, hurt, neglected, cheated, almost naked. But he was a savage, even though he was a sensitive one, and did not mind nakedness. What had happened? Had they refused to come or had he left them behind? Something had happened. But it was not desertion nor young insurgency. It was death. Even as the last scion of a famous line prances out this day and dies and is set aside with his ancestors in their cold whited sepulcher, so had his masters marched with flags and banners flying all their wonderful, trenchant, critical, satirical, mind-sharpening, pity-evoking, constructive ideas of ultimate social righteousness, into the vast international cemetery of this century.

Dreams of patterns of words achieving form. What would he ever do with the words he had acquired? Were they adequate to tell the thoughts he felt, describe the impressions that reached him vividly? What were men making of words now? During the war he had been startled by James Joyce in *The Little Review*. Sherwood Anderson had reached him with *Winesburg, Ohio*. He had read, fascinated, all that D. H. Lawrence published. And wondered if there was not a great Lawrence reservoir of words too terrible and too terrifying for nice printing. Henri Barbusse's *Le Feu* burnt like a flame in his memory. Ray loved the book because it was such a grand anti-romantic presentation of mind and behavior in that hell-pit of life. And literature, story-telling, had little interest for him now if thought and feeling did not wrestle and sprawl with appetite and dark desire all over the pages.

Dreams of making something with words. What could he make . . . and fashion? Could he ever create Art? Art, around which vague, incomprehensible words and phrases stormed? What was art, anyway? Was it more than a clear-cut presentation of a vivid impression of life? Only the Russians of the late era seemed to stand up like giants in the new. Gogol, Dostoievski, Tolstoy, Chekhov, Turgeniev. When he read them now he thought: Here were elements that the grand carnage swept over and touched not. The soil of life saved their roots from the fire. They were so saturated, so deep-down rooted in it.

Thank God and Uncle Sam that the old dreams were shattered. Nevertheless, he still felt more than ever the utter blinding nakedness and violent coloring of life. But what of it? Could he create out of the fertile reality around him? Of Jake nosing through life, a handsome hound, quick to snap up any tempting morsel of poisoned meat thrown carelessly on the pavement? Of a work pal he had visited in the venereal ward of Bellevue, where youths lolled sadly about? And the misery that overwhelmed him there, until life appeared like one big disease and the world a vast hospital?

A Practical Prank

XVI

MY DEAR HONEY-STICK

"I was riding in Fairmount Park one afternoon, just taking the air as usual, when I saw your proper-speaking friend with a mess of books. He told me you were sick and I was so mortified for I am giving a big evening soon and was all set on fixing it on a night when you would certain sure be laying over in Philadelphia. Because you are such good company I may as well say how much you are appreciated here. I guess I'll put it off till you are okay again, for as I am putting my hand in my own pocket to give all of my friends and wellwishers a dandy time it won't be no fun for *me* if I leave out the *principal* one. Guess who!

"I am expecting to come to New York soon on shopping bent. You know all us weak women who can afford it have got the Fifth Avenue fever, my dear. If I come I'll sure look you up, you can bank on it.

"Bye, bye, honeystick and be good and quiet and better yourself soon. Philadelphia is lonesome without you.

"Lovingly, LAURA."

Billy Biasse, calling by Jake's former lodging, found this letter for him, lying there among a pile of others, on the little black round table in the hall. . . .

"Here you is, boh. Whether youse well or sick, them's after you."

"Is they? Lemme see. Hm . . . Philly." . . .

"Who is you' pen-pusher?" asked Billy.

"A queen in Philly. Says she might pay me a visit here. I ain't send out no invitation foh no womens yet."

"Is she the goods?"

"She's a wang, boh. Queen o' Philly, I tell you. And foh me, everything with her is f. o. c. But I don't want that yaller piece o' business come nosing after me here in Harlem."

"She ain't got to find you, boh. Jest throws her a bad lead."

"Tha's the stuff to give 'm. Ain't you a buddy with a haid on, though?"

" 'Deed I is. And all you niggers knows it who done frequent mah place."

And so Jake, in a prankish mood, replied to Madame Laura on a picture post-card saying he would be well and up soon and be back on the road and on the job again, and he gave Congo Rose's address.

Madame Laura made her expected trip to New York, traveling "Chair," as was her custom when she traveled. She wore a mauve dress, vermilion-shot at the throat, and short enough to show the curved plumpness of her legs encased in fine unrumpled rose-tinted stockings. Her modish overcoat was lilac-gray lined with green and a large marine-blue rosette was bunched at the side of her neat gray hat.

In the Fifth Avenue shops she was waited upon as if she were a dark foreign lady of title visiting New York. In the afternoon she took a taxi-cab to Harlem.

Now all the fashionable people who called at Rose's house were generally her friends. And so Rose always went herself to let them in. She could look out from her window, one flight up, and ho-ho down to them.

When Madame Laura rang the bell, Rose popped her head out. Nobody I know, she thought, but the attractive woman in expensive clothes piqued her curiosity. Hastily she dabbed her face with powder pad, patted her hair into shape, and descended.

"Is Mr. Jacob Brown living here?" Madame Laura asked.

"Well, he was—I mean—" This luxurious woman demanding Jake tantalized Rose. She still referred to him as her man since his disappearance. No reports of his living with another woman having come to her, she had told her friends that Jake's mother had come between them.

"He always had a little some'n' of a mamma's boy about him, you know."

Poor Jake. Since he left home, his mother had become for him a loving memory only. When you saw him, talked to him, he stood forth as one of those unique types of humanity who lived alone and were never lonely. You would hardly wonder who were his father and mother and what they were like. He, in his frame and atmosphere, was the Alpha and Omega himself.

"I mean— Can you tell me what you want?" asked Rose.

"Must I? I didn't know he—Why, he wrote to me. Said he was ill. And sent his friend to tell me he was ill. Can't I see him?"

"Did he write to you from this here address?"

"Why, certainly. I have his card here." Madame Laura was fumbling in her handbag.

A triumphant smile stole into Rose's face. Jake had no real home and had to use her address.

"Is you his sister or what?"

"I'm a friend," Madame Laura said, sharply.

"Well, he's got a nearve." Rose jerked herself angrily. "He's mah man."

"I didn't come all the way here to hear that," said Madame Laura. "I thought he was sick and wanting attention."

"Ain't I good enough to give him all the attention required without another woman come chasing after him?"

"Disgusting!" cried Madame Laura. "I would think this was a spohting house."

"Gwan with you before I spit in you' eye," cried Rose. "You look like some'n just outa one you'self."

"You're no lady," retorted Madame Laura, and she hurried down the steps.

Rose amplified the story exceedingly in telling it to her friends. "I slapped her face for insulting me," she said.

Billy Biasse heard of it from the boy dancer of the Congo. When Billy went again to see Jake, one of the patrons of his gaming joint went with him. It was that yellow youth, the same one that had first invited Zeddy over to Gin-head Susy's place. He was a prince of all the day joints and night holes of the Belt. All the shark players of Dixie Red's pool-room were proud of losing a game to him, and at the Congo the waiters danced around to catch his orders. For Yaller Prince, so they affectionately called him, was living easy and sweet. Three girls, they said, were engaged in the business of keeping him princely—one chocolate-to-the-bone, one teasing-brown, and one yellow. He was always well dressed in a fine nigger-brown or bottle-green suit, excessively creased, and spats. Also he was happy-going and very generous. But there was something slimy about him.

Yaller Prince had always admired Jake, in the way a common-bred admires a thorough-bred, and hearing from Billy that he was ill, he had brought him fruit, cake, and ice cream and six packets of Camels. Yaller Prince was more intimate with Jake's world than Billy, who swerved off at a different angle and was always absorbed in the games and winnings of men.

Jake and Yaller had many loose threads to pick up again and follow for a while. Were the gin parties going on still at Susy's? What had become of Miss Curdy? Yaller didn't know. He had dropped Myrtle Avenue before Zeddy did.

"Susy was free with the gin all right, but, gee whizzard! She was sure black and ugly, buddy," remarked Yaller.

"You said it, boh," agreed Jake. "They was some pair all right, them two womens. Black and ugly is exactly Susy, and that there other Curdy creachur all streaky yaller and ugly. I couldn't love them theah kind."

Yaller uttered a little goat laugh. "I kain't stand them ugly grannies, either. But sometimes they does pay high, buddy, and when the paying is good, I can always transfer mah mind."

"I couldn't foh no price, boh," said Jake. "Gimme a nice sweet-skin brown. I ain't got no time foh none o' you' ugly hard-hided dames."

Jake asked for Strawberry Lips. He was living in Harlem again and working longshore. Up in Yonkers Zeddy was endeavoring to overcome his passion for gambling and start housekeeping with a steady home-loving woman. He was beginning to realize that he was not big enough to carry two strong passions, each pulling him in opposite directions. Some day a grandson of his born in Harlem might easily cope with both passions, might even come to sacrifice woman to gambling. But Zeddy himself was too close to the savage swell of life.

Ray entered with a friend whom he introduced as James Grant. He was also a student working his way through college. But lacking funds to continue, he had left college to find a job. He was fourth waiter on Ray's diner, succeeding the timid boy from Georgia. As both chairs were in use, Grant sat on the edge of the bed and Ray tipped up Jake's suitcase. . . .

Conversation veered off to the railroad.

"I am getting sick of it," Ray said. "It's a crazy, clattering, nerve-shattering life. I think I'll fall down for good."

"Why, ef you quit, chappie, I'll nevah go back on that there white man's sweet chariot," said Jake.

"Whasmat?" asked Billy Biasse. "Kain't you git along on theah without him?"

"It's a whole lot the matter you can't understand, Billy. The white folks' railroad ain't like Lenox Avenue. You can tell on theah when a pal's a real pal."

"I got a pal, I got a gal," chanted Billy, "heah in mah pocket-book." He patted his breast pocket.

"Go long from here with you' lonesome haht, you wolf," cried Jake.

"Wolf is mah middle name, but . . . I ain't bad as I hear, and ain't you mah buddy, too?" Billy said to Jake. "Git you'self going quick and come on down to mah place, son. The bones am lonesome foh you."

Billy and Yaller Prince left.

"Who is the swell strutter?" Ray's friend asked.

"Hm! . . . I knowed him long time in Harlem," said Jake. "He's a good guy. Just brought me all them eats and cigarettes."

"What does he work at?" asked Ray.

"Nothing menial. He's a p-i.". . .

"Low-down yaller swine," said Ray's friend. "Harlem is stinking with them."

"Oh, Yaller is all right, though," said Jake. "A real good-hearted scout."

"Good-hearted!" Grant sneered. "A man's heart is cold dead when he has women doing that for him. How can a man live that way and strut in public, instead of hiding himself underground like a worm?" He turned indignantly to Ray.

"Search me!" Ray laughed a little. "You might as well ask why all mulattoes have unpleasant voices."

Grant was slightly embarrassed. He was yellow-skinned and his voice was hard and grainy. Jake he-hawed.

"Not all, chappie, I know some with sweet voice."

"Mula*ttress, mon ami*." Ray lifted a finger. "That's an exception. And now, James, let us forget Jake's kind friend."

"Oh, I don't mind him talking," said Jake. "I don't approve of Yaller's trade mahself, but ef he can do it, well—It's because you don't know how many womens am running after the fellahs jest begging them to do that. They been after me moh time I can remember. There's lots o' folks living easy and living sweet, but . . ."

"There are as many forms of parasitism as there are ways of earning a living," said Ray.

"But to live the life of carrion," sneered Grant, "fatten on rotting human flesh. It's the last ditch, where dogs go to die. When you drop down in that you cease being human."

"You done said it straight out, brother," said Jake. "It's a stinking life and I don't like stinks."

"Your feeling against that sort of thing is fine, James," said Ray. "But that's the most I could say for it. It's all right to start out with nice theories from an advantageous point in life. But when you get a chance to learn life for yourself, it's quite another thing. The things you call fine human traits don't belong to any special class or nation or race of people. Nobody can pull that kind of talk now and get away with it, least of all a Negro."

"Why not?" asked Grant. "Can't a Negro have fine feelings about life?"

"Yes, but not the old false-fine feelings that used to be monopolized by educated and cultivated people. You should educate yourself away from that sort of thing."

"But education is something to make you fine!"

"No, modern education is planned to make you a sharp, snouty, rooting hog. A Negro getting it is an anachronism. We ought to get something new, we Negroes. But we get our education like—like our houses. When the whites move out, we move in and take possession of the old dead stuff. Dead stuff that this age has no use for."

"How's that?"

"Can you ask? You and I were born in the midst of the illness of this age and have lived through its agony. . . . Keep your fine feelings, indeed, but don't try to make a virtue of them. You'll lose them, then. They'll become all hollow inside, false and dry as civilization itself. And civilization is rotten. We are all rotten who are touched by it."

"I am not rotten," retorted Grant, "and I couldn't bring myself and my ideas down to the level of such filthy parasites."

"All men have the disease of pimps in their hearts," said Ray. "We can't be civilized and not. I have seen your high and mighty civilized people do things that some pimps would be ashamed of—"

"You said it, then, and most truly," cried Jake, who, lying on the bed, was intently following the dialogue.

"Do it in the name of civilization," continued Ray. "And I have been forced down to the level of pimps and found some of them more than human. One of them was so strange. . . . I never thought he could feel anything. Never thought he could do what he did. Something so strange and wonderful and awful, it just lifted me up out of my little straight thoughts into a big whirl where all of life seemed hopelessly tangled and colored without point or purpose."

"Tell us about it," said Grant.

"All right," said Ray. "I'll tell it."

He Also Loved

XVII

It was in the winter of 1916 when I first came to New York to hunt for a job. I was broke. I was afraid I would have to pawn my clothes, and it was dreadfully cold. I didn't even know the right way to go about looking for a job. I was always timid about that. For five weeks I had not paid my rent. I was worried, and Ma Lawton, my landlady, was also worried. She had her bills to meet. She was a good-hearted old woman from South Carolina. Her face was all wrinkled and sensitive like finely-carved mahogany.

Every bed-space in the flat was rented. I was living in the small hall bedroom. Ma Lawton asked me to give it up. There were four men sleeping in the front room; two in an old, chipped-enameled brass bed, one on a davenport, and the other in a folding chair. The old lady put a little canvas cot in that same room, gave me a pillow and a heavy quilt, and said I should try and make myself comfortable there until I got work.

The cot was all right for me. Although I hate to share a room with another person and the fellows snoring disturbed my rest. Ma Lawton moved into the little room that I had had, and rented out hers—it was next to the front room—to a man and a woman.

The woman was above ordinary height, chocolate-colored. Her skin was smooth, too smooth, as if it had been pressed and fashioned out for ready sale like chocolate candy. Her hair was straightened out into an Indian Straight after the present style among Negro ladies. She had a mongoose sort of a mouth, with two top front teeth showing. She wore a long mink coat.

The man was darker than the woman. His face was longish, with the right cheek somewhat caved in. It was an interesting face, an attractive, salacious mouth, with the lower lip protruding. He wore a bottle-green peg-top suit, baggy at the hips. His coat hung loose from his shoulders and it was much longer than the prevailing style. He wore also a Mexican hat, and in his breast pocket he carried an Ingersoll watch attached to a heavy gold chain. His name was Jericho Jones, and they called him Jerco for short. And she was Miss Whicher—Rosalind Whicher.

Ma Lawton introduced me to them and said I was broke, and they were both awfully nice to me. They took me to a big feed of corned beef and cabbage at Burrell's on Fifth Avenue. They gave me a good appetizing drink of gin to commence with. And we had beer with the eats; not ordinary beer, either, but real Budweiser, right off the ice.

And as good luck sometimes comes pouring down like a shower, the next day Ma Lawton got me a job in the little free-lunch saloon right under her flat. It wasn't a paying job as far as money goes in New York, but I was glad to have it. I had charge of the free-lunch counter. You know the little dry crackers that go so well with beer, and the cheese and fish and the potato salad. And I served, besides, spare-ribs and whole boiled potatoes and corned beef and cabbage for those customers who could afford to pay for a lunch. I got no wages at all, but I got my eats twice a day. And I made a few tips, also. For there were about six big black men with plenty of money who used to eat lunch with us, specially for our spare-ribs and sweet potatoes. Each one of them gave me a quarter. I made enough to pay Ma Lawton for my canvas cot.

Strange enough, too, Jerco and Rosalind took a liking to me. And sometimes they came and ate lunch perched up there at the counter, with Rosalind the only woman there, all made up and rubbing her mink coat against the men. And when they got through eating, Jerco would toss a dollar bill at me.

We got very friendly, we three. Rosalind would bring up squabs and canned stuff from the German delicatessen in One Hundred and Twenty-fifth Street, and sometimes they asked me to dinner in their room and gave me good liquor.

I thought I was pretty well fixed for such a hard winter. All I had to do as extra work was keeping the saloon clean. . . .

One afternoon Jerco came into the saloon with a man who looked pretty near white. Of course, you never can tell for sure about a person's race in Harlem, nowadays, when there are so many high-yallers floating round—colored folks that would make Italian and Spanish people look like Negroes beside them. But I figured out from his way of talking and acting that the man with Jerco belonged to the white race. They went in through the family entrance into the back room, which was unusual, for the family room of a saloon, as you know, is only for women in the business and the men they bring in there with them. Real men don't sit in a saloon here as they do at home. I suppose it would be sissified. There's a bar for them to lean on and drink and joke as long as they feel like.

The boss of the saloon was a little fidgety about Jerco and his friend sitting there in the back. The boss was a short pumpkin-bellied brown man, a little bald off the forehead. Twice he found something to attend to in the back room, although there was nothing at all there that wanted attending to. . . . I felt better, and the boss, too, I guess, when Rosalind came along and gave the family room its respectable American character. I served Rosalind a Martini cocktail extra dry, and afterward all three of them, Rosalind, Jerco, and their friend, went up to Ma Lawton's.

The two fellows that slept together were elevator operators in a department store, so they had their Sundays free. On the afternoon of the Sunday of the same week that the white-looking man had been

in the saloon with Jerco, I went upstairs to change my old shoes—
they'd got soaking wet behind the counter—and I found Ma Lawton
talking to the two elevator fellows.

The boys had given Ma Lawton notice to quit. They said they
couldn't sleep there comfortably together on account of the goings-on
in Rosalind's room. The fellows were members of the Colored
Y.M.C.A. and were queerly quiet and pious. One of them was studying to be a preacher. They were the sort of fellows that thought going
to cabarets a sin, and that parlor socials were leading Harlem straight
down to hell. They only went to church affairs themselves. They had
been rooming with Ma Lawton for over a year. She called them her
gentlemen lodgers.

Ma Lawton said to me: "Have you heard anything phony outa the
next room, dear?"

"Why, no, Ma," I said, "nothing more unusual than you can hear
all over Harlem. Besides, I work so late, I am dead tired when I turn
in to bed, so I sleep heavy."

"Well, it's the truth I do like that there Jerco an' Rosaline," said
Ma Lawton. "They did seem quiet as lambs, although they was always havin' company. But Ise got to speak to them, 'cause I doana
wanta lose ma young mens. . . . But theyse a real nice-acting couple. Jerco him treats me like him was mah son. It's true that they
doan work like all poah niggers, but they pays that rent down good
and prompt ehvery week."

Jerco was always bringing in ice-cream and cake or something for
Ma Lawton. He had a way about him, and everybody liked him. He
was a sympathetic type. He helped Ma Lawton move beds and com-
modes and he fixed her clothes lines. I had heard somebody talking
about Jerco in the saloon, however, saying that he could swing a
mean fist when he got his dander up, and that he had been mixed
up in more than one razor cut-up. He did have a nasty long razor
scar on the back of his right hand.

The elevator fellows had never liked Rosalind and Jerco. The one
who was studying to preach Jesus said he felt pretty sure that they
were an ungodly-living couple. He said that late one night he had
pointed out their room to a woman that looked white. He said the
woman looked suspicious. She was perfumed and all powdered up
and it appeared as if she didn't belong among colored people.

"There's no sure telling white from high-yaller these days," I said.
"There are so many swell-looking quadroons and octoroons of the
race."

But the other elevator fellow said that one day in the tenderloin section he had run up against Rosalind and Jerco together with a petty officer of marines. And that just put the lid on anything favorable that could be said about them.

But Ma Lawton said: "Well, Ise got to run mah flat right an' try mah utmost to please youall, but I ain't wanta dip mah nose too deep in a lodger's affairs."

Late that night, toward one o'clock, Jerco dropped in at the saloon and told me that Rosalind was feeling badly. She hadn't eaten a bite all day and he had come to get a pail of beer, because she had asked specially for draught beer. Jerco was worried, too.

"I hopes she don't get bad," he said. "For we ain't got a cent o' money. Wese just in on a streak o' bad luck."

"I guess she'll soon be all right," I said.

The next day after lunch I stole a little time and went up to see Rosalind. Ma Lawton was just going to attend to her when I let my-self in, and she said to me: "Now the poor woman is sick, poor chile, ahm so glad mah conscience is free and that I hadn't a said nothing evil t' her."

Rosalind was pretty sick. Ma Lawton said it was the grippe. She gave Rosalind hot whisky drinks and hot milk, and she kept her feet warm with a hot-water bottle. Rosalind's legs were lead-heavy. She had a pain that pinched her side like a pair of pincers. And she cried out for thirst and begged for draught beer.

Ma Lawton said Rosalind ought to have a doctor. "You'd better go an' scares up a white one," she said to Jerco. "Ise nevah had no faith in these heah nigger doctors."

"I don't know how we'll make out without money," Jerco whined. He was sitting in the old Morris chair with his head heavy on his left hand.

"You kain pawn my coat," said Rosalind. "Old man Greenbaum will give you two hundred down without looking at it."

"I won't put a handk'chief o' yourn in the hock shop," said Jerco. "You'll need you' stuff soon as you get better. Specially you' coat. You kain't go anywheres without it."

"S'posin' I don't get up again," Rosalind smiled. But her counte-nance changed suddenly as she held her side and moaned. Ma Law-ton bent over and adjusted the pillows.

Jerco pawned his watch chain and his own overcoat, and called in a Jewish doctor from the upper Eighth Avenue fringe of the Belt. But Rosalind did not improve under medical treatment. She lay there with a sad, tired look, as if she didn't really care what happened to her. Her lower limbs were apparently paralyzed. Jerco told the doctor that she had been sick unto death like that before. The doctor shot a lot of stuff into her system. But Rosalind lay there heavy and fading like a felled tree.

The elevator operators looked in on her. The student one gave her a Bible with a little red ribbon marking the chapter in St. John's Gospel about the woman taken in adultery. He also wanted to pray for her recovery. Jerco wanted the prayer, but Rosalind said no. Her refusal shocked Ma Lawton, who believed in God's word.

The doctor stopped Rosalind from drinking beer. But Jerco slipped it in to her when Ma Lawton was not around. He said he couldn't refuse it to her when beer was the only thing she cared for. He had an expensive sweater. He pawned it. He also pawned their large suitcase. It was real leather and worth a bit of money.

One afternoon Jerco sat alone in the back room of the saloon and began to cry.

"I'd do anything. There ain't anything too low I wouldn't do to raise a little money," he said.

"Why don't you hock Rosalind's fur coat?" I suggested. "That'll give you enough money for a while."

"Gawd, no! I wouldn't touch none o' Rosalind's clothes. I jest kain't," he said. "She'll need them as soon as she's better."

"Well, you might try and find some sort of a job, then," I said.

"Me find a job? What kain I do? I ain't no good foh no job. I kain't work. I don't know how to ask for no job. I wouldn't know how. I wish I was a woman."

"Good God! Jerco," I said, "I don't see any way out for you but some sort of a job."

"What kain I do? What kain I do?" he whined. "I kain't do nothing. That's why I don't wanta hock Rosalind's fur coat. She'll need it soon as she's better. Rosalind's so wise about picking up good money. Just like that!" He snapped his fingers.

I left Jerco sitting there and went into the saloon to serve a customer a plate of corned beef and cabbage.

After lunch I thought I'd go up to see how Rosalind was making out. The door was slightly open, so I slipped in without knocking. I saw Jerco kneeling down by the open wardrobe and kissing the toe of one of her brown shoes. He started as he saw me, and looked queer kneeling there. It was a high old-fashioned wardrobe that Ma Lawton must have picked up at some sale. Rosalind's coat was hanging there, and it gave me a spooky feeling, for it looked so much more like the real Rosalind than the woman that was dozing there on the bed.

Her other clothes were hanging there, too. There were three gowns—a black silk, a glossy green satin, and a flimsy chiffon-like yellow thing. In a corner of the lowest shelf was a bundle of soiled champagne-colored silk stockings and in the other four pairs of shoes—one black velvet, one white kid, and another gold-finished. Jerco regarded the lot with dog-like affection.

"I wouldn't touch not one of her things until she's better," he said. "I'd sooner hock the shirt off mah back."

Which he was preparing to do. He had three expensive striped silk shirts, presents from Rosalind. He had just taken two out of the wardrobe and the other off his back, and made a parcel of them for old Greenbaum. . . . Rosalind woke up and murmured that she wanted some beer. . . .

A little later Jerco came to the saloon with the pail. He was shivering. His coat collar was turned up and fastened with a safety pin, for he only had an undershirt on.

"I don't know what I'd do if anything happens to Rosalind," he said. "I kain't live without her."

"Oh yes, you can," I said in a not very sympathetic tone. Jerco gave me such a reproachful pathetic look that I was sorry I said it.

The tall big fellow had turned into a scared, trembling baby. "You ought to buck up and hold yourself together," I told him. "Why, you ought to be game if you like Rosalind, and don't let her know you're down in the dumps."

"I'll try," he said. "She don't know how miserable I am. When I hooks up with a woman I treat her right, but I never let her know everything about me. Rosalind is an awful good woman. The straightest woman I ever had, honest."

I gave him a big glass of strong whisky.

Ma Lawton came in the saloon about nine o'clock that evening and said that Rosalind was dead. "I told Jerco we'd have to sell that theah coat to give the poah woman a decent fun'ral, an' he jest brokes down crying like a baby."

That night Ma Lawton slept in the kitchen and put Jerco in her little hall bedroom. He was all broken up. I took him up a pint of whisky.

"I'll nevah find another one like Rosalind," he said, "nevah!" He sat on an old black-framed chair in which a new yellow-varnished bottom had just been put. I put my hand on his shoulder and tried to cheer him up: "Buck up, old man. Never mind, you'll find somebody else." He shook his head. "Perhaps you didn't like the way me and Rosalind was living. But she was one naturally good woman, all good inside her."

I felt foolish and uncomfortable. "I always liked Rosalind, Jerco," I said, "and you, too. You were both awfully good scouts to me. I have nothing against her. I am nothing myself."

Jerco held my hand and whimpered: "Thank you, old top. Youse all right. Youse always been a regular fellar."

It was late, after two a. m. I went to bed. And, as usual, I slept soundly.

Ma Lawton was an early riser. She made excellent coffee and she gave the two elevator runners and another lodger, a porter who worked on Ellis Island, coffee and hot homemade biscuits every morning. The next morning she shook me abruptly out of my sleep.

"Ahm scared to death. Thar's moah tur'ble trouble. I kain't git in the barfroom and the hallway's all messy."

I jumped up, hauled on my pants, and went to the bathroom. A sickening purplish liquid coming from under the door had trickled down the hall toward the kitchen. I took Ma Lawton's rolling-pin and broke through the door.

Jerco had cut his throat and was lying against the bowl of the water-closet. Some empty coke papers were on the floor. And he sprawled there like a great black boar in a mess of blood.

A Farewell Feed

XVIII

Ray and Grant had found jobs on a freighter that was going down across the Pacific to Australia and from there to Europe. Ray had reached the point where going any further on the railroad was impossible. He had had enough to vomit up of Philadelphia and Baltimore, Pittsburgh and Washington. More than enough of the bar-to-bar camaraderie of railroad life.

And Agatha was acting wistfully. He knew what would be the inevitable outcome of meeting that subtle wistful yearning halfway. Soon he would become one of the contented hogs in the pigpen of Harlem, getting ready to litter little black piggies. If he could have felt about things as Jake, how different his life might have been! Just to hitch up for a short while and be irresponsible! But he and Agatha were slaves of the civilized tradition. . . . Harlem nigger strutting his stuff. . . . Harlem niggers! How often he had listened to those phrases, like jets of saliva, spewing from the lips of his work pals. They pursued, scared, and haunted him. He was afraid that some day the urge of the flesh and the mind's hankering after the pattern of respectable comfort might chase his high dreams out of him and deflate him to the contented animal that was a Harlem nigger strutting his stuff. "No happy-nigger strut for me," he would mutter, when the feeling for

Agatha worked like a fever in his flesh. He saw destiny working in her large, dream-sad eyes, filling them with the passive softness of resignation to life, and seeking to encompass and yoke him down as just one of the thousand niggers of Harlem. And he hated Agatha and, for escape, wrapped himself darkly in self-love.

Oh, he was scared of that long red steel cage whose rumbling rollers were eternally heavy-lipped upon shining, continent-circling rods. If he forced himself to stay longer he would bang right off his head. Once upon a time he used to wonder at that great body of people who worked in nice cages: bank clerks in steel-wire cages, others in wooden cages, salespeople behind counters, neat, dutiful, respectful, all of them. God! how could they carry it on from day to day and remain quietly obliging and sane? If the railroad had not been cacophonous and riotous enough to balance the dynamo roaring within him, he would have jumped it long ago.

Life burned in Ray perhaps more intensely than in Jake. Ray felt more and his range was wider and he could not be satisfied with the easy, simple things that sufficed for Jake. Sometimes he felt like a tree with roots in the soil and sap flowing out and whispering leaves drinking in the air. But he drank in more of life than he could distill into active animal living. Maybe that was why he felt he had to write.

He was a reservoir of that intense emotional energy so peculiar to his race. Life touched him emotionally in a thousand vivid ways. Maybe his own being was something of a touchstone of the general emotions of his race. Any upset—a terror-breathing, Negro-baiting headline in a metropolitan newspaper or the news of a human bonfire in Dixie—could make him miserable and despairingly despondent like an injured child. While any flash of beauty or wonder might lift him happier than a god. It was the simple, lovely touch of life that charmed and stirred him most. . . . The warm, rich-brown face of a Harlem girl seeking romance . . . a late wet night on Lenox Avenue, when all forms are soft-shadowy and the street gleams softly like a still, dim stream under the misted yellow lights. He remembered once the melancholy-comic notes of a "Blues" rising out of a Harlem basement before dawn. He was going to catch an early train and all that trip he was sweetly, deliciously happy humming the refrain and imagining what the interior of the little dark den he heard it in was like. "Blues" . . . melancholy-comic. That was the key to himself and to his race. That strange, child-like capacity for wistfulness-and-laughter. . . .

No wonder the whites, after five centuries of contact, could not understand his race. How could they when the instinct of comprehension had been cultivated out of them? No wonder they hated them, when out of their melancholy environment the blacks could create mad, contagious music and high laughter. . . .

Going away from Harlem. . . . Harlem! How terribly Ray could hate it sometimes. Its brutality, gang rowdyism, promiscuous thickness. Its hot desires. But, oh, the rich blood-red color of it! The warm accent of its composite voice, the fruitiness of its laughter, the trailing rhythm of its "blues" and the improvised surprises of its jazz. He had known happiness, too, in Harlem, joy that glowed gloriously upon him like the high-noon sunlight of his tropic island home.

How long would he be able to endure the life of a cabin boy or mess boy on a freighter? Jake had tried to dissuade him. "A seaman's life is no good, chappie, and it's easier to jump off a train in the field than offn a ship gwine across the pond."

"Maybe it's not so bad in the mess," suggested Ray.

" 'Deed it's worse foh mine, chappie. Stoking and A. B. S. is cleaner work than messing with raw meat and garbage. I never was in love with no kitchen job. And tha's why I ain't none crazy about the white man's chuchuing buggy."

Going away from Harlem. . . .

Jake invited Ray and Grant to a farewell feed, for which Billy Biasse was paying. Billy was a better pal for Jake than Zeddy. Jake was the only patron of his gambling house that Billy really chummed with. They made a good team. Their intimate interests never clashed. And it never once entered Jake's head that there was anything ugly about Billy's way of earning a living. Tales often came roundabout to Billy of patrons grumbling that "he was swindling poah hardworking niggers outa their wages." But he had never heard of Jake backbiting.

"The niggers am swindling themselves," Billy always retorted. "I runs a gambling place foh the gang and they pays becas they love to gamble. I plays even with them mahself. I ain't no miser hog like Nije Gridley."

Billy liked Jake because Jake played for the fun of the game and then quit. Gambling did not have a strangle hold upon him any more than dope or desire did. Jake took what he wanted of whatever he fancied and . . . kept going.

The feed was spread at Aunt Hattie's cookshop. Jake maintained that Aunt Hattie's was the best place for good eats in Harlem. A bottle of Scotch whisky was on the table and a bottle of gin.

While the boys sampled the fine cream tomato soup, Aunt Hattie bustled in and out of the kitchen, with a senile-fond look for Jake and an affectionate phrase, accompanied by a salacious lick of her tongue.

"Why, it's good and long sence you ain't been in reg'lar to see me, chile. Whar's you been keeping you'self?"

"Ain't been no reg'lar chile of Harlem sence I done jump on the white man's chu-chu," said Jake.

"And is you still on that theah business?" Aunt Hattie asked.

"I don't know ef I is and I don't know ef I ain't. Ise been laid off sick."

"Sick! Poah chile, and I nevah knowed so I could come off'ring you a li'l' chicken broth. You jest come heah and eats any time you wanta, whether youse got money or not."

Aunt Hattie shuffled back to the kitchen to pick the nicest piece of fried chicken for Jake.

"Always in luck, Jakey," said Billy. "It's no wonder you nevah see niggers in the bread line. And you'll nevah so long as theah's good black womens like Aunt Hattie in Harlem."

Jake poured Scotch for three.

"Gimme gin," said Billy.

Jake called to Aunt Hattie to bring her glass. "What you gwine to have, Auntie?"

"Same thing youse having, chile," replied Aunt Hattie.

"This heah stuff is from across the pond."

"Lemme taste it, then. Ef youse always so eye-filling drinking it, it might ginger up mah bones some."

"Well, here's to us, fellahs," cried Billy. "Let's hope that hard luck nevah turn our glasses down or shet the door of a saloon in our face."

Glasses clinked and Aunt Hattie touched Jake's twice and closed her eyes as with trembling hand she guzzled.

"You had better said, 'Le's hope that this heah Gawd's own don't shut the pub in our face'," replied Jake. "Prohibition is right under our tail."

Everybody laughed. . . . Ray bit into the tender leg of his fried chicken. The candied sweet potatoes were sweeter than honey to his palate.

"Drink up, fellahs," said Billy.

"Got to leave you, Harlem," Ray sang lightly. "Got to turn our backs on you."

"And our black moon on the Pennsy," added Jake.

"Tomorrow the big blue beautiful ocean," said Ray.

"You'll puke in it," Jake grinned devilishly. "Why not can the idea, chappie? The sea is hell and when you hits shore it's the same life all ovah."

"I guess you are right," replied Ray. "Goethe said the same thing in *Werther*."

"Who is that?" Jake asked.

"A German—"

"A boche?"

"Yes, a great one who made books instead of war. He was mighty and contented like a huge tame elephant. Genteel lovers of literature call that Olympian."

Jake gripped Ray's shoulder: "Chappie, I wish I was edjucated mahself."

"Christ! What for?" demanded Ray.

"Becaz I likes you." Like a black Pan out of the woods Jake looked into Ray's eyes with frank savage affection and Billy Biasse exclaimed:

"Lawdy in heaben" A li'l' foreign booze gwine turn you all soft?"

"Can't you like me just as well as you are?" asked Ray. "I can't feel any difference at all. If I was famous as Jack Johnson and rich as Madame Walker I'd prefer to have you as my friend than—President Wilson."

"Like bumbole you would!" retorted Jake. "Ef I was edjucated, I could understand things better and be proper-speaking like you is. . . . And I mighta helped mah li'l' sister to get edjucated, too (she must be a li'l' woman, now), and she would be nice-speaking like you' sweet brown, good enough foh you to hitch up with. Then we could all settle down and make money like edjucated people do, instead a you gwine off to throw you'self away on some lousy dinghy and me chasing around all the time lak a hungry dawg."

"Oh, you heart-breaking, slobbering nigger!" cried Billy Biasse. "That's the stuff youse got tuck away there under your tough black hide."

"Muzzle you' mouf," retorted Jake. "Sure Ise human. I ain't no lonesome wolf lak you is."

"A wolf is all right ef he knows the jungle."

"The fact is, Jake," Ray said, "I don't know what I'll do with my little education. I wonder sometimes if I could get rid of it and go and lose myself in some savage culture in the jungles of Africa. I am a misfit—as the doctors who dole out newspaper advice to the well-fit might say—a misfit with my little education and constant dreaming, when I should be getting the nightmare habit to hog in a whole lot of dough like everybody else in this country. Would you like to be educated to be like me?"

"If I had your edjucation I wouldn't be slinging no hash on the white man's chu-chu," Jake responded.

"Nobody knows, Jake. Anyway, you're happier than I as you are. The more I learn the less I understand and love life. All the learning in this world can't answer this little question, Why are we living?"

"Why, becaz Gawd wants us to, chappie," said Billy Biasse.

"Come on le's all go to Uncle Doc's," said Jake, "and finish the night with a li'l' sweet jazzing. This is you last night, chappie. Make the most of it, foh there ain't no jazzing like Harlem jazzing over the other side."

They went to Uncle Doc's, where they drank many ceremonious rounds. Later they went to Leroy's Cabaret. . . .

The next afternoon the freighter left with Ray signed on as a mess boy.

THIRD PART

Spring in Harlem
XIX

The lovely trees of Seventh Avenue were a vivid flame-green. Children, lightly clad, skipped on the pavement. Light open coats prevailed and the smooth bare throats of brown girls were a token as charming as the first pussy-willows. Far and high over all, the sky was a grand blue benediction, and beneath it the wonderful air of New York tasted like fine dry champagne.

Jake loitered along Seventh Avenue. Crossing to Lenox, he lazied northward and over the One Hundred and Forty-ninth Street bridge into the near neighborhood of the Bronx. Here, just a step from compactly-built, teeming Harlem, were frame houses and open lots and people digging. A colored couple dawdled by, their arms fondly caressing each other's hips. A white man forking a bit of ground stopped and stared expressively after them.

Jake sat down upon a mound thick-covered with dandelions. They glittered in the sun away down to the rear of a rusty-gray shack. They filled all the green spaces. Oh, the common little things were glorious there under the sun in the tender spring grass. Oh, sweet to be alive in that sun beneath that sky! And to be in love—even for one hour of such rare hours! One day! One night! Somebody with spring charm, like a dandelion, seasonal and haunting like a lovely dream that never repeats itself. . . . There are hours, there are days, and nights whose sheer beauty overwhelm us with happiness, that we seek to make even more beautiful by comparing them with rare human contacts. . . . It was a day like this we romped in the grass . . . a night as soft and intimate as this on which we forgot the world and ourselves. . . . Hours of pagan abandon, celebrating ourselves. . . .

And Jake felt as all men who love love for love's sake can feel. He thought of the surging of desire in his boy's body and of his curious pure nectarine beginnings, without pain, without disgust, down home in Virginia. Of his adolescent breaking-through when the fever-and-pain of passion gave him a wonderful strange-sweet taste of love that he had never known again. Of rude contacts and swift satisfactions in Norfolk, Baltimore, and other coast ports. . . . Havre. . . . The West India Dock districts of London. . . .

"Only that cute heart-breaking brown of the Baltimore," he mused. "A day like this sure feels like her. Didn't even get her name. O Lawdy! what a night that theah night was. Her and I could sure make a hallelujah picnic outa a day like this." . . .

Jake and Billy Biasse, leaving Dixie Red's pool-room together, shuffled into a big excited ring of people at the angle of Fifth Avenue and One Hundred and Thirty-third Street. In the ring three bad actors were staging a rough play—a yellow youth, a chocolate youth, and a brown girl.

The girl had worked herself up to the highest pitch of obscene frenzy and was sicking the dark strutter on to the yellow with all the filthiest phrases at her command. The two fellows pranced round, menacing each other with comic gestures.

"Why, ef it ain't Yaller Prince!" said Jake.

"Him sure enough," responded Billy Biasse. "Guess him done laid off from that black gal why she's shooting her stinking mouth off at him."

"Is she one of his producing goods?"

"She was. But I hcard she done beat up anether gal of hisn—a fair-brown that useta hand over moh change than her and Yaller turn' her loose foh it." . . .

"You lowest-down face-artist!" the girl shrieked at Yaller Prince. "I'll bawl it out so all a Harlem kain know what you is." And ravished by the fact that she was humiliating her one-time lover, she gesticulated wildly.

"Hit him, Obadiah!" she yelled to the chocolate chap. "Hit him I tell you. Beat his mug up foh him, beat his mug and bleed his mouf." Over and over again she yelled: "Bleed his mouf!" As if that was the thing in Yaller Prince she had desired most. For it she had given herself up to the most unthinkable acts of degradation. Nothing had been impossible to do. And now she would cut and bruise and bleed that mouth that had once loved her so well so that he should not smile upon her rivals for many a day.

"Two-faced yaller nigger, you does ebery low-down thing, but you nevah done a lick of work in you lifetime. Show him, Obadiah. Beat his face and bleed his mouf."

"Yaller nigger," cried the extremely bandy-legged and grim-faced Obadiah, "Ise gwine kick you pants."

"I ain't scared a you, black buzzard," Yaller Prince replied in a thin, breathless voice, and down he went on his back, no one knowing whether he fell or was tripped up. Obadiah lifted a bottle and swung it down upon his opponent. Yaller Prince moaned and blood bubbled from his nose and his mouth.

"He's a sweet-back, all right, but he ain't a strong one," said some one in the crowd. The police had been conspicuously absent during the fracas, but now a baton tap-tapped upon the pavement and two of them hurried up. The crowd melted away.

Jake had pulled Yaller Prince against the wall and squatted to rest the bleeding head against his knee.

"What's matter here now? What's matter?" the first policeman, with revolver drawn, asked harshly.

"Nigger done beat this one up and gone away from heah, tha's whatsmat," said Billy Biasse.

They carried Yaller Prince into a drugstore for first aid, and the policeman telephoned for an ambulance. . . .

"We gotta look out foh him in hospital. He was a pretty good skate for a sweetman," Billy Biasse said.

"Poor Yaller!" Jake, shaking his head, commented; "it's a bad business."

"He's plumb crazy gwine around without a gun when he's a-playing that theah game," said Billy, "with all these cut-thwoat niggers in Harlem ready to carve up one another foh a li'l' insisnificant humpy."

"It's the same ole life everywhere," responded Jake. "In white man's town or nigger town. Same bloody-sweet life across the pond. I done lived through the same blood-battling foh womens ovah theah in London. Between white and white and between white and black. Done see it in the froggies' country, too. A mess o' fat-headed white soldiers them was knocked off by apaches. Don't tell *me* about cut-thwoat niggers in Harlem. The whole wul' is bloody-crazy—"

"But Harlem is the craziest place foh that, I bet you, boh," Billy laughed richly. "The stuff it gives the niggers brain-fevah, so far as I see, and this heah wolf has got a big-long horeezon. Wese too thick together in Harlem. Wese all just lumped together without a chanst to choose and so we nacherally hate one another. It's nothing to wonder that you' buddy Ray done runned away from it. Why, jest the other night I witnessed a nasty stroke. You know that spade prof that's always there on the Avenue handing out the big stuff about niggers and their rights and the wul' and bolschism. . . . He was passing by the pool-room with a bunch o' books when a bad nigger jest lunges out and socks him bif! in the jaw. The poah frightened prof started picking up his books without a word said, so I ups and asks the boxer what was the meaning o' that pass. He laughed and asked me ef I really wanted to know, and before he could squint I landed him one in the eye and pulled mah gun on him. I chased him off that corner all right. I tell you, boh, Harlem is lousy with crazy-bad niggers, as tough as Hell's Kitchen, and I always travel with mah gun ready."

"And ef all the niggers did as you does," said Jake, "theah'd be a regular gun-toting army of us up here in the haht of the white man's city. . . . Guess ef a man stahts gunning after you and means to git you he will someways—"

"But you might git him fierst, too, boh, ef youse in luck."

"I mean ef you don't know he's gunning after you," said Jake. "I don't carry no weapons nonetall, but mah two long hands."

"Youse a punk customer, then, I tell you," declared Billy Biasse, "and no real buddy o' mine. Ise got a A number one little barker I'll give it to you. You kain't lay you'self wide open lak thataways in this heah burg. No boh!"

Jake went home alone in a mood different from the lyrical feelings that had fevered his blood among the dandelions. "Niggers fixing to slice one another's throats. Always fighting. Got to fight if youse a man. It ain't because Yaller was a p-i. . . . It coulda been me or anybody else. Wese too close and thick in Harlem. Need some moh fresh air between us. . . . Hitting out at a edjucated nigger minding his own business and without a word said. . . . Guess Billy is right toting his silent dawg around with him. He's gotta, though, when he's running a gambling joint. All the same, I gambles mahself and you nevah know when niggers am gwineta git crazy-mad. Guess I'll take the li'l' dawg offn Billy, all right. It ain't costing me nothing." . . .

In the late afternoon he lingered along Seventh Avenue in a new nigger-brown suit. The fine gray English suit was no longer service-able for parade. The American suit did not fit him so well. Jake saw and felt it. . . . The only thing he liked better about the American suit was the pantaloons made to wear with a belt. And the two hip pockets. If you have the American habit of carrying your face-cloth on the hip instead of sticking it up in your breast pocket like a funny decoration, and if, like Billy Biasse, you're accustomed to toting some steely thing, what is handier than two hip pockets?

Except for that, Jake had learned to prefer the English cut of clothes. Such first-rate tweed stuff, and so cheap and durable com-pared with American clothes! Jake knew nothing of tariff laws and naïvely wondered why the English did not spread their fine cloth all over the American clothes market. . . . He worked up his shoulders in his nigger-brown coat. It didn't feel right, didn't hang so well. There was something a little too chic in American clothes. Not nearly as awful as French, though, Jake horse-laughed, vividly remembering the popular French styles. Broad-pleated, long-waisted, tight-bottomed pants and close-waisted coats whose breast pockets stick out their little comic signs of color. . . . Better color as a savage wears it, or none at all, instead of the Frenchman's peeking bit. The French must consider the average bantam male killing handsome, and so they make clothes to emphasize all the angular elevated rounded and pendulated parts of the anatomy. . . .

The broad pavements of Seventh Avenue were colorful with promenaders. Brown babies in white carriages pushed by little black brothers wearing nice sailor suits. All the various and varying pigmentation of the human race were assembled there: dim brown, clear brown, rich brown, chestnut, copper, yellow, near-white, mahogany, and gleaming anthracite. Charming brown matrons, proud yellow matrons, dark nursemaids pulled a zigzag course by their restive little charges. . . .

And the elegant strutters in faultless spats; West Indians, carrying canes and wearing trousers of a different pattern from their coats and vests, drawing sharp comments from their Afro-Yank rivals.

Jake mentally noted: "A dickty gang sure as Harlem is black, but—"

The girls passed by in bright batches of color, according to station and calling. High class, menial class, and the big trading class, flaunting a front of chiffon-soft colors framed in light coats, seizing the fashion of the day to stage a lovely leg show and spilling along the Avenue the perfume of Djer-kiss, Fougère, and Brown Skin.

"These heah New York gals kain most sartainly wear some moh clothes," thought Jake, "jest as nifty as them French gals." . . .

Twilight was enveloping the Belt, merging its life into a soft blue-black symphony. . . . The animation subsided into a moment's pause, a muffled, tremulous soul-stealing note . . . then electric lights flared everywhere, flooding the scene with dazzling gold.

Jake went to Aunt Hattie's to feed. Billy Biasse was there and a gang of longshoremen who had boozed and fed and were boozing again and, touched by the tender spring night, were swapping love stories and singing:

"Back home in Dixie is a brown gal there,
Back home in Dixie is a brown gal there,

Back home in Dixie is a brown gal there,
Back home in Dixie I was bawn in.

"Back home in Dixie is a gal I know,
Back home in Dixie is a gal I know,
Back home in Dixie is a gal I know,
   And I wonder what nigger is saying to her a bootiful good
      mawnin.'."

A red-brown West Indian among them volunteered to sing a
Port-of-Spain song. It immortalized the drowning of a
young black sailor. It was made up by the bawdy colored
girls of the port, with whom the deceased had been a favorite, and became very popular among the stevedores and
sailors of the island.

"Ring the bell again,
Ring the bell again,
Ring the bell again,
But the sharks won't puke him up.
Oh, ring the bell again.

"Empty is you' room,
Empty is you' room,
Empty is you' room,
But you find one in the sea.
Oh, empty is you' room.

"Ring the bell again,
Ring the bell again,
Ring the bell again,
But we know who feel the pain.
Oh, ring the bell again."

The song was curious, like so many Negro songs of its kind, for
the strange strengthening of its wistful melody by a happy rhythm that
was suitable for dancing.

Aunt Hattie, sitting on a low chair, was swaying to the music and
licking her lips, her wrinkled features wearing an expression of ecstatic delight. Billy Biasse offered to stand a bottle of gin. Jake said he
would also sing a sailor song he had picked up in Limehouse. And
so he sang the chanty of Bullocky Bill who went up to town to see a
fair young maiden. But he could not remember most of the words,

therefore Bullocky Bill cannot be presented here. But Jake was bois-
terously applauded for the scraps of it that he rendered.

The singing finished, Jake confided to Billy: "I sure don't feel lak
spending a lonesome night this heah mahvelous night."

"Ain't nobody evah lonely in Harlem that don't wanta be," retorted
Billy. "Even yours truly lone Wolf ain't nevah lonesome."

"But I want something as mahvelous as mah feelings."

Billy laughed and fingered his kinks: "Harlem has got the right
stuff, boh, for all feelings."

"Youse right enough," Jake agreed, and fell into a reverie of full
brown mouth and mischievous brown eyes all composing a perfect
whole for his dark-brown delight.

"You wanta take a turn down the Congo?" asked Billy.

"Ah no."

"Rose ain't there no moh."

Rose had stepped up a little higher in her profession and had been
engaged to tour the West in a Negro company.

"All the same, I don't feel like the Congo tonight," said Jake. "Le's
go to Sheba Palace and jazz around a little."

Sheba Palace was an immense hall that was entirely monopolized
for the amusements of the common workaday Negroes of the Belt.
Longshoremen, kitchen-workers, laundresses, and W. C. tenders—
all gravitated to the Sheba Palace, while the upper class of servitors—
bell-boys, butlers, some railroad workers and waiters, waitresses and
maids of all sorts—patronized the Casino and those dancings that
were given under the auspices of the churches.

The walls of Sheba Palace were painted with garish gold, and tables
and chairs were screaming green. There were green benches also
lined round the vast dancing space. The music stopped with an
abrupt clash just as Jake entered. Couples and groups were drinking
at tables. Deftly, quickly the waiters slipped a way through the tables
to serve and collect the money before the next dance. . . . Little
white-filled glasses, little yellow-filled glasses, general guzzling of gin
and whisky. Little saucy brown lips, rouged maroon, sucking up iced
crème de menthe through straws, and many were sipping the golden
Virginia Dare, in those days the favorite wine of the Belt. On the
green benches couples lounged, sprawled, and, with the juicy love of
spring and the liquid of Bacchus mingled in fascinating white eyes
curious in their dark frames, apparently oblivious of everything outside of themselves, were loving in every way but . . .

The orchestra was tuning up. . . . The first notes fell out like a
general clapping for merrymaking and chased the dancers running,

sliding, shuffling, trotting to the floor. Little girls energetically chewing Spearmint and showing all their teeth dashed out on the floor and started shivering amorously, itching for their partners to come. Some lads were quickly on their feet, grinning gayly and improvising new steps with snapping of fingers while their girls were sucking up the last of their crème de menthe. The floor was large and smooth enough for anything.

They had a new song-and-dance at the Sheba and the black fellows were playing it with *éclat*.

> Brown gal crying on the corner,
>   Yaller gal done stole her candy,
> Buy him spats and feed him cream,
>   Keep him strutting fine and dandy.
>
>   Tell me, pa-pa, Ise you' ma-ma,
>   Yaller gal can't make you fall,
>   For Ise got some loving pa-pa
>   Yaller gal ain't got atall.

"Tell me, pa-pa, Ise you' ma-ma." The black players grinned and swayed and let the music go with all their might. The yellow in the music must have stood out in their imagination like a challenge, conveying a sense of that primitive, ancient, eternal, inexplicable antagonism in the color taboo of sex and society. The dark dancers picked up the refrain and jazzed and shouted with delirious joy, "Tell me, pa-pa, Ise you' ma-ma." The handful of yellow dancers in the crowd were even more abandoned to the spirit of the song. "White," "green," or "red" in place of "yaller" might have likewise touched the same deep-sounding, primitive chord. . . .

> Yaller gal sure wants mah pa-pa,
>   But mah chocolate turns her down,
> 'Cause he knows there ain't no loving
>   Sweeter than his loving brown.
>
>   Tell me, pa-pa, Ise you' ma-ma,
>   Yaller gal can't make you fall,
>   For Ise got some loving pa-pa
>   Yaller gal ain't got atall.

Jake was doing his dog with a tall, shapely quadroon girl when, glancing up at the balcony, he spied the little brown that he had entirely given over as lost. She was sitting at a table while "Tell me pa-pa" was tickling everybody to the uncontrollable point—she was sitting with her legs crossed and well exposed, and, with the aid of the mirror attached to her vanity case, was saucily and nonchalantly powdering her nose.

The quadroon girl nearly fell as Jake, without a word of explanation, dropped her in the midst of a long slide and, dashing across the floor, bounded up the stairs.

"Hello, sweetness! What youse doing here?"

The girl started and knocked over a glass of whisky on the floor: "O my Gawd! it's mah heartbreaking daddy! Where was you all this time?"

Jake drew a chair up beside her, but she jumped up: "Lawdy, no! Le's get outa here quick, 'cause Ise got somebody with me and now I don't want see him no moh."

" 'Sawright, I kain take care of mahself," said Jake.

"Oh, honey, no! I don't want no trouble and he's a bad actor, that nigger. See, I done break his glass o' whisky and tha's bad luck. Him's just theah in the lav'try. Come quick. I don't want him to ketch us."

And the flustered little brown heart hustled Jake down the stairs and out of the Sheba Palace.

"Tell me, pa-pa, Ise you' ma-ma . . ."

The black shouting chorus pursued them outside.

"There ain't no yaller gal gwine get mah honey daddy thisanight."
She took Jake's arm and cuddled up against his side.

"Aw no, sweetness. I was dogging it with one and jest drops her flat when I seen you."

"And there ain't no nigger in the wul' I wouldn't ditch foh you, daddy. O Lawdy! How Ise been crazy longing to meet you again."

Felice

XX

"Whar's we gwine?" Jake asked.

They had walked down Madison Avenue, turned on One Hundred and Thirtieth Street, passing the solid gray-grim mass of the whites' Presbyterian church, and were under the timidly whispering trees of the decorously silent and distinguished Block Beautiful. . . . The whites had not evacuated that block yet. The black invasion was threatening it from One Hundred and Thirty-first Street, from Fifth Avenue, even from behind in One Hundred and Twenty-ninth

Street. But desperate, frightened, blanch-faced, the ancient sepulchral Respectability held on. And giving them moral courage, the Presbyterian church frowned on the corner like a fortress against the invasion. The Block Beautiful was worth a struggle. With its charming green lawns and quaint white-fronted houses, it preserved the most Arcadian atmosphere in all New York. When there was a flat to let in that block, you would have to rubber-neck terribly before you saw in the corner of a window-pane a neat little sign worded, Vacancy. But groups of loud-laughing-and-acting black swains and their sweethearts had started in using the block for their afternoon promenade. That was the limit: the desecrating of that atmosphere by black love in the very shadow of the gray, gaunt Protestant church! The Ancient Respectability was getting ready to flee. . . .

The beautiful block was fast asleep. Up in the branches the little elfin green things were barely whispering. The Protestant church was softened to a shadow. The atmosphere was perfect, the moment sweet for something sacred.

The burning little brownskin cuddled up against Jake's warm tall person: "Kiss me, daddy," she said. He folded her closely to him and caressed her. . . .

"But whar was you all this tur'bly long time?" demanded Jake.

Light-heartedly, she frisky like a kitten, they sauntered along Seventh Avenue, far from the rough environment of Sheba Palace.

"Why, daddy, I waited foh you all that day after you went away and all that night! Oh, I had a heart-break on foh you, I was so tur'bly disappointed. I nev' been so crazy yet about no man. Why didn't you come back, honey?"

Jake felt foolish, remembering why. He said that shortly after leaving her he had discovered the money and the note. He had met some of his buddies of his company who had plenty of money, and they all went celebrating until that night, and by then he had forgotten the street.

"Mah poor daddy!"

"Even you' name, sweetness, I didn't know. Ise Jake Brown—Jake for ev'body. What is you', sweetness?"

"They calls me Felice."

"Felice. . . . But I didn't fohget the cabaret nonatall. And I was back theah hunting foh you that very night and many moh after, but I nevah finds you. Where was you?"

"Why, honey, I don't lives in cabarets all mah nights 'cause Ise got to work. Furthermore, I done went away that next week to Palm Beach—"

"Palm Beach! What foh?"

"Work of course. What you think? You done brokes mah heart in one mahvelous night and neveh returns foh moh. And I was jest right down sick and tiahd of Harlem. So I went away to work. I always work. . . . I know what youse thinking, honey, but I ain't in the reg'lar business. 'Cause Ise a funny gal. I kain't go with a fellah ef I don't like him some. And ef he kain make me like him enough I won't take nothing off him and ef he kain make me fall the real way, I guess I'd work like a wop for him."

"Youse the baby I been waiting foh all along," said Jake. "I knowed you was the goods."

"Where is we gwine, daddy?"

"Ise got a swell room, sweetness, up in 'Fortiet' Street whar all them dicky shines live."

"But kain you take me there?"

"Sure thing, baby. Ain't no nigger renting a room in Harlem whar he kain't have his li'l company."

"Oh, goody, goody, honey-stick!"

Jake took Felice home to his room. She was delighted with it. It was neat and orderly.

"Your landlady must be one of them proper persons," she remarked. "How did you find such a nice place way up here?"

"A chappie named Ray got it foh me when I was sick—"

"O Lawdy! was it serious? Did they all take good care a you?"

"It wasn't nothing much and the fellahs was all awful good spohts, especially Ray."

"Who is this heah Ray?"

Jake told her. She smoothed out the counterpane on the bed, making a mental note that it was just right for two. She admired the geraniums in the window that looked on the large court.

"These heah new homes foh niggers am sure nice," she commented.

She looked behind the curtain where his clothes were hanging and remarked his old English suit. Then she regarded archly his new nigger-brown rig-out.

"You was moh illegant in that other, but I likes you in this all the same."

Jake laughed. "Everything's gotta wear out some day."

Felice hung round his neck, twiddling her pretty legs.

He held her as you might hold a child and she ruffled his thick mat of hair and buried her face in it. She wriggled down with a little scream:

"Oh, I gotta go get mah bag!"

"I'll come along with you," said Jake.

"No, lemme go alone. I kain manage better by mahself."

"But suppose that nigger is waiting theah foh you? You better lemme come along."

"No, honey, I done figure he's waiting still in Sheba Palace, or boozing. Him and some friends was all drinking befoh and he was kinder full. Ise sure he ain't gone home. Anyway, I kain manage by mahself all right, but ef you comes along and we runs into him— No, honey, you stays right here. I don't want messing up in no blood-baff. Theah's too much a that in Harlem."

They compromised, Felice agreeing that Jake should accompany her to the corner of Seventh Avenue and One Hundred and Thirty-fifth Street and wait for her there. She had not the faintest twinge of conscience herself. She had met the male that she preferred and gone with him, leaving the one that she was merely makeshifting with. It was a very simple and natural thing to her. There was nothing mean about it. She was too nice to be mean. However, she was aware that in her world women scratched and bit into each other's flesh and men razored and gunned at each other over such things. . . .

Felice recalled one memorable afternoon when two West Indian women went for each other in the back yard of a house in One Hundred and Thirty-second Street. One was a laundress, a whopping brown woman who had come to New York from Colon, and the other was a country girl, a buxom Negress from Jamaica. They were quarreling over a vain black bantam, one of the breed that delight in women's scratching over them. The laundress had sent for him to come over from the Canal Zone to New York. They had lived together there and she had kept him, making money in all the ways that a gay and easy woman can on the Canal Zone. But now the laundress bemoaned the fact that "sence mah man come to New Yawk, him jest gone back on me in the queerest way you can imagine."

Her man, in turn, blamed the situation upon her, said she was too aggressive and mannish and had harried the energy out of him. But the other girl seemed to endow him again with virility. . . . After keeping him in Panama and bringing him to New York, the laundress hesitated about turning her male loose in Harlem, although he was apparently of no more value to her. But his rejuvenating experience with the younger girl had infuriated the laundress. A sister worker from Alabama, to whom she had confided her secret tragedy, had hinted: "Lawdy! sistah, that sure sounds phony-like. Mebbe you' man is jest playing 'possum with you." And the laundress was crazy with suspicion and jealousy and a feeling for revenge. She challenged her rival to fight the affair out. They were all living in the same house. . . .

Felice also lived in that house. And one afternoon she was startled by another girl from an adjoining room pounding on her door and shrieking: "Open foh the love of Jesus! . . . Theah's sweet hell playing in the back yard."

The girls rushed to the window and saw the two black women squaring off at each other down in the back yard. They were stark naked.

After the challenge, the women had decided to fight with their clothes off. An old custom, perhaps a survival of African tribalism, had been imported from some remote West Indian hillside into a New York back yard. Perhaps, the laundress had thought, that with her heavy and powerful limbs she could easily get her rival down and sit on her, mauling her properly. But the black girl was as nimble as a wild goat. She dodged away from the laundress who was trying to get ahold of her big bush of hair, and suddenly sailing fullfront into her, she seized the laundress, shoulder and neck, and butted her twice on the forehead as only a rough West Indian country girl can butt. The laundress staggered backward, groggy, into a bundle of old carpets. But she rallied and came back at the grinning Negress again. The laundress had never learned the brutal art of butting. The girl bounded up at her forehead with another well-aimed butt and sent her reeling flop on her back among the carpets. The girl planted her knees upon the laundress's high chest and wrung her hair.

"You don't know me, but I'll make you remember me foreber. I'll beat you' mug ugly. There!" Bam! Bam! She slapped the laundress's face.

"Git off mah stomach, nigger gal, and leave me in peace," the laundress panted. The entire lodging-house was in a sweet fever over the event. Those lodgers whose windows gave on the street had crowded into their neighbors' rear rooms and some had descended into the basement for a close-up view. Apprised of the naked exhibition, the landlord hurried in from the corner saloon and threatened the combatants with the police. But there was nothing to do. The affair was settled and the women had already put their shifts on.

The women lodgers cackled gayly over the novel staging of the fight.

"It sure is better to disrobe like that, befoh battling," one declared. "It turn you' hands and laigs loose for action."

"And saves you' clothes being ripped into ribbons," said another.

A hen-fight was more fun than a cock-fight, thought Felice, as she hastily threw her things into her bag. The hens pluck feathers, but they never wring necks like the cocks.

And Jake. Standing on the corner, he waited, restive, nervous. But, unlike Felice, his thought was not touched by the faintest fear of a blood battle. His mind was a circle containing the girl and himself only, making a thousand plans of the joys they would create together. She was a prize to hold. Had slipped through his fingers once, but he wasn't ever going to lose her again. That little model of warm brown flesh. Each human body has its own peculiar rhythm, shallow or deep or profound. Transient rhythms that touch and pass you, unrememberable, and rhythms unforgetable. Imperial rhythms whose vivid splendor blinds your sight and destroys your taste for lesser ones.

Jake possessed a sure instinct for the right rhythm. He was connoisseur enough. But although he had tasted such a varied many, he was not raw animal enough to be undiscriminating, nor civilized enough to be cynical. . . .

Felice came hurrying as much as she could along One Hundred and Thirty-fifth Street, bumping a cumbersome portmanteau on the pavement and holding up one unruly lemon-bright silk stocking with her left hand. Jake took the bag from her. They went into a delicatessen store and bought a small cold chicken, ham, mustard, olives, and bread. They stopped in a sweet shop and bought a box of chocolate-and-vanilla ice-cream and cake. Felice also took a box of chocolate candy. Their last halt was at a United Cigar Store, where Jake stocked his pockets with a half a dozen packets of Camels. . . .

Felice had just slipped out of her charming strawberry frock when her hands flew down to her pretty brown leg. "O Gawd! I done fohget something!" she cried in a tone that intimated something very precious.

"What's it then?" demanded Jake.

"It's mah luck," she said. "It's the fierst thing that was gived to me when I was born. Mah gran'ma gived it and I wears it always foh good luck."

This lucky charm was an old plaited necklace, leathery in appearance, with a large, antique blue bead attached to it, that Felice's grandmother (who had superintended her coming into the world) had given to her immediately after that event. Her grandmother had dipped the necklace into the first water that Felice was washed in. Felice had religiously worn her charm around her neck all during her childhood. But since she was grown to ripe girlhood and low-cut frocks were the fashion and she loved them so much, she had transferred the unsightly necklace from her throat to her leg. But before going to the Sheba Palace she had unhooked the thing. And she had forgotten it there in the closet, hanging by a little nail against the wash-bowl.

"I gotta go get it," she said.

"Aw no, you won't bother," drawled Jake. And he drew the little agitated brown body to him and quieted it. "It was good luck you fohget it, sweetness, for it made us find one another."

"Something to that, daddy," Felice said, and her mouth touched his mouth.

They wove an atmosphere of dreams around them and were lost in it for a week. Felice asked the landlady to let her use the kitchen to cook their meals at home. They loitered over the wide field and lay in the sweet grass of Van Cortlandt Park. They went to the Negro Picture Theater and held each other's hand, gazing in raptures at the crude pictures. It was odd that all these cinematic pictures about the blacks were a broad burlesque of their home and love life. These colored screen actors were all dressed up in expensive evening clothes, with automobiles, and menials, to imitate white society people. They laughed at themselves in such roles and the laughter was good on the screen. They pranced and grinned like good-nigger servants, who know that "mas'r" and "missus," intent on being amused, are watching their antics from an upper window. It was quite a little funny and the audience enjoyed it. Maybe that was the stuff the Black Belt wanted.

The Gift that Billy Gave

XXI

"We gotta celebrate to-night," said Felice when Saturday came round again. Jake agreed to do anything she wanted. Monday they would have to think of working. He wanted to dine at Aunt Hattie's, but Felice preferred a "niftier" place. So they dined at the Nile Queen restaurant on Seventh Avenue. After dinner they subwayed down to Broadway. They bought tickets for the nigger heaven of a theater, whence they watched high-class people make luxurious love on the screen. They enjoyed the exhibition. There is no better angle from which one can look down on a motion picture than that of the nigger heaven.

They returned to Harlem after the show in a mood to celebrate until morning. Should they go to Sheba Palace where chance had been so good to them, or to a cabaret? Sentiment was in favor of Sheba Palace but her love of the chic and novel inclined Felice toward an attractive new Jewish-owned Negro cabaret. She had never been there and could not go under happier circumstances.

The cabaret was a challenge to any other in Harlem. There were one or two cabarets in the Belt that were distinguished for their impolite attitude toward the average Negro customer, who could not afford to swill expensive drinks. He was pushed off into a corner and neglected, while the best seats and service were reserved for notorious little gangs of white champagne-guzzlers from downtown.

The new cabaret specialized in winning the good will of the average blacks and the approval of the fashionable set of the Belt. The owner had obtained a college-bred Negro to be manager, and the cashier was a genteel mulatto girl. On the opening night the management had sent out special invitations to the high lights of the Negro theatrical world and free champagne had been served to them. The new cabaret was also drawing nightly a crowd of white pleasure-seekers from downtown. The war was just ended and people were hungry for any amusements that were different from the stale stock things.

Besides its spacious floor, ladies' room, gentlemen's room and coat-room, the new cabaret had a bar with stools, where men could get together away from their women for a quick drink and a little stag conversation. The bar was a paying innovation. The old-line cabarets were falling back before their formidable rival. . . .

The fashionable Belt was enjoying itself there on this night. The press, theatrical, and music world were represented. Madame Mulberry was there wearing peacock blue with patches of yellow. Madame Mulberry was a famous black beauty in the days when Fifty-third Street was the hub of fashionable Negro life. They called her then, Brown Glory. She was the wife of Dick Mulberry, a promoter of Negro shows. She had no talent for the stage herself, but she knew all the celebrated stage people of her race. She always gossiped reminiscently of Bert Williams, George Walker and Aida Overton Walker, Anita Patti Brown and Cole and Johnson.

With Madame Mulberry sat Maunie Whitewing with a dapper cocoa-brown youth by her side, who was very much pleased by his own person and the high circle to which it gained him admission. Maunie was married to a nationally-known Negro artist, who lived simply and quietly. But Maunie was notorious among the scandal sets of Brooklyn, New York, and Washington. She was always creating scandals wherever she went, gallivanting around with improper persons at improper places, such as this new cabaret. Maunie's beauty was Egyptian in its exoticism and she dared to do things in the manner of ancient courtesans. Dignified colored matrons frowned upon her ways, but they had to invite her to their homes, nevertheless, when they asked her husband. But Maunie seldom went.

The sports editor of *Colored Life* was also there, with a prominent

Negro pianist. It was rumored that Bert Williams might drop in after midnight. Madame Mulberry was certain he would.

James Reese Europe, the famous master of jazz, was among a group of white admirers. He had just returned from France, full of honors, with his celebrated band. New York had acclaimed him and America was ready to applaud. . . . That was his last appearance in a Harlem cabaret before his heart was shot out during a performance in Boston by a savage buck of his race. . . .

Prohibition was on the threshold of the country and drinking was becoming a luxury, but all the joy-pacers of the Belt who adore the novel and the fashionable and had a dollar to burn had come together in a body to fill the new cabaret.

The owner of the cabaret knew that Negro people, like his people, love the pageantry of life, the expensive, the fine, the striking, the showy, the trumpet, the blare—sumptuous settings and luxurious surroundings. And so he had assembled his guests under an enchanting-blue ceiling of brilliant chandeliers and a dome of artificial roses bowered among green leaves. Great mirrors reflected the variegated colors and poses. Shaded, multi-colored side-lights glowed softly along the golden walls.

It was a scene of blazing color. Soft, barbaric, burning, savage, clashing, planless colors—all rioting together in wonderful harmony. There is no human sight so rich as an assembly of Negroes ranging from lacquer black through brown to cream, decked out in their ceremonial finery. Negroes are like trees. They wear all colors naturally. And Felice, rouged to a ravishing maroon, and wearing a close-fitting, chrome-orange frock and cork-brown slippers, just melted into the scene.

They were dancing as Felice entered and she led Jake right along into it.

"Tell me, pa-pa, Ise you ma-ma . . ."

Every cabaret and dancing-hall was playing it. It was the tune for the season. It had carried over from winter into spring and was still the favorite. Oh, ma-ma! Oh, pa-pa!

The dancing stopped. . . . A brief interval and a dwarfish, shiny black man wearing a red-brown suit, with kinks straightened and severely plastered down in the Afro-American manner, walked into the center of the floor and began singing. He had a massive mouth, which he opened wide, and a profoundly big and quite good voice came out of it.

"I'm so doggone fed up, I don't know what to do.
Can't find a pal that's constant, can't find a gal that's true.
But I ain't gwine to worry 'cause mah buddy was a ham;
Ain't gwine to cut mah throat 'cause mah gal ain't worf a damn.
Ise got the blues all ovah, the coal-black biting blues,
Like a prowling tom-cat that's got the low-down mews.

'I'm gwine to lay me in a good supply a gin,
Foh gunning is a crime, but drinking ain't no sin.
I won't do a crazy deed 'cause of a two-faced pal,
Ain't gwineta break mah heart ovah a no-'count gal
Ise got the blues all ovah, the coal-black biting blues,
Like a prowling tom-cat that's got the low-down mews."

There was something of the melancholy charm of Tschaikovsky in
the melody. The black singer made much of the triumphant note of
strength that reigned over the sad motif. When he sang, "I ain't gwine
to cut mah throat," "Ain't gwine to break mah heart," his face became grim and full of will as a bulldog's.

He conquered his audience and at the finish he was greeted with
warm applause and a shower of silver coins ringing on the tiled pavement. An enthusiastic white man waved a dollar note at the singer
and, to show that Negroes could do just as good or better, Maunie
Whitewing's sleek escort imitated the gesture with a two-dollar note.
That started off the singer again.

"Ain't gwine to cut mah throat . . .
Ain't gwine to break mah heart . . ."

"That zigaboo is a singing fool," remarked Jake.
Billy Biasse entered resplendent in a new bottle-green suit, and
joined Jake and Felice at their table.
"What you say, Billy?" Jake's greeting.
"I say Ise gwineta blow. Toss off that theah liquor, you two. Ise
gwineta blow champagne as mah compliments, old top." . . .
"Heah's good luck t'you, boh, and plenty of joy-stuff and happiness," continued Billy, when the champagne was poured. "You sure
been hugging it close this week."
Jake smiled and looked foolish. . . . The second cook, whom he
had not seen since he quitted the railroad, entered the cabaret with a
mulatto girl on his arm and looked round for seats. Jake stood up and
beckoned him over to his table.
"It's awright, ain't it Billy?" he asked his friend.

"Sure. Any friend a yourn is awright."

The two girls began talking fashion around the most striking dresses in the place. Jake asked about the demoted rhinoceros. He was still on the railroad, the second cook said, taking orders from another chef, "jest as savage and mean as ever, but not so moufy. I hear you friend Ray done quit us for the ocean, Jakey." . . .

There was still champagne to spare, nevertheless the second cook invited the boys to go up to the bar for a stiff drink of real liquor.

Negroes, like all good Americans, love a bar. I should have said, Negroes under Anglo-Saxon civilization. A bar has a charm all of its own that makes drinking there pleasanter. We like to lean up against it, with a foot on the rail. We will leave our women companions and choice wines at the table to snatch a moment of exclusive sex solidarity over a thimble of gin at the bar.

The boys left the girls to the fashions for a little while. Billy Biasse, being a stag as always, had accepted the invitation with alacrity. He loved to indulge in naked man-stuff talk, which would be too raw even for Felice's ears. As they went out Maunie Whitewing (she was a traveled woman of the world and had been abroad several times with and without her husband) smiled upon Jake with a bold stare and remarked to Madame Mulberry: "*Quel beau garçon! J'aimerais beaucoup faire l'amour avec lui.*"

"Superb!" agreed Madame Mulberry, appreciating Jake through her lorgnette.

Felice caught Maunie Whitewing's carnal stare at her man and said to the mulatto girl: "Jest look at that high-class hussy!"

And the dapper escort tried to be obviously unconcerned.

At the bar the three pals had finished one round and the bar-man was in the act of pouring another when a loud scream tore through music and conversation. Jake knew that voice and dashed down the stairs. What he saw held him rooted at the foot of the stairs for a moment. Zeddy had Felice's wrists in a hard grip and she was trying to wrench herself away.

"Leggo a me, I say," she bawled.

"I ain't gwineta do no sich thing. Youse mah woman."

"You lie! I ain't and you ain't mah man, black nigger."

"We'll see ef I ain't. Youse gwine home wif me right now."

Jake strode up to Zeddy. "Turn that girl loose."

"Whose gwineta make me?" growled Zeddy.

"I is. She's mah woman. I knowed her long before you. For Gawd's sake quit you' fooling and don't let's bust up the man's cabaret."

All the fashionable folk had already fled.

"She's *my* woman and I'll carve any damn-fool nigger for her." Lightning-quick Zeddy released the girl and moved upon Jake like a terrible bear with open razor.

"Don't let him kill him, foh Gawd's sake don't," a woman shrieked, and there was a general stampede for the exit.

But Zeddy had stopped like a cowed brute in his tracks, for leveled straight at his heart was the gift that Billy gave.

"Drop that razor and git you' hands up," Jake commanded, "and don't make a fool move or youse a dead nigger."

Zeddy obeyed. Jake searched him and found nothing. "I gotta good mind fixing you tonight, so you won't evah pull a razor on another man."

Zeddy looked Jake steadily in the face and said: "You kain kill me, nigger, ef you wanta. You come gunning at me, but you didn't go gunning after the Germans. Nosah! You was scared and runned away from the army."

Jake looked bewildered, sick. He was hurt now to his heart and he was dumb. The waiters and a few rough customers that the gun did not frighten away looked strangely at him.

"Yes, mah boy," continued Zeddy, "that's what life is everytime. When youse good to a buddy, he steals you woman and pulls a gun on you. Tha's what I get for prohceeding a slacker. A-llll right, boh, I was a good sucker, but—I ain't got no reason to worry sence youse down in the white folks' books." And he ambled away.

Jake shuffled off by himself. Billy Biasse tried to say a decent word, but he waved him away.

These miserable cock-fights, beastly, tigerish, bloody. They had always sickened, saddened, unmanned him. The wild, shrieking mad woman that is sex seemed jeering at him. Why should love create terror? Love should be joy lifting man out of the humdrum ways of life. He had always managed to delight in love and yet steer clear of the hate and violence that govern it in his world. His love nature was generous and warm without any vestige of the diabolical or sadistic.

Yet here he was caught in the thing that he despised so thoroughly. . . . Brest, London, and his America. Their vivid brutality tortured his imagination. Oh, he was infinitely disgusted with himself to think that he had just been moved by the same savage emotions as those vile, vicious, villainous white men who, like hyenas and rattlers, had fought, murdered, and clawed the entrails out of black men over the common, commercial flesh of women. . . .

He reached home and sat brooding in the shadow upon the stoop.

"Zeddy. My own friend in some ways. Naturally lied about me and the army, though. Playing martyr. How in hell did *he* get hooked up with her? Thought he was up in Yonkers. Would never guess one in a hundred it was he. What a crazy world! He must have passed us drinking at the bar. Wish I'd seen him. Would have had him drinking with us. And maybe we would have avoided that stinking row. Maybe and maybe not. Can't tell about Zeddy. He was always a bad-acting razor-flashing nigger."

A little hand timidly took his arm.

"Honey, you ain't mad at you sweetness, is you?"

"No. . . . I'm jest sick and tiah'd a everything."

"I nevah know you knowed one anether, honey. Oh, I was so scared. . . . But how could I know?"

"No, you couldn't. I ain't blaming nothing on you. I nevah would guess it was him mahself. I ain't blaming nobody at all."

Felice cuddled closer to Jake and fondled his face. "It was a good thing you had you' gun, though, honey, or—O Lawd! what mighta happened!"

"Oh, I woulda been a dead nigger this time or a helpless one," Jake laughed and hugged her closer to him. "It was Billy gived me that gun and I didn't even wanta take it."

"Didn't you? Billy is a good friend, eh?"

"You bet he is. Nevah gets mixed up with—in scraps like that."

"Honest, honey, I nevah liked Zeddy, but—"

"Oh, you don't have to explain me nothing. I know it's jest connexidence. It coulda been anybody else. That don't worry mah skin."

"I really didn't like him, though, honey. Lemme tell you. I was kinder sorry for him. It was jest when I got back from Palm Beach I seen him one night at a buffet flat. And he was that nice to me. He paid drinks for the whole houseful a people and all because a me. I couldn't act mean, so I had to be nice mahself. And the next day he ups and buys me two pair a shoes and silk stockings and a box a chocolate candy. So I jest stayed on and gived him a li'l' loving, honey, but I nevah did tuk him to mah haht."

"It's awright, sweetness. What do I care so long as wese got one another again?"

She drew down his head and sought his mouth. . . .

"But what is we gwineta do, daddy? Sence they say that youse a slacker or deserter, I don't [know] which is which—"

"He done lied about that, though," Jake said, angrily. "I didn't run away because I was scared a them Germans. But I beat it away from Brest because they wouldn't give us a chance at them, but kept us in that rainy, sloppy, Gawd-forsaken burg working like wops. They didn't seem to want us niggers foh no soldiers. We was jest a bunch a despised hod-carriers, and Zeddy know that."

Now it was Felice's turn. "You ain't telling me a thing, daddy. I'll be slack with you and desert with you. What right have niggers got to shoot down a whole lot a Germans for? Is they worse than Americans or any other nation a white people? You done do the right thing, honey, and Ise with you and I love you the more for that. . . . But all the same, we can't stay in Harlem no longer, for the bulls will sure get you."

"I been thinking a gitting away from the stinking mess and go on off to sea again."

"Ah no, daddy," Felice tightened her hold on his arm. "And what'll become a me? I kain't go 'board a ship with you and I needs you."

Jake said nothing.

"What you wanta go knocking around them foreign countries again for like swallow come and swallow go from year to year and nevah settling down no place? This heah is you' country, daddy. What you gwine away from it for?"

"And what kain I do?"

"Do? Jest le's beat it away from Harlem, daddy. This heah country is good and big enough for us to git lost in. You know Chicago?"

"Haven't made that theah burg yet."

"Why, le's go to Chicago, then. I hear it's a mahvelous place foh niggers. Chicago, honey."

"When?"

"This heah very night. Ise ready. Ain't nothing in Harlem holding *me*, honey. Come on. Le's pack."

Zeddy rose like an apparition out of the shadow. Automatically Jake's hand went to his pocket.

"Don't shoot!" Zeddy threw up his hands. "I ain't here foh no trouble. I jest wanta ast you' pahdon, Jake. Excuse me, boh. I was crazy-mad and didn't know what I was saying. Ahm bloody well ashamed a mahself. But you know how it is when a gal done make a fool outa you. I done think it ovah and said to mah inner man: Why, you fool fellah, whasmat with you? Ef Zeddy slit his buddy's thwoat for a gal, that won't give back the gal to Zeddy. . . . So I jest had to come and tell it to you and ast you pahdon. You kain stay in Harlem as long as you wanta. Zeddy ain'ta gwineta open his mouf against you. You was always a good man-to-man buddy and nevah did wears you face bahind you. Don't pay no mind to what I done said in that theah cabaret. Them niggers hanging around was all drunk and wouldn't shoot their mouf off about you nohow. You ain't no moh slacker than me. What you done was all right, Jakey, and I woulda did it mahself ef I'd a had the guts to."

"It's all right, Zeddy," said Jake. "It was jest a crazy mix-up we all got into. I don't bear you no grudge."

"Will you take the paw on it?"

"Sure!" Jake gripped Zeddy's hand.

"So long, buddy, and fohgit it."

"So long, Zeddy, ole top." And Zeddy bear-walked off, without a word or a look at Felice, out of Jake's life forever. Felice was pleased, yet, naturally, just a little piqued. He might have said good-by to *me*, too, she thought. I would even have kissed him for the last time. She took hold of Jake's hands and swung them meditatively: "It's all right daddy, but—"

"But what?"

"I think we had better let Harlem miss us foh a little while."

"Scared?"

"Yes, daddy, but for you only. Zeddy won't go back on you. I guess not. But news is like a traveling agent, honey, going from person to person. I wouldn't take no chances."

"I guess youse right, sweetness. Come on, le's get our stuff together."

The two leather cases were set together against the wall. Felice sat upon the bed dangling her feet and humming "Tell me, pa-pa, Ise you ma-ma." Jake, in white shirt-sleeves, was arranging in the mirror a pink-yellow-and-blue necktie.

"ALL set! What you say, sweetness?"

"I say, honey, le's go to the Baltimore and finish the night and ketch the first train in the morning."

"Why, the Baltimore is padlocked!" said Jake.

"It was, daddy, but it's open again and going strong. White folks can't padlock niggers outa joy forever. Let's go, daddy."

She jumped down from the bed and jazzed around.

"Oh, I nearly made a present of these heah things to the landlady!" She swept from the bed a pink coverlet edged with lace, and pillow-slips of the same fantasy (they were her own make), with which she had replaced the flat, rooming-house-white ones, and carefully folded them to fit in the bag that Jake had ready open for her. He slid into his coat, made certain of his pocket-book, and picked up the two bags.

The Baltimore was packed with happy, grinning wrigglers. Many pleasure-seekers who had left the new cabaret, on account of the Jake-

Zeddy incident, had gone there. It was brighter than before the raid. The ceiling and walls were kalsomined in white and lilac and the lights glared stronger from new chandeliers.

The same jolly, compact manager was there, grinning a welcome to strange white visitors, who were pleased and never guessed what cautious reserve lurked under that grin.

Tell me, pa-pa, Ise you' ma-ma. . . .

Jake and Felice squeezed a way in among the jazzers. They were all drawn together in one united mass, wriggling around to the same primitive, voluptuous rhythm.

Tell me, pa-pa, Ise you' ma-ma. . . .

Haunting rhythm, mingling of naïve wistfulness and charming gayety, now sheering over into mad riotous joy, now, like a jungle mask, strange, unfamiliar, disturbing, now plunging headlong into the far, dim depths of profundity and rising out as suddenly with a simple, childish grin. And the white visitors laugh. They see the grin only. Here are none of the well-patterned, well-made emotions of the respectable world. A laugh might finish in a sob. A moan end in hilarity. That gorilla type wriggling there with his hands so strangely hugging his mate, may strangle her tonight. But he has no thought of that now. He loves the warm wriggle and is lost in it. Simple, raw emotions and real. They may frighten and repel refined souls, because they are too intensely real, just as a simple savage stands dismayed before nice emotions that he instantly perceives are false.

Tell me, pa-pa, Ise you' ma-ma. . . .

Jake was the only guest left in the Baltimore. The last wriggle was played. The waiters were picking up things and settling accounts.

"Whar's the little hussy?" irritated and perplexed, Jake wondered.

Felice was not in the cabaret nor outside on the pavement. Jake could not understand how she had vanished from his side.

"Maybe she was making a high sign when you was asleep," a waiter laughed.

"Sleep hell!" retorted Jake. He was in no joking mood.

"We gwineta lock up now, big boy," the manager said.

Jake picked up the bags and went out on the sidewalk again. "I kain't believe she'd ditch me like that at the last moment," he said aloud. "Anyhow, I'm bound foh Chicago. I done made up mah mind to go all becausing a her, and I ain'ta gwineta change it whether she throws me down or not. But sure she kain'ta run off and leaves her suitcase. What the hell is I gwine do with it?"

Felice came running up to him, panting, from Lenox Avenue.

"Where in hell you been all this while?" he growled.

"Oh, daddy, don't get mad!"

"Whar you been I say?"

"I done been to look for mah good-luck necklace. I couldn't go to Chicago without it."

Jake grinned. "Whyn't you tell me you was gwine? Weren't you scared a Zeddy?"

"I was and I wasn't. Ef I'd a told you, you woulda said it wasn't worth troubling about. So I jest made up mah mind to slip off and git it. The door wasn't locked and Zeddy wasn't home. It was hanging same place where I left it and I slipped it on mah leg and left the keys on the table. You know I had the keys. Ah, daddy, ef I'd a had mah luck with me, we nevah woulda gotten into a fight at that cabaret."

"You really think so, sweetness?"

They were walking to the subway station along Lenox Avenue.

"I ain't thinking, honey. I knows it. I'll nevah fohgit it again and it'll always give us good luck."

THE END

RUDOLPH FISHER
Photographs and Prints Division,
Shomburg Center for Research in Black Culture,
The New York Public Library,
Astor, Lenox and Tilden Foundations.

RUDOLPH FISHER

n a short story entitled "Blades of Steel" (1927), Rudolph Fisher locates "the heart and soul" of Harlem in 135th Street, a popular thoroughfare that links low-class Lenox Avenue, "the boulevard of the unperfumed," with Seventh Avenue, "the promenade of high-toned 'dicties' and strivers." One Hundred Thirty-fifth Street thus becomes "common ground, the natural scene of unusual contacts, a region that disregards class. It neutralizes, equilibrates, binds, rescues union out of diversity." In an important sense, providing a common ground, a venue in which some unifying bond could be discerned amid Harlem's often conflicting diversity, was one of Fisher's central concerns as a fiction writer. Unlike 135th Street, however, Fisher would never disregard class in his writing, for the sophisticated tone and point of view that he brought to storytelling owed much to his own birth and breeding in the privileged world of what once was known as the black "talented tenth." What made Fisher unusual among his literary compatriots from the black bourgeoisie during the Harlem Renaissance was a comic insight into the pitfalls of class and caste consciousness among blacks and a genuine appreciation of the resilience and resourcefulness of the average black man and woman.

Rudolph Fisher was born in Washington, D.C. on May 9, 1897, the son of the Reverend John W. and Glendora Williamson Fisher. Reared in Providence, Rhode Island, Rudolph was an outstanding student; in 1919 he earned a degree with honors from Brown University, where he studied English and biology. Careers as a writer and as a physician evolved out of Fisher's undergraduate majors. After an M.S. degree in biology at Brown, Fisher went to Howard University Medical School, receiving his M.D. in 1924. While a medical student he began writing short stories, the first of which, "The City of Refuge," appeared in the *Atlantic*

Monthly in 1925 and later that year in Alain Locke's *The New Negro*. In the same year another of Fisher's short stories, "High Yaller," won a prize in a literary contest sponsored by *The Crisis*. As Fisher was establishing himself as a research fellow in biology at Columbia University Medical College in New York, he continued to publish short stories distinguished by his unsentimental but not unsympathetic portrayal of the lives of black migrants from the South trying to adjust to the urban realities of Harlem. He soon won a reputation as one of the wittiest and most promising of the New Negro writers.

In 1927 Fisher opened up his own medical practice as a radiologist while also serving as superintendent of the International Hospital in Harlem. A year later *The Walls of Jericho*, his first novel, was published. Hailed by some as the first genuinely comic novel of African American life, *The Walls of Jericho* earned favorable reviews because of a balanced satire of class and color prejudice among black New Yorkers that neither degenerated into caricature of one class nor engaged in special pleading for another. In 1932 Fisher brought out his second novel, *The Conjure Man Dies*, often referred to as the first African American detective novel. A man of many talents, Fisher staged a dramatic version of his second novel and arranged Negro spirituals for Paul Robeson, the most dynamic black American singer of the era. Fisher's death from cancer the day after Christmas 1934, deprived African American literature of one of its most admired and respected voices just as he was reaching his artistic maturity.

"Miss Cynthie," one of Fisher's last short stories and often considered his best, appeared in *Story* magazine in the summer of 1933. In the story Fisher makes a characteristic effort to reconcile and integrate seeming differences, even oppositions, in African American life. What makes Miss Cynthie different from her grandson Dave Tappen is what, in conventional thinking, put the sacred at odds with the secular and the traditional in conflict with the modern in the Harlem Renaissance. Yet Fisher makes it clear that elderly Miss Cynthie from the small-town South holds much in common with her transplanted and transformed, but still quite respectful, grandson in New York. It is the continuity, not the contrast, between Dave Tappen's success as an artist-entertainer in Harlem and the spiritual ideals and social goals represented by Miss Cynthie's ambitions for her grandson that climaxes Fisher's story. "Miss Cynthie" suggests that art, whether Dave Tappen's theater or Rudolph Fisher's fiction, can furnish the conduit, the crucial interlink, that allows the dualities of African American life to inform and enlighten each other so as to attain a mutually fulfilling synthesis.

McCluskey, John, Jr., ed. *The City of Refuge: The Collected Stories of Rudolph Fisher*. Columbia: University of Missouri Press, 1987.

For additional critical resources on Fisher's life and writing, please consult the books on African American fiction and the histories of the Harlem Renaissance listed in the "Suggestions for Further Reading" following the introduction to this anthology.

MISS CYNTHIE

For the first time in her life somebody had called her "madam."

She had been standing, bewildered but unafraid, while innumerable Red Caps appropriated piece after piece of the baggage arrayed on the platform. Neither her brief seventy years' journey through life nor her long two days' travel northward had dimmed the live brightness of her eyes, which, for all their bewilderment, had accurately selected her own treasures out of the row of luggage and guarded them vigilantly.

"These yours, madam?"

The biggest Red Cap of all was smiling at her. He looked for all the world like Doc Crinshaw's oldest son back home. Her little brown face relaxed; she smiled back at him.

"They got to be. You all done took all the others."

He laughed aloud. Then—"Carry 'em in for you?"

She contemplated his bulk. "Reckon you can manage it—puny little feller like you?"

Thereupon they were friends. Still grinning broadly, he surrounded himself with her impedimenta, the enormous brown extension-case on one shoulder, the big straw suitcase in the opposite hand, the carpet-bag under one arm. She herself held fast to the umbrella.

"Always like to have sump'm in my hand when I walk. Can't never tell when you'll run across a snake."

"There aren't any snakes in the city."

"There's snakes everywhere, chile."

They began the tedious hike up the interminable platform. She was small and quick. Her carriage was surprisingly erect, her gait astonishingly spry. She said:

"You liked to took my breath back yonder, boy, callin' me 'madam.' Back home everybody call me 'Miss Cynthie.' Even my own chillun. Even their chillun. Black folks, white folks too. 'Miss Cynthie.' Well, when you come up with that 'madam' o' yourn, I say to myself, 'Now, I wonder who that chile's a-grinnin' at? 'Madam' stand for mist'ess o' the house, and I sho' ain' mist'ess o' nothin' in this hyeh New York."

"Well, you see, we call everybody 'madam.' "

"Everybody?—Hm." The bright eyes twinkled. "Seem like that'd worry me some—if I was a man."

He acknowledged his slip and observed, "I see this isn't your first trip to New York."

"First trip any place, son. First time I been over fifty mile from Waxhaw. Only travelin' I've done is in my head. Ain' seen many places, but I's seen a passel o' people. Reckon places is pretty much alike after people been in 'em awhile."

"Yes, ma'am. I guess that's right."

"You ain' no reg'lar bag-toter, is you?"

"Ma'am?"

"You talk too good."

"Well, I only do this in vacation-time. I'm still in school."

"You is. What you aimin' to be?"

"I'm studying medicine."

"You is?" She beamed. "Aimin' to be a doctor, huh? Thank the Lord for that. That's what I always wanted my David to be. My grandchile hyeh in New York. He's to meet me hyeh now."

"I bet you'll have a great time."

"Mussn't bet, chile. That's sinful. I tole him 'fo' he left home, I say, 'Son, you the only one o' the chillun what's got a chance to amount to sump'm. Don' th'ow it away. Be a preacher or a doctor. Work yo' way up and don' stop short. If the Lord don' see fit for you to doctor the soul, then doctor the body. If you don' get to be a reg'lar doctor, be a tooth-doctor. If you jes' can't make that, be a foot-doctor. And if you don' get that fur, be a undertaker. That's the least you must be. That ain' so bad. Keep you acquainted with the house of the Lord. Always mind the house o' the Lord—whatever you do, di like a church-steeple: aim high and go straight.' "

"Did he get to be a doctor?"

"Don' b'lieve he did. Too late startin', I reckon. But he's done succeeded at sump'm. Mus' be at least a undertaker, 'cause he started sendin' the home-folks money, and he come home las' year dressed like Judge Pettiford's boy what went off to school in Virginia. Wouldn't tell none of us 'zackly what he was doin', but he said he wouldn't never be happy till I come and see for myself. So hyeh I is." Something softened her voice. "His mammy died befo' he knowed her. But he was always sech a good chile—" The something was apprehension. "Hope he *is* a undertaker."

They were mounting a flight of steep stairs leading to an exit-gate, about which clustered a few people still hoping to catch sight of arriving friends. Among these a tall young brown-skinned man in a light grey suit suddenly waved his panama and yelled, "Hey, Miss Cynthie!"

Miss Cynthie stopped, looked up, and waved back with a delighted umbrella. The Red Cap's eyes lifted too. His lower jaw sagged.

"Is that your grandson?"

"It sho' is," she said and distanced him for the rest of the climb. The grandson, with an abandonment that superbly ignored on-lookers, folded the little woman in an exultant, smothering embrace. As soon as she could, she pushed him off with breathless mock impatience.

"Go 'way, you fool, you. Aimin' to squeeze my soul out my body befo' I can get a look at this place?" She shook herself into the semblance of composure. "Well. You don' look hungry, anyhow."

"Ho-ho! Miss Cynthie in New York! Can y'imagine this? Come on. I'm parked on Eighth Avenue."

The Red Cap delivered the outlandish luggage into a robin's egg blue open Packard with scarlet wheels, accepted the grandson's dollar and smile, and stood watching the car roar away up Eighth Avenue.

Another Red Cap came up. "Got a break, hey, boy?"

"Dave Tappen himself—can you beat that?"

"The old lady hasn't seen the station yet—starin' at him."

"That's not the half of it, bozo. That's Dave Tappen's grandmother. And what do you s'pose she hopes?"

"What?"

"She hopes that Dave has turned out to be a successful undertaker!"

"Undertaker? Undertaker!"

They stared at each other a gaping moment, then doubled up with laughter.

"Look—through there—that's the Chrysler Building. Oh, hell-elujah! I meant to bring you up Broadway—"

"David—"

"Ma'am?"

"This hyeh wagon yourn?"

"Nobody else's. Sweet buggy, ain't it?"

"David—you ain't turned out to be one of them moonshiners, is you?"

"Moonshiners—? Moon—Ho! No indeed, Miss Cynthie. I got a better racket 'n that."

"Better which?"

"Game. Business. Pick-up."

"Tell me, David. What is yo' racket?"

"Can't spill it yet, Miss Cynthie. Rather show you. Tomorrow night you'll know the worst. Can't you make out till tomorrow night?"

"David, you know I always wanted you to be a doctor, even if 'twasn' nothin' but a foot-doctor. The very leas' I wanted you to be was a undertaker."

"Undertaker! Oh, Miss Cynthie!—with my sunny disposition?"

"Then you ain' even a undertaker?"

"Listen, Miss Cynthie. Just forget 'bout what I am for awhile. Just till tomorrow night. I want you to see for yourself. Tellin' you will spoil it. Now stop askin', you hear?—because I'm not answerin'—I'm surprisin' you. And don't expect anybody you meet to tell you. It'll mess up the whole works. Understand? Now give the big city a break. There's the elevated train going up Columbus Avenue. Ain't that hot stuff?"

Miss Cynthie looked. "Humph!" she said. "'Tain' half high as that trestle two mile from Waxhaw."

She thoroughly enjoyed the ride up Central Park West. The stagger lights, the extent of the park, the high, close, kingly dwellings, remarkable because their stoves cooled them in summer as well as heated them in winter, all drew nods of mild interest. But what gave her special delight was not these: it was that David's car so effortlessly sped past the headlong drove of vehicles racing northward.

They stopped for a red light; when they started again their machine leaped forward with a triumphant eagerness that drew from her an unsuppressed "Hot you, David! That's it!"

He grinned appreciatively. "Why, you're a regular New Yorker already."

"New Yorker nothin'! I done the same thing fifty years ago—befo' I knowed they was a New York."

"What!"

" 'Deed so. Didn' I use to tell you 'bout my young mare, Betty? Chile, I'd hitch Betty up to yo' grandpa's buggy and pass anything on the road. Betty never knowed what another horse's dust smelt like. No 'ndeedy. Shuh, boy, this ain' nothin' new to me. Why that broke-down Fo'd you' uncle Jake's got ain' nothin'—nothin' but a sorry mess. Done got so slow I jes' won' ride in it—I declare I'd rather walk. But this hyeh thing, now, this is right nice." She settled back in complete, complacent comfort, and they sped on, swift and silent.

Suddenly she sat erect with abrupt discovery.

"David—well—bless my soul!"

"What's the matter, Miss Cynthie?"

Then he saw what had caught her attention. They were traveling up Seventh Avenue now, and something was miraculously different. Not the road; that was as broad as ever, wide, white gleaming in the sun. Not the houses; they were lofty still, lordly, disdainful, supercilious. Not the cars; they continued to race impatiently onward, innumerable, precipitate, tumultuous. Something else, something at once obvious and subtle, insistent, pervasive, compelling.

"David—this mus' be Harlem!"

"Good Lord, Miss Cynthie—!"

"Don' use the name of the Lord in vain, David."

"But I mean—gee!—you're no fun at all. You get everything before a guy can tell you."

"You got plenty to tell me, David. But don' nobody need to tell me this. Look a yonder."

Not just a change of complexion. A completely dissimilar atmosphere. Sidewalks teeming with leisurely strollers, at once strangely dark and bright. Boys in white trousers, berets, and green shirts, with slickened black heads and proud swagger. Bareheaded girls in crisp organdie dresses, purple, canary, gay scarlet. And laughter, abandoned strong Negro laughter, some falling full on the ear, some not heard at all, yet sensed—the warm life-breath of the tireless carnival to which Harlem's heart quickens in summer.

"This is it," admitted David. "Get a good eyeful. Here's One Hundred and Twenty-fifth Street—regular little Broadway. And here's the Alhambra, and up ahead we'll pass the Lafayette."

"What's them?"

"Theatres."

"Theatres? Theatres. Humph! Look, David—is that a colored folks church?" They were passing a fine gray-stone edifice.

"That? Oh. Sure it is. So's this one on this side."

"No! Well, ain' that fine? Splendid big church like that for colored folks."

Taking his cue from this, her first tribute to the city, he said, "You ain't seen nothing yet. Wait a minute."

They swung left through a side-street and turned right on a boulevard. "What do you think o' that?" And he pointed to the quarter-million-dollar St. Mark's.

"That a colored church, too?"

" 'Tain' no white one. And they built it themselves, you know. Nobody's hand-me-down gift."

She heaved a great happy sigh. "Oh, yes, it was a gift, David. It was a gift from on high." Then, "Look a hyeh—which a one you belong to?"

"Me? Why, I don't belong to any—that is, none o' these. Mine's over in another section. Y'see, mine's Baptist. These are all Methodist. See?"

"M-m. Uh-huh. I see."

They circled a square and slipped into a quiet narrow street overlooking a park, stopping before the tallest of the apartment-houses in the single commanding row.

Alighting, Miss Cynthie gave this imposing structure one sidewise, upward glance, and said, "Y'all live like bees in a hive, don't y'?—I boun' the women does all the work, too." A moment later, "So this is a elevator? Feel like I'm glory-bound sho' nuff."

Along a tiled corridor and into David's apartment. Rooms leading into rooms. Luxurious couches, easy-chairs, a brown-walnut grand piano, gay-shaded floor lamps, panelled walls, deep rugs, treacherous glass-wood floors—and a smiling golden-skinned girl in a gingham house-dress, approaching with outstretched hands.

"This is Ruth, Miss Cynthie."

"Miss Cynthie!" said Ruth.

They clasped hands. "Been wantin' to see David's girl ever since he first wrote us 'bout her."

"Come—here's your room this way. Here's the bath. Get out of your things and get comfy. You must be worn out with the trip."

"Worn out? Worn out? Shuh. How you gon' get worn out on a train? Now if 'twas a horse, maybe, or Jake's no-'count Fo'd—but a train—didn' but one thing bother me on that train."

"What?"

"When the man made them beds down, I jes' couldn' manage to undress same as at home. Why, s'posin' sump'm bus' the train open—where'd you be? Naked as a jay-bird in dew-berry time."

David took in her things and left her to get comfortable. He returned, and Ruth, despite his reassuring embrace, whispered:

"Dave, you can't fool old folks—why don't you go ahead and tell her about yourself? Think of the shock she's going to get—at her age."

David shook his head. "She'll get over the shock if she's there looking on. If we just told her, she'd never understand. We've got to railroad her into it. Then she'll be happy."

"She's nice. But she's got the same ideas as all old folks—"

"Yea—but with her you can change 'em. Specially if everything is really all right. I know her. She's for church and all, but she believes in good times too, if they're right. Why, when I was a kid—" He broke off. "Listen!"

Miss Cynthie's voice came quite distinctly to them, singing a jaunty little rhyme:

> "Oh I danced with the gal with the hole in her stockin',
> And her toe kep' a-kickin' and her heel kep' a-knockin'—
>
> Come up, Jesse, and get a drink o' gin,
> 'Cause you near to the heaven as you'll ever get ag'in."

"She taught me that when I wasn't knee-high to a cricket," David said.

Miss Cynthie still sang softly and merrily:

> "Then I danced with the gal with the dimple in her cheek,
> And if she'd 'a' kep' a-smilin', I'd a' danced for a week—"

"God forgive me," prayed Miss Cynthie as she discovered David's purpose the following night. She let him and Ruth lead her, like an early Christian martyr, into the Lafayette Theatre. The blinding glare of the lobby produced a merciful self-anaesthesia, and she entered the sudden dimness of the interior as involuntarily as in a dream—

Attendants outdid each other for Mr. Dave Tappen. She heard him tell them, "Fix us up till we go on," and found herself sitting between Ruth and David in the front row of a lower box. A miraculous device of the devil, a motion-picture that talked, was just ending. At her feet the orchestra was assembling. The motion-picture faded out amid a scattered round of applause. Lights blazed and the orchestra burst into an ungodly rumpus.

She looked out over the seated multitude, scanning row upon row of illumined faces, black faces, white faces, yellow, tan, brown; bald heads, bobbed heads, kinky and straight heads; and upon every countenance, expectancy,—scowling expectancy in this case, smiling in that, complacent here, amused there, commentative elsewhere, but everywhere suspense, abeyance, anticipation.

Half a dozen people were ushered down the nearer aisle to reserved seats in the second row. Some of them caught sight of David and Ruth and waved to them. The chairs immediately behind them in the box were being shifted. "Hello, Tap!" Miss Cynthie saw David turn, rise, and shake hands with two men. One of them was large, bald and pink, emanating good cheer; the other short, thin, sallow with thick black hair and a sour mien. Ruth also acknowledged their greeting. "This is my grandmother," David said proudly. "Miss Cynthie, meet my managers, Lou and Lee Goldman." "Pleased to meet you," managed Miss Cynthie. "Great lad, this boy of yours," said Lou Goldman. "Great little partner he's got, too," added Lee. They also settled back expectantly.

"Here we go!"

The curtain rose to reveal a cotton-field at dawn. Pickers in blue denim overalls, bandanas, and wide-brimmed straws, or in gingham aprons and sun-bonnets, were singing as they worked. Their voices, from clearest soprano to richest bass, blended in low concordances, first simply humming a series of harmonies, until, gradually, came words, like figures forming in mist. As the sound grew, the mist cleared, the words came round and full, and the sun rose bringing light as if in answer to the song. The chorus swelled, the radiance grew, the two, as if emanating from a single source, fused their crescendos, till at last they achieved a joint transcendence of tonal and visual brightness.

"Swell opener," said Lee Goldman.

"Ripe," agreed Lou.

David and Ruth arose. "Stay here and enjoy the show, Miss Cynthie. You'll see us again in a minute."

"Go to it, kids," said Lou Goldman.

"Yea—burn 'em up," said Lee.

Miss Cynthie hardly noted that she had been left, so absorbed was she in the spectacle. To her, the theatre had always been the antithesis of the church. As the one was the refuge of righteousness, so the other was the stronghold of transgression. But this first scene awakened memories, captured and held her attention by offering a blend of truth and novelty. Having thus baited her interest, the show now proceeded to play it like the trout through swift-flowing waters of wickedness. Resist as it might, her mind was caught and drawn into the impious subsequences.

The very music that had just rounded out so majestically now distorted itself into ragtime. The singers came forward and turned to dancers; boys, a crazy, swaying background, threw up their arms and kicked out their legs in a rhythmic jamboree; girls, an agile, brazen foreground, caught their skirts up to their hips and displayed their copper calves, knees, thighs, in shameless, incredible steps. Miss Cynthie turned dismayed eyes upon the audience, to discover that mob of sinners devouring it all with fond satisfaction. Then the dancers separated and with final abandon flung themselves off the stage in both directions.

Lee Goldman commented through the applause, "They work easy, them babies."

"Yea," said Lou. "Savin' the hot stuff for later."

Two black-faced cotton-pickers appropriated the scene, indulging in dialogue that their hearers found uproarious,

"Ah'm tired."

"Ah'm hongry."

"Dis job jes' wears me out."

"Starves me to death."

"Ah'm so tired—you know what Ah'd like to do?"

"What?"

"Ah'd like to go to sleep and dream I was sleepin'."

"What good dat do?"

"Den I could wake up and still be 'sleep."

"Well y' know what Ah'd like to do?"

"No. What?"

"Ah'd like to swaller me a hog and a hen."

"What good dat do?"

"Den Ah'd always be full o' ham and eggs."

"Ham? Shuh. Don't you know a hog has to be smoked 'fo' he's a ham?"

"Well, if I swaller him, he'll have a smoke all around him, won' he?"

Presently Miss Cynthie was smiling like everyone else, but her smile soon fled. For the comics departed, and the dancing girls returned, this time in scant travesties on their earlier voluminous costumes—tiny sunbonnets perched jauntily on one side of their glistening bobs, bandanas reduced to scarlet neck-ribbons, waists mere brassieres, skirts mere gingham sashes.

And now Miss Cynthie's whole body stiffened with a new and surpassing shock; her bright eyes first widened with unbelief, then slowly grew dull with misery. In the midst of a sudden great volley of applause her grandson had broken through that bevy of agile wantons and begun to sing.

He too was dressed as a cotton-picker, but a Beau Brummel among cotton-pickers; his hat bore a pleated green band, his bandana was silk, his overalls blue satin, his shoes black patent leather. His eyes flashed, his teeth gleamed, his body swayed, his arms waved, his words came fast and clear. As he sang, his companions danced a concerted tap, uniformly wild, ecstatic. When he stopped singing, he himself began to dance, and without sacrificing crispness of execution, seemed to absorb into himself every measure of the energy which the girls, now merely standing off and swaying, had relinquished.

"Look at that boy go," said Lee Goldman.

"He ain't started yet," said Lou.

But surrounding comment, Dave's virtuosity, the eager enthusiasm of the audience were all alike lost on Miss Cynthie. She sat with stricken eyes watching this boy whom she'd raised from a babe, taught right from wrong, brought up in the church, and endowed with her prayers, this child whom she had dreamed of seeing a preacher, a regular doctor, a tooth-doctor, a foot-doctor, at the very least an undertaker—sat watching him disport himself for the benefit of a sinsick, flesh-hungry mob of lost souls, not one of whom knew or cared to know the loving kindness of God; sat watching a David she'd never foreseen, turned tool of the devil, disciple of lust, unholy prince among sinners.

For a long time she sat there watching with wretched eyes, saw portrayed on the stage David's arrival in Harlem, his escape from "old friends" who tried to dupe him; saw him working as a trap-drummer in a night-club, where he fell in love with Ruth, a dancer; not the gentle Ruth Miss Cynthie knew, but a wild and shameless young savage who danced like seven devils—in only a girdle and breastplates; saw the two of them join in a song-and-dance act that eventually made them Broadway headliners, an act presented *in toto* as the pre-finale of this show. And not any of the melodies, not any of the sketches, not all the comic philosophy of the tired-and-hungry duo, gave her figure a moment's relaxation or brightened the dull defeat in her staring eyes. She sat apart, alone in the box, the symbol, the epitome of supreme failure. Let the rest of the theatre be riotous, clamoring for more and more of Dave Tappen, "Tap," the greatest tapster of all time, idol of uptown and downtown New York. For her, they were lauding simply an exhibition of sin which centered about her David.

"This'll run a year on Broadway," said Lee Goldman.

"Then we'll take it to Paris."

Encores and curtains with Ruth, and at last David came out on the stage alone. The clamor dwindled. And now he did something quite unfamiliar to even the most consistent of his followers. Softly, delicately, he began to tap a routine designed to fit a particular song. When he had established the rhythm, he began to sing the song:

> "Oh I danced with the gal with the hole in her stockin',
> And her toe kep' a-kickin' and her heel kep' a-knockin'

Come up, Jesse, and get a drink o' gin,
'Cause you near to the heaven as you'll ever get ag'in—"

As he danced and sang this song, frequently smiling across at Miss Cynthie, a visible change transformed her. She leaned forward incredulously, listened intently, then settled back in limp wonder. Her bewildered eyes turned on the crowd, on those serried rows of shriftless sinners. And she found in their faces now an overwhelmingly curious thing: a grin, a universal grin, a gleeful and sinless grin such as not the nakedest chorus in the performance had produced. In a few seconds, with her own song, David had dwarfed into unimportance, wiped off their faces, swept out of their minds every trace of what had seemed to be sin; had reduced it all to mere trivial detail and revealed these revelers as a crowd of children, enjoying the guileless antics of another child. And Miss Cynthie whispered her discovery aloud:

"Bless my soul! They didn't mean nothin' . . . They jes' didn't see no harm in it—"

"Then I danced with the gal with the dimple in her cheek,
And if she'd 'a' kep' a-smilin' I'd 'a' danced for a week—

Come up, Jesse—"

The crowd laughed, clapped their hands, whistled. Someone threw David a bright yellow flower. "From Broadway!"

He caught the flower. A hush fell. He said:

"I'm really happy tonight, folks. Y'see this flower? Means success, don't it? Well, listen. The one who is really responsible for my success is here tonight with me. Now what do you think o' that?"

The hush deepened.

"Y'know folks, I'm sump'm like Adam—I never had no mother. But I've got a grandmother. Down home everybody calls her Miss Cynthie. And everybody loves her. Take that song I just did for you. Miss Cynthie taught me that when I wasn't knee-high to a cricket. But that wasn't all she taught me. For back as I can remember, she used to always say one thing: 'Son, do like a church steeple—aim high and go straight.' And for doin' it—" he grinned, contemplating the flower—"I get this."

He strode across to the edge of the stage that touched Miss Cynthie's box. He held up the flower.

"So y'see, folks, this isn't mine. It's really Miss Cynthie's." He leaned over to hand it to her. Miss Cynthie's last trace of doubt was swept away. She drew a deep breath of revelation; her bewilderment vanished, her redoubtable composure returned, her eyes lighted up; and no one but David, still holding the flower toward her, heard her sharply whispered reprimand:

"Keep it, you fool you. Where's yo' manners—givin' 'way what somebody give you?"

David grinned:

"Take it, tyro. What you tryin' to do—crab my act?"

Thereupon, Miss Cynthie, smiling at him with bright, meaningful eyes, leaned over without rising from her chair, jerked a tiny twig off the stem of the flower, then sat decisively back, resolutely folding her arms, with only a leaf in her hand.

"This'll do me," she said.

The finale didn't matter. People filed out of the theatre. Miss Cynthie sat awaiting her children, her foot absently patting time to the orchestra's jazz recessional. Perhaps she was thinking, "God moves in a mysterious way," but her lips were unquestionably forming the words:

> "—danced with the gal—hole in her stockin'—
> —toe kep' a-kickin'—heel kep' a-knockin'—"

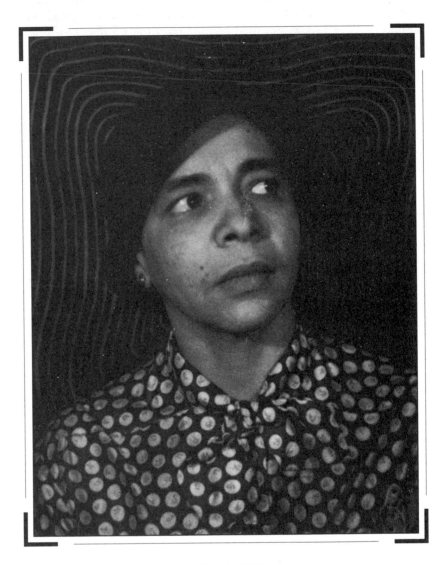

NELLA LARSEN
Photograph by Carl Van Vechten.
By permission of the Estate of Carl Van Vechten.
Joseph Solomon, Executor.

NELLA LARSEN

1891 TO 1964

Nella Larsen has been called, with some justification, the "mystery woman of the Harlem Renaissance." When she burst on the literary scene in 1928 with her first novel *Quicksand*, and quickly followed up its critical success with a second novel *Passing*, in 1929, Larsen seemed destined for leadership in contemporary African American literature, especially among black women writers. She impressed her friends and associates with her desire for serious literary recognition, her focus and hard work, and her determination to disclose hard truths about the dilemmas of middle-class women of color, regardless of what was fashionable in either black or white circles. *Quicksand* won Larsen a coveted Harmon medal for literature, and *Passing* helped her garner a creative writing fellowship from the Guggenheim Foundation, the first grant of its kind ever awarded an African American woman. Yet with the exception of a single short story in 1930, Nella Larsen never published fiction again in her life. For reasons that have never been entirely clear, after a stormy marriage and divorce in 1933 and failure to complete a third book, Larsen gave up on her literary career. Needing a means of support after her ex-husband's death in 1941, she returned to the nursing profession in which she had been trained and worked more than twenty years earlier. Thereafter she courted obscurity until her death in Brooklyn, New York, in 1964.

In part the "mystery" of Nella Larsen was of her own making. Biographical research done by Thadious Davis and other scholars has revealed a number of discrepancies between the personal myth Larsen cultivated for the Harlem Renaissance and the person she actually was. Nella Marian Larsen was born into a working-class immigrant family in Chicago in 1891. But when she made her bid for membership among the Harlem literati of the 1920s, Larsen endowed herself with a more youthful and exotic aura by claiming that she was born in 1893 in the Virgin Islands. To Larsen the Harlem Renaissance represented not merely an artistic advance for the race but a once-in-a-lifetime chance to make a name for herself. Thus the woman who had been satisfied to be known as Nella Imes after her 1919 marriage to black physicist Elmer Samuel Imes renamed herself Nella Larsen after the publication of her first novel. Larsen was not the only Harlem Renaissance writer to reinvent herself in these ways. But her willingness to engage in this kind of self-promotion gives useful clues to the personal and social agendas of her art.

The female protagonists of Nella Larsen's two novels are haunted by conflicting identifications and ambitions that their creator knew all too well from personal experience. In Irene Redfield and Clare Kendry, the central characters in *Passing*, Larsen depicts the social anxieties, repressions, and deceptions to which upwardly mobile mixed-race women fall prey in their attempts to reconcile their desires for sexual fulfillment with their struggle to maintain the respectable image their class demands of them. The melodramatic life and death of Clare Kendry, who passes for white but cannot resist dabbling in the Harlem scene in the 1920s, have little direct reference to Larsen's own autobiography. But the distinctions between the inhibited, family-oriented Redfield and the selfish, amoral Kendry define the polarities of standard literary images of black women that Larsen had to confront as an African American woman and writer from the same class as that of Redfield and Kendry.

Affinities between Helga Crane, the restless heroine of *Quicksand*, and Larsen allow readers of that novel a glimpse into the author's personal sense of what it meant to be a sophisticated New Negro woman trying to find her own way according to the supposedly liberated racial and sexual ground rules of the modern era. Like Larsen, Helga Crane is a woman of mixed race, the product of a liaison between a Scandinavian woman and an African American man. Though Larsen was not born out of wedlock, as Crane is in *Quicksand*, both women share an acute awareness of growing up different from, and quite literally beyond the pale of, the families that their mothers created with men of their own race after, in Larsen's case, the death of her West Indian father when she was two, or, in Helga Crane's story, the desertion of her mother's lover. Given Larsen's intimate but attenuated connections to both sides of the color line, one is hardly surprised to find Helga Crane negotiating a similarly difficult set of allegiances in *Quicksand*.

In 1907, apparently intent on orienting herself racially, Larsen entered the predominately black world of Fisk University in Nashville, Tennessee, as a sixteen-year-old high school student. At the opening of *Quicksand*, we find Helga Crane teaching at a similar all-black southern institution, Naxos (an anagram of Saxon), which she soon finds obnoxious. Just as Larsen left Fisk in 1908 to travel to Denmark, where she lived with relatives in Copenhagen for approximately the next three years, so Crane leaves Naxos after a short time, and following a year in Harlem, goes on to Copenhagen herself. Throughout her story, Crane oscillates between black and white society, respectable and rebellious female behavior, a desire for release and sensual fulfillment and a need for security and sexual legitimacy.

Larsen's investment in her unconventional protagonist is evident in the detailed and sympathetic insights that accompany her narrative of Crane's resistance to the socially mandated status and role of a mixed-race woman in the United States. To readers knowledgeable of the traditional stereotyping of mixed-race figures in American fiction, Helga Crane might have seemed a prime candidate for 1928's "tragic mulatta" of the year award simply by virtue of the troubling sense of in-betweenness that nags her through much of the novel. But the author of *Quicksand* knew from experience that a modern mixed-race woman like Helga Crane (or Nella Larsen) could and would not be as easily disposed of as the Victorian-era "tragic mulatta," who, though a sexual object, routinely chooses death before settling for anything less than honorable marriage. Unlike the tragic mulatta, Crane has choices, alternatives, and social and economic freedom virtually unprecedented in African American fiction concerned with black women. She is not burdened by the pinched set of proprieties that govern what black women in earlier African American fiction say and do. Like Larsen herself, Helga Crane can and does claim the relative privilege and opportunity of a well-connected middle-class African American woman of the 1920s. Yet the best Crane can do for herself by the end of *Quicksand* is alienation and exhaustion within a stifling sham of a marriage. The multiple ironies of Crane's appalling outcome in *Quicksand*, particularly the revolting view of marriage and motherhood as Crane comes to know it, make this novel the most provocative study of gender roles and female sexuality produced by the Harlem Renaissance.

SUGGESTIONS FOR FURTHER READING

Larsen, Nella. *Quicksand and Passing.* Ed. Deborah E. McDowell. New Brunswick, NJ: Rutgers University Press, 1986.

For additional critical resources on Larsen's life and writing, please consult the books on African American fiction and the histories of the Harlem Renaissance listed in the "Suggestions for Further Reading" following the introduction to this anthology.

QUICKSAND

One

Helga Crane sat alone in her room, which at that hour, eight in the evening, was in soft gloom. Only a single reading lamp, dimmed by a great black and red shade, made a pool of light on the blue Chinese carpet, on the bright covers of the books which she had taken down from their long shelves, on the white pages of the opened one selected, on the shining brass bowl crowded with many-colored nasturtiums beside her on the low table, and on the oriental silk which covered the stool at her slim feet. It was a comfortable room, furnished with rare and intensely personal taste, flooded with Southern sun in the day, but shadowy just then with the drawn curtains and single shaded light. Large, too. So large that the spot where Helga sat was a small oasis in a desert of darkness. And eerily quiet. But that was what she liked after her taxing day's work, after the hard classes, in which she gave willingly and unsparingly of herself with no apparent return. She loved this tranquillity, this quiet, following the fret and strain of the long hours spent among fellow members of a carelessly unkind and gossiping faculty, following the strenuous rigidity of conduct required in this huge educational community of which she was an insignificant part. This was her rest, this intentional isolation for a short while in the evening, this little time in her own attractive room with her own books. To the rapping of other teachers, bearing fresh scandals, or seeking information, or other more concrete favors, or merely talk, at that hour Helga Crane never opened her door.

An observer would have thought her well fitted to that framing of light and shade. A slight girl of twenty-two years, with narrow, sloping shoulders and delicate, but well-turned, arms and legs, she had, none the less, an air of radiant, careless health. In vivid green and gold negligee and glistening brocaded mules, deep sunk in the big high-backed chair, against whose dark tapestry her sharply cut face, with skin like yellow satin, was distinctly outlined, she was—to use a hackneyed word—attractive. Black, very broad brows over soft, yet penetrating, dark eyes, and a pretty mouth, whose sensitive and sensuous lips had a slight questioning petulance and a tiny dissatisfied droop, were the features on which the observer's attention would fasten; though her nose was good, her ears delicately chiseled, and her curly blue-black hair plentiful and always straying in a little wayward, delightful way. Just then it was tumbled, falling unrestrained about her face and on to her shoulders.

Helga Crane tried not to think of her work and the school as she sat there. Ever since her arrival in Naxos she had striven to keep these ends of the days from the intrusion of irritating thoughts and worries. Usually she was successful. But not this evening. Of the books which she had taken from their places she had decided on Marmaduke Pickthall's *Saïd the Fisherman*. She wanted forgetfulness, complete mental relaxation, rest from thought of any kind. For the day had been more than usually crowded with distasteful encounters and stupid perversities. The sultry hot Southern spring had left her strangely tired, and a little unnerved. And annoying beyond all other happenings had been that affair of the noon period, now again thrusting itself on her already irritated mind.

She had counted on a few spare minutes in which to indulge in the sweet pleasure of a bath and a fresh, cool change of clothing. And instead her luncheon time had been shortened, as had that of everyone else, and immediately after the hurried gulping down of a heavy hot meal the hundreds of students and teachers had been herded into the sun-baked chapel to listen to the banal, the patronizing, and even the insulting remarks of one of the renowned white preachers of the state.

Helga shuddered a little as she recalled some of the statements made by that holy white man of God to the black folk sitting so respectfully before him.

This was, he had told them with obvious sectional pride, the finest school for Negroes anywhere in the country, north or south; in fact, it was better even than a great many schools for white children. And he had dared any Northerner to come south and after looking upon this great institution to say that the Southerner mistreated the Negro. And he had said that if all Negroes would only take a leaf out of the book of Naxos and conduct themselves in the manner of the Naxos products, there would be no race problem, because Naxos Negroes knew what was expected of them. They had good sense and they had good taste. They knew enough to stay in their places, and that, said the preacher, showed good taste. He spoke of his great admiration for the Negro race, no other race in so short a time had made so much progress, but he had urgently besought them to know when and where to stop. He hoped, he sincerely hoped, that they wouldn't become avaricious and grasping, thinking only of adding to their earthly goods, for that would be a sin in the sight of Almighty God. And then he had spoken of contentment, embellishing his words with scriptural quotations and pointing out to them that it was their duty to be satisfied in the estate to which they had been called, hewers of wood and drawers of water. And then he had prayed.

Sitting there in her room, long hours after, Helga again felt a surge of hot anger and seething resentment. And again it subsided in amazement at the memory of the considerable applause which had greeted the speaker just before he had asked his God's blessing upon them.

The South. Naxos. Negro education. Suddenly she hated them all. Strange, too, for this was the thing which she had ardently desired to share in, to be a part of this monument to one man's genius and vision. She pinned a scrap of paper about the bulb under the lamp's shade, for, having discarded her book in the certainty that in such a mood even *Saïd* and his audacious villainy could not charm her, she wanted an even more soothing darkness. She wished it were vacation, so that she might get away for a time.

"No, forever!" she said aloud.

The minutes gathered into hours, but still she sat motionless, a disdainful smile or an angry frown passing now and then across her face. Somewhere in the room a little clock ticked time away. Somewhere outside, a whippoorwill wailed. Evening died. A sweet smell of early Southern flowers rushed in on a newly-risen breeze which suddenly parted the thin silk curtains at the opened windows. A slender, frail glass vase fell from the sill with a tingling crash, but Helga Crane did not shift her position. And the night grew cooler, and older.

At last she stirred, uncertainly, but with an overpowering desire for action of some sort. A second she hesitated, then rose abruptly and pressed the electric switch with determined firmness, flooding suddenly the shadowy room with a white glare of light. Next she made a quick nervous tour to the end of the long room, paused a moment before the old bow-legged secretary that held with almost articulate protest her school-teacher paraphernalia of drab books and papers. Frantically Helga Crane clutched at the lot and then flung them violently, scornfully toward the wastebasket. It received a part, allowing the rest to spill untidily over the floor. The girl smiled ironically, seeing in the mess a simile of her own earnest endeavor to inculcate knowledge into her indifferent classes.

Yes, it was like that; a few of the ideas which she tried to put into the minds behind those baffling ebony, bronze, and gold faces reached their destination. The others were left scattered about. And, like the gay, indifferent wastebasket, it wasn't their fault. No, it wasn't the fault of those minds back of the diverse colored faces. It was, rather, the fault of the method, the general idea behind the system. Like her own hurried shot at the basket, the aim was bad, the material drab and badly prepared for its purpose.

This great community, she thought, was no longer a school. It had grown into a machine. It was now a show place in the black belt, exemplification of the white man's magnanimity, refutation of the black man's inefficiency. Life had died out of it. It was, Helga decided, now only a big knife with cruelly sharp edges ruthlessly cutting all to a pattern, the white man's pattern. Teachers as well as students were subjected to the paring process, for it tolerated no innovations, no individualisms. Ideas it rejected, and looked with open hostility on one and all who had the temerity to offer a suggestion or ever so mildly express a disapproval. Enthusiasm, spontaneity, if not actually suppressed, were at least openly regretted as unladylike or ungentlemanly qualities. The place was smug and fat with self-satisfaction.

A peculiar characteristic trait, cold, slowly accumulated unreason in which all values were distorted or else ceased to exist, had with surprising ferociousness shaken the bulwarks of that self-restraint which was also, curiously, a part of her nature. And now that it had waned as quickly as it had risen, she smiled again, and this time the smile held a faint amusement, which wiped away the little hardness which had congealed her lovely face. Nevertheless she was soothed by the impetuous discharge of violence, and a sigh of relief came from her.

She said aloud, quietly, dispassionately: "Well, I'm through with that," and, shutting off the hard, bright blaze of the overhead lights, went back to her chair and settled down with an odd gesture of sudden soft collapse, like a person who had been for months fighting the devil and then unexpectedly had turned round and agreed to do his bidding.

Helga Crane had taught in Naxos for almost two years, at first with the keen joy and zest of those immature people who have dreamed dreams of doing good to their fellow men. But gradually this zest was blotted out, giving place to a deep hatred for the trivial hypocrisies and careless cruelties which were, unintentionally perhaps, a part of the Naxos policy of uplift. Yet she had continued to try not only to teach, but to befriend those happy singing children, whose charm and distinctiveness the school was so surely ready to destroy. Instinctively Helga was aware that their smiling submissiveness covered many poignant heartaches and perhaps much secret contempt for their instructors. But she was powerless. In Naxos between teacher and student, between condescending authority and smoldering resentment, the gulf was too great, and too few had tried to cross it. It couldn't be spanned by one sympathetic teacher. It was useless to offer her atom of friendship, which under the existing conditions was neither wanted nor understood.

Nor was the general atmosphere of Naxos, its air of self-rightness and intolerant dislike of difference, the best of mediums for a pretty, solitary girl with no family connections. Helga's essentially likable and charming personality was smudged out. She had felt this for a long time. Now she faced with determination that other truth which she had refused to formulate in her thoughts, the fact that she was utterly unfitted for teaching, even for mere existence, in Naxos. She was a failure here. She had, she conceded now, been silly, obstinate, to persist for so long. A failure. Therefore, no need, no use, to stay longer. Suddenly she longed for immediate departure. How good, she thought, to go now, tonight!—and frowned to remember how impossible that would be. "The dignitaries," she said, "are not in their offices, and there will be yards and yards of red tape to unwind, gigantic, impressive spools of it."

And there was James Vayle to be told, and much-needed money to be got. James, she decided, had better be told at once. She looked at the clock racing indifferently on. No, too late. It would have to be tomorrow.

She hated to admit that money was the most serious difficulty. Knowing full well that it was important, she nevertheless rebelled at the unalterable truth that it could influence her actions, block her desires. A sordid necessity to be grappled with. With Helga it was almost a superstition that to concede to money its importance magnified its power. Still, in spite of her reluctance and distaste, her financial situation would have to be faced, and plans made, if she were to get away from Naxos with anything like the haste which she now so ardently desired.

Most of her earnings had gone into clothes, into books, into the furnishings of the room which held her. All her life Helga Crane had loved and longed for nice things. Indeed, it was this craving, this urge for beauty which had helped to bring her into disfavor in Naxos— "pride" and "vanity" her detractors called it.

The sum owing to her by the school would just a little more than buy her ticket back to Chicago. It was too near the end of the school term to hope to get teaching-work anywhere. If she couldn't find something else, she would have to ask Uncle Peter for a loan. Uncle

Peter was, she knew, the one relative who thought kindly, or even calmly, of her. Her step-father, her step-brothers and sisters, and the numerous cousins, aunts, and other uncles could not be even remotely considered. She laughed a little, scornfully, reflecting that the antagonism was mutual, or, perhaps, just a trifle keener on her side than on theirs. They feared and hated her. She pitied and despised them. Uncle Peter was different. In his contemptuous way he was fond of her. Her beautiful, unhappy mother had been his favorite sister. Even so, Helga Crane knew that he would be more likely to help her because her need would strengthen his oft-repeated conviction that because of her Negro blood she would never amount to anything, than from motives of affection or loving memory. This knowledge, in its present aspect of truth, irritated her to an astonishing degree. She regarded Uncle Peter almost vindictively, although always he had been extraordinarily generous with her and she fully intended to ask his assistance. "A beggar," she thought ruefully, "cannot expect to choose."

Returning to James Vayle, her thoughts took on the frigidity of complete determination. Her resolution to end her stay in Naxos would of course inevitably end her engagement to James. She had been engaged to him since her first semester there, when both had been new workers, and both were lonely. Together they had discussed their work and problems in adjustment, and had drifted into a closer relationship. Bitterly she reflected that James had speedily and with entire ease fitted into his niche. He was now completely "naturalized," as they used laughingly to call it. Helga, on the other hand, had never quite achieved the unmistakable Naxos mold, would never achieve it, in spite of much trying. She could neither conform, nor be happy in her unconformity. This she saw clearly now, and with cold anger at all the past futile effort. What a waste! How pathetically she had struggled in those first months and with what small success. A lack somewhere. Always she had considered it a lack of understanding on the part of the community, but in her present new revolt she realized that the fault had been partly hers. A lack of acquiescence. She hadn't really wanted to be made over. This thought bred a sense of shame, a feeling of ironical disillusion. Evidently there were parts of her she couldn't be proud of. The revealing picture of her past striving was too humiliating. It was as if she had deliberately planned to steal an ugly thing, for which she had no desire, and had been found out.

Ironically she visualized the discomfort of James Vayle. How her maladjustment had bothered him! She had a faint notion that it was behind his ready assent to her suggestion anent a longer engagement than, originally, they had planned. He was liked and approved of in Naxos and loathed the idea that the girl he was to marry couldn't manage to win liking and approval also. Instinctively Helga had known that secretly he had placed the blame upon her. How right he had been! Certainly his attitude had gradually changed, though he still gave her his attentions. Naxos pleased him and he had become content with life as it was lived there. No longer lonely, he was now one of the community and so beyond the need or the desire to discuss its affairs and its failings with an outsider. She was, she knew, in a queer indefinite way, a disturbing factor. She knew too that a something held him, a something against which he was powerless. The idea that she was in but one nameless way necessary to him filled her with a sensation amounting almost to shame. And yet his mute helplessness against that ancient appeal by which she held him pleased her and fed her vanity—gave her a feeling of power. At the same time she shrank away from it, subtly aware of possibilities she herself couldn't predict.

Helga's own feelings defeated inquiry, but honestly confronted, all pretense brushed aside, the dominant one, she suspected, was relief. At least, she felt no regret that tomorrow would mark the end of any claim she had upon him. The surety that the meeting would be a clash annoyed her, for she had no talent for quarreling—when possible she preferred to flee. That was all.

The family of James Vayle, in near-by Atlanta, would be glad. They had never liked the engagement, had never liked Helga Crane. Her own lack of family disconcerted them. No family. That was the crux of the whole matter. For Helga, it accounted for everything, her failure here in Naxos, her former loneliness in Nashville. It even accounted for her engagement to James. Negro society, she had learned, was as complicated. and as rigid in its ramifications as the highest strata of white society. If you couldn't prove your ancestry and connections, you were tolerated, but you didn't "belong." You could be queer, or even attractive, or bad, or brilliant, or even love beauty and such nonsense if you were a Rankin, or a Leslie, or a Scoville; in other words, if you had a family. But if you were just plain Helga Crane, of whom nobody had ever heard, it was presumptuous of you to be anything but inconspicuous and conformable.

To relinquish James Vayle would most certainly be social suicide, for the Vayles were people of consequence. The fact that they were a "first family" had been one of James's attractions for the obscure Helga. She had wanted social background, but—she had not imagined that it could be so stuffy.

She made a quick movement of impatience and stood up. As she did so, the room whirled about her in an impish, hateful way. Familiar objects seemed suddenly unhappily distant. Faintness closed about her like a vise. She swayed, her small, slender hands gripping the chair arms for support. In a moment the faintness receded, leaving in its wake a sharp resentment at the trick which her strained nerves had played upon her. And after a moment's rest she got hurriedly into bed, leaving her room disorderly for the first time.

Books and papers scattered about the floor, fragile stockings and underthings and the startling green and gold negligee dripping about on chairs and stool, met the encounter of the amazed eyes of the girl who came in the morning to awaken Helga Crane.

Two

She woke in the morning unrefreshed and with that feeling of half-terrified apprehension peculiar to Christmas and birthday mornings. A long moment she lay puzzling under the sun streaming in a golden flow through the yellow curtains. Then her mind returned to the night before. She had decided to leave Naxos. That was it.

Sharply she began to probe her decision. Reviewing the situation carefully, frankly, she felt no wish to change her resolution. Except— that it would be inconvenient. Much as she wanted to shake the dust of the place from her feet forever, she realized that there would be difficulties. Red tape. James Vayle. Money. Other work. Regretfully she was forced to acknowledge that it would be vastly better to wait until June, the close of the school year. Not so long, really. Half of March, April, May, some of June. Surely she could endure for that much longer conditions which she had borne for nearly two years. By an effort of will, her will, it could be done.

But this reflection, sensible, expedient, though it was, did not reconcile her. To remain seemed too hard. Could she do it? Was it possible in the present rebellious state of her feelings? The uneasy sense of being engaged with some formidable antagonist, nameless and ununderstood, startled her. It wasn't, she was suddenly aware, merely the school and its ways and its decorous stupid people that oppressed her. There was something else, some other more ruthless force, a quality within herself, which was frustrating her, had always frustrated her, kept her from getting the things she had wanted. Still wanted.

But just what did she want? Barring a desire for material security, gracious ways of living, a profusion of lovely clothes, and a goodly share of envious admiration, Helga Crane didn't know, couldn't tell.

But there was, she knew, something else. Happiness, she supposed. Whatever that might be. What, exactly, she wondered, was happiness. Very positively she wanted it. Yet her conception of it had no tangibility. She couldn't define it, isolate it, and contemplate it as she could some other abstract things. Hatred, for instance. Or kindness.

The strident ringing of a bell somewhere in the building brought back the fierce resentment of the night. It crystallized her wavering determination.

From long habit her biscuit-coloured feet had slipped mechanically out from under the covers at the bell's first unkind jangle. Leisurely she drew them back and her cold anger vanished as she decided that, now, it didn't at all matter if she failed to appear at the monotonous distasteful breakfast which was provided for her by the school as part of her wages.

In the corridor beyond her door was a medley of noises incident to the rising and preparing for the day at the same hour of many school-girls—foolish giggling, indistinguishable snatches of merry conversation, distant gurgle of running water, patter of slippered feet, low-pitched singing, good-natured admonitions to hurry, slamming of doors, clatter of various unnamable articles, and—suddenly—calamitous silence.

Helga ducked her head under the covers in the vain attempt to shut out what she knew would fill the pregnant silence—the sharp sarcastic voice of the dormitory matron. It came.

"Well! Even if every last one of you did come from homes where you weren't taught any manners, you might at least try to pretend that you're capable of learning some here, now that you have the opportunity. Who slammed the shower-baths door?"

Silence.

"Well, you needn't trouble to answer. It's rude, as all of you know. But it's just as well, because none of you can tell the truth. Now hurry up. Don't let me hear of a single one of you being late for breakfast. If I do there'll be extra work for everybody on Saturday. And *please* at least try to act like ladies and not like savages from the backwoods."

On her side of the door, Helga was wondering if it had ever occurred to the lean and desiccated Miss MacGooden that most of her charges had actually come from the backwoods. Quite recently too. Miss MacGooden, humorless, prim, ugly, with a face like dried leather, prided herself on being a "lady" from one of the best families—an uncle had been a congressman in the period of the Reconstruction. She was therefore, Helga Crane reflected, perhaps unable to perceive that the inducement to act like a lady, her own acrimonious example, was slight, if not altogether negative. And thinking on Miss MacGooden's "ladyness," Helga grinned a little as she remembered that one's expressed reason for never having married, or intending to marry. There were, so she had been given to understand, things in the matrimonial state that were of necessity entirely too repulsive for a lady of delicate and sensitive nature to submit to.

Soon the forcibly shut-off noises began to be heard again, as the evidently vanishing image of Miss MacGooden evaporated from the short memories of the ladies-in-making. Preparations for the intake of the day's quota of learning went on again. Almost naturally.

"So much for that!" said Helga, getting herself out of bed.

She walked to the window and stood looking down into the great quadrangle below, at the multitude of students streaming from the six big dormitories which, two each, flanked three of its sides, and assembling into neat phalanxes preparatory to marching in military order to the sorry breakfast in Jones Hall on the fourth side. Here and there a male member of the faculty, important and resplendent in the regalia of an army officer, would pause in his prancing or strutting, to jerk a negligent or offending student into the proper attitude or place. The massed phalanxes increased in size and number, blotting out pavements, bare earth, and grass. And about it all was a depressing silence, a sullenness almost, until with a horrible abruptness the waiting band blared into "The Star Spangled Banner." The goose-step began. Left, right. Left, right. Forward! March! The automatons moved. The squares disintegrated into fours. Into twos. Disappeared into the gaping doors of Jones Hall. After the last pair of marchers had entered, the huge doors were closed. A few unlucky latecomers, apparently already discouraged, tugged half-heartedly at the knobs, and finding, as they had evidently expected, that they were indeed barred out, turned resignedly away.

Helga Crane turned away from the window, a shadow dimming the pale amber loveliness of her face. Seven o'clock it was now. At twelve those children who by some accident had been a little minute or two late would have their first meal after five hours of work and so-called education. Discipline, it was called.

There came a light knocking on her door.

"Come in," invited Helga unenthusiastically. The door opened to admit Margaret Creighton, another teacher in the English department and to Helga the most congenial member of the whole Naxos faculty. Margaret, she felt, appreciated her.

Seeing Helga still in night robe seated on the bedside in a mass of cushions, idly dangling a mule across bare toes like one with all the time in the world before her, she exclaimed in dismay: "Helga Crane, do you know what time it is? Why, it's long after half past seven. The students—"

"Yes, I know," said Helga defiantly, "the students are coming out from breakfast. Well, let them. I, for one, wish that there was some way that they could forever stay out from the poisonous stuff thrown at them, literally thrown at them, Margaret Creighton, for food. Poor things."

Margaret laughed. "That's just ridiculous sentiment, Helga, and you know it. But you haven't had any breakfast, yourself. Jim Vayle asked if you were sick. Of course nobody knew. You never tell anybody anything about yourself. I said I'd look in on you."

"Thanks awfully," Helga responded, indifferently. She was watching the sunlight dissolve from thick orange into pale yellow. Slowly it crept across the room, wiping out in its path the morning shadows. She wasn't interested in what the other was saying.

"If you don't hurry, you'll be late to your first class. Can I help you?" Margaret offered uncertainly. She was a little afraid of Helga. Nearly everyone was.

"No. Thanks all the same." Then quickly in another, warmer tone: "I do mean it. Thanks, a thousand times, Margaret. I'm really awfully grateful, but—you see, it's like this, I'm not going to be late to my class. I'm not going to be there at all."

The visiting girl, standing in relief, like old walnut against the buff-colored wall, darted a quick glance at Helga. Plainly she was curious. But she only said formally: "Oh, then you *are* sick." For something there was about Helga which discouraged questionings.

No, Helga wasn't sick. Not physically. She was merely disgusted. Fed up with Naxos. If that could be called sickness. The truth was that she had made up her mind to leave. That very day. She could no longer abide being connected with a place of shame, lies, hypocrisy, cruelty, servility, and snobbishness. "It ought," she concluded, "to be shut down by law."

"But, Helga, you can't go now. Not in the middle of the term." The kindly Margaret was distressed.

"But I can. And I am. Today."

"They'll never let you," prophesied Margaret.

"*They* can't stop me. Trains leave here for civilization every day. All that's needed is money," Helga pointed out.

"Yes, of course. Everybody knows that. What I mean is that you'll only hurt yourself in your profession. They won't give you a reference if you jump up and leave like this now. At this time of the year. You'll be put on the black list. And you'll find it hard to get another teaching-job. Naxos has enormous influence in the South. Better wait till school closes."

"Heaven forbid," answered Helga fervently, "that I should ever again want work anywhere in the South! I hate it." And fell silent, wondering for the hundredth time just what form of vanity it was that had induced an intelligent girl like Margaret Creighton to turn what was probably nice live crinkly hair, perfectly suited to her smooth dark skin and agreeable round features, into a dead straight, greasy, ugly mass.

Looking up from her watch, Margaret said: "Well, I've really got to run, or I'll be late myself. And since I'm staying—Better think it over, Helga. There's no place like Naxos, you know. Pretty good salaries, decent rooms, plenty of men, and all that. Ta-ta." The door slid to behind her.

But in another moment it opened. She was back. "I do wish you'd stay. It's nice having you here, Helga. We all think so. Even the dead ones. We need a few decorations to brighten our sad lives." And again she was gone.

Helga was unmoved. She was no longer concerned with what anyone in Naxos might think of her, for she was now in love with the piquancy of leaving. Automatically her fingers adjusted the Chinese-looking pillows on the low couch that served for her bed. Her mind was busy with plans for departure. Packing, money, trains, and—could she get a berth?

Three

On one side of the long, white, hot sand road that split the flat green, there was a little shade, for it was bordered with trees. Helga Crane walked there so that the sun could not so easily get at her. As she went slowly across the empty campus she was conscious of a vague tenderness for the scene spread out before her. It was so incredibly lovely, so appealing, and so facile. The trees in their spring beauty sent through her restive mind a sharp thrill of pleasure. Seductive, charming, and beckoning as cities were, they had not this easy unhuman loveliness. The trees, she thought, on city avenues and boulevards, in city parks and gardens, were tamed, held prisoners in a surrounding maze of human beings. Here they were free. It was human beings who were prisoners. It was too bad. In the midst of all this radiant life. They weren't, she knew, even conscious of its presence.

Perhaps there was too much of it, and therefore it was less than nothing.

In response to her insistent demand she had been told that Dr. Anderson could give her twenty minutes at eleven o'clock. Well, she supposed that she could say all that she had to say in twenty minutes, though she resented being limited. Twenty minutes. In Naxos, she was as unimportant as that.

He was a new man, this principal, for whom Helga remembered feeling unaccountably sorry, when last September he had first been appointed to Naxos as its head. For some reason she had liked him, although she had seen little of him; he was so frequently away on publicity and money-raising tours. And as yet he had made but few and slight changes in the running of the school. Now she was a little irritated at finding herself wondering just how she was going to tell him of her decision. What did it matter to him? Why should she mind if it did? But there returned to her that indistinct sense of sympathy for the remote silent man with the tired gray eyes, and she wondered again by what fluke of fate such a man, apparently a humane and understanding person, had chanced into the command of this cruel educational machine. Suddenly, her own resolve loomed as an almost direct unkindness. This increased her annoyance and discomfort. A sense of defeat, of being cheated of justification, closed down on her. Absurd!

She arrived at the administration building in a mild rage, as unreasonable as it was futile, but once inside she had a sudden attack of nerves at the prospect of traversing that great outer room which was the workplace of some twenty odd people. This was a disease from which Helga had suffered at intervals all her life, and it was a point of honor, almost, with her never to give way to it. So, instead of turning away, as she felt inclined, she walked on, outwardly indifferent. Half-way down the long aisle which divided the room, the principal's secretary, a huge black man, surged toward her.

"Good-morning, Miss Crane, Dr. Anderson will see you in a few moments. Sit down right here."

She felt the inquiry in the shuttered eyes. For some reason this dissipated her self-consciousness and restored her poise. Thanking him, she seated herself, really careless now of the glances of the stenographers, book-keepers, clerks. Their curiosity and slightly veiled hostility no longer touched her. Her coming departure had released her from the need for conciliation which had irked her for so long. It was pleasant to Helga Crane to be able to sit calmly looking out of the window on to the smooth lawn, where a few leaves quite prematurely fallen dotted the grass, for once uncaring whether the frock which she wore roused disapproval or envy.

Turning from the window, her gaze wandered contemptuously over the dull attire of the women workers. Drab colors, mostly navy blue, black, brown, unrelieved, save for a scrap of white or tan about the hands and necks. Fragments of a speech made by the dean of women floated through her thoughts—"Bright colors are vulgar"—"Black, gray, brown, and navy blue are the most becoming colors for colored people"—"Dark-complected people shouldn't wear yellow, or green or red."—The dean was a woman from one of the "first families"—a great "race" woman; she, Helga Crane, a despised mulatto, but something intuitive, some unanalyzed driving spirit of loyalty to the inherent racial need for gorgeousness told her that bright colours *were* fitting and that dark-complexioned people *should* wear yellow, green, and red. Black, brown, and gray were ruinous to them, actually destroyed the luminous tones lurking in their dusky skins. One of the loveliest sights Helga had ever seen had been a sooty black girl decked out in a flaming orange dress, which a horrified matron had next day consigned to the dyer. Why, she wondered, didn't someone write *A Plea for Color?*

These people yapped loudly of race, of race consciousness, of race pride, and yet suppressed its most delightful manifestations, love of color, joy of rhythmic motion, naïve, spontaneous laughter. Harmony, radiance, and simplicity, all the essentials of spiritual beauty in the race they had marked for destruction.

She came back to her own problems. Clothes had been one of her difficulties in Naxos. Helga Crane loved clothes, elaborate ones. Nevertheless, she had tried not to offend. But with small success, for, although she had affected the deceptively simple variety, the hawk eyes of dean and matrons had detected the subtle difference from their own irreproachably conventional garments. Too, they felt that the colors were queer; dark purples, royal blues, rich greens, deep reds, in soft, luxurious woolens, or heavy, clinging silks. And the trimmings—when Helga used them at all—seemed to them odd. Old laces, strange embroideries, dim brocades. Her faultless, slim shoes made them uncomfortable and her small plain hats seemed to them positively indecent. Helga smiled inwardly at the thought that whenever there was an evening affair for the faculty, the dear ladies probably held their breaths until she had made her appearance. They existed in constant fear that she might turn out in an evening dress. The proper evening wear in Naxos was afternoon attire. And one could, if one wished, garnish the hair with flowers.

Quick, muted footfalls sounded. The secretary had returned.

"Dr. Anderson will see you now, Miss Crane."

She rose, followed, and was ushered into the guarded sanctum, without having decided just what she was to say. For a moment she felt behind her the open doorway and then the gentle impact of its closing. Before her at a great desk her eyes picked out the figure of a man, at first blurred slightly in outline in that dimmer light. At his "Miss Crane?" her lips formed for speech, but no sound came. She was aware of inward confusion. For her the situation seemed charged, unaccountably, with strangeness and something very like hysteria. An almost overpowering desire to laugh seized her. Then, miraculously, a complete ease, such as she had never known in Naxos, possessed her. She smiled, nodded in answer to his questioning salutation, and with a gracious "Thank you" dropped into the chair which he indicated. She looked at him frankly now, this man still young, thirty-five perhaps, and found it easy to go on in the vein of a simple statement.

"Dr. Anderson, I'm sorry to have to confess that I've failed in my job here. I've made up my mind to leave. Today."

A short, almost imperceptible silence, then a deep voice of peculiarly pleasing resonance, asking gently: "You don't like Naxos, Miss Crane?"

She evaded. "Naxos, the place? Yes, I like it. Who wouldn't like it? It's so beautiful. But I—well—I don't seem to fit here."

The man smiled, just a little. "The school? You don't like the school?"

The words burst from her. "No, I don't like it. I hate it!"

"Why?" The question was detached, too detached.

In the girl blazed a desire to wound. There he sat, staring dreamily out of the window, blatantly unconcerned with her or her answer. Well, she'd tell him. She pronounced each word with deliberate slowness.

"Well, for one thing, I hate hypocrisy. I hate cruelty to students, and to teachers who can't fight back. I hate backbiting, and sneaking, and petty jealousy. Naxos? It's hardly a place at all. It's more like some loathsome, venomous disease. Ugh! Everybody spending his time in a malicious hunting for the weaknesses of others, spying, grudging, scratching."

"I see. And you don't think it might help to cure us, to have someone who doesn't approve of these things stay with us? Even just one person, Miss Crane?"

She wondered if this last was irony. She suspected it was humor and so ignored the half-pleading note in his voice.

"No, I don't! It doesn't do the disease any good. Only irritates it. And it makes me unhappy, dissatisfied. It isn't pleasant to be always made to appear in the wrong, even when I know I'm right."

His gaze was on her now, searching. "Queer," she thought, "how some brown people have gray eyes. Gives them a strange, unexpected appearance. A little frightening."

The man said, kindly: "Ah, you're unhappy. And for the reasons you've stated?"

"Yes, partly. Then, too, the people here don't like me. They don't think I'm in the spirit of the work. And I'm not, not if it means suppression of individuality and beauty."

"And does it?"

"Well, it seems to work out that way."

"How old are you, Miss Crane?"

She resented this, but she told him, speaking with what curtness she could command only the bare figure: "Twenty-three."

"Twenty-three. I see. Some day you'll learn that lies, injustice, and hypocrisy are a part of every ordinary community. Most people achieve a sort of protective immunity, a kind of callousness, toward them. If they didn't, they couldn't endure. I think there's less of these evils here than in most places, but because we're trying to do such a big thing, to aim so high, the ugly things show more, they irk some of us more. Service is like clean white linen, even the tiniest speck shows." He went on, explaining, amplifying, pleading.

Helga Crane was silent, feeling a mystifying yearning which sang and throbbed in her. She felt again that urge for service, not now for her people, but for this man who was talking so earnestly of his work, his plans, his hopes. An insistent need to be a part of them sprang in her. With compunction tweaking at her heart for even having entertained the notion of deserting him, she resolved not only to remain until June, but to return next year. She was shamed, yet stirred. It was not sacrifice she felt now, but actual desire to stay, and to come back next year.

He came, at last, to the end of the long speech, only part of which she had heard. "You see, you understand?" he urged.

"Yes, oh yes, I do."

"What we need is more people like you, people with a sense of values, and proportion, an appreciation of the rarer things of life. You have something to give which we badly need here in Naxos. You mustn't desert us, Miss Crane."

She nodded, silent. He had won her. She knew that she would stay. "It's an elusive something," he went on. "Perhaps I can best explain it by the use of that trite phrase, 'You're a lady.' You have dignity and breeding."

At these words turmoil rose again in Helga Crane. The intricate pattern of the rug which she had been studying escaped her. The shamed feeling which had been her penance evaporated. Only a lacerated pride remained. She took firm hold of the chair arms to still the trembling of her fingers.

"If you're speaking of family, Dr. Anderson, why, I haven't any. I was born in a Chicago slum."

The man chose his words, carefully he thought. "That doesn't at all matter, Miss Crane. Financial, economic circumstances can't destroy tendencies inherited from good stock. You yourself prove that!"

Concerned with her own angry thoughts, which scurried here and there like trapped rats, Helga missed the import of his words. Her own words, her answer, fell like drops of hail.

"The joke is on you, Dr. Anderson. My father was a gambler who deserted my mother, a white immigrant. It is even uncertain that they were married. As I said at first, I don't belong here. I shall be leaving at once. This afternoon. Good-morning."

Four

Long, soft white clouds, clouds like shreds of incredibly fine cotton, streaked the blue of the early evening sky. Over the flying landscape hung a very faint mist, disturbed now and then by a languid breeze. But no coolness invaded the heat of the train rushing north. The open windows of the stuffy day coach, where Helga Crane sat with others of her race, seemed only to intensify her discomfort. Her head ached with a steady pounding pain. This, added to her wounds of the spirit, made traveling something little short of a medieval torture. Desperately she was trying to right the confusion in her mind. The temper of the morning's interview rose before her like an ugly mutilated creature crawling horribly over the flying landscape of her thoughts. It was no use. The ugly thing pressed down on her, held her. Leaning back, she tried to doze as others were doing. The futility of her effort exasperated her.

Just what had happened to her there in that cool dim room under the quizzical gaze of those piercing gray eyes? Whatever it was had been so powerful, so compelling, that but for a few chance words she would still be in Naxos. And why had she permitted herself to be jolted into a rage so fierce, so illogical, so disastrous, that now after it was spent she sat despondent, sunk in shameful contrition? As she reviewed the manner of her departure from his presence, it seemed increasingly rude.

She didn't, she told herself, after all, like this Dr. Anderson. He was too controlled, too sure of himself and others. She detested cool, perfectly controlled people. Well, it didn't matter. He didn't matter.

But she could not put him from her mind. She set it down to annoyance because of the cold discourtesy of her abrupt action. She disliked rudeness in anyone.

She had outraged her own pride, and she had terribly wronged her mother by her insidious implication. Why? Her thoughts lingered with her mother, long dead. A fair Scandinavian girl in love with life, with love, with passion, dreaming, and risking all in one blind surrender. A cruel sacrifice. In forgetting all but love she had forgotten, or had perhaps never known, that some things the world never forgives. But as Helga knew, she had remembered, or had learned in suffering and longing all the rest of her life. Her daughter hoped she had been happy, happy beyond most human creatures, in the little time it had lasted, the little time before that gay suave scoundrel, Helga's father, had left her. But Helga Crane doubted it. How could she have been? A girl gently bred, fresh from an older, more polished civilization, flung into poverty, sordidness, and dissipation. She visualized her now, sad, cold, and—yes, remote. The tragic cruelties of the years had left her a little pathetic, a little hard, and a little unapproachable.

That second marriage, to a man of her own race, but not of her own kind—so passionately, so instinctively resented by Helga even at the trivial age of six—she now understood as a grievous necessity. Even foolish, despised women must have food and clothing; even unloved little Negro girls must be somehow provided for. Memory, flown back to those years following the marriage, dealt her torturing stabs. Before her rose the pictures of her mother's careful management to avoid those ugly scarifying quarrels which even at this far-off time caused an uncontrollable shudder, her own childish self-effacement, the savage unkindness of her stepbrothers and sisters, and the jealous, malicious hatred of her mother's husband. Summers, winters, years, passing in one long, changeless stretch of aching misery of soul. Her mother's death, when Helga was fifteen. Her rescue by Uncle Peter, who had sent her to school, a school for Negroes, where for the first time she could breathe freely, where she discovered that because one was dark, one was not necessarily loathsome, and could, therefore, consider oneself without repulsion.

Six years. She had been happy there, as happy as a child unused to happiness dared be. There had been always a feeling of strangeness, of outsideness, and one of holding her breath for fear that it wouldn't last. It hadn't. It had dwindled gradually into eclipse of painful isolation. As she grew older, she became gradually aware of a difference between herself and the girls about her. They had mothers, fathers, brothers, and sisters of whom they spoke frequently, and who

sometimes visited them. They went home for the vacations which
Helga spent in the city where the school was located. They visited
each other and knew many of the same people. Discontent for which
there was no remedy crept upon her, and she was glad almost when
these most peaceful years which she had yet known came to their
end. She had been happier, but still horribly lonely.

She had looked forward with pleasant expectancy to working in
Naxos when the chance came. And now this! What was it that stood
in her way? Helga Crane couldn't explain it, put a name to it. She
had tried in the early afternoon in her gentle but staccato talk with
James Vayle. Even to herself her explanation had sounded inane and
insufficient; no wonder James had been impatient and unbelieving.
During their brief and unsatisfactory conversation she had had an odd
feeling that he felt somehow cheated. And more than once she had
been aware of a suggestion of suspicion in his attitude, a feeling that
he was being duped, that he suspected her of some hidden purpose
which he was attempting to discover.

Well, that was over. She would never be married to James Vayle
now. It flashed upon her that, even had she remained in Naxos, she
would never have been married to him. She couldn't have married
him. Gradually, too, there stole into her thoughts of him a curious
sensation of repugnance, for which she was at a loss to account. It
was new, something unfelt before. Certainly she had never loved him
overwhelmingly, not, for example, as her mother must have loved
her father, but she *had* liked him, and she had expected to love him,
after their marriage. People generally did love then, she imagined.
No, she had not loved James, but she had wanted to. Acute nausea
rose in her as she recalled the slight quivering of his lips sometimes
when her hands had unexpectedly touched his; the throbbing vein in
his forehead on a gay day when they had wandered off alone across
the low hills and she had allowed him frequent kisses under the shelter of some low-hanging willows. Now she shivered a little, even in
the hot train, as if she had suddenly come out from a warm scented
place into cool, clear air. She must have been mad, she thought; but
she couldn't tell why she thought so. This, too, bothered her.

Laughing conversation buzzed about her. Across the aisle a bronze
baby, with bright staring eyes, began a fretful whining, which its young
mother essayed to silence by a low droning croon. In the seat just beyond, a black and tan young pair were absorbed in the eating of a cold
fried chicken, audibly crunching the ends of the crisp, browned bones.
A little distance away a tired laborer slept noisily. Near him two children dropped the peelings of oranges and bananas on the already soiled
floor. The smell of stale food and ancient tobacco irritated Helga like a

physical pain. A man, a white man, strode through the packed car and spat twice, once in the exact centre of the dingy door panel, and once into the receptacle which held the drinking-water. Instantly Helga became aware of stinging thirst. Her eyes sought the small watch at her wrist. Ten hours to Chicago. Would she be lucky enough to prevail upon the conductor to let her occupy a berth, or would she have to remain here all night, without sleep, without food, without drink, and with that disgusting door panel to which her purposely averted eyes were constantly, involuntarily straying?

Her first effort was unsuccessful. An ill-natured "No, you know you can't," was the answer to her inquiry. But farther on along the road, there was a change of men. Her rebuff had made her reluctant to try again, but the entry of a farmer carrying a basket containing live chickens, which he deposited on the seat (the only vacant one) beside her, strengthened her weakened courage. Timidly, she approached the new conductor, an elderly gray-mustached man of pleasant appearance, who subjected her to a keen, appraising look, and then promised to see what could be done. She thanked him, gratefully, and went back to her shared seat, to wait anxiously. After half an hour he returned, saying he could "fix her up," there was a section she could have, adding: "It'll cost you ten dollars." She murmured: "All right. Thank you." It was twice the price, and she needed every penny, but she knew she was fortunate to get it even at that, and so was very thankful, as she followed his tall, loping figure out of that car and through seemingly endless others, and at last into one where she could rest a little.

She undressed and lay down, her thoughts still busy with the morning's encounter. Why hadn't she grasped his meaning? Why, if she had said so much, hadn't she said more about herself and her mother? He would, she was sure, have understood, even sympathized. Why had she lost her temper and given way to angry half-truths?—Angry half-truths—Angry half- -

Five

Gray Chicago seethed, surged, and scurried about her. Helga shivered a little, drawing her light coat closer. She had forgotten how cold March could be under the pale skies of the North. But she liked it, this blustering wind. She would even have welcomed snow, for it would more clearly have marked the contrast between this freedom and the cage which Naxos had been to her. Not but what it was marked plainly enough by the noise, the dash, the crowds.

Helga Crane, who had been born in this dirty, mad, hurrying city, had no home here. She had not even any friends here. It would have to be, she decided, the Young Women's Christian Association. "Oh dear! The uplift. Poor, poor colored people. Well, no use stewing about it. I'll get a taxi to take me out, bag and baggage, then I'll have a hot bath and a really good meal, peep into the shops—mustn't buy anything—and then for Uncle Peter. Guess I won't phone. More effective if I surprise him."

It was late, very late, almost evening, when finally Helga turned her steps northward, in the direction of Uncle Peter's home. She had put it off as long as she could, for she detested her errand. The fact that that one day had shown her its acute necessity did not decrease her distaste. As she approached the North Side, the distaste grew. Arrived at last at the familiar door of the old stone house, her confidence in Uncle Peter's welcome deserted her. She gave the bell a timid push and then decided to turn away, to go back to her room and phone, or, better yet, to write. But before she could retreat, the door was opened by a strange red-faced maid, dressed primly in black and white. This increased Helga's mistrust. Where, she wondered, was the ancient Rose, who had, ever since she could remember, served her uncle.

The hostile "Well?" of this new servant forcibly recalled the reason for her presence there. She said firmly: "Mr. Nilssen, please."

"Mr. Nilssen's not in," was the pert retort. "Will you see Mrs. Nilssen?"

Helga was startled. "Mrs. Nilssen! I beg your pardon, did you say Mrs. Nilssen?"

"I did," answered the maid shortly, beginning to close the door.

"What is it, Ida?" A woman's soft voice sounded from within.

"Someone for Mr. Nilssen, m'am." The girl looked embarrassed.

In Helga's face the blood rose in a deep-red stain. She explained: "Helga Crane, his niece."

"She says she's his niece, m'am."

"Well, have her come in."

There was no escape. She stood in the large reception hall, and was annoyed to find herself actually trembling. A woman, tall, exquisitely gowned, with shining gray hair piled high, came forward murmuring in a puzzled voice: "His niece, did you say?"

"Yes, Helga Crane. My mother was his sister, Karen Nilssen. I've been away. I didn't know Uncle Peter had married." Sensitive to atmosphere, Helga had felt at once the latent antagonism in the woman's manner.

"Oh, yes! I remember about you now. I'd forgotten for a moment.

Well, he isn't exactly your uncle, is he? Your mother wasn't married, was she? I mean, to your father?"

"I—I don't know," stammered the girl, feeling pushed down to the uttermost depths of ignominy.

"Of course she wasn't." The clear, low voice held a positive note. "Mr. Nilssen has been very kind to you, supported you, sent you to school. But you mustn't expect anything else. And you mustn't come here any more. It—well, frankly, it isn't convenient. I'm sure an intelligent girl like yourself can understand that."

"Of course," Helga agreed, coldly, freezingly, but her lips quivered. She wanted to get away as quickly as possible. She reached the door. There was a second of complete silence, then Mrs. Nilssen's voice, a little agitated: "And please remember that my husband is not your uncle. No indeed! Why, that, that would make me your aunt! He's not—"

But at last the knob had turned in Helga's fumbling hand. She gave a little unpremeditated laugh and slipped out. When she was in the street, she ran. Her only impulse was to get as far away from her uncle's house, and this woman, his wife, who so plainly wished to dissociate herself from the outrage of her very existence. She was torn with mad fright, an emotion against which she knew but two weapons: to kick and scream, or to flee.

The day had lengthened. It was evening and much colder, but Helga Crane was unconscious of any change, so shaken she was and burning. The wind cut her like a knife, but she did not feel it. She ceased her frantic running, aware at last of the curious glances of passers-by. At one spot, for a moment less frequented than others, she stopped to give heed to her disordered appearance. Here a man, well groomed and pleasant-spoken, accosted her. On such occasions she was wont to reply scathingly, but, tonight, his pale Caucasian face struck her breaking faculties as too droll. Laughing harshly, she threw at him the words: "You're not my uncle."

He retired in haste, probably thinking her drunk, or possibly a little mad.

Night fell, while Helga Crane in the rushing swiftness of a roaring elevated train sat numb. It was as if all the bogies and goblins that had beset her unloved, unloving, and unhappy childhood had come to life with tenfold power to hurt and frighten. For the wound was deeper in that her long freedom from their presence had rendered her the more vulnerable. Worst of all was the fact that under the stinging hurt she understood and sympathized with Mrs. Nilssen's point of view, as always she had been able to understand her mother's, her stepfather's, and his children's points of view. She saw herself for an obscene sore in all their lives, at all costs to be hidden. She understood, even while she resented. It would have been easier if she had not.

Later in the bare silence of her tiny room she remembered the unaccomplished object of her visit. Money. Characteristically, while admitting its necessity, and even its undeniable desirability, she dismissed its importance. Its elusive quality she had as yet never known. She would find work of some kind. Perhaps the library. The idea clung. Yes, certainly the library. She knew books and loved them.

She stood intently looking down into the glimmering street, far below, swarming with people, merging into little eddies and disengaging themselves to pursue their own individual ways. A few minutes later she stood in the doorway, drawn by an uncontrollable desire to mingle with the crowd. The purple sky showed tremulous clouds piled up, drifting here and there with a sort of endless lack of purpose. Very like the myriad human beings pressing hurriedly on. Looking at these, Helga caught herself wondering who they were, what they did, and of what they thought. What was passing behind those dark molds of flesh. Did they really think at all? Yet, as she stepped out into the moving multi-colored crowd, there came to her a queer feeling of enthusiasm, as if she were tasting some agreeable, exotic food—sweetbreads, smothered with truffles and mushrooms—perhaps. And, oddly enough, she felt, too, that she had come home. She, Helga Crane, who had no home.

Six

Helga woke to the sound of rain. The day was leaden gray, and misty black, and dullish white. She was not surprised, the night had promised it. She made a little frown, remembering that it was today that she was to search for work.

She dressed herself carefully, in the plainest garments she possessed, a suit of fine blue twill faultlessly tailored, from whose left pocket peeped a gay kerchief, an unadorned, heavy silk blouse, a small, smart, fawn-colored hat, and slim, brown oxfords, and chose a brown umbrella. In a near-by street she sought out an appealing little restaurant, which she had noted in her last night's ramble through the neighborhood, for the thick cups and the queer dark silver of the Young Women's Christian Association distressed her.

After a slight breakfast she made her way to the library, that ugly gray building, where was housed much knowledge and a little wisdom, on interminable shelves. The friendly person at the desk in the hall bestowed on her a kindly smile when Helga stated her business and asked for directions.

"The corridor to your left, then the second door to your right," she was told.

Outside the indicated door, for half a second she hesitated, then braced herself and went in. In less than a quarter of an hour she came out, in surprised disappointment. "Library training"—"civil service"—"library school"—"classification"—"cataloguing"—"training class"—"examination"—"probation period"—flitted through her mind.

"How erudite they must be!" she remarked sarcastically to herself, and ignored the smiling curiosity of the desk person as she went through the hall to the street. For a long moment she stood on the high stone steps above the avenue, then shrugged her shoulders and stepped down. It *was* a disappointment, but of course there were other things. She would find something else. But what? Teaching, even substitute teaching, was hopeless now, in March. She had no business training, and the shops didn't employ colored clerks or salespeople, not even the smaller ones. She couldn't sew, she couldn't cook. Well, she *could* do housework, or wait on table, for a short time at least. Until she got a little money together. With this thought she remembered that the Young Women's Christian Association maintained an employment agency.

"Of course, the very thing!" She exclaimed, aloud. "I'll go straight back."

But, though the day was still drear, rain had ceased to fall, and Helga, instead of returning, spent hours in aimless strolling about the hustling streets of the Loop district. When at last she did retrace her steps, the business day had ended, and the employment office was closed. This frightened her a little, this and the fact that she had spent money, too much money, for a book and a tapestry purse, things which she wanted, but did not need and certainly could not afford. Regretful and dismayed, she resolved to go without her dinner, as a self-inflicted penance, as well as an economy—and she would be at the employment office the first thing tomorrow morning.

But it was not until three days more had passed that Helga Crane sought the Association, or any other employment office. And then it was sheer necessity that drove her there, for her money had dwindled to a ridiculous sum. She had put off the hated moment, had assured herself that she was tired, needed a bit of vacation, was due one. It had been pleasant, the leisure, the walks, the lake, the shops and streets with their gay colors, their movement, after the great quiet of Naxos. Now she was panicky.

In the office a few nondescript women sat scattered about on the long rows of chairs. Some were plainly uninterested, others wore an air of acute expectancy, which disturbed Helga. Behind a desk two alert young women, both wearing a superior air, were busy writing upon and filing countless white cards. Now and then one stopped to answer the telephone.

"Y.W.C.A. employment. . . . Yes. . . . Spell it, please. . . . Sleep in or out? Thirty dollars? . . . Thank you, I'll send one right over."

Or, "I'm awfully sorry, we haven't anybody right now, but I'll send you the first one that comes in."

Their manners were obtrusively business-like, but they ignored the already embarrassed Helga. Diffidently she approached the desk. The darker of the two looked up and turned on a little smile.

"Yes?" she inquired.

"I wonder if you can help me? I want work," Helga stated simply.

"Maybe. What kind? Have you references?"

Helga explained. She was a teacher. A graduate of Devon. Had been teaching in Naxos.

The girl was not interested. "Our kind of work wouldn't do for you," she kept repeating at the end of each of Helga's statements. "Domestic mostly."

When Helga said that she was willing to accept work of any kind, a slight, almost imperceptible change crept into her manner and her perfunctory smile disappeared. She repeated her question about the reference. On learning that Helga had none, she said sharply, finally: "I'm sorry, but we never send out help without references."

With a feeling that she had been slapped, Helga Crane hurried out. After some lunch she sought out an employment agency on State Street. An hour passed in patient sitting. Then came her turn to be interviewed. She said, simply, that she wanted work, work of any kind. A competent young woman, whose eyes stared frog-like from great tortoise-shell-rimmed glasses, regarded her with an appraising look and asked for her history, past and present, not forgetting the "references." Helga told her that she was a graduate of Devon, had taught in Naxos. But even before she arrived at the explanation of the lack of references, the other's interest in her had faded.

"I'm sorry, but we have nothing that you would be interested in," she said and motioned to the next seeker, who immediately came forward, proffering several much worn papers.

"References," thought Helga, resentfully, bitterly, as she went out the door into the crowded garish street in search of another agency, where her visit was equally vain.

Days of this sort of thing. Weeks of it. And of the futile scanning and answering of newspaper advertisements. She traversed acres of streets, but it seemed that in that whole energetic place nobody wanted her services. At least not the kind that she offered. A few men, both white and black, offered her money, but the price of the money was too dear. Helga Crane did not feel inclined to pay it.

She began to feel terrified and lost. And she was a little hungry too, for her small money was dwindling and she felt the need to economize somehow. Food was the easiest.

In the midst of her search for work she felt horribly lonely too. This sense of loneliness increased, it grew to appalling proportions, encompassing her, shutting her off from all of life around her. Devastated she was, and always on the verge of weeping. It made her feel small and insignificant that in all the climbing massed city no one cared one whit about her.

Helga Crane was not religious. She took nothing on trust. Nevertheless on Sundays she attended the very fashionable, very high services in the Negro Episcopal church on Michigan Avenue. She hoped that some good Christian would speak to her, invite her to return, or inquire kindly if she was a stranger in the city. None did, and she became bitter, distrusting religion more than ever. She was herself unconscious of that faint hint of offishness which hung about her and repelled advances, an arrogance that stirred in people a peculiar irritation. They noticed her, admired her clothes, but that was all, for the self-sufficient uninterested manner adopted instinctively as a protective measure for her acute sensitiveness, in her child days, still clung to her.

An agitated feeling of disaster closed in on her, tightened. Then, one afternoon, coming in from the discouraging round of agencies and the vain answering of newspaper wants to the stark neatness of her room, she found between door and sill a small folded note. Spreading it open, she read:

Miss Crane:

Please come into the employment office as soon as you return.

Ida Ross

Helga spent some time in the contemplation of this note. She was afraid to hope. Its possibilities made her feel a little hysterical. Finally, after removing the dirt of the dusty streets, she went down, down to that room where she had first felt the smallness of her commercial value. Subsequent failures had augmented her feeling of incompetence, but she resented the fact that these clerks were evidently aware of her unsuccess. It required all the pride and indifferent hauteur she could summon to support her in their presence. Her additional arrogance passed unnoticed by those for whom it was assumed. They were interested only in the business for which they had summoned her, that of procuring a traveling-companion for a lecturing female on her way to a convention.

"She wants," Miss Ross told Helga, "someone intelligent, someone who can help her get her speeches in order on the train. We thought of you right away. Of course, it isn't permanent. She'll pay your expenses and there'll be twenty-five dollars besides. She leaves tomorrow. Here's her address. You're to go to see her at five o'clock. It's after four now. I'll phone that you're on your way."

The presumptuousness of their certainty that she would snatch at the opportunity galled Helga. She became aware of a desire to be disagreeable. The inclination to fling the address of the lecturing female in their face stirred in her, but she remembered the lone five dollar bill in the rare old tapestry purse swinging from her arm. She couldn't afford anger. So she thanked them very politely and set out for the home of Mrs. Hayes-Rore on Grand Boulevard, knowing full well that she intended to take the job, if the lecturing one would take her. Twenty-five dollars was not to be looked at with nose in air when one was the owner of but five. And meals—meals for four days at least.

Mrs. Hayes-Rore proved to be a plump lemon-colored woman with badly straightened hair and dirty finger-nails. Her direct, penetrating gaze was somewhat formidable. Notebook in hand, she gave Helga the impression of having risen early for consultation with other harassed authorities on the race problem, and having been in conference on the subject all day. Evidently, she had had little time or thought for the careful donning of the five-years-behind-the-mode garments which covered her, and which even in their youth could hardly have fitted or suited her. She had a tart personality, and prying. She approved of Helga, after asking her endless questions about her education and her opinions on the race problem, none of which she was permitted to answer, for Mrs. Hayes-Rore either went on to the next or answered the question herself by remarking: "Not that it matters, if you can only do what I want done, and the girls at the 'Y' said that you could. I'm on the Board of Managers, and I know they wouldn't send me anybody who wasn't all right." After this had been repeated twice in a booming, oratorical voice, Helga felt that the Association secretaries had taken an awful chance in sending a person about whom they knew as little as they did about her.

"Yes, I'm sure you'll do. I don't really need ideas, I've plenty of my own. It's just a matter of getting someone to help me get my speeches in order, correct and condense them, you know. I leave at eleven in the morning. Can you be ready by then? . . . That's good. Better be here at nine. Now, don't disappoint me. I'm depending on you."

As she stepped into the street and made her way skillfully through the impassioned human traffic, Helga reviewed the plan which she had formed, while in the lecturing one's presence, to remain in New York. There would be twenty-five dollars, and perhaps the amount of her return ticket. Enough for a start. Surely she could get work there. Everybody did. Anyway, she would have a reference.

With her decision she felt reborn. She began happily to paint the future in vivid colors. The world had changed to silver, and life ceased to be a struggle and became a gay adventure. Even the advertisements in the shop windows seemed to shine with radiance.

Curious about Mrs. Hayes-Rore, on her return to the "Y" she went into the employment office, ostensibly to thank the girls and to report that that important woman would take her. Was there, she inquired, anything that she needed to know? Mrs. Hayes-Rore had appeared to put such faith in their recommendation of her that she felt almost obliged to give satisfaction. And she added: "I didn't get much chance to ask questions. She seemed so—er—busy."

Both the girls laughed. Helga laughed with them, surprised that she hadn't perceived before how really likable they were.

"We'll be through here in ten minutes. If you're not busy, come in and have your supper with us and we'll tell you about her," promised Miss Ross.

Seven

Having finally turned her attention to Helga Crane, Fortune now seemed determined to smile, to make amends for her shameful neglect. One had, Helga decided, only to touch the right button, to press the right spring, in order to attract the jade's notice.

For Helga that spring had been Mrs. Hayes-Rore. Ever afterwards on recalling that day on which with wellnigh empty purse and apprehensive heart she had made her way from the Young Women's Christian Association to the Grand Boulevard home of Mrs. Hayes-Rore, always she wondered at her own lack of astuteness in not seeing in the woman someone who by a few words was to have a part in the shaping of her life.

The husband of Mrs. Hayes-Rore had at one time been a dark

thread in the soiled fabric of Chicago's South Side politics, who, departing this life hurriedly and unexpectedly and a little mysteriously, and somewhat before the whole of his suddenly acquired wealth had had time to vanish, had left his widow comfortably established with money and some of that prestige which in Negro circles had been his. All this Helga had learned from the secretaries at the "Y." And from numerous remarks dropped by Mrs. Hayes-Rore herself she was able to fill in the details more or less adequately.

On the train that carried them to New York, Helga had made short work of correcting and condensing the speeches, which Mrs. Hayes-Rore as a prominent "race" woman and an authority on the problem was to deliver before several meetings of the annual convention of the Negro Women's League of Clubs, convening the next week in New York. These speeches proved to be merely patchworks of others' speeches and opinions. Helga had heard other lecturers say the same things in Devon and again in Naxos. Ideas, phrases, and even whole sentences and paragraphs were lifted bodily from previous orations and published works of Wendell Phillips, Frederick Douglass, Booker T. Washington, and other doctors of the race's ills. For variety Mrs. Hayes-Rore had seasoned hers with a peppery dash of Du Bois and a few vinegary statements of her own. Aside from these it was, Helga reflected, the same old thing.

But Mrs. Hayes-Rore was to her, after the first short, awkward period, interesting. Her dark eyes, bright and investigating, had, Helga noted, a humorous gleam, and something in the way she held her untidy head gave the impression of a cat watching its prey so that when she struck, if she so decided, the blow would be unerringly effective. Helga, looking up from a last reading of the speeches, was aware that she was being studied. Her employer sat leaning back, the tips of her fingers pressed together, her head a bit on one side, her small inquisitive eyes boring into the girl before her. And as the train hurled itself frantically toward smoke-infested Newark, she decided to strike.

"Now tell me," she commanded, "how is it that a nice girl like you can rush off on a wildgoose chase like this at a moment's notice. I should think your people'd object, or'd make inquiries, or something."

At that command Helga Crane could not help sliding down her eyes to hide the anger that had risen in them. Was she to be forever explaining her people—or lack of them? But she said courteously enough, even managing a hard little smile: "Well you see, Mrs. Hayes-Rore, I haven't any people. There's only me, so I can do as I please."

"Ha!" said Mrs. Hayes-Rore.

Terrific, thought Helga Crane, the power of that sound from the lips of this woman. How, she wondered, had she succeeded in investing it with so much incredulity.

"If you didn't have people, you wouldn't be living. Everybody has people, Miss Crane. Everybody."

"I haven't, Mrs. Hayes-Rore."

Mrs. Hayes-Rore screwed up her eyes. "Well, that's mighty mysterious, and I detest mysteries." She shrugged, and into those eyes there now came with alarming quickness an accusing criticism.

"It isn't," Helga said defensively, "a mystery. It's a fact and a mighty unpleasant one. Inconvenient too," and she laughed a little, not wishing to cry.

Her tormentor, in sudden embarrassment, turned her sharp eyes to the window. She seemed intent on the miles of red clay sliding past. After a moment, however, she asked gently: "You wouldn't like to tell me about it, would you? It seems to bother you. And I'm interested in girls."

Annoyed, but still hanging, for the sake of the twenty-five dollars, to her self-control, Helga gave her head a little toss and flung out her hands in a helpless, beaten way. Then she shrugged. What did it matter? "Oh, well, if you really want to know. I assure you, it's nothing interesting. Or nasty," she added maliciously. "It's just plain horrid. For me." And she began mockingly to relate her story.

But as she went on, again she had that sore sensation of revolt, and again the torment which she had gone through loomed before her as something brutal and undeserved. Passionately, tearfully, incoherently, the final words tumbled from her quivering petulant lips.

The other woman still looked out of the window, apparently so interested in the outer aspect of the drab sections of the Jersey manufacturing city through which they were passing that, the better to see, she had now so turned her head that only an ear and a small portion of cheek were visible.

During the little pause that followed Helga's recital, the faces of the two women, which had been bare, seemed to harden. It was almost as if they had slipped on masks. The girl wished to hide her turbulent feeling and to appear indifferent to Mrs. Hayes-Rore's opinion of her story. The woman felt that the story, dealing as it did with race intermingling and possibly adultery, was beyond definite discussion. For among black people, as among white people, it is tacitly understood that these things are not mentioned—and therefore they do not exist.

Sliding adroitly out from under the precarious subject to a safer, more decent one, Mrs. Hayes-Rore asked Helga what she was thinking of doing when she got back to Chicago. Had she anything in mind?

Helga, it appeared, hadn't. The truth was she had been thinking of staying in New York. Maybe she could find something there. Everybody seemed to. At least she could make the attempt.

Mrs. Hayes-Rore sighed, for no obvious reason. "Um, maybe I can help you. I know people in New York. Do you?"

"No."

"New York's the lonesomest place in the world if you don't know anybody."

"It couldn't possibly be worse than Chicago," said Helga savagely, giving the table support a violent kick.

They were running into the shadow of the tunnel. Mrs. Hayes-Rore murmured thoughtfully: "You'd better come uptown and stay with me a few days. I may need you. Something may turn up."

It was one of those vicious mornings, windy and bright. There seemed to Helga, as they emerged from the depths of the vast station, to be a whirling malice in the sharp air of this shining city. Mrs. Hayes-Rore's words about its terrible loneliness shot through her mind. She felt its aggressive unfriendliness. Even the great buildings, the flying cabs, and the swirling crowds seemed manifestations of purposed malevolence. And for that first short minute she was awed and frightened and inclined to turn back to that other city, which, though not kind, was yet not strange. This New York seemed somehow more appalling, more scornful, in some inexplicable way even more terrible and uncaring than Chicago. Threatening almost. Ugly. Yes, perhaps she'd better turn back.

The feeling passed, escaped in the surprise of what Mrs. Hayes-Rore was saying. Her oratorical voice boomed above the city's roar. "I suppose I ought really to have phoned Anne from the station. About you, I mean. Well, it doesn't matter. She's got plenty of room. Lives alone in a big house, which is something Negroes in New York don't do. They fill 'em up with lodgers usually. But Anne's funny. Nice, though. You'll like her, and it will be good for you to know her if you're going to stay in New York. She's a widow, my husband's sister's son's wife. The war, you know."

"Oh," protested Helga Crane, with a feeling of acute misgiving, "but won't she be annoyed and inconvenienced by having me brought in on her like this? I supposed we were going to the 'Y' or a hotel or something like that. Oughtn't we really to stop and phone?"

The woman at her side in the swaying cab smiled, a peculiar invincible, self-reliant smile, but gave Helga Crane's suggestion no other attention. Plainly she was a person accustomed to having things her way. She merely went on talking of other plans. "I think maybe I can get you some work. With a new Negro insurance company. They're after me to put quite a tidy sum into it. Well, I'll just tell them that they may as well take you with the money," and she laughed.

"Thanks awfully," Helga said, "but will they like it? I mean being made to take me because of the money."

"They're not being made," contradicted Mrs. Hayes-Rore. "I intended to let them have the money anyway, and I'll tell Mr. Darling so—after he takes you. They ought to be glad to get you. Colored organizations always need more brains as well as more money. Don't worry. And don't thank me again. You haven't got the job yet, you know."

There was a little silence, during which Helga gave herself up to the distraction of watching the strange city and the strange crowds, trying hard to put out of her mind the vision of an easier future which her companion's words had conjured up; for, as had been pointed out, it was, as yet, only a possibility.

Turning out of the park into the broad thoroughfare of Lenox Avenue, Mrs. Hayes-Rore said in a too carefully casual manner: "And, by the way, I wouldn't mention that my people are white, if I were you. Colored people won't understand it, and after all it's your own business. When you've lived as long as I have, you'll know that what others don't know can't hurt you. I'll just tell Anne that you're a friend of mine whose mother's dead. That'll place you well enough and it's all true. I never tell lies. She can fill in the gaps to suit herself and anyone else curious enough to ask."

"Thanks," Helga said again. And so great was her gratitude that she reached out and took her new friend's slightly soiled hand in one of her own fastidious ones, and retained it until their cab turned into a pleasant tree-lined street and came to a halt before one of the dignified houses in the center of the block. Here they got out.

In after years Helga Crane had only to close her eyes to see herself standing apprehensively in the small cream-colored hall, the floor of which was covered with deep silver-hued carpet; to see Mrs. Hayes-Rore pecking the cheek of the tall slim creature beautifully dressed in a cool green tailored frock; to hear herself being introduced to "my niece, Mrs. Grey" as "Miss Crane, a little friend of mine whose mother's died, and I think perhaps a while in New York will be good for her"; to feel her hand grasped in quick sympathy, and to hear Anne Grey's pleasant voice, with its faint note of wistfulness, saying:

"I'm so sorry, and I'm glad Aunt Jeanette brought you here. Did you have a good trip? I'm sure you must be worn out. I'll have Lillie take you right up." And to feel like a criminal.

Eight

A year thick with various adventures had sped by since that spring day on which Helga Crane had set out away from Chicago's indifferent unkindness for New York in the company of Mrs. Hayes-Rore. New York she had found not so unkind, not so unfriendly, not so indifferent. There she had been happy, and secured work, had made acquaintances and another friend. Again she had had that strange transforming experience, this time not so fleetingly, that magic sense of having come home. Harlem, teeming black Harlem, had welcomed her and lulled her into something that was, she was certain, peace and contentment.

The request and recommendation of Mrs. Hayes-Rore had been sufficient for her to obtain work with the insurance company in which that energetic woman was interested. And through Anne it had been possible for her to meet and to know people with tastes and ideas similar to her own. Their sophisticated cynical talk, their elaborate parties, the unobtrusive correctness of their clothes and homes, all appealed to her craving for smartness, for enjoyment. Soon she was able to reflect with a flicker of amusement on that constant feeling of humiliation and inferiority which had encompassed her in Naxos. Her New York friends looked with contempt and scorn on Naxos and all its works. This gave Helga a pleasant sense of avengement. Any shreds of self-consciousness or apprehension which at first she may have felt vanished quickly, escaped in the keenness of her joy at seeming at last to belong somewhere. For she considered that she had, as she put it, "found herself."

Between Anne Grey and Helga Crane there had sprung one of those immediate and peculiarly sympathetic friendships. Uneasy at first, Helga had been relieved that Anne had never returned to the uncomfortable subject of her mother's death so intentionally mentioned on their first meeting by Mrs. Hayes-Rore, beyond a tremulous brief: "You won't talk to me about it, will you? I can't bear the thought of death. Nobody ever talks to me about it. My husband, you know." This Helga discovered to be true. Later, when she knew Anne better, she suspected that it was a bit of a pose assumed for the purpose of doing away with the necessity of speaking regretfully of a husband who had been perhaps not too greatly loved.

After the first pleasant weeks, feeling that her obligation to Anne was already too great, Helga began to look about for a permanent place to live. It was, she found, difficult. She eschewed the "Y" as too bare, impersonal, and restrictive. Nor did furnished rooms or the idea of a solitary or a shared apartment appeal to her. So she rejoiced when one day Anne, looking up from her book, said lightly: "Helga, since you're going to be in New York, why don't you stay here with me? I don't usually take people. It's too disrupting. Still, it *is* sort of pleasant having somebody in the house and I don't seem to mind you. You don't bore me, or bother me. If you'd like to stay—Think it over."

Helga didn't, of course, require to think it over, because lodgment in Anne's home was in complete accord with what she designated as her "æsthetic." Even Helga Crane approved of Anne's house and the furnishings which so admirably graced the big cream-colored rooms. Beds with long, tapering posts to which tremendous age lent dignity and interest, bonneted old highboys, tables that might be by Duncan Phyfe, rare spindle-legged chairs, and others whose ladder backs gracefully climbed the delicate wall panels. These historic things mingled harmoniously and comfortably with brass-bound Chinese tea-chests, luxurious deep chairs and davenports, tiny tables of gay color, a lacquered jade-green settee with gleaming black satin cushions, lustrous Eastern rugs, ancient copper, Japanese prints, some fine etchings, a profusion of precious bric-a-brac, and endless shelves filled with books.

Anne Grey herself was, as Helga expressed it, "almost too good to be true." Thirty, maybe, brownly beautiful, she had the face of a golden Madonna, grave and calm and sweet, with shining black hair and eyes. She carried herself as queens are reputed to bear themselves, and probably do not. Her manners were as agreeably gentle as her own soft name. She possessed an impeccably fastidious taste in clothes, knowing what suited her and wearing it with an air of unconscious assurance. The unusual thing, a native New Yorker, she was also a person of distinction, financially independent, well connected and much sought after. And she was interesting, an odd confusion of wit and intense earnestness; a vivid and remarkable person. Yes, undoubtedly, Anne was almost too good to be true. She was almost perfect.

Thus established, secure, comfortable, Helga soon became thoroughly absorbed in the distracting interests of life in New York. Her secretarial work with the Negro insurance company filled her day. Books, the theater, parties, used up the nights. Gradually in the charm of this new and delightful pattern of her life she lost that tantalizing oppression of loneliness and isolation which always, it seemed, had been a part of her existence.

But, while the continuously gorgeous panorama of Harlem fascinated her, thrilled her, the sober mad rush of white New York failed entirely to stir her. Like thousands of other Harlem dwellers, she patronized its shops, its theaters, its art galleries, and its restaurants, and read its papers, without considering herself a part of the monster. And she was satisfied, unenvious. For her this Harlem was enough. Of that white world, so distant, so near, she asked only indifference. No, not at all did she crave, from those pale and powerful people, awareness. Sinister folk, she considered them, who had stolen her birthright. Their past contribution to her life, which had been but shame and grief, she had hidden away from brown folk in a locked closet, "never," she told herself, "to be reopened."

Some day she intended to marry one of those alluring brown or yellow men who danced attendance on her. Already financially successful, any one of them could give to her the things which she had now come to desire, a home like Anne's, cars of expensive makes such as lined the avenue, clothes and furs from Bendel's and Revillon Frères', servants, and leisure.

Always her forehead wrinkled in distaste whenever, involuntarily, which was somehow frequently, her mind turned on the speculative gray eyes and visionary uplifting plans of Dr. Anderson. That other, James Vayle, had slipped absolutely from her consciousness. Of him she never thought. Helga Crane meant, now, to have a home and perhaps laughing, appealing dark-eyed children in Harlem. Her existence was bounded by Central Park, Fifth Avenue, St. Nicholas Park, and One Hundred and Forty-fifth street. Not at all a narrow life, as Negroes live it, as Helga Crane knew it. Everything was there, vice and goodness, sadness and gayety, ignorance and wisdom, ugliness and beauty, poverty and richness. And it seemed to her that somehow of goodness, gayety, wisdom, and beauty always there was a little more than of vice, sadness, ignorance, and ugliness. It was only riches that did not quite transcend poverty.

"But," said Helga Crane, "what of that? Money isn't everything. It isn't even the half of everything. And here we have so much else— and by ourselves. It's only outside of Harlem among those others that money really counts for everything."

In the actuality of the pleasant present and the delightful vision of an agreeable future she was contented, and happy. She did not analyze this contentment, this happiness, but vaguely, without putting it into words or even so tangible a thing as a thought, she knew it sprang from a sense of freedom, a release from the feeling of smallness which had hedged her in, first during her sorry, unchildlike childhood among hostile white folk in Chicago, and later during her uncomfortable sojourn among snobbish black folk in Naxos.

Nine

But it didn't last, this happiness of Helga Crane's.

Little by little the signs of spring appeared, but strangely the enchantment of the season, so enthusiastically, so lavishly greeted by the gay dwellers of Harlem, filled her only with restlessness. Somewhere, within her, in a deep recess, crouched discontent. She began to lose confidence in the fullness of her life, the glow began to fade from her conception of it. As the days multiplied, her need of something, something vaguely familiar, but which she could not put a name to and hold for definite examination, became almost intolerable. She went through moments of overwhelming anguish. She felt shut in, trapped. "Perhaps I'm tired, need a tonic, or something," she reflected. So she consulted a physician, who, after a long, solemn examination, said that there was nothing wrong, nothing at all. "A change of scene, perhaps for a week or so, or a few days away from work," would put her straight most likely. Helga tried this, tried them both, but it was no good. All interest had gone out of living. Nothing seemed any good. She became a little frightened, and then shocked to discover that, for some unknown reason, it was of herself she was afraid.

Spring grew into summer, languidly at first, then flauntingly. Without awareness on her part, Helga Crane began to draw away from those contacts which had so delighted her. More and more she made lonely excursions to places outside of Harlem. A sensation of estrangement and isolation encompassed her. As the days became hotter and the streets more swarming, a kind of repulsion came upon her. She recoiled in aversion from the sight of the grinning faces and from the sound of the easy laughter of all these people who strolled, aimlessly now, it seemed, up and down the avenues. Not only did the crowds of nameless folk on the street annoy her, she began also actually to dislike her friends.

Even the gentle Anne distressed her. Perhaps because Anne was obsessed by the race problem and fed her obsession. She frequented all the meetings of protest, subscribed to all the complaining magazines, and read all the lurid newspapers spewed out by the Negro yellow press. She talked, wept, and ground her teeth dramatically about the wrongs and shames of her race. At times she lashed her fury to surprising heights for one by nature so placid and gentle. And, though she would not, even to herself, have admitted it, she reveled in this orgy of protest.

"Social equality," "Equal opportunity for all," were her slogans, often and emphatically repeated. Anne preached these things and honestly thought that she believed them, but she considered it an affront to the race, and to all the vari-colored peoples that made Lenox and Seventh Avenues the rich spectacles which they were, for any Negro to receive on terms of equality any white person.

"To me," asserted Anne Grey, "the most wretched Negro prostitute that walks One Hundred and Thirty-fifth Street is more than any president of these United States, not excepting Abraham Lincoln." But she turned up her finely carved nose at their lusty churches, their picturesque parades, their naïve clowning on the streets. She would not have desired or even have been willing to live in any section outside the black belt, and she would have refused scornfully, had they been tendered, any invitation from white folk. She hated white people with a deep and burning hatred, with the kind of hatred which, finding itself held in sufficiently numerous groups, was capable some day, on some great provocation, of bursting into dangerously malignant flames.

But she aped their clothes, their manners, and their gracious ways of living. While proclaiming loudly the undiluted good of all things Negro, she yet disliked the songs, the dances, and the softly blurred speech of the race. Toward these things she showed only a disdainful contempt, tinged sometimes with a faint amusement. Like the despised people of the white race, she preferred Pavlova to Florence Mills, John McCormack to Taylor Gordon, Walter Hampden to Paul Robeson. Theoretically, however, she stood for the immediate advancement of all things Negroid, and was in revolt against social inequality.

Helga had been entertained by this racial ardor in one so little affected by racial prejudice as Anne, and by her inconsistencies. But suddenly these things irked her with a great irksomeness and she wanted to be free of this constant prattling of the incongruities, the injustices, the stupidities, the viciousness of white people. It stirred memories, probed hidden wounds, whose poignant ache bred in her surprising oppression and corroded the fabric of her quietism. Sometimes it took all her self-control to keep from tossing sarcastically at Anne Ibsen's remark about there being assuredly something very wrong with the drains, but after all there were other parts of the edifice.

It was at this period of restiveness that Helga met again Dr. Anderson. She was gone, unwillingly, to a meeting, a health meeting, held in a large church—as were most of Harlem's uplift activities—as a substitute for her employer, Mr. Darling. Making her tardy arrival during a tedious discourse by a pompous saffron-hued physician, she was led by the irritated usher, whom she had roused from a nap in which he had been pleasantly freed from the intricacies of Negro health statistics, to a very front seat. Complete silence ensued while she subsided into her chair. The offended doctor looked at the ceiling, at the floor, and accusingly at Helga, and finally continued his lengthy discourse. When at last he had ended and Helga had dared to remove her eyes from his sweating face and look about, she saw with a sudden thrill that Robert Anderson was among her nearest neighbors. A peculiar, not wholly disagreeable, quiver ran down her spine. She felt an odd little faintness. The blood rushed to her face. She tried to jeer at herself for being so moved by the encounter.

He, meanwhile, she observed, watched her gravely. And having caught her attention, he smiled a little and nodded.

When all who so desired had spouted to their hearts' content—if to little purpose—and the meeting was finally over, Anderson detached himself from the circle of admiring friends and acquaintances that had gathered around him and caught up with Helga half-way down the long aisle leading out to fresher air.

"I wondered if you were really going to cut me. I see you were," he began, with that half-quizzical smile which she remembered so well.

She laughed. "Oh, I didn't think you'd remember me." Then she added: "Pleasantly, I mean."

The man laughed too. But they couldn't talk yet. People kept breaking in on them. At last, however, they were at the door, and then he suggested that they share a taxi "for the sake of a little breeze." Helga assented.

Constraint fell upon them when they emerged into the hot street, made seemingly hotter by a low-hanging golden moon and the hundreds of blazing electric lights. For a moment, before hailing a taxi, they stood together looking at the slow moving mass of perspiring human beings. Neither spoke, but Helga was conscious of the man's steady gaze. The prominent gray eyes were fixed upon her, studying her, appraising her. Many times since turning her back on Naxos she had in fancy rehearsed this scene, this re-encounter. Now she found that rehearsal helped not at all. It was so absolutely different from anything that she had imagined.

In the open taxi they talked of impersonal things, books, places, the fascination of New York, of Harlem. But underneath the exchange of small talk lay another conversation of which Helga Crane was sharply aware. She was aware, too, of a strange ill-defined emotion, a vague yearning rising within her. And she experienced a sensation of consternation and keen regret when with a lurching jerk the cab pulled up before the house in One Hundred and Thirty-ninth Street. So soon, she thought.

But she held out her hand calmly, coolly. Cordially she asked him to call some time. "It is," she said, "a pleasure to renew our acquaintance." Was it, she was wondering, merely an acquaintance?

He responded seriously that he too thought it a pleasure, and added: "You haven't changed. You're still seeking for something, I think."

At his speech there dropped from her that vague feeling of yearning, that longing for sympathy and understanding which his presence evoked. She felt a sharp stinging sensation and a recurrence of that anger and defiant desire to hurt which had so seared her on that past morning in Naxos. She searched for a biting remark, but, finding none venomous enough, she merely laughed a little rude and scornful laugh and, throwing up her small head, bade him an impatient good-night and ran quickly up the steps.

Afterwards she lay for long hours without undressing, thinking angry self-accusing thoughts, recalling and reconstructing that other explosive contact. That memory filled her with a sort of aching delirium. A thousand indefinite longings beset her. Eagerly she desired to see him again to right herself in his thoughts. Far into the night she lay planning speeches for their next meeting, so that it was long before drowsiness advanced upon her.

When he did call, Sunday, three days later, she put him off on Anne and went out, pleading an engagement, which until then she had not meant to keep. Until the very moment of his entrance she had had no intention of running away, but something, some imp of contumacy, drove her from his presence, though she longed to stay. Again abruptly had come the uncontrollable wish to wound. Later, with a sense of helplessness and inevitability, she realized that the weapon which she had chosen had been a boomerang, for she herself had felt the keen disappointment of the denial. Better to have stayed and hurled polite sarcasms at him. She might then at least have had the joy of seeing him wince.

In this spirit she made her way to the corner and turned into Seventh Avenue. The warmth of the sun, though gentle on that afternoon, had nevertheless kissed the street into marvelous light and color. Now and then, greeting an acquaintance, or stopping to chat with a friend, Helga was all the time seeing its soft shining brightness on the buildings along its sides or on the gleaming bronze, gold, and copper faces of its promenaders. And another vision, too, came haunting Helga Crane; level gray eyes set down in a brown face which stared out at her, coolly, quizzically, disturbingly. And she was not happy.

The tea to which she had so suddenly made up her mind to go she found boring beyond endurance, insipid drinks, dull conversation, stupid men. The aimless talk glanced from John Wellinger's lawsuit for discrimination because of race against a downtown restaurant and the advantages of living in Europe, especially in France, to the significance, if any, of the Garvey movement. Then it sped to a favorite Negro dancer who had just then secured a foothold on the stage of a current white musical comedy, to other shows, to a new book touching on Negroes. Thence to costumes for a coming masquerade dance, to a new jazz song, to Yvette Dawson's engagement to a Boston lawyer who had seen her one night at a party and proposed to her the next day at noon. Then back again to racial discrimination.

Why, Helga wondered, with unreasoning exasperation, didn't they find something else to talk of? Why must the race problem always creep in? She refused to go on to another gathering. It would, she thought, be simply the same old thing.

On her arrival home she was more disappointed than she cared to admit to find the house in darkness and even Anne gone off somewhere. She would have liked that night to have talked with Anne. Get her opinion of Dr. Anderson.

Anne it was who the next day told her that he had given up his work in Naxos; or rather that Naxos had given him up. He had been too liberal, too lenient, for education as it was inflicted in Naxos. Now he was permanently in New York, employed as welfare worker by some big manufacturing concern, which gave employment to hundreds of Negro men.

"Uplift," sniffed Helga contemptuously, and fled before the on slaught of Anne's harangue on the needs and ills of the race.

Ten

With the waning summer the acute sensitiveness of Helga Crane's frayed nerves grew keener. There were days when the mere sight of the serene tan and brown faces about her stung her like a personal insult. The care-free quality of their laughter roused in her the desire to scream at them: "Fools, fools! Stupid fools!" This passionate and unreasoning protest gained in intensity, swallowing up all else like some dense fog. Life became for her only a hateful place where one lived in intimacy with people one would not have chosen had one been given choice. It was, too, an excruciating agony. She was continually out of temper. Anne, thank the gods! was away, but her nearing return filled Helga with dismay.

Arriving at work one sultry day, hot and dispirited, she found waiting a letter, a letter from Uncle Peter. It had originally been sent to Naxos, and from there it had made the journey back to Chicago to the Young Women's Christian Association, and then to Mrs. Hayes-Rore. That busy woman had at last found time between conventions and lectures to readdress it and had sent it on to New York. Four months, at least, it had been on its travels. Helga felt no curiosity as to its contents, only annoyance at the long delay, as she ripped open the thin edge of the envelope, and for a space sat staring at the peculiar foreign script of her uncle.

> 715 Sheridan Road
> Chicago, Ill.

Dear Helga:

It is now over a year since you made your unfortunate call here. It was unfortunate for us all, you, Mrs. Nilssen, and myself. But of course you couldn't know. I blame myself. I should have written you of my marriage.

I have looked for a letter, or some word from you; evidently, with your usual penetration, you understood thoroughly that I must terminate my outward relation with you. You were always a keen one.

Of course I am sorry, but it can't be helped. My wife must be considered, and she feels very strongly about this.

You know, of course, that I wish you the best of luck. But take an old man's advice and don't do as your mother did. Why don't you run over and visit your Aunt Katrina? She always wanted you. Maria Kirkeplads, No. 2, will find her.

I enclose what I intended to leave you at my death. It is better and more convenient that you get it now. I wish it were more, but even this little may come in handy for a rainy day.

Best wishes for your luck.

> *Peter Nilssen*

Beside the brief, friendly, but none the less final, letter there was a check for five thousand dollars. Helga Crane's first feeling was one of unreality. This changed almost immediately into one of relief, of liberation. It was stronger than the mere security from present financial worry which the check promised. Money as money was still not very important to Helga. But later, while on an errand in the big general office of the society, her puzzled bewilderment fled. Here the inscrutability of the dozen or more brown faces, all cast from the same indefinite mold, and so like her own, seemed pressing forward against her. Abruptly it flashed upon her that the harrowing irritation of the past weeks was a smoldering hatred. Then, she was overcome by another, so actual, so sharp, so horribly painful, that forever afterwards she preferred to forget it. It was as if she were shut up, boxed up, with hundreds of her race, closed up with that something in the racial character which had always been to her, inexplicable, alien. Why, she demanded in fierce rebellion, should she be yoked to these despised black folk?

Back in the privacy of her own cubicle, self-loathing came upon her. "They're my own people, my own people," she kept repeating over and over to herself. It was no good. The feeling would not be routed. "I can't go on like this," she said to herself. "I simply can't."

There were footsteps. Panic seized her. She'd have to get out. She terribly needed to. Snatching hat and purse, she hurried to the narrow door, saying in a forced, steady voice, as it opened to reveal her employer: "Mr. Darling, I'm sorry, but I've got to go out. Please, may I be excused?"

At his courteous "Certainly, certainly. And don't hurry. It's much too hot," Helga Crane had the grace to feel ashamed, but there was no softening of her determination. The necessity for being alone was too urgent. She hated him and all the others too much.

Outside, rain had begun to fall. She walked bare-headed, bitter with self-reproach. But she rejoiced too. She didn't, in spite of her racial markings, belong to these dark segregated people. She was different. She felt it. It wasn't merely a matter of color. It was something broader, deeper, that made folk kin.

And now she was free. She would take Uncle Peter's money and advice and revisit her aunt in Copenhagen. Fleeting pleasant memories of her childhood visit there flew through her excited mind. She had been only eight, yet she had enjoyed the interest and the admiration which her unfamiliar color and dark curly hair, strange to those pink, white, and gold people, had evoked. Quite clearly now she recalled that her Aunt Katrina had begged for her to be allowed to remain. Why, she wondered, hadn't her mother consented? To Helga it seemed that it would have been the solution to all their problems, her mother's, her stepfather's, her own.

At home in the cool dimness of the big chintz-hung living-room, clad only in a fluttering thing of green chiffon, she gave herself up to day-dreams of a happy future in Copenhagen, where there were no Negroes, no problems, no prejudice, until she remembered with perturbation that this was the day of Anne's return from her vacation at the sea-shore. Worse. There was a dinner-party in her honor that very night. Helga sighed. She'd have to go. She couldn't possibly get out of a dinner-party for Anne, even though she felt that such an event on a hot night was little short of an outrage. Nothing but a sense of obligation to Anne kept her from pleading a splitting headache as an excuse for remaining quietly at home.

Her mind trailed off to the highly important matter of clothes. What should she wear? White? No, everybody would, because it was hot. Green? She shook her head, Anne would be sure to. The blue thing. Reluctantly she decided against it; she loved it, but she had worn it too often. There was that cobwebby black net touched with orange, which she had bought last spring in a fit of extravagance and never worn, because on getting it home both she and Anne had considered it too *décolleté*, and too *outré*. Anne's words: "There's not enough of it, and what there is gives you the air of something about to fly," came back to her, and she smiled as she decided that she would certainly wear the black net. For her it would be a symbol. She was about to fly.

She busied herself with some absurdly expensive roses which she had ordered sent in, spending an interminable time in their arrangement. At last she was satisfied with their appropriateness in some blue Chinese jars of great age. Anne *did* have such lovely things, she thought, as she began conscientiously to prepare for her return, although there was really little to do; Lillie seemed to have done everything. But Helga dusted the tops of the books, placed the magazines in ordered carelessness, redressed Anne's bed in fresh-smelling sheets of cool linen, and laid out her best pale-yellow pajamas of *crêpe de Chine*. Finally she set out two tall green glasses and made a great pitcher of lemonade, leaving only the ginger-ale and claret to be added on Anne's arrival. She was a little conscience-stricken, so she wanted to be particularly nice to Anne, who had been so kind to her when first she came to New York, a forlorn friendless creature. Yes, she was grateful to Anne; but, just the same, she meant to go. At once.

Her preparations over, she went back to the carved chair from which the thought of Anne's home-coming had drawn her. Characteristically she writhed at the idea of telling Anne of her impending departure and shirked the problem of evolving a plausible and inoffensive excuse for its suddenness. "That," she decided lazily, "will have to look out for itself; I can't be bothered just now. It's too hot."

She began to make plans and to dream delightful dreams of change, of life somewhere else. Some place where at last she would be permanently satisfied. Her anticipatory thoughts waltzed and eddied about to the sweet silent music of change. With rapture almost, she let herself drop into the blissful sensation of visualizing herself in different, strange places, among approving and admiring people, where she would be appreciated, and understood.

Eleven

It was night. The dinner-party was over, but no one wanted to go home. Half-past eleven was, it seemed, much too early to tumble into bed on a Saturday night. It was a sulky, humid night, a thick furry night, through which the electric torches shone like silver fuzz—an atrocious night for cabareting, Helga insisted, but the others wanted to go, so she went with them, though half unwillingly. After much consultation and chatter they decided upon a place and climbed into two patiently waiting taxis, rattling things which jerked, wiggled, and groaned, and threatened every minute to collide with others of their kind, or with inattentive pedestrians. Soon they pulled up before a tawdry doorway in a narrow crosstown street and stepped out. The night was far from quiet, the streets far from empty. Clanging trolley bells, quarreling cats, cackling phonographs, raucous laughter, complaining motor-horns, low singing, mingled in the familiar medley that is Harlem. Black figures, white figures, little forms, big forms, small groups, large groups, sauntered, or hurried by. It was gay, grotesque, and a little weird. Helga Crane felt singularly apart from it all. Entering the waiting door-way, they descended through a furtive, narrow passage, into a vast subterranean room. Helga smiled, thinking that this was one of those places characterized by the righteous as a hell.

A glare of light struck her eyes, a blare of jazz split her ears. For a moment everything seemed to be spinning round; even she felt that she was circling aimlessly, as she followed with the others the black giant who led them to a small table, where, when they were seated, their knees and elbows touched. Helga wondered that the waiter, indefinitely carved out of ebony, did not smile as he wrote their order— "four bottles of White Rock, four bottles of ginger-ale." Bah! Anne giggled, the others smiled and openly exchanged knowing glances, and under the tables flat glass bottles were extracted from the women's evening scarfs and small silver flasks drawn from the men's hip pockets. In a little moment she grew accustomed to the smoke and din.

They danced, ambling lazily to a crooning melody, or violently twisting their bodies, like whirling leaves, to a sudden streaming rhythm, or shaking themselves ecstatically to a thumping of unseen tomtoms. For the while, Helga was oblivious of the reek of flesh, smoke, and alcohol, oblivious of the oblivion of other gyrating pairs, oblivious of the color, the noise, and the grand distorted childishness of it all. She was drugged, lifted, sustained, by the extraordinary music, blown out, ripped out, beaten out, by the joyous, wild, murky orchestra. The essence of life seemed bodily motion. And when suddenly the music died, she dragged herself back to the present with a conscious effort; and a shameful certainty that not only had she been in the jungle, but that she had enjoyed it, began to taunt her. She hardened her determination to get away. She wasn't, she told herself, a jungle creature. She cloaked herself in a faint disgust as she watched the entertainers throw themselves about to the bursts of syncopated jangle, and when the time came again for the patrons to dance, she declined. Her rejected partner excused himself and sought an acquaintance a few tables removed. Helga sat looking curiously about her as the buzz of conversation ceased, strangled by the savage strains of music, and the crowd became a swirling mass. For the hundredth time she marveled at the gradations within this oppressed race of hers. A dozen shades slid by. There was sooty black, shiny black, taupe, mahogany, bronze, copper, gold, orange, yellow, peach, ivory, pinky white, pastry white. There was yellow hair, brown hair, black hair; straight hair, straightened hair, curly hair, crinkly hair, woolly hair. She saw black eyes in white faces, brown eyes in yellow faces, gray eyes in brown faces, blue eyes in tan faces. Africa, Europe, perhaps with a pinch of Asia, in a fantastic motley of ugliness and beauty, semi-barbaric, sophisticated, exotic, were here. But she was blind to its charm, purposely aloof and a little contemptuous, and soon her interest in the moving mosaic waned.

She had discovered Dr. Anderson sitting at a table on the far side of the room, with a girl in a shivering apricot frock. Seriously he returned her tiny bow. She met his eyes, gravely smiling, then blushed, furiously, and averted her own. But they went back immediately to the girl beside him, who sat indifferently sipping a colorless liquid from a high glass, or puffing a precariously hanging cigarette. Across dozens of tables, littered with corks, with ashes, with shriveled sandwiches, through slits in the swaying mob, Helga Crane studied her.

She was pale, with a peculiar, almost deathlike pallor. The brilliantly red, softly curving mouth was somehow sorrowful. Her pitch-black eyes, a little aslant, were veiled by long, drooping lashes and surmounted by broad brows, which seemed like black smears. The short dark hair was brushed severely back from the wide forehead. The extreme *décolleté* of her simple apricot dress showed a skin of unusual color, a delicate, creamy hue, with golden tones. "Almost like an alabaster," thought Helga.

Bang! Again the music died. The moving mass broke, separated. The others returned. Anne had rage in her eyes. Her voice trembled as she took Helga aside to whisper: "There's your Dr. Anderson over there, with Audrey Denney."

"Yes, I saw him. She's lovely. Who is she?"

"She's Audrey Denney, as I said, and she lives downtown. West Twenty-second Street. Hasn't much use for Harlem any more. It's a wonder she hasn't some white man hanging about. The disgusting creature! I wonder how she inveigled Anderson? But that's Audrey! If there is any desirable man about, trust her to attach him. She ought to be ostracized."

"Why?" asked Helga curiously, noting at the same time that three of the men in their own party had deserted and were now congregated about the offending Miss Denney.

"Because she goes about with white people," came Anne's indignant answer, "and they know she's colored."

"I'm afraid I don't quite see, Anne. Would it be all right if they didn't know she was colored?"

"Now, don't be nasty, Helga. You know very well what I mean." Anne's voice was shaking. Helga didn't see, and she was greatly interested, but she decided to let it go. She didn't want to quarrel with Anne, not now, when she had that guilty feeling about leaving her. But Anne was off on her favorite subject, race. And it seemed, too, that Audrey Denney was to her particularly obnoxious.

"Why, she gives parties for white and colored people together. And she goes to white people's parties. It's worse than disgusting, it's positively obscene."

"Oh, come, Anne, you haven't been to any of the parties, I know, so how can you be so positive about the matter?"

"No, but I've heard about them. I know people who've been."

"Friends of yours, Anne?"

Anne admitted that they were, some of them.

"Well, then, they can't be so bad. I mean, if your friends sometimes go, can they? Just what goes on that's so terrible?"

"Why, they drink, for one thing. Quantities, they say."

"So do we, at the parties here in Harlem," Helga responded. An idiotic impulse seized her to leave the place, Anne's presence, then, forever. But of course she couldn't. It would be foolish, and so ugly.

"And the white men dance with the colored women. Now you know, Helga Crane, that can mean only one thing." Anne's voice was trembling with cold hatred. As she ended, she made a little clicking noise with her tongue, indicating an abhorrence too great for words.

"Don't the colored men dance with the white women, or do they sit about, impolitely, while the other men dance with their women?" inquired Helga very softly, and with a slowness approaching almost to insolence. Anne's insinuations were too revolting. She had a slightly sickish feeling, and a flash of anger touched her. She mastered it and ignored Anne's inadequate answer.

"It's the principle of the thing that I object to. You can't get round the fact that her behavior is outrageous, treacherous, in fact. That's what's the matter with the Negro race. They won't stick together. She certainly ought to be ostracized. I've nothing but contempt for her, as has every other self-respecting Negro."

The other women and the lone man left to them—Helga's own escort—all seemingly agreed with Anne. At any rate, they didn't protest. Helga gave it up. She felt that it would be useless to tell them that what she felt for the beautiful, calm, cool girl who had the assurance, the courage, so placidly to ignore racial barriers and give her attention to people, was not contempt, but envious admiration. So she remained silent, watching the girl.

At the next first sound of music Dr. Anderson rose. Languidly the girl followed his movement, a faint smile parting her sorrowful lips at some remark he made. Her long, slender body swayed with an eager pulsing motion. She danced with grace and abandon, gravely, yet with obvious pleasure, her legs, her hips, her back, all swaying gently, swung by that wild music from the heart of the jungle. Helga turned her glance to Dr. Anderson. Her disinterested curiosity passed. While she still felt for the girl envious admiration, that feeling was now augmented by another, a more primitive emotion. She forgot the garish crowded room. She forgot her friends. She saw only two figures, closely clinging. She felt her heart throbbing. She felt the room receding. She went out the door. She climbed endless stairs. At last, panting, confused, but thankful to have escaped, she found herself again out in the dark night alone, a small crumpled thing in a fragile, flying black and gold dress. A taxi drifted toward her, stopped. She stepped into it, feeling cold, unhappy, misunderstood, and forlorn.

Twelve

Helga Crane felt no regret as the cliff-like towers faded. The sight thrilled her as beauty, grandeur, of any kind always did, but that was all.

The liner drew out from churning slate-colored waters of the river into the open sea. The small seething ripples on the water's surface became little waves. It was evening. In the western sky was a pink and mauve light, which faded gradually into a soft gray-blue obscurity. Leaning against the railing, Helga stared into the approaching night, glad to be at last alone, free of that great superfluity of human beings, yellow, brown, and black, which, as the torrid summer burnt to its close, had so oppressed her. No, she hadn't belonged there. Of her attempt to emerge from that inherent aloneness which was part of her very being, only dullness had come, dullness and a great aversion.

Almost at once it was time for dinner. Somewhere a bell sounded. She turned and with buoyant steps went down. Already she had begun to feel happier. Just for a moment, outside the dining-salon, she hesitated, assailed with a tiny uneasiness which passed as quickly as it had come. She entered softly, unobtrusively. And, after all, she had had her little fear for nothing. The purser, a man grown old in the service of the Scandinavian-American Line, remembered her as the little dark girl who had crossed with her mother years ago, and so she must sit at his table. Helga liked that. It put her at her ease and made her feel important.

Everyone was kind in the delightful days which followed, and her first shyness under the politely curious glances of turquoise eyes of her fellow travelers soon slid from her. The old forgotten Danish of her childhood began to come, awkwardly at first, from her lips, under their agreeable tutelage. Evidently they were interested, curious, and perhaps a little amused about this Negro girl on her way to Denmark alone.

Helga was a good sailor, and mostly the weather was lovely with the serene calm of the lingering September summer, under whose sky the sea was smooth, like a length of watered silk, unruffled by the stir of any wind. But even the two rough days found her on deck, reveling like a released bird in her returned feeling of happiness and freedom, that blessed sense of belonging to herself alone and not to a race. Again, she had put the past behind her with an ease which astonished even herself. Only the figure of Dr. Anderson obtruded itself with surprising vividness to irk her because she could get no meaning from that keen sensation of covetous exasperation that had so surprisingly risen within her on the night of the cabaret party. This question Helga Crane recognized as not entirely new; it was but a revival of the puzzlement experienced when she had fled so abruptly from Naxos more than a year before. With the recollection of that previous flight and subsequent half-questioning a dim disturbing notion came to her. She wasn't, she couldn't be, in love with the man. It was a thought too humiliating, and so quickly dismissed. Nonsense! Sheer nonsense! When one is in love, one strives to please. Never, she decided, had she made an effort to be pleasing to Dr. Anderson. On the contrary, she had always tried, deliberately, to irritate him. She was, she told herself, a sentimental fool.

Nevertheless, the thought of love stayed with her, not prominent, definite; but shadowy, incoherent. And in a remote corner of her consciousness lurked the memory of Dr. Anderson's serious smile and gravely musical voice.

On the last morning Helga rose at dawn, a dawn outside old Copenhagen. She lay lazily in her long chair watching the feeble sun creeping over the ship's great green funnels with sickly light; watching the purply gray sky change to opal, to gold, to pale blue. A few other passengers, also early risen, excited by the prospect of renewing old attachments, of glad home-comings after long years, paced nervously back and forth. Now, at the last moment, they were impatient, but apprehensive fear, too, had its place in their rushing emotions. Impatient Helga Crane was not. But she *was* apprehensive. Gradually, as the ship drew into the lazier waters of the dock, she became prey to sinister fears and memories. A deep pang of misgiving nauseated her at the thought of her aunt's husband, acquired since Helga's childhood visit. Painfully, vividly, she remembered the frightened anger of Uncle Peter's new wife, and looking back at her precipitate departure from America, she was amazed at her own stupidity. She had not even considered the remote possibility that her aunt's husband might be like Mrs. Nilssen. For the first time in nine days she wished herself back in New York, in America.

The little gulf of water between the ship and the wharf lessened. The engines had long ago ceased their whirring, and now the buzz of conversation, too, died down. There was a sort of silence. Soon the welcoming crowd on the wharf stood under the shadow of the great sea-monster, their faces turned up to the anxious ones of the passengers who hung over the railing. Hats were taken off, handkerchiefs were shaken out and frantically waved. Chatter. Deafening shouts. A little quiet weeping. Sailors and laborers were yelling and rushing about. Cables were thrown. The gangplank was laid.

Silent, unmoving, Helga Crane stood looking intently down into the gesticulating crowd. Was anyone waving to her? She couldn't tell. She didn't in the least remember her aunt, save as a hazy pretty lady. She smiled a little at the thought that her aunt, or anyone waiting there in the crowd below, would have no difficulty in singling her out. But—had she been met? When she descended the gangplank she was still uncertain and was trying to decide on a plan of procedure in the event that she had not. A telegram before she went through the customs? Telephone? A taxi?

But, again, she had all her fears and questionings for nothing. A smart woman in olive-green came toward her at once. And, even in the fervent gladness of her relief, Helga took in the carelessly trailing purple scarf and correct black hat that completed the perfection of her aunt's costume, and had time to feel herself a little shabbily dressed. For it was her aunt; Helga saw that at once, the resemblance to her own mother was unmistakable. There was the same long nose, the same beaming blue eyes, the same straying pale-brown hair so like sparkling beer. And the tall man with the fierce mustache who followed carrying hat and stick must be Herr Dahl, Aunt Katrina's husband. How gracious he was in his welcome, and how anxious to air his faulty English, now that her aunt had finished kissing her and exclaimed in Danish: "Little Helga! Little Helga! Goodness! But how you have grown!"

Laughter from all three.

"Welcome to Denmark, to Copenhagen, to our home," said the new uncle in queer, proud, oratorical English. And to Helga's smiling, grateful "Thank you," he returned: "Your trunks? Your checks?" also in English, and then lapsed into Danish.

"Where in the world are the Fishers? We must hurry the customs."

Almost immediately they were joined by a breathless couple, a young gray-haired man and a fair, tiny, doll-like woman. It developed that they had lived in England for some years and so spoke English, real English, well. They were both breathless, all apologies and explanations.

"So early!" sputtered the man, Herr Fisher, "We inquired last night and they said nine. It was only by accident that we called again this morning to be sure. Well, you can imagine the rush we were in when they said eight! And of course we had trouble in finding a cab. One always does if one is late." All this in Danish. Then to Helga in English: "You see, I was especially asked to come because Fru Dahl didn't know if you remembered your Danish, and your uncle's English—well—"

More laughter.

At last, the customs having been hurried and a cab secured, they were off, with much chatter, through the toy-like streets, weaving perilously in and out among the swarms of bicycles.

It had begun, a new life for Helga Crane.

Thirteen

She liked it, this new life. For a time it blotted from her mind all else. She took to luxury as the proverbial duck to water. And she took to admiration and attention even more eagerly.

It was pleasant to wake on that first afternoon, after the insisted-upon nap, with that sensation of lavish contentment and well-being enjoyed only by impecunious sybarites waking in the houses of the rich. But there was something more than mere contentment and well-being. To Helga Crane it was the realization of a dream that she had dreamed persistently ever since she was old enough to remember such vague things as day-dreams and longings. Always she had wanted, not money, but the things which money could give, leisure, attention, beautiful surroundings. Things. Things. Things.

So it was more than pleasant, it was important, this awakening in the great high room which held the great high bed on which she lay, small but exalted. It was important because to Helga Crane it was the day, so she decided, to which all the sad forlorn past had led, and from which the whole future was to depend. This, then, was where she belonged. This was her proper setting. She felt consoled at last for the spiritual wounds of the past.

A discreet knocking on the tall paneled door sounded. In response to Helga's "Come in" a respectful rosy-faced maid entered and Helga lay for a long minute watching her adjust the shutters. She was conscious, too, of the girl's sly curious glances at her, although her general attitude was quite correct, willing and disinterested. In New York, America, Helga would have resented this sly watching. Now, here, she was only amused. Marie, she reflected, had probably never seen a Negro outside the pictured pages of her geography book.

Another knocking. Aunt Katrina entered, smiling at Helga's quick, lithe spring from the bed. They were going out to tea, she informed Helga. What, the girl inquired, did one wear to tea in Copenhagen, meanwhile glancing at her aunt's dark purple dress and bringing forth a severely plain blue *crêpe* frock. But no! It seemed that that wouldn't at all do.

"Too sober," pronounced Fru Dahl. "Haven't you something lively, something bright?" And, noting Helga's puzzled glance at her own subdued costume, she explained laughingly: "Oh, I'm an old married lady, and a Dane. But you, you're young. And you're a foreigner, and different. You must have bright things to set off the color of your lovely brown skin. Striking things, exotic things. You must make an impression."

"I've only these," said Helga Crane, timidly displaying her wardrobe on couch and chairs. "Of course I intend to buy here. I didn't want to bring over too much that might be useless."

"And you were quite right too. Umm. Let's see. That black there, the one with the cerise and purple trimmings. Wear that."

Helga was shocked. "But for tea, Aunt! Isn't it too gay? Too— too—*outré?*"

"Oh dear, no. Not at all, not for you. Just right." Then after a little pause she added: "And we're having people in to dinner tonight, quite a lot. Perhaps we'd better decide on our frocks now." For she was, in spite of all her gentle kindness, a woman who left nothing to chance. In her own mind she had determined the role that Helga was to play in advancing the social fortunes of the Dahls of Copenhagen, and she meant to begin at once.

At last, after much trying on and scrutinizing, it was decided that Marie should cut a favorite emerald-green velvet dress a little lower in the back and add some gold and mauve flowers, "to liven it up a bit," as Fru Dahl put it.

"Now that," she said, pointing to the Chinese red dressing-gown in which Helga had wrapped herself when at last the fitting was over, "suits you. Tomorrow we'll shop. Maybe we can get something that color. That black and orange thing there is good too, but too high. What a prim American maiden you are, Helga, to hide such a fine back and shoulders. Your feet are nice too, but you ought to have higher heels—and buckles."

Left alone, Helga began to wonder. She was dubious, too, and not a little resentful. Certainly she loved color with a passion that perhaps only Negroes and Gypsies know. But she had a deep faith in the perfection of her own taste, and no mind to be bedecked in flaunting flashy things. Still—she had to admit that Fru Dahl was right about the dressing-gown. It did suit her. Perhaps an evening dress. And she knew that she had lovely shoulders, and her feet *were* nice.

When she was dressed in the shining black taffeta with its bizarre trimmings of purple and cerise, Fru Dahl approved her and so did Herr Dahl. Everything in her responded to his "She's beautiful; beautiful!" Helga Crane knew she wasn't that, but it pleased her that he could think so, and say so. Aunt Katrina smiled in her quiet, assured way, taking to herself her husband's compliment to her niece. But a little frown appeared over the fierce mustache, as he said, in his precise, faintly feminine voice: "She ought to have ear-rings, long ones. Is it too late for Garborg's? We could call up."

And call up they did. And Garborg, the jeweler, in Fredericksgaarde waited for them. Not only were ear-rings bought, long ones brightly enameled, but glittering shoe-buckles and two great bracelets. Helga's sleeves being long, she escaped the bracelets for the moment. They were wrapped to be worn that night. The ear-rings, however, and the buckles came into immediate use and Helga felt like a veritable savage as they made their leisurely way across the pavement from the shop to the waiting motor. This feeling was intensified by the many pedestrians who stopped to stare at the queer dark creature, strange to their city. Her cheeks reddened, but both Herr and Fru Dahl seemed oblivious of the stares or the audible whispers in which Helga made out the one frequently recurring word "*sorte*," which she recognized as the Danish word for "black."

Her Aunt Katrina merely remarked: "A high color becomes you, Helga. Perhaps tonight a little rouge—" To which her husband nodded in agreement and stroked his mustache meditatively. Helga Crane said nothing.

They were pleased with the success she was at the tea, or rather the coffee—for no tea was served—and later at dinner. Helga herself felt like nothing so much as some new and strange species of pet dog being proudly exhibited. Everyone was very polite and very friendly, but she felt the massed curiosity and interest, so discreetly hidden under the polite greetings. The very atmosphere was tense with it. "As if I had horns, or three legs," she thought. She was really nervous and a little terrified, but managed to present an outward smiling composure. This was assisted by the fact that it was taken for granted that she knew nothing or very little of the language. So she had only to bow and look pleasant. Herr and Fru Dahl did the talking, answered the questions. She came away from the coffee feeling that she had acquitted herself well in the first skirmish. And, in spite of the mental strain, she had enjoyed her prominence.

If the afternoon had been a strain, the evening was something more. It was more exciting too. Marie had indeed "cut down" the prized green velvet, until, as Helga put it, it was "practically nothing but a skirt." She was thankful for the barbaric bracelets, for the dangling ear-rings, for the beads about her neck. She was even thankful for the rouge on her burning cheeks and for the very powder on her back. No other woman in the stately pale-blue room was so greatly exposed. But she liked the small murmur of wonder and admiration which rose when Uncle Poul brought her in. She liked the compliments in the men's eyes as they bent over her hand. She liked the subtle half-understood flattery of her dinner partners. The women too were kind, feeling no need for jealousy. To them this girl, this Helga Crane, this mysterious niece of the Dahls, was not to be reckoned seriously in their scheme of things. True, she was attractive, unusual, in an exotic, almost savage way, but she wasn't one of them. She didn't at all count.

Near the end of the evening, as Helga sat effectively posed on a red satin sofa, the center of an admiring group, replying to questions about America and her trip over, in halting, inadequate Danish, there came a shifting of the curious interest away from herself. Following the others' eyes, she saw that there had entered the room a tallish man with a flying mane of reddish blond hair. He was wearing a great black cape, which swung gracefully from his huge shoulders, and in his long, nervous hand he held a wide soft hat. An artist, Helga decided at once, taking in the broad streaming tie. But how affected! How theatrical!

With Fru Dahl he came forward and was presented. "Herr Olsen, Herr Axel Olsen." To Helga Crane that meant nothing. The man, however, interested her. For an imperceptible second he bent over her hand. After that he looked intently at her for what seemed to her an incredibly rude length of time from under his heavy drooping lids. At last, removing his stare of startled satisfaction, he wagged his leonine head approvingly.

"Yes, you're right. She's amazing. Marvelous," he muttered.

Everyone else in the room was deliberately not staring. About Helga there sputtered a little staccato murmur of manufactured conversation. Meanwhile she could think of no proper word of greeting to the outrageous man before her. She wanted, very badly, to laugh. But the man was as unaware of her omission as of her desire. His words flowed on and on, rising and rising. She tried to follow, but his rapid Danish eluded her. She caught only words, phrases, here and there. "Superb eyes . . . color . . . neck column . . . yellow . . . hair . . . alive . . . wonderful. . . ." His speech was for Fru Dahl. For a bit longer he lingered before the silent girl, whose smile had become a fixed aching mask, still gazing appraisingly, but saying no word to her, and then moved away with Fru Dahl, talking rapidly and excitedly to her and her husband, who joined them for a moment at the far side of the room. Then he was gone as suddenly as he had come.

"Who is he?" Helga put the question timidly to a hovering young army officer, a very smart captain just back from Sweden. Plainly he was surprised.

"Herr Olsen, Herr Axel Olsen, the painter. Portraits, you know."

"Oh," said Helga, still mystified.

"I guess he's going to paint you. You're lucky. He's queer. Won't do everybody."

"Oh, no. I mean, I'm sure you're mistaken. He didn't ask, didn't say anything about it."

The young man laughed. "Ha ha! That's good! He'll arrange that with Herr Dahl. He evidently came just to see you, and it was plain that he was pleased." He smiled, approvingly.

"Oh," said Helga again. Then at last she laughed. It was too funny. The great man hadn't addressed a word to her. Here she was, a curiosity, a stunt, at which people came and gazed. And was she to be treated like a secluded young miss, a Danish *frøkken*, not to be consulted personally even on matters affecting her personally? She, Helga Crane, who almost all her life had looked after herself, was she now to be looked after by Aunt Katrina and her husband? It didn't seem real.

It was late, very late, when finally she climbed into the great bed after having received an auntly kiss. She lay long awake reviewing the events of the crowded day. She was happy again. Happiness covered her like the lovely quilts under which she rested. She was mystified too. Her aunt's words came back to her. "You're young and a foreigner and—and different." Just what did that mean, she wondered. Did it mean that the difference was to be stressed, accented? Helga wasn't so sure that she liked that. Hitherto all her efforts had been toward similarity to those about her.

"How odd," she thought sleepily, "and how different from America!"

Fourteen

The young officer had been right in his surmise. Axel Olsen was going to paint Helga Crane. Not only was he going to paint her, but he was to accompany her and her aunt on their shopping expedition. Aunt Katrina was frankly elated. Uncle Poul was also visibly pleased. Evidently they were not above kotowing to a lion. Helga's own feelings were mixed; she was amused, grateful, and vexed. It had all been decided and arranged without her, and, also she was a little afraid of Olsen. His stupendous arrogance awed her.

The day was an exciting, not easily to be forgotten one. Definitely, too, it conveyed to Helga her exact status in her new environment. A decoration. A curio. A peacock. Their progress through the shops was an event; an event for Copenhagen as well as for Helga Crane. Her dark, alien appearance was to most people an astonishment. Some stared surreptitiously, some openly, and some stopped dead in front of her in order more fully to profit by their stares. *"Den Sorte"* dropped freely, audibly, from many lips.

The time came when she grew used to the stares of the population. And the time came when the population of Copenhagen grew used to her outlandish presence and ceased to stare. But at the end of that first day it was with thankfulness that she returned to the sheltering walls of the house on Maria Kirkplads.

They were followed by numerous packages, whose contents all had been selected or suggested by Olsen and paid for by Aunt Katrina. Helga had only to wear them. When they were opened and the things spread out upon the sedate furnishings of her chamber, they made a rather startling array. It was almost in a mood of rebellion that Helga faced the fantastic collection of garments incongruously laid out in the quaint, stiff, pale old room. There were batik dresses in which mingled indigo, orange, green, vermilion, and black; dresses of velvet and chiffon in screaming colors, blood-red, sulphur-yellow, sea-green; and one black and white thing in striking combination. There was a black Manila shawl strewn with great scarlet and lemon flowers, a leopardskin coat, a glittering opera-cape. There were turban-like hats of metallic silks, feathers and furs, strange jewelry, enameled or set with odd semi-precious stones, a nauseous Eastern perfume, shoes with dangerously high heels. Gradually Helga's perturbation subsided in the unusual pleasure of having so many new and expensive clothes at one time. She began to feel a little excited, incited.

Incited. That was it, the guiding principle of her life in Copenhagen. She was incited to make an impression, a voluptuous impression. She was incited to inflame attention and admiration. She was dressed for it, subtly schooled for it. And after a little while she gave herself up wholly to the fascinating business of being seen, gaped at, desired. Against the solid background of Herr Dahl's wealth and generosity she submitted to her aunt's arrangement of her life to one end, the amusing one of being noticed and flattered. Intentionally she kept to the slow, faltering Danish. It was, she decided, more attractive than a nearer perfection. She grew used to the extravagant things with which Aunt Katrina chose to dress her. She managed, too, to retain that air of remoteness which had been in America so disastrous to her friendships. Here in Copenhagen it was merely a little mysterious and added another clinging wisp of charm.

Helga Crane's new existence was intensely pleasant to her; it gratified her augmented sense of self-importance. And it suited her. She had to admit that the Danes had the right idea. To each his own milieu. Enhance what was already in one's possession. In America Negroes sometimes talked loudly of this, but in their hearts they repudiated it. In their lives too. They didn't want to be like themselves. What they wanted, asked for, begged for, was to be like their white overlords. They were ashamed to be Negroes, but not ashamed to beg to be something else. Something inferior. Not quite genuine. Too bad!

Helga Crane didn't, however, think often of America, excepting in unfavorable contrast to Denmark. For she had resolved never to return to the existence of ignominy which the New World of opportunity and promise forced upon Negroes. How stupid she had been ever to have thought that she could marry and perhaps have children in a land where every dark child was handicapped at the start by the shroud of color! She saw, suddenly, the giving birth to little, helpless, unprotesting Negro children as a sin, an unforgivable outrage. More black folk to suffer indignities. More dark bodies for mobs to lynch. No, Helga Crane didn't think often of America. It was too humiliating, too disturbing. And she wanted to be left to the peace which had come to her. Her mental difficulties and questionings had become simplified. She now believed sincerely that there was a law of compensation, and that sometimes it worked. For all those early desolate years she now felt recompensed. She recalled a line that had impressed her in her lonely school-days, "The far-off interest of tears."

To her, Helga Crane, it had come at last, and she meant to cling to it. So she turned her back on painful America, resolutely shutting out the griefs, the humiliations, the frustrations, which she had endured there.

Her mind was occupied with other and nearer things.

The charm of the old city itself, with its odd architectural mixture of medievalism and modernity, and the general air of well-being which pervaded it, impressed her. Even in the so-called poor sections there was none of that untidiness and squalor which she remembered as the accompaniment of poverty in Chicago, New York, and the Southern cities of America. Here the door-steps were always white from constant scrubbings, the women neat, and the children washed and provided with whole clothing. Here were no tatters and rags, no beggars. But, then, begging, she learned, was an offense punishable by law. Indeed, it was unnecessary in a country where everyone considered it a duty somehow to support himself and his family by honest work; or, if misfortune and illness came upon one, everyone else, including the State, felt bound to give assistance, a lift on the road to the regaining of independence.

After the initial shyness and consternation at the sensation caused by her strange presence had worn off, Helga spent hours driving or walking about the city, at first in the protecting company of Uncle Poul or Aunt Katrina or both, or sometimes Axel Olsen. But later, when she had become a little familiar with the city, and its inhabitants a little used to her, and when she had learned to cross the streets in safety, dodging successfully the innumerable bicycles like a true Copenhagener, she went often alone, loitering on the long bridge which spanned the placid lakes, or watching the pageant of the blue-clad, sprucely tailored soldiers in the daily parade at Amielenborg Palace, or in the historic vicinity of the long, low-lying Exchange, a picturesque structure in picturesque surroundings, skirting as it did the great canal, which always was alive with many small boats, flying broad white sails and pressing close on the huge ruined pile of the Palace of Christiansborg. There was also the Gammelstrand, the congregating-place of the venders of fish, where daily was enacted a spirited and interesting scene between sellers and buyers, and where Helga's appearance always roused lively and audible, but friendly, interest, long after she became in other parts of the city an accepted curiosity. Here it was that one day an old countrywoman asked her to what manner of mankind she belonged and at Helga's replying: "I'm a Negro," had become indignant, retorting angrily that, just because she was old and a countrywoman she could not be so easily fooled, for she knew as well as everyone else that Negroes were black and had woolly hair.

Against all this walking the Dahls had at first uttered mild protest. "But, Aunt dear, I have to walk, or I'll get fat," Helga asserted. "I've never, never in all my life, eaten so much." For the accepted style of entertainment in Copenhagen seemed to be a round of dinner-parties, at which it was customary for the hostess to tax the full capacity not only of her dining-room, but of her guests as well. Helga enjoyed these dinner-parties, as they were usually spirited affairs, the conversation brilliant and witty, often in several languages. And always she came in for a goodly measure of flattering attention and admiration.

There were, too, those popular afternoon gatherings for the express purpose of drinking coffee together, where between much talk, interesting talk, one sipped the strong and steaming beverage from exquisite cups fashioned of Royal Danish porcelain and partook of an infinite variety of rich cakes and *smørrebrød*. This *smørrebrød*, dainty sandwiches of an endless and tempting array, was distinctly a Danish institution. Often Helga wondered just how many of these delicious sandwiches she had consumed since setting foot on Denmark's soil. Always, wherever food was served, appeared the inevitable *smørrebrød*, in the home of the Dahls, in every other home that she visited, in hotels, in restaurants.

At first she had missed, a little, dancing, for, though excellent dancers, the Danes seemed not to care a great deal for that pastime, which so delightfully combines exercise and pleasure. But in the winter there was skating, solitary, or in gay groups. Helga liked this sport, though she was not very good at it. There were, however, always plenty of efficient and willing men to instruct and to guide her over the glittering ice. One could, too, wear such attractive skating-things.

But mostly it was with Axel Olsen that her thoughts were occupied. Brilliant, bored, elegant, urbane, cynical, worldly, he was a type entirely new to Helga Crane, familiar only, and that but little, with the restricted society of American Negroes. She was aware, too, that this amusing, if conceited, man was interested in her. They were, because he was painting her, much together. Helga spent long mornings in the eccentric studio opposite the Folkemuseum, and Olsen came often to the Dahl home, where, as Helga and the man himself knew, he was something more than welcome. But in spite of his expressed interest and even delight in her exotic appearance, in spite of his constant attendance upon her, he gave no sign of the more personal kind of concern which—encouraged by Aunt Katrina's mild insinuations and Uncle Poul's subtle questionings—she had tried to secure. Was it, she wondered, race that kept him silent, held him back. Helga Crane frowned on this thought, putting it furiously from her, because it disturbed her sense of security and permanence in her new life, pricked her self-assurance.

Nevertheless she was startled when on a pleasant afternoon while drinking coffee in the Hotel Vivili, Aunt Katrina mentioned, almost casually, the desirability of Helga's making a good marriage.

"Marriage, Aunt dear!"

"Marriage," firmly repeated her aunt, helping herself to another anchovy and olive sandwich. "You are," she pointed out, "twenty-five."

"Oh, Aunt, I couldn't! I mean, there's nobody here for me to marry." In spite of herself and her desire not to be, Helga was shocked.

"Nobody?" There was, Fru Dahl asserted, Captain Frederick Skaargaard—and very handsome he was too—and he would have money. And there was Herr Hans Tietgen, not so handsome, of course, but clever and a good business man; he too would be rich, very rich, some day. And there was Herr Karl Pedersen, who had a good berth with the Landmands-bank and considerable shares in a prosperous cement-factory at Aalborg. There was, too, Christian Lende, the young owner of the new Odin Theater. Any of these Helga might marry, was Aunt Katrina's opinion. "And," she added, "others." Or maybe Helga herself had some ideas.

Helga had. She didn't, she responded, believe in mixed marriages, "between races, you know." They brought only trouble—to the children—as she herself knew but too well from bitter experience.

Fru Dahl thoughtfully lit a cigarette. Eventually, after a satisfactory glow had manifested itself, she announced: "Because your mother was a fool. Yes, she was! If she'd come home after she married, or after you were born, or even after your father—er—went off like that, it would have been different. If even she'd left you when she was here. But why in the world she should have married again, and a person like that, I can't see. She wanted to keep you, she insisted on it, even over his protest, I think. She loved you so much, she said.—And so she made you unhappy. Mothers, I suppose, are like that. Selfish. And Karen was always stupid. If you've got any brains at all they came from your father."

Into this Helga would not enter. Because of its obvious partial truths she felt the need for disguising caution. With a detachment that amazed herself she asked if Aunt Katrina didn't think, really, that miscegenation was wrong, in fact as well as principle.

"Don't," was her aunt's reply, "be a fool too, Helga. We don't think of those things here. Not in connection with individuals, at least." And almost immediately she inquired: "Did you give Herr Olsen my message about dinner tonight?"

"Yes, Aunt." Helga was cross, and trying not to show it.

"He's coming?"

"Yes, Aunt," with precise politeness.

"What about him?"

"I don't know. *What* about him?"

"He likes you?"

"I don't know. How can I tell that?" Helga asked with irritating reserve, her concentrated attention on the selection of a sandwich. She had a feeling of nakedness. Outrage.

Now Fru Dahl was annoyed and showed it. "What nonsense! Of course you know. Any girl does," and her satin-covered foot tapped, a little impatiently, the old tiled floor.

"Really, I don't know, Aunt," Helga responded in a strange voice, a strange manner, coldly formal, levelly courteous. Then suddenly contrite, she added: "Honestly, I don't. I can't tell a thing about him," and fell into a little silence. "Not a thing," she repeated. But the phrase, though audible, was addressed to no one. To herself.

She looked out into the amazing orderliness of the street. Instinctively she wanted to combat this searching into the one thing which, here, surrounded by all other things which for so long she had so positively wanted, made her a little afraid. Started vague premonitions.

Fru Dahl regarded her intently. It would be, she remarked with a return of her outward casualness, by far the best of all possibilities.

Particularly desirable. She touched Helga's hand with her fingers in a little affectionate gesture. Very lightly.

Helga Crane didn't immediately reply. There was, she knew, so much reason—from one viewpoint—in her aunt's statement. She could only acknowledge it. "I know that," she told her finally. Inwardly she was admiring the cool, easy way in which Aunt Katrina had brushed aside the momentary acid note of the conversation and resumed her customary pitch. It took, Helga thought, a great deal of security. Balance.

"Yes," she was saying, while leisurely lighting another of those long, thin, brown cigarettes which Helga knew from distressing experience to be incredibly nasty tasting, "it would be the ideal thing for you, Helga." She gazed penetratingly into the masked face of her niece and nodded, as though satisfied with what she saw there. "And you of course realize that you are a very charming and beautiful girl. Intelligent too. If you put your mind to it, there's no reason in the world why you shouldn't—" Abruptly she stopped, leaving her implication at once suspended and clear. Behind her there were footsteps. A small gloved hand appeared on her shoulder. In the short moment before turning to greet Fru Fischer she said quietly, meaningly: "Or else stop wasting your time, Helga."

Helga Crane said: "Ah, Fru Fischer. It's good to see you." She meant it. Her whole body was tense with suppressed indignation. Burning inside like the confined fire of a hot furnace. She was so harassed that she smiled in self-protection. And suddenly she was oddly cold. An intimation of things distant, but none the less disturbing, oppressed her with a faintly sick feeling. Like a heavy weight, a stone weight, just where, she knew, was her stomach.

Fru Fischer was late. As usual. She apologized profusely. Also as usual. And, yes, she would have some coffee. And some smørrebrød. Though she must say that the coffee here at the Vivili was atrocious. Simply atrocious. "I don't see how you stand it." And the place was getting so common, always so many Bolsheviks and Japs and things. And she didn't—"begging your pardon, Helga"—like that hideous American music they were forever playing, even if it was considered very smart. "Give me," she said, "the good old-fashioned Danish melodies of Gade and Heise. Which reminds me, Herr Olsen says that Nielsen's "Helios" is being performed with great success just now in England. But I suppose you know all about it, Helga. He's already told you. What?" This last was accompanied with an arch and insinuating smile.

A shrug moved Helga Crane's shoulders. Strange she'd never before noticed what a positively disagreeable woman Fru Fischer was. Stupid, too.

Fifteen

Well into Helga's second year in Denmark, came an indefinite discontent. Not clear, but vague, like a storm gathering far on the horizon. It was long before she would admit that she was less happy than she had been during her first year in Copenhagen, but she knew that it was so. And this subconscious knowledge added to her growing restlessness and little mental insecurity. She desired ardently to combat this wearing down of her satisfaction with her life, with herself. But she didn't know how.

Frankly the question came to this: what was the matter with her? Was there, without her knowing it, some peculiar lack in her? Absurd. But she began to have a feeling of discouragement and hopelessness. Why couldn't she be happy, content, somewhere? Other people managed, somehow, to be. To put it plainly, didn't she know how? Was she incapable of it?

And then on a warm spring day came Anne's letter telling of her coming marriage to Anderson, who retained still his shadowy place in Helga Crane's memory. It added, somehow, to her discontent, and to her growing dissatisfaction with her peacock's life. This, too, annoyed her.

What, she asked herself, was there about that man which had the power always to upset her? She began to think back to her first encounter with him. Perhaps if she hadn't come away— She laughed. Derisively. "Yes, if I hadn't come away, I'd be stuck in Harlem. Working every day of my life. Chattering about the race problem."

Anne, it seemed, wanted her to come back for the wedding. This, Helga had no intention of doing. True, she had liked and admired Anne better than anyone she had ever known, but even for her she wouldn't cross the ocean.

Go back to America, where they hated Negroes! To America, where Negroes were not people. To America, where Negroes were allowed to be beggars only, of life, of happiness, of security. To America, where everything had been taken from those dark ones, liberty, respect, even the labor of their hands. To America, where if one had Negro blood, one mustn't expect money, education, or, sometimes, even work whereby one might earn bread. Perhaps she was wrong to bother about it now that she was so far away. Helga couldn't, however, help it. Never could she recall the shames and often the absolute horrors of the black man's existence in America without the quickening of her heart's beating and a sensation of disturbing nausea. It was too awful. The sense of dread of it was almost a tangible thing in her throat.

And certainly she wouldn't go back for any such idiotic reason as Anne's getting married to that offensive Robert Anderson. Anne was really too amusing. Just why, she wondered, and how had it come about that he was being married to Anne. And why did Anne, who had so much more than so many others—more than enough—want Anderson too? Why couldn't she— "I think," she told herself, "I'd better stop. It's none of my business. I don't care in the least. Besides," she added irrelevantly, "I hate such nonsensical soul-searching."

One night not long after the arrival of Anne's letter with its curious news, Helga went with Olsen and some other young folk to the great Circus, a vaudeville house, in search of amusement on a rare off night. After sitting through several numbers they reluctantly arrived at the conclusion that the whole entertainment was dull, unutterably dull, and apparently without alleviation, and so not to be borne. They were reaching for their wraps when out upon the stage pranced two black men, American Negroes undoubtedly, for as they danced and cavorted, they sang in the English of America an old rag-time song that Helga remembered hearing as a child, "Everybody Gives Me Good Advice." At its conclusion the audience applauded with delight. Only Helga Crane was silent, motionless.

More songs, old, all of them old, but new and strange to that audience. And how the singers danced, pounding their thighs, slapping their hands together, twisting their legs, waving their abnormally long arms, throwing their bodies about with a loose ease! And how the enchanted spectators clapped and howled and shouted for more!

Helga Crane was not amused. Instead she was filled with a fierce hatred for the cavorting Negroes on the stage. She felt shamed, betrayed, as if these pale pink and white people among whom she lived had suddenly been invited to look upon something in her which she had hidden away and wanted to forget. And she was shocked at the avidity at which Olsen beside her drank it in.

But later, when she was alone, it became quite clear to her that all along they had divined its presence, had known that in her was something, some characteristic, different from any that they themselves possessed. Else why had they decked her out as they had? Why subtly indicated that she was different? And they hadn't despised it. No, they had admired it, rated it as a precious thing, a thing to be enhanced, preserved. Why? She, Helga Crane, didn't admire it. She suspected that no Negroes, no Americans, did. Else why their constant slavish imitation of traits not their own? Why their constant begging to be considered as exact copies of other people? Even the enlightened, the intelligent ones demanded nothing more. They were all beggars like the motley crowd in the old nursery rhyme:

> *Hark! Hark!*
> *The dogs do bark.*
> *The beggars are coming to town.*
>
> *Some in rags,*
> *Some in tags,*
> *And some in velvet gowns.*

The incident left her profoundly disquieted. Her old unhappy questioning mood came again upon her, insidiously stealing away more of the contentment from her transformed existence.

But she returned again and again to the Circus, always alone, gazing intently and solemnly at the gesticulating black figures, an ironical and silently speculative spectator. For she knew that into her plan for her life had thrust itself a suspensive conflict in which were fused doubts, rebellion, expediency, and urgent longings.

It was at this time that Axel Olsen asked her to marry him. And now Helga Crane was surprised. It was a thing that at one time she had much wanted, had tried to bring about, and had at last relinquished as impossible of achievement. Not so much because of its apparent hopelessness as because of a feeling, intangible almost, that, excited and pleased as he was with her, her origin a little repelled him, and that, prompted by some impulse of racial antagonism, he had retreated into the fastness of a protecting habit of self-ridicule. A mordantly personal pride and sensitiveness deterred Helga from further efforts at incitation.

True, he had made, one morning, while holding his brush poised for a last, a very last stroke on the portrait, one admirably draped suggestion, speaking seemingly to the pictured face. Had he insinuated marriage, or something less—and easier? Or had he paid her only a rather florid compliment, in somewhat dubious taste? Helga, who had not at the time been quite sure, had remained silent, striving to appear unhearing.

Later, having thought it over, she flayed herself for a fool. It wasn't, she should have known, in the manner of Axel Olsen to pay florid compliments in questionable taste. And had it been marriage that he had meant, he would, of course, have done the proper thing. He wouldn't have stopped—or, rather, have begun—by making his wishes known to her when there was Uncle Poul to be formally consulted. She had been, she told herself, insulted. And a goodly measure of contempt and wariness was added to her interest in the man. She was able, however, to feel a gratifying sense of elation in the remembrance that she had been silent, ostensibly unaware of his utterance, and therefore, as far as he knew, not affronted.

This simplified things. It did away with the quandary in which the confession to the Dahls of such a happening would have involved her, for she couldn't be sure that they, too, might not put it down to the difference of her ancestry. And she could still go attended by him, and envied by others, to openings in Konigen's Nytorv, to showings at the Royal Academy or Charlottenborg's Palace. He could still call for her and Aunt Katrina of an afternoon or go with her to Magasin du Nord to select a scarf or a length of silk, of which Uncle Poul could say casually in the presence of interested acquaintances: "Um, pretty scarf"—or "frock"—"you're wearing, Helga. Is that the new one Olsen helped you with?"

Her outward manner toward him changed not at all, save that gradually she became, perhaps, a little more detached and indifferent. But definitely Helga Crane had ceased, even remotely, to consider him other than as someone amusing, desirable, and convenient to have about—if one was careful. She intended, presently, to turn her attention to one of the others. The decorative Captain of the Hussars, perhaps. But in the ache of her growing nostalgia, which, try as she might, she could not curb, she no longer thought with any seriousness on either Olsen or Captain Skaargaard. She must, she felt, see America again first. When she returned—

Therefore, where before she would have been pleased and proud at Olsen's proposal, she was now truly surprised. Strangely, she was aware also of a curious feeling of repugnance, as her eyes slid over his face, as smiling, assured, with just the right note of fervor, he made his declaration and request. She was astonished. Was it possible? Was it really this man that she had thought, even wished, she could marry?

He was, it was plain, certain of being accepted, as he was always certain of acceptance, of adulation, in any and every place that he deigned to honor with his presence. Well, Helga was thinking, that wasn't as much his fault as her own, her aunt's, everyone's. He was spoiled, childish almost.

To his words, once she had caught their content and recovered from her surprise, Helga paid not much attention. They would, she knew, be absolutely appropriate ones, and they didn't at all matter. They meant nothing to her—now. She was too amazed to discover suddenly how intensely she disliked him, disliked the shape of his head, the mop of his hair, the line of his nose, the tones of his voice, the nervous grace of his long fingers; disliked even the very look of his irreproachable clothes. And for some inexplicable reason, she was a little frightened and embarrassed, so that when he had finished speaking, for a short space there was only stillness in the small room, into which Aunt Katrina had tactfully had him shown. Even Thor, the enormous Persian, curled on the window ledge in the feeble late afternoon sun, had rested for the moment from his incessant purring under Helga's idly stroking fingers.

Helga, her slight agitation vanished, told him that she was surprised. His offer was, she said, unexpected. Quite.

A little sardonically, Olsen interrupted her. He smiled too. "But of course I expected surprise. It is, is it not, the proper thing? And always you are proper, Frøkken Helga, always."

Helga, who had a stripped, naked feeling under his direct glance, drew herself up stiffly. Herr Olsen needn't, she told him, be sarcastic. She *was* surprised. He must understand that she was being quite sincere, quite truthful about that. Really, she hadn't expected him to do her so great an honor.

He made a little impatient gesture. Why, then, had she refused, ignored, his other, earlier suggestion?

At that Helga Crane took a deep indignant breath and was again, this time for an almost imperceptible second, silent. She had, then, been correct in her deduction. Her sensuous, petulant mouth hardened. That he should so frankly—so insolently, it seemed to her—admit his outrageous meaning was too much. She said, coldly: "Because, Herr Olsen, in my country the men, of my race, at least, don't make such suggestions to decent girls. And thinking that you were a gentleman, introduced to me by my aunt, I chose to think myself mistaken, to give you the benefit of the doubt."

"Very commendable, my Helga—and wise. Now you have your reward. Now I offer you marriage."

"Thanks," she answered, "thanks, awfully."

"Yes," and he reached for her slim cream hand, now lying quiet on Thor's broad orange and black back. Helga let it lie in his large pink one, noting their contrast. "Yes, because I, poor artist that I am, cannot hold out against the deliberate lure of you. You disturb me. The longing for you does harm to my work. You creep into my brain and madden me," and he kissed the small ivory hand. Quite decorously, Helga thought, for one so maddened that he was driven, against his inclination, to offer her marriage. But immediately, in extenuation, her mind leapt to the admirable casualness of Aunt Katrina's expressed desire for this very thing, and recalled the unruffled calm of Uncle Poul under any and all circumstances. It was, as she had long ago decided, security. Balance.

"But," the man before her was saying, "for me it will be an experience. It may be that with you, Helga, for wife, I will become great. Immortal. Who knows? I didn't want to love you, but I had to. That is the truth. I make of myself a present to you. For love." His voice held a theatrical note. At the same time he moved forward putting out his arms. His hands touched air. For Helga had moved back. Instantly he dropped his arms and took a step away, repelled by something suddenly wild in her face and manner. Sitting down, he passed a hand over his face with a quick, graceful gesture.

Tameness returned to Helga Crane. Her ironic gaze rested on the face of Axel Olsen, his leonine head, his broad nose—"broader than my own"—his bushy eyebrows, surmounting thick, drooping lids, which hid, she knew, sullen blue eyes. He stirred sharply, shaking off his momentary disconcertion.

In his assured, despotic way he went on: "You know, Helga, you are a contradiction. You have been, I suspect, corrupted by the good Fru Dahl, which is perhaps as well. Who knows? You have the warm impulsive nature of the women of Africa, but, my lovely, you have, I fear, the soul of a prostitute. You sell yourself to the highest buyer. I should of course be happy that it is I. And I am." He stopped, contemplating her, lost apparently, for the second, in pleasant thoughts of the future.

To Helga he seemed to be the most distant, the most unreal figure in the world. She suppressed a ridiculous impulse to laugh. The effort sobered her. Abruptly she was aware that in the end, in some way, she would pay for this hour. A quick brief fear ran through her, leaving in its wake a sense of impending calamity. She wondered if for this she would pay all that she'd had.

And, suddenly, she didn't at all care. She said, lightly, but firmly: "But you see, Herr Olsen, I'm not for sale. Not to you. Not to any white man. I don't at all care to be owned. Even by you."

The drooping lids lifted. The look in the blue eyes was, Helga thought, like the surprised stare of a puzzled baby. He hadn't at all grasped her meaning.

She proceeded, deliberately: "I think you don't understand me. What I'm trying to say is this, I don't want you. I wouldn't under any circumstances marry you," and since she was, as she put it, being brutally frank, she added: "*Now!*"

He turned a little away from her, his face white but composed, and looked down into the gathering shadows in the little park before the house. At last he spoke, in a queer frozen voice: "You refuse me?"

"Yes," Helga repeated with intentional carelessness. "I refuse you."

The man's full upper lip trembled. He wiped his forehead, where the gold hair was now lying flat and pale and lusterless. His eyes still avoided the girl in the high-backed chair before him. Helga felt a shiver of compunction. For an instant she regretted that she had not been a little kinder. But wasn't it after all the greatest kindness to be cruel? But more gently, less indifferently, she said: "You see, I couldn't marry a white man. I simply couldn't. It isn't just you, not just personal, you understand. It's deeper, broader than that. It's racial. Some day maybe you'll be glad. We can't tell, you know; if we were married, you might come to be ashamed of me, to hate me, to hate all dark people. My mother did that."

"I have offered you marriage, Helga Crane, and you answer me with some strange talk of race and shame. What nonsense is this?"

Helga let that pass because she couldn't, she felt, explain. It would be too difficult, too mortifying. She had no words which could adequately, and without laceration to her pride, convey to him the pitfalls into which very easily they might step. "I might," she said, "have considered it once—when I first came. But you, hoping for a more informal arrangement, waited too long. You missed the moment. I had time to think. Now I couldn't. Nothing is worth the risk. We might come to hate each other. I've been through it, or something like it. I know. I couldn't do it. And I'm glad."

Rising, she held out her hand, relieved that he was still silent. "Good afternoon," she said formally. "It has been a great honor—"

"A tragedy," he corrected, barely touching her hand with his moist finger-tips.

"Why?" Helga countered, and for an instant felt as if something sinister and internecine flew back and forth between them like poison.

"I mean," he said, and quite solemnly, "that though I don't entirely understand you, yet in a way I do too. And—" He hesitated. Went on. "I think that my picture of you is, after all, the true Helga Crane. Therefore—a tragedy. For someone. For me? Perhaps."

"Oh, the picture!" Helga lifted her shoulders in a little impatient motion.

Ceremoniously Axel Olsen bowed himself out, leaving her grateful for the urbanity which permitted them to part without too much awkwardness. No other man, she thought, of her acquaintance could have managed it so well—except, perhaps, Robert Anderson.

"I'm glad," she declared to herself in another moment, "that I refused him. And," she added honestly, "I'm glad that I had the chance. He took it awfully well, though—for a tragedy." And she made a tiny frown.

The picture—she had never quite, in spite of her deep interest in him, and her desire for his admiration and approval, forgiven Olsen for that portrait. It wasn't, she contended, herself at all, but some disgusting sensual creature with her features. Herr and Fru Dahl had not exactly liked it either, although collectors, artists, and critics had been unanimous in their praise and it had been hung on the line at an annual exhibition, where it had attracted much flattering attention and many tempting offers.

Now Helga went in and stood for a long time before it, with its creator's parting words in mind: ". . . a tragedy . . . my picture is, after all, the true Helga Crane." Vehemently she shook her head. "It isn't, it isn't at all," she said aloud. Bosh! Pure artistic bosh and conceit. Nothing else. Anyone with half an eye could see that it wasn't, at all, like her.

"Marie," she called to the maid passing in the hall, "do you think this is a good picture of me?"

Marie blushed. Hesitated. "Of course, Frøkken, I know Herr Olsen is a great artist, but no, I don't like that picture. It looks bad, wicked. Begging your pardon, Frøkken."

"Thanks, Marie, I don't like it either."

Yes, anyone with half an eye could see that it wasn't she.

Sixteen

Glad though the Dahls may have been that their niece had had the chance of refusing the hand of Axel Olsen, they were anything but glad that she had taken that chance. Very plainly they said so, and quite firmly they pointed out to her the advisability of retrieving the opportunity, if, indeed, such a thing were possible. But it wasn't, even had Helga been so inclined, for, they were to learn from the columns of *Politikken*, Axel Olsen had gone off suddenly to some queer place in the Balkans. To rest, the newspapers said. To get Frøkken Crane out of his mind, the gossips said.

Life in the Dahl ménage went on, smoothly as before, but not so pleasantly. The combined disappointment and sense of guilt of the Dahls and Helga colored everything. Though she had resolved not to think that they felt that she had, as it were, "let them down," Helga knew that they did. They had not so much expected as hoped that she would bring down Olsen, and so secure the link between the merely fashionable set to which they belonged and the artistic one after which they hankered. It was of course true that there were others, plenty of them. But there was only one Olsen. And Helga, for some idiotic reason connected with race, had refused him. Certainly there was no use in thinking, even, of the others. If she had refused him, she would refuse any and all for the same reason. It was, it seemed, all-embracing.

"It isn't," Uncle Poul had tried to point out to her, "as if there were hundreds of mulattoes here. That, I can understand, might make it a little different. But there's only you. You're unique here, don't you see? Besides, Olsen has money and enviable position. Nobody'd dare to say, or even to think anything odd or unkind of you or him. Come now, Helga, it isn't this foolishness about race. Not here in Denmark. You've never spoken of it before. It can't be just that. You're too sensible. It must be something else. I wish you'd try to explain. You don't perhaps like Olsen?"

Helga had been silent, thinking what a severe wrench to Herr Dahl's ideas of decency was this conversation. For he had an almost fanatic regard for reticence, and a peculiar shrinking from what he looked upon as indecent exposure of the emotions.

"Just what is it, Helga?" he asked again, because the pause had grown awkward, for him.

"I can't explain any better than I have," she had begun tremulously, "it's just something—something deep down inside of me," and had turned away to hide a face convulsed by threatening tears.

But that, Uncle Poul had remarked with a reasonableness that was wasted on the miserable girl before him, was nonsense, pure nonsense.

With a shaking sigh and a frantic dab at her eyes, in which had come a despairing look, she had agreed that perhaps it was foolish, but she couldn't help it. "Can't you, won't you understand, Uncle Poul?" she begged, with a pleading look at the kindly worldly man who at that moment had been thinking that this strange exotic niece of his wife's was indeed charming. He didn't blame Olsen for taking it rather hard.

The thought passed. She was weeping. With no effort at restraint. Charming, yes. But insufficiently civilized. Impulsive. Imprudent. Selfish.

"Try, Helga, to control yourself," he had urged gently. He detested tears. "If it distresses you so, we won't talk of it again. You, of course, must do as you yourself wish. Both your aunt and I want only that you should be happy." He had wanted to make an end of this fruitless wet conversation.

Helga had made another little dab at her face with the scrap of lace and raised shining eyes to his face. She had said, with sincere regret: "You've been marvelous to me, you and Aunt Katrina. Angelic. I don't want to seem ungrateful. I'd do anything for you, anything in the world but this."

Herr Dahl had shrugged. A little sardonically he had smiled. He had refrained from pointing out that this was the only thing she could do for them, the only thing that they had asked of her. He had been too glad to be through with the uncomfortable discussion.

So life went on. Dinners, coffees, theaters, pictures, music, clothes. More dinners, coffees, theaters, clothes, music. And that nagging aching for America increased. Augmented by the uncomfortableness of Aunt Katrina's and Uncle Poul's disappointment with her, that tormenting nostalgia grew to an unbearable weight. As spring came on with many gracious tokens of following summer, she found her thoughts straying with increasing frequency to Anne's letter and to Harlem, its dirty streets, swollen now, in the warmer weather, with dark, gay humanity.

Until recently she had had no faintest wish ever to see America again. Now she began to welcome the thought of a return. Only a visit, of course. Just to see, to prove to herself that there was nothing there for her. To demonstrate the absurdity of even thinking that there could be. And to relieve the slight tension here. Maybe when she came back—

Her definite decision to go was arrived at with almost bewildering suddenness. It was after a concert at which Dvořák's "New World Symphony" had been wonderfully rendered. Those wailing undertones of "Swing Low, Sweet Chariot" were too poignantly familiar. They struck into her longing heart and cut away her weakening defenses. She knew at least what it was that had lurked formless and undesignated these many weeks in the back of her troubled mind. Incompleteness.

"I'm homesick, not for America, but for Negroes. That's the trouble."

For the first time Helga Crane felt sympathy rather than contempt and hatred for that father, who so often and so angrily she had blamed for his desertion of her mother. She understood, now, his rejection, his repudiation, of the formal calm her mother had represented. She understood his yearning, his intolerable need for the inexhaustible humor and the incessant hope of his own kind, his need for those things, not material, indigenous to all Negro environments. She understood and could sympathize with his facile surrender to the irresistible ties of race, now that they dragged at her own heart. And as she attended parties, the theater, the opera, and mingled with people on the streets, meeting only pale serious faces when she longed for brown laughing ones, she was able to forgive him. Also, it was as if in this understanding and forgiving she had come upon knowledge of almost sacred importance.

Without demur, opposition, or recrimination Herr and Fru Dahl accepted Helga's decision to go back to America. She had expected that they would be glad and relieved. It was agreeable to discover that she had done them less than justice. They were, in spite of their extreme worldliness, very fond of her, and would, as they declared, miss her greatly. And they did want her to come back to them, as they repeatedly insisted. Secretly they felt as she did, that perhaps when she returned— So it was agreed upon that it was only for a brief visit, "for your friend's wedding," and that she was to return in the early fall.

The last day came. The last good-byes were said. Helga began to regret that she was leaving. Why couldn't she have two lives, or why couldn't she be satisfied in one place? Now that she was actually off, she felt heavy at heart. Already she looked back with infinite regret at the two years in the country which had given her so much, of pride, of happiness, of wealth, and of beauty.

Bells rang. The gangplank was hoisted. The dark strip of water widened. The running figures of friends suddenly grown very dear grew smaller, blurred into a whole, and vanished. Tears rose in Helga Crane's eyes, fear in her heart.

Good-bye Denmark! Good-bye. Good-bye!

Seventeen

A summer had ripened and fall begun. Anne and Dr. Anderson had returned from their short Canadian wedding journey. Helga Crane, lingering still in America, had tactfully removed herself from the house in One Hundred and Thirty-ninth Street to a hotel. It was, as she could point out to curious acquaintances, much better for the newly-married Andersons not to be bothered with a guest, not even with such a close friend as she, Helga, had been to Anne.

Actually, though she herself had truly wanted to get out of the house when they came back, she had been a little surprised and a great deal hurt that Anne had consented so readily to her going. She might at least, thought Helga indignantly, have acted a little bit as if she had wanted her to stay. After writing for her to come, too.

Pleasantly unaware was Helga that Anne, more silently wise than herself, more determined, more selfish, and less inclined to leave anything to chance, understood perfectly that in a large measure it was the voice of Robert Anderson's inexorable conscience that had been the chief factor in bringing about her second marriage—his ascetic protest against the sensuous, the physical. Anne had perceived that the decorous surface of her new husband's mind regarded Helga Crane with that intellectual and aesthetic appreciation which attractive and intelligent women would always draw from him, but that underneath that well-managed section, in a more lawless place where she herself never hoped or desired to enter, was another, a vagrant primitive groping toward something shocking and frightening to the cold asceticism of his reason. Anne knew also that though she herself was lovely—more beautiful than Helga—and interesting, with her he had not to struggle against that nameless and to him shameful impulse, that sheer delight, which ran through his nerves at mere proximity to Helga. And Anne intended that her marriage should be a success. She intended that her husband should be happy. She was sure that it could be managed by tact and a little cleverness on her own part. She was truly fond of Helga, but seeing how she had grown more charming, more aware of her power, Anne wasn't so sure that her sincere and urgent request to come over for her wedding hadn't been a mistake. She was, however, certain of herself. She could look out for her husband. She could carry out what she considered her obligation to him, keep him undisturbed, unhumiliated. It was impossible that she could fail. Unthinkable.

Helga, on her part, had been glad to get back to New York. How glad, or why, she did not truly realize. And though she sincerely meant to keep her promise to Aunt Katrina and Uncle Poul and return to Copenhagen, summer, September, October, slid by and she made no move to go. Her uttermost intention had been a six or eight weeks' visit, but the feverish rush of New York, the comic tragedy of Harlem, still held her. As time went on, she became a little bored, a little restless, but she stayed on. Something of that wild surge of gladness that had swept her on the day when with Anne and Anderson she had again found herself surrounded by hundreds, thousands, of dark-eyed brown folk remained with her. *These* were her people. Nothing, she had come to understand now, could ever change that. Strange that she had never truly valued this kinship until distance had shown her its worth. How absurd she had been to think that another country, other people, could liberate her from the ties which bound her forever to these mysterious, these terrible, these fascinating, these lovable, dark hordes. Ties that were of the spirit. Ties not only superficially entangled with mere outline of features or color of skin. Deeper. Much deeper than either of these.

Thankful for the appeasement of that loneliness which had again tormented her like a fury, she gave herself up to the miraculous joyousness of Harlem. The easement which its heedless abandon brought to her was a real, a very definite thing. She liked the sharp contrast to her pretentious stately life in Copenhagen. It was as if she had passed from the heavy solemnity of a church service to a gorgeous care-free revel.

Not that she intended to remain. No. Helga Crane couldn't, she told herself and others, live in America. In spite of its glamour, existence in America, even in Harlem, was for Negroes too cramped, too uncertain, too cruel; something not to be endured for a lifetime if one could escape; something demanding a courage greater than was in her. No. She couldn't stay. Nor, she saw now, could she remain away. Leaving, she would have to come back.

This knowledge, this certainty of the division of her life into two parts in two lands, into physical freedom in Europe and spiritual freedom in America, was unfortunate, inconvenient, expensive. It was, too, as she was uncomfortably aware, even a trifle ridiculous, and mentally she caricatured herself moving shuttle-like from continent to continent. From the prejudiced restrictions of the New World to the easy formality of the Old, from the pale calm of Copenhagen to the colorful lure of Harlem.

Nevertheless she felt a slightly pitying superiority over those Negroes who were apparently so satisfied. And she had a fine contempt for the blatantly patriotic black Americans. Always when she encountered one of those picturesque parades in the Harlem streets, the Stars and Stripes streaming ironically, insolently, at the head of the procession tempered for her, a little, her amusement at the childish seriousness of the spectacle. It was too pathetic.

But when mental doors were deliberately shut on those skeletons that stalked lively and in full health through the consciousness of every person of Negro ancestry in America—conspicuous black, obvious brown, or indistinguishable white—life was intensely amusing, interesting, absorbing, and enjoyable; singularly lacking in that tone of anxiety which the insecurities of existence seemed to ferment in other peoples.

Yet Helga herself had an acute feeling of insecurity, for which she could not account. Sometimes it amounted to fright almost. "I must," she would say then, "get back to Copenhagen." But the resolution gave her not much pleasure. And for this she now blamed Axel

Olsen. It was, she insisted, he who had driven her back, made her unhappy in Denmark. Though she knew well that it wasn't. Misgivings, too, rose in her. Why hadn't she married him? Anne was married—she would not say Anderson—Why not she? It would serve Anne right if she married a white man. But she knew in her soul that she wouldn't. "Because I'm a fool," she said bitterly.

Eighteen

One November evening, impregnated still with the kindly warmth of the dead Indian summer, Helga Crane was leisurely dressing in pleasant anticipation of the party to which she had been asked for that night. It was always amusing at the Tavenors'. Their house was large and comfortable, the food and music always of the best, and the type of entertainment always unexpected and brilliant. The drinks, too, were sure to be safe.

And Helga, since her return, was more than ever popular at parties. Her courageous clothes attracted attention, and her deliberate lure—as Olsen had called it—held it. Her life in Copenhagen had taught her to expect and accept admiration as her due. This attitude, she found, was as effective in New York as across the sea. It was, in fact, even more so. And it was more amusing too. Perhaps because it was somehow a bit more dangerous.

In the midst of curious speculation as to the possible identity of the other guests, with an indefinite sense of annoyance she wondered if Anne would be there. There was of late something about Anne that was to Helga distinctly disagreeable, a peculiar half-patronizing attitude, mixed faintly with distrust. Helga couldn't define it, couldn't account for it. She had tried. In the end she had decided to dismiss it, to ignore it.

"I suppose," she said aloud, "it's because she's married again. As if anybody couldn't get married. Anybody. That is, if mere marriage is all one wants."

Smoothing away the tiny frown from between the broad black brows, she got herself into a little shining, rose-colored slip of a frock knotted with a silver cord. The gratifying result soothed her ruffled feelings. It didn't really matter, this new manner of Anne's. Nor did the fact that Helga knew that Anne disapproved of her. Without words Anne had managed to make that evident. In her opinion, Helga had lived too long among the enemy, the detestable pale faces. She understood them too well, was too tolerant of their ignorant stupidities. If they had been Latins, Anne might conceivably have forgiven the disloyalty. But Nordics! Lynchers! It was too traitorous. Helga smiled a little, understanding Anne's bitterness and hate, and a little of its cause. It was a piece with that of those she so virulently hated. Fear. And then she sighed a little, for she regretted the waning of Anne's friendship. But, in view of diverging courses of their lives, she felt that even its complete extinction would leave her undevastated. Not that she wasn't still grateful to Anne for many things. It was only that she had other things now. And there would, forever, be Robert Anderson between them. A nuisance. Shutting them off from their previous confident companionship and understanding. "And anyway," she said again, aloud, "he's nobody much to have married. Anybody could have married him. Anybody. If a person wanted only to be married— If it had been somebody like Olsen— That would be different—something to crow over, perhaps."

The party was even more interesting than Helga had expected. Helen, Mrs. Tavenor, had given vent to a malicious glee, and had invited representatives of several opposing Harlem political and social factions, including the West Indian, and abandoned them helplessly to each other. Helga's observing eyes picked out several great and near-great sulking or obviously trying hard not to sulk in widely separated places in the big rooms. There were present, also, a few white people, to the open disapproval or discomfort of Anne and several others. There too, poised, serene, certain, surrounded by masculine black and white, was Audrey Denney.

"Do you know, Helen," Helga confided, "I've never met Miss Denney. I wish you'd introduce me. Not this minute. Later, when you can manage it. Not so—er—apparently by request, you know."

Helen Tavenor laughed. "No, you wouldn't have met her, living as you did with Anne Grey. Anderson, I mean. She's Anne's particular pet aversion. The mere sight of Audrey is enough to send her into a frenzy for a week. It's too bad, too, because Audrey's an awfully interesting person and Anne's said some pretty awful things about her. You'll like her, Helga."

Helga nodded. "Yes, I expect to. And I know about Anne. One night—" She stopped, for across the room she saw, with a stab of surprise, James Vayle. "Where, Helen did you get him?"

"Oh, that? That's something the cat brought in. Don't ask which one. He came with somebody, I don't remember who. I think he's shocked to death. Isn't he lovely? The dear baby. I was going to introduce him to Audrey and tell her to do a good job of vamping on him as soon as I could remember the darling's name, or when it got noisy enough so he wouldn't hear what I called him. But you'll do just as well. Don't tell me you know him!" Helga made a little nod. "Well!

And I suppose you met him at some shockingly wicked place in Europe. That's always the way with those innocent-looking men."

"Not quite. I met him ages ago in Naxos. We were engaged to be married. Nice, isn't he? His name's Vayle. James Vayle."

"Nice," said Helen throwing out her hands in a characteristic dramatic gesture—she had beautiful hands and arms—"is exactly the word. Mind if I run off? I've got somebody here who's going to sing. *Not* spirituals. And I haven't the faintest notion where he's got to. The cellar, I'll bet."

James Vayle hadn't, Helga decided, changed at all. Someone claimed her for a dance and it was some time before she caught his eyes, half questioning, upon her. When she did, she smiled in a friendly way over her partner's shoulder and was rewarded by a dignified little bow. Inwardly she grinned, flattered. He hadn't forgotten. He was still hurt. The dance over, she deserted her partner and deliberately made her way across the room to James Vayle. He was for the moment embarrassed and uncertain. Helga Crane, however, took care of that, thinking meanwhile that Helen was right. Here he did seem frightfully young and delightfully unsophisticated. He must be, though, every bit of thirty-two or more.

"They say," was her bantering greeting, "that if one stands on the corner of One Hundred and Thirty-fifth Street and Seventh Avenue long enough, one will eventually see all the people one has ever known or met. It's pretty true, I guess. Not literally of course." He was, she saw, getting himself together. "It's only another way of saying that everybody, almost, some time sooner or later comes to Harlem, even you."

He laughed. "Yes, I guess that is true enough. I didn't come to stay, though." And then he was grave, his earnest eyes searchingly upon her.

"Well, anyway, you're here now, so let's find a quiet corner if that's possible, where we can talk. I want to hear all about you."

For a moment he hung back and a glint of mischief shone in Helga's eyes. "I see," she said, "you're just the same. However, you needn't be anxious. This isn't Naxos, you know. Nobody's watching us, or if they are, they don't care a bit what we do."

At that he flushed a little, protested a little, and followed her. And when at last they had found seats in another room, not so crowded, he said: "I didn't expect to see you here. I thought you were still abroad."

"Oh, I've been back some time, ever since Dr. Anderson's marriage. Anne, you know, is a great friend of mine. I used to live with her. I came for the wedding. But, of course, I'm not staying. I didn't think I'd be here this long."

"You don't mean that you're going to live over there? Do you really like it so much better?"

"Yes and no, to both questions. I was awfully glad to get back, but I wouldn't live here always. I couldn't. I don't think that any of us who've lived abroad for any length of time would ever live here altogether again if they could help it."

"Lot of them do, though," James Vayle pointed out.

"Oh, I don't mean tourists who rush over to Europe and rush all over the continent and rush back to America thinking they know Europe. I mean people who've actually lived there, actually lived among the people."

"I still maintain that they nearly all come back here eventually to live."

"That's because they can't help it," Helga Crane said firmly. "Money, you know."

"Perhaps, I'm not so sure. I was in the war. Of course, that's not really living over there, but I saw the country and the difference in treatment. But, I can tell you, I was pretty darn glad to get back. All the fellows were." He shook his head solemnly. "I don't think anything, money or lack of money, keeps us here. If it was only that, if we really wanted to leave, we'd go all right. No, it's something else, something deeper than that."

"And just what do you think it is?"

"I'm afraid it's hard to explain, but I suppose it's just that we like to be together. I simply can't imagine living forever away from colored people."

A suspicion of a frown drew Helga's brows. She threw out rather tartly: "I'm a Negro too, you know."

"Well, Helga, you were always a little different, a little dissatisfied, though I don't pretend to understand you at all. I never did," he said a little wistfully.

And Helga, who was beginning to feel that the conversation had taken an impersonal and disappointing tone, was reassured and gave him her most sympathetic smile and said almost gently: "And now let's talk about you. You're still at Naxos?"

"Yes I'm still there. I'm assistant principal now."

Plainly it was a cause for enthusiastic congratulation, but Helga could only manage a tepid "How nice!" Naxos was to her too remote, too unimportant. She did not even hate it now.

How long, she asked, would James be in New York?

He couldn't say. Business, important business for the school, had brought him. It was, he said, another tone creeping into his voice, another look stealing over his face, awfully good to see her. She was looking tremendously well. He hoped he would have the opportunity of seeing her again.

But of course. He must come to see her. Any time, she was always in, or would be for him. And how did he like New York, Harlem?

He didn't, it seemed, like it. It was nice to visit, but not to live in. Oh, there were so many things he didn't like about it, the rush, the lack of home life, the crowds, the noisy meaninglessness of it all.

On Helga's face there had come that pityingly sneering look peculiar to imported New Yorkers when the city of their adoption is attacked by alien Americans. With polite contempt she inquired: "And is that all you don't like?"

At her tone the man's bronze face went purple. He answered coldly, slowly, with a faint gesture in the direction of Helen Tavenor, who stood conversing gayly with one of her white guests: "And I don't like that sort of thing. In fact I detest it."

"Why?" Helga was striving hard to be casual in her manner.

James Vayle, it was evident, was beginning to be angry. It was also evident that Helga Crane's question had embarrassed him. But he seized the bull by the horns and said: "You know as well as I do, Helga, that it's the colored girls these men come up here to see. They wouldn't think of bringing their wives." And he blushed furiously at his own implication. The blush restored Helga's good temper. James was really too funny.

"That," she said softly, "is Hugh Wentworth, the novelist, you know." And she indicated a tall olive-skinned girl being whirled about to the streaming music in the arms of a towering black man. "And that is his wife. She isn't colored, as you've probably been thinking. And now let's change the subject again."

"All right! And this time let's talk about you. You say you don't intend to live here. Don't you ever intend to marry, Helga?"

"Some day, perhaps. I don't know. Marriage—that means children, to me. And why add more suffering to the world? Why add any more unwanted, tortured Negroes to America? Why do Negroes have children? Surely it must be sinful. Think of the awfulness of being responsible for the giving of life to creatures doomed to endure such wounds to the flesh, such wounds to the spirit, as Negroes have to endure."

James was aghast. He forgot to be embarrassed. "But Helga! Good heavens! Don't you see that if we—I mean people like us—don't have children, the others will still have. That's one of the things that's the matter with us. The race is sterile at the top. Few, very few Negroes of the better class have children, and each generation has to wrestle again with the obstacles of the preceding ones, lack of money, education, and background. I feel very strongly about this. We're the ones who must have the children if the race is to get anywhere."

"Well, I for one don't intend to contribute any to the cause. But how serious we are! And I'm afraid that I've really got to leave you. I've already cut two dances for your sake. Do come to see me."

"Oh, I'll come to see you all right. I've got several things that I want to talk to you about and one thing especially."

"Don't," Helga mocked, "tell me you're going to ask me again to marry you."

"That," he said, "is just what I intend to do."

Helga Crane was suddenly deeply ashamed and very sorry for James Vayle, so she told him laughingly that it was shameful of him to joke with her like that, and before he could answer, she had gone tripping off with a handsome coffee-colored youth whom she had beckoned from across the room with a little smile.

Later she had to go upstairs to pin up a place in the hem of her dress which had caught on a sharp chair corner. She finished the temporary repair and stepped out into the hall, and somehow, she never quite knew exactly just how, into the arms of Robert Anderson. She drew back and looked up smiling to offer an apology.

And then it happened. He stooped and kissed her, a long kiss, holding her close. She fought against him with all her might. Then, strangely, all power seemed to ebb away, and a long-hidden, half-understood desire welled up in her with the suddenness of a dream. Helga Crane's own arms went up about the man's neck. When she drew away, consciously confused and embarrassed, everything seemed to have changed in a space of time which she knew to have been only seconds. Sudden anger seized her. She pushed him indignantly aside and with a little pat for her hair and dress went slowly down to the others.

Nineteen

That night riotous and colorful dreams invaded Helga Crane's prim hotel bed. She woke in the morning weary and a bit shocked at the uncontrolled fancies which had visited her. Catching up a filmy scarf, she paced back and forth across the narrow room and tried to think. She recalled her flirtations and her mild engagement with James Vayle. She was used to kisses. But none had been like that of last night. She lived over those brief seconds, thinking not so much of the man whose arms had held her as of the ecstasy which had flooded her. Even recollection brought a little onrush of emotion that made her sway a little. She pulled herself together and began to fasten on the solid fact of Anne and experienced a pleasant sense of shock in the realization that Anne was to her exactly what she had been before the incomprehensible experience of last night. She still liked her in the same degree and in the same manner. She still felt slightly annoyed with her. She still did not envy her marriage with Anderson. By some mysterious process the emotional upheaval which had racked her had left all the rocks of her existence unmoved. Outwardly nothing had changed.

Days, weeks, passed; outwardly serene; inwardly tumultous. Helga met Dr. Anderson at the social affairs to which often they were both asked. Sometimes she danced with him, always in perfect silence. She couldn't, she absolutely couldn't, speak a word to him when they were thus alone together, for at such times lassitude encompassed her; the emotion which had gripped her retreated, leaving a strange tranquillity, troubled only by a soft stir of desire. And shamed by his silence, his apparent forgetting, always after these dances she tried desperately to persuade herself to believe what she wanted to believe: that it had not happened, that she had never had that irrepressible longing. It was of no use.

As the weeks multiplied, she became aware that she must get herself out of the mental quagmire into which that kiss had thrown her. And she should be getting herself back to Copenhagen, but she had now no desire to go.

Abruptly one Sunday in a crowded room, in the midst of teacups and chatter, she knew that she couldn't go, that she hadn't since that kiss intended to go without exploring to the end that unfamiliar path into which she had strayed. Well, it was of no use lagging behind or pulling back. It was of no use trying to persuade herself that she didn't want to go on. A species of fatalism fastened on her. She felt that, ever since that last day in Naxos long ago, somehow she had known that this thing would happen. With this conviction came an odd sense of elation. While making a pleasant assent to some remark of a fellow guest she put down her cup and walked without haste, smiling and nodding to friends and acquaintances on her way to that part of the room where he stood looking at some examples of African carvings. Helga Crane faced him squarely. As he took the hand which she held out with elaborate casualness, she noted that his trembled slightly. She was secretly congratulating herself on her own calm when it failed her. Physical weariness descended on her. Her knees wobbled. Gratefully she slid into the chair which he hastily placed for her. Timidity came over her. She was silent. He talked. She did not listen. He came at last to the end of his long dissertation on African sculpture, and Helga Crane felt the intentness of his gaze upon her.

"Well?" she questioned.

"I want very much to see you, Helga. Alone."

She held herself tensely on the edge of her chair, and suggested: "Tomorrow?"

He hesitated a second and then said quickly: "Why, yes, that's all right."

"Eight o'clock?"

"Eight o'clock," he agreed.

Eight o'clock tomorrow came. Helga Crane never forgot it. She had carried away from yesterday's meeting a feeling of increasing elation. It had seemed to her that she hadn't been so happy, so exalted, in years, if ever. All night, all day, she had mentally prepared herself for the coming consummation; physically too, spending hours before the mirror.

Eight o'clock had come at last and with it Dr. Anderson. Only then had uneasiness come upon her and a feeling of fear for possible exposure. For Helga Crane wasn't, after all, a rebel from society, Negro society. It did mean something to her. She had no wish to stand alone. But these late fears were overwhelmed by the hardiness of insistent desire; and she had got herself down to the hotel's small reception room.

It was, he had said, awfully good of her to see him. She instantly protested. No, she had wanted to see him. He looked at her surprised. "You know, Helga," he had begun with an air of desperation, "I can't forgive myself for acting such a swine at the Tavenors' party. I don't at all blame you for being angry and not speaking to me except when you had to."

But that, she exclaimed, was simply too ridiculous. "I wasn't angry a bit." And it had seemed to her that things were not exactly going forward as they should. It seemed that he had been very sincere, and very formal. Deliberately. She had looked down at her hands and inspected her bracelets, for she had felt that to look at him would be, under the circumstances, too exposing.

"I was afraid," he went on, "that you might have misunderstood; might have been unhappy about it. I could kick myself. It was, it must have been, Tavenor's rotten cocktails."

Helga Crane's sense of elation had abruptly left her. At the same time she had felt the need to answer carefully. No, she replied, she hadn't thought of it at all. It had meant nothing to her. She had been kissed before. It was really too silly of him to have been at all bothered about it. "For what," she had asked, "is one kiss more or less, these days, between friends?" She had even laughed a little.

Dr. Anderson was relieved. He had been, he told her, no end upset. Rising, he said: "I see you're going out. I won't keep you."

Helga Crane too had risen. Quickly. A sort of madness had swept over her. She felt that he had belittled and ridiculed her. And thinking this, she had suddenly savagely slapped Robert Anderson with all her might, in the face.

For a short moment they had both stood stunned, in the deep silence which had followed that resounding slap. Then, without a word of contrition or apology, Helga Crane had gone out of the room and upstairs.

She had, she told herself, been perfectly justified in slapping Dr. Anderson, but she was not convinced. So she had tried hard to make herself very drunk in order that sleep might come to her, but had managed only to make herself very sick.

Not even the memory of how all living had left his face, which had gone a taupe gray hue, or the despairing way in which he had lifted his head and let it drop, or the trembling hands which he had pressed into his pockets, brought her any scrap of comfort. She had ruined everything. Ruined it because she had been so silly as to close her eyes to all indications that pointed to the fact that no matter what the intensity of his feelings or desires might be, he was not the sort of man who would for any reason give up one particle of his own good opinion of himself. Not even for her. Not even though he knew that she had wanted so terribly something special from him.

Something special. And now she had forfeited it forever. Forever. Helga had an instantaneous shocking perception of what forever meant. And then, like a flash, it was gone, leaving an endless stretch of dreary years before her appalled vision.

Twenty

The day was a rainy one. Helga Crane, stretched out on her bed, felt herself so broken physically, mentally, that she had given up thinking. But back and forth in her staggered brain wavering, incoherent thoughts shot shuttle-like. Her pride would have shut out these humiliating thoughts and painful visions of herself. The effort was too great. She felt alone, isolated from all other human beings, separated even from her own anterior existence by the disaster of yesterday.

Over and over, she repeated: "There's nothing left but to go now." Her anguish seemed unbearable.

For days, for weeks, voluptuous visions had haunted her. Desire had burned in her flesh with uncontrollable violence. The wish to give herself had been so intense that Dr. Anderson's surprising, trivial apology loomed as a direct refusal of the offering. Whatever outcome she had expected, it had been something else than this, this mortification, this feeling of ridicule and self-loathing, this knowledge that she had deluded herself. It was all, she told herself, as unpleasant as possible.

Almost she wished she could die. Not quite. It wasn't that she was afraid of death, which had, she thought, its picturesque aspects. It was rather that she knew she would not die. And death, after the debacle, would but intensify its absurdity. Also, it would reduce her, Helga Crane, to unimportance, to nothingness. Even in her unhappy present state, that did not appeal to her. Gradually, reluctantly, she began to know that the blow to her self-esteem, the certainty of having proved herself a silly fool, was perhaps the severest hurt which she had suffered. It was her self-assurance that had gone down in the crash. After all, what Dr. Anderson thought didn't matter. She could escape from the discomfort of his knowing gray eyes. But she couldn't escape from sure knowledge that she had made a fool of herself. This angered her further and she struck the wall with her hands and jumped up and began hastily to dress herself. She couldn't go on with the analysis. It was too hard. Why bother, when she could add nothing to the obvious fact that she had been a fool?

"I can't stay in this room any longer. I must get out or I'll choke." Her self-knowledge had increased her anguish. Distracted, agitated, incapable of containing herself, she tore open drawers and closets trying desperately to take some interest in the selection of her apparel.

It was evening and still raining. In the streets, unusually deserted, the electric lights cast dull glows. Helga Crane, walking rapidly, aimlessly, could decide on no definite destination. She had not thought to take umbrella or even rubbers. Rain and wind whipped cruelly about her, drenching her garments and chilling her body. Soon the foolish little satin shoes which she wore were sopping wet. Unheeding these physical discomforts, she went on, but at the open corner of One Hundred and Thirty-eighth Street a sudden more ruthless gust of wind ripped the small hat from her head. In the next minute the black clouds opened wider and spilled their water with unusual fury. The streets became swirling rivers. Helga Crane, forgetting her mental torment, looked about anxiously for a sheltering taxi. A few taxis sped by, but inhabited, so she began desperately to struggle through wind and rain toward one of the buildings, where she could take shelter in a store or a doorway. But another whirl of wind lashed her and, scornful of her slight strength, tossed her into the swollen gutter.

Now she knew beyond all doubt that she had no desire to die, and certainly not there nor then. Not in such a messy wet manner. Death had lost all of its picturesque aspects to the girl lying soaked and soiled in the flooded gutter. So, though she was very tired and very weak, she dragged herself up and succeeded finally in making her way to the store whose blurred light she had marked for her destination.

She had opened the door and had entered before she was aware that, inside, people were singing a song which she was conscious of having heard years ago—hundreds of years it seemed. Repeated over and over, she made out the words:

> . . . *Showers of blessings,*
> *Showers of blessings* . . .

She was conscious too of a hundred pairs of eyes upon her as she stood there, drenched and disheveled, at the door of this improvised meeting-house.

> . . . *Showers of blessings* . . .

The appropriateness of the song, with its constant reference to showers, the ridiculousness of herself in such surroundings, was too much for Helga Crane's frayed nerves. She sat down on the floor, a dripping heap, and laughed and laughed and laughed.

It was into a shocked silence that she laughed. For at the first hysterical peal the words of the song had died in the singers' throats, and the wheezy organ had lapsed into stillness. But in a moment there were hushed solicitous voices; she was assisted to her feet and led haltingly to a chair near the low platform at the far end of the room. On one side of her a tall angular black woman under a queer hat sat down, on the other a fattish yellow man with huge outstanding ears and long, nervous hands.

The singing began again, this time a low wailing thing:

> *Oh, the bitter shame and sorrow*
> *That a time could ever be,*
> *When I let the Savior's pity*
> *Plead in vain, and proudly answered:*

> *"All of self and none of Thee,*
> *All of self and none of Thee."*

> *Yet He found me, I beheld Him,*
> *Bleeding on the cursed tree;*
> *Heard Him pray: "Forgive them, Father."*
> *And my wistful heart said faintly,*
> *"Some of self and some of Thee,*
> *Some of self and some of Thee."*

There were, it appeared, endless moaning verses. Behind Helga a woman had begun to cry audibly, and soon, somewhere else, another. Outside, the wind still bellowed. The wailing singing went on:

> *. . . Less of self and more of Thee,*
> *Less of self and more of Thee.*

Helga too began to weep, at first silently, softly; then with great racking sobs. Her nerves were so torn, so aching, her body so wet, so cold! It was a relief to cry unrestrainedly, and she gave herself freely to soothing tears, not noticing that the groaning and sobbing of those about her had increased, unaware that the grotesque ebony figure at her side had begun gently to pat her arm to the rhythm of the singing and to croon softly: "Yes, chile, yes, chile." Nor did she notice the furtive glances that the man on her other side cast at her between his fervent shouts of "Amen!" and "Praise God for a sinner!"

She did notice, though, that the tempo, the atmosphere of the place, had changed, and gradually she ceased to weep and gave her attention to what was happening about her. Now they were singing:

> *. . . Jesus knows all about my troubles . . .*

Men and women were swaying and clapping their hands, shouting and stamping their feet to the frankly irreverent melody of the song. Without warning the woman at her side threw off her hat, leaped to her feet, waved her long arms, and shouted shrilly: "Glory! Hallelujah!" and then, in wild, ecstatic fury jumped up and down before Helga clutching at the girl's soaked coat, and screamed: "Come to Jesus, you pore los' sinner!" Alarmed for the fraction of a second, involuntarily Helga had shrunk from her grasp, wriggling out of the wet coat when she could not loosen the crazed creature's hold. At the sight of the bare arms and neck growing out of the clinging red dress, a shudder shook the swaying man at her right. On the face of the dancing woman before her a disapproving frown gathered. She shrieked: "A scarlet 'oman. Come to Jesus, you pore los' Jezebel!"

At this the short brown man on the platform raised a placating hand and sanctimoniously delivered himself of the words: "Remembah de words of our Mastah: 'Let him that is without sin cast de first stone.' Let us pray for our errin' sistah."

Helga Crane was amused, angry, disdainful, as she sat there, listening to the preacher praying for her soul. But though she was contemptuous, she was being too well entertained to leave. And it was, at least, warm and dry. So she stayed, listening to the fervent exhortation to God to save her and to the zealous shoutings and groanings of the congregation. Particularly she was interested in the writhings and weepings of the feminine portion, which seemed to predominate. Little by little the performance took on an almost Bacchic vehemence. Behind her, before her, beside her, frenzied women gesticulated, screamed, wept, and tottered to the praying of the preacher, which had gradually become a cadenced chant. When at last he ended, another took up the plea in the same moaning chant, and then another. It went on and on without pause with the persistence of some unconquerable faith exalted beyond time and reality.

Fascinated, Helga Crane watched until there crept upon her an indistinct horror of an unknown world. She felt herself in the presence of a nameless people, observing rites of a remote obscure origin. The faces of the men and women took on the aspect of a dim vision. "This," she whispered to herself, "is terrible. I must get out of here." But the horror held her. She remained motionless, watching, as if she lacked the strength to leave the place—foul, vile, and terrible, with its mixture of breaths, its contact of bodies, its concerted convulsions, all in wild appeal for a single soul. Her soul.

And as Helga watched and listened, gradually a curious influence penetrated her; she felt an echo of the weird orgy resound in her own heart; she felt herself possessed by the same madness; she too felt a brutal desire to shout and to sling herself about. Frightened at the strength of the obsession, she gathered herself for one last effort to escape, but vainly. In rising, weakness and nausea from last night's unsuccessful attempt to make herself drunk overcame her. She had eaten nothing since yesterday. She fell forward against the crude railing which enclosed the little platform. For a single moment she remained there in silent stillness, because she was afraid she was going to be sick. And in that moment she was lost—or saved. The yelling figures about her pressed forward, closing her in on all sides. Mad-

dened, she grasped at the railing, and with no previous intention began to yell like one insane, drowning every other clamor, while torrents of tears streamed down her face. She was unconscious of the
words she uttered, or their meaning: "Oh God, mercy, mercy. Have
mercy on me!" but she repeated them over and over.

From those about her came a thunderclap of joy. Arms were
stretched toward her with savage frenzy. The women dragged themselves upon their knees or crawled over the floor like reptiles, sobbing
and pulling their hair and tearing off their clothing. Those who succeeded in getting near to her leaned forward to encourage the unfortunate sister, dropping hot tears and beads of sweat upon her bare
arms and neck.

The thing became real. A miraculous calm came upon her. Life
seemed to expand, and to become very easy. Helga Crane felt within
her a supreme aspiration toward the regaining of simple happiness, a
happiness unburdened by the complexities of the lives she had
known. About her the tumult and the shouting continued, but in a
lesser degree. Some of the more exuberant worshipers had fainted
into inert masses, the voices of others were almost spent. Gradually
the room grew quiet and almost solemn, and to the kneeling girl time
seemed to sink back into the mysterious grandeur and holiness of far-
off simpler centuries.

Twenty-one

On leaving the mission Helga Crane had started straight back to her
room at the hotel. With her had gone the fattish yellow man who
had sat beside her. He had introduced himself as the Reverend Mr.
Pleasant Green in proffering his escort for which Helga had been
grateful because she had still felt a little dizzy and much exhausted.
So great had been this physical weariness that as she had walked beside him, without attention to his verbose information about his own
"field," as he called it, she had been seized with a hateful feeling of
vertigo and obliged to lay firm hold on his arm to keep herself from
falling. The weakness had passed as suddenly as it had come. Silently
they had walked on. And gradually Helga had recalled that the man
beside her had himself swayed slightly at their close encounter, and
that frantically for a fleeting moment he had gripped at a protruding
fence railing. That man! Was it possible? As easy as that?

Instantly across her still half-hypnotized consciousness little burning darts of fancy had shot themselves. No. She couldn't. It would be

too awful. Just the same, what or who was there to hold her back? Nothing. Simply nothing. Nobody. Nobody at all.

Her searching mind had become in a moment quite clear. She cast at the man a speculative glance, aware that for a tiny space she had looked into his mind, a mind striving to be calm. A mind that was certain that it was secure because it was concerned only with things of the soul, spiritual things, which to him meant religious things. But actually a mind by habit at home amongst the mere material aspect of things, and at that moment consumed by some longing for the ecstasy that might lurk behind the gleam of her cheek, the flying wave of her hair, the pressure of her slim fingers on his heavy arm. An instant's flashing vision it had been and it was gone at once. Escaped in the aching of her own senses and the sudden disturbing fear that she herself had perhaps missed the supreme secret of life.

After all, there was nothing to hold her back. Nobody to care. She stopped sharply, shocked at what she was on the verge of considering. Appalled at where it might lead her.

The man—what was his name?—thinking that she was almost about to fall again, had reached out his arms to her. Helga Crane had deliberately stopped thinking. She had only smiled, a faint pro-vocative smile, and pressed her fingers deep into his arms until a wild look had come into his slightly bloodshot eyes.

The next morning she lay for a long while, scarcely breathing, while she reviewed the happenings of the night before. Curious. She couldn't be sure that it wasn't religion that had made her feel so ut-terly different from dreadful yesterday. And gradually she became a little sad, because she realized that with every hour she would get a little farther away from this soothing haziness, this rest from her long trouble of body and of spirit; back into the clear bareness of her own small life and being, from which happiness and serenity always faded just as they had shaped themselves. And slowly bitterness crept into her soul. Because, she thought, all I've ever had in life has been things—except just this one time. At that she closed her eyes, for even remembrance caused her to shiver a little.

Things, she realized, hadn't been, weren't, enough for her. She'd have to have something else besides. It all came back to that old question of happiness. Surely this was it. Just for a fleeting moment Helga Crane, her eyes watching the wind scattering the gray-white clouds and so clearing a speck of blue sky, questioned her ability to retain, to bear, this happiness at such cost as she must pay for it. There was, she knew, no getting round that. The man's agitation and sincere conviction of sin had been too evident, too illuminating. The question returned in a slightly new form. Was it worth the risk? Could she take it? Was she able? Though what did it matter—now?

And all the while she knew in one small corner of her mind that such thinking was useless. She had made her decision. Her resolution. It was a chance at stability, at permanent happiness, that she meant to take. She had let so many other things, other chances, escape her. And anyway there was God. He would perhaps make it come out all right. Still confused and not so sure that it wasn't the fact that she was "saved" that had contributed to this after feeling of well-being, she clutched the hope, the desire to believe that now at last she had found some One, some Power, who was interested in her. Would help her.

She meant, however, for once in her life to be practical. So she would make sure of both things, God and man.

Her glance caught the calendar over the little white desk. The tenth of November. The steamer *Oscar II* sailed today. Yesterday she had half thought of sailing with it. Yesterday. How far away!

With the thought of yesterday came the thought of Robert Anderson and a feeling of elation, revenge. She had put herself beyond the need of help from him. She had made it impossible for herself ever again to appeal to him. Instinctively she had the knowledge that he would be shocked. Grieved. Horribly hurt even. Well, let him!

The need to hurry suddenly obsessed her. She must. The morning was almost gone. And she meant, if she could manage it, to be married today. Rising, she was seized with a fear so acute that she had to lie down again. For the thought came to her that she might fail. Might not be able to confront the situation. That would be too dreadful. But she became calm again. How could he, a naïve creature like that, hold out against her? If she pretended to distress? To fear? To remorse? He couldn't. It would be useless for him even to try. She screwed up her face into a little grin, remembering that even if protestations were to fail, there were other ways.

And, too, there was God.

Twenty-two

And so in the confusion of seductive repentance Helga Crane was married to the grandiloquent Reverend Mr. Pleasant Green, that rattish yellow man, who had so kindly, so unctuously, proffered his escort to her hotel on the memorable night of her conversion. With him she willingly, even eagerly, left the sins and temptations of New

York behind her to, as he put it, "labor in the vineyard of the Lord" in the tiny Alabama town where he was pastor to a scattered and primitive flock. And where, as the wife of the preacher, she was a person of relative importance. Only relative.

Helga did not hate him, the town, or the people. No. Not for a long time.

As always, at first the novelty of the thing, the change, fascinated her. There was a recurrence of the feeling that now, at last, she had found a place for herself, that she was really living. And she had her religion, which in her new status as a preacher's wife had of necessity become real to her. She believed in it. Because in its coming it had brought this other thing, this anæsthetic satisfaction for her senses. Hers was, she declared to herself, a truly spiritual union. This one time in her life, she was convinced, she had not clutched a shadow and missed the actuality. She felt compensated for all previous humiliations and disappointments and was glad. If she remembered that she had had something like this feeling before, she put the unwelcome memory from her with the thought: "This time I know I'm right. This time it will last."

Eagerly she accepted everything, even that bleak air of poverty which, in some curious way, regards itself as virtuous, for no other reason than that it is poor. And in her first hectic enthusiasm she intended and planned to do much good to her husband's parishioners. Her young joy and zest for the uplifting of her fellow men came back to her. She meant to subdue the cleanly scrubbed ugliness of her own surroundings to soft inoffensive beauty, and to help the other women to do likewise. Too, she would help them with their clothes, tactfully point out that sunbonnets, no matter how gay, and aprons, no matter how frilly, were not quite the proper things for Sunday church wear. There would be a sewing circle. She visualized herself instructing the children, who seemed most of the time to run wild, in ways of gentler deportment. She was anxious to be a true helpmate, for in her heart was a feeling of obligation, of humble gratitude.

In her ardor and sincerity Helga even made some small beginnings. True, she was not very successful in this matter of innovations. When she went about to try to interest the women in what she considered more appropriate clothing and in inexpensive ways of improving their homes according to her ideas of beauty, she was met, always, with smiling agreement and good-natured promises. "Yuh all is right, Mis' Green," and "Ah suttinly will, Mis' Green," fell courteously on her ear at each visit.

She was unaware that afterwards they would shake their heads sullenly over their wash-tubs and ironing-boards. And that among themselves they talked with amusement, or with anger, of "dat uppity, meddlin' No'the'nah," and "pore Reve'end," who in their opinion "would 'a done bettah to a ma'ied Clementine Richards." Knowing, as she did, nothing of this, Helga was unperturbed. But even had she known, she would not have been disheartened. The fact that it was difficult but increased her eagerness, and made the doing of it seem only the more worth while. Sometimes she would smile to think how changed she was.

And she was humble too. Even with Clementine Richards, a strapping black beauty of magnificent Amazon proportions and bold shining eyes of jet-like hardness. A person of awesome appearance. All chains, strings of beads, jingling bracelets, flying ribbons, feathery neck-pieces, and flowery hats. Clementine was inclined to treat Helga with an only partially concealed contemptuousness, considering her a poor thing without style, and without proper understanding of the worth and greatness of the man, Clementine's own adored pastor, whom Helga had somehow had the astounding good luck to marry. Clementine's admiration of the Reverend Mr. Pleasant Green was open. Helga was at first astonished. Until she learned that there was really no reason why it should be concealed. Everybody was aware of it. Besides, open adoration was the prerogative, the almost religious duty, of the female portion of the flock. If this unhidden and exaggerated approval contributed to his already oversized pomposity, so much the better. It was what they expected, liked, wanted. The greater his own sense of superiority became, the more flattered they were by his notice and small attentions, the more they cast at him killing glances, the more they hung enraptured on his words.

In the days before her conversion, with its subsequent blurring of her sense of humor, Helga might have amused herself by tracing the relation of this constant ogling and flattering on the proverbially large families of preachers; the often disastrous effect on their wives of this constant stirring of the senses by extraneous women. Now, however, she did not even think of it.

She was too busy. Every minute of the day was full. Necessarily. And to Helga this was a new experience. She was charmed by it. To be mistress in one's own house, to have a garden, and chickens, and a pig; to have a husband—and to be "right with God"—what pleasure did that other world which she had left contain that could surpass these? Here, she had found, she was sure, the intangible thing for which, indefinitely, always she had craved. It had received embodiment.

Everything contributed to her gladness in living. And so for a time she loved everything and everyone. Or thought she did. Even the weather. And it was truly lovely. By day a glittering gold sun was set in an unbelievably bright sky. In the evening silver buds sprouted in a Chinese blue sky, and the warm day was softly soothed by a slight, cool breeze. And night! Night, when a languid moon peeped through the wide-opened windows of her little house, a little mockingly, it may be. Always at night's approach Helga was bewildered by a disturbing medley of feelings. Challenge. Anticipation. And a small fear.

In the morning she was serene again. Peace had returned. And she could go happily, inexpertly, about the humble tasks of her household, cooking, dish-washing, sweeping, dusting, mending, and darning. And there was the garden. When she worked there, she felt that life was utterly filled with the glory and the marvel of God.

Helga did not reason about this feeling, as she did not at that time reason about anything. It was enough that it was there, coloring all her thoughts and acts. It endowed the four rooms of her ugly brown house with a kindly radiance, obliterating the stark bareness of its white plaster walls and the nakedness of its uncovered painted floors. It even softened the choppy lines of the shiny oak furniture and subdued the awesome horribleness of the religious pictures.

And all the other houses and cabins shared in this illumination. And the people. The dark undecorated women unceasingly concerned with the actual business of life, its rounds of births and christenings, of loves and marriages, of deaths and funerals, were to Helga miraculously beautiful. The smallest, dirtiest, brown child, barefooted in the fields or muddy roads, was to her an emblem of the wonder of life, of love, and of God's goodness.

For the preacher, her husband, she had a feeling of gratitude, amounting almost to sin. Beyond that, she thought of him not at all. But she was not conscious that she had shut him out from her mind. Besides, what need to think of him? He was there. She was at peace, and secure. Surely their two lives were one, and the companionship in the Lord's grace so perfect that to think about it would be tempting providence. She had done with soul-searching.

What did it matter that he consumed his food, even the softest varieties, audibly? What did it matter that, though he did no work with his hands, not even in the garden, his fingernails were always rimmed with black? What did it matter that he failed to wash his fat body, or to shift his clothing, as often as Helga herself did? There were things that more than outweighed these. In the certainty of his goodness, his righteousness, his holiness, Helga somehow overcame her first disgust at the odor of sweat and stale garments. She was even able to be unaware of it. Herself, Helga had come to look upon as a finicky, showy thing of unnecessary prejudices and fripperies. And when she sat in the dreary structure, which had once been a stable belonging to the estate of a wealthy horse-racing man and about which the odor of manure still clung, now the church and social center of the Negroes of the town, and heard him expound with verbal extravagance the gospel of blood and love, of hell and heaven, of fire and gold streets, pounding with clenched fists the frail table before him or shaking those fists in the faces of the congregation like direct personal threats, or pacing wildly back and forth and even sometimes shedding great tears as he besought them to repent, she was, she told herself, proud and gratified that he belonged to her. In some strange way she was able to ignore the atmosphere of self-satisfaction which poured from him like gas from a leaking pipe.

And night came at the end of every day. Emotional, palpitating, amorous, all that was living in her sprang like rank weeds at the tingling thought of night, with a vitality so strong that it devoured all shoots of reason.

Twenty-three

After the first exciting months Helga was too driven, too occupied, and too sick to carry out any of the things for which she had made such enthusiastic plans, or even to care that she had made only slight progress toward their accomplishment. For she, who had never thought of her body save as something on which to hang lovely fabrics, had now constantly to think of it. It had persistently to be pampered to secure from it even a little service. Always she felt extraordinarily and annoyingly ill, having forever to be sinking into chairs. Or, if she was out, to be pausing by the roadside, clinging desperately to some convenient fence or tree, waiting for the horrible nausea and hateful faintness to pass. The light, care-free days of the past, when she had not felt heavy and reluctant or weak and spent, receded more and more and with increasing vagueness, like a dream passing from a faulty memory.

The children used her up. There were already three of them, all born within the short space of twenty months. Two great healthy twin boys, whose lovely bodies were to Helga like rare figures carved out of amber, and in whose sleepy and mysterious black eyes all that was puzzling, evasive, and aloof in life seemed to find expression. No matter how often or how long she looked at these two small sons of hers, never did she lose a certain delicious feeling in which were mingled pride, tenderness, and exaltation. And there was a girl, sweet, delicate, and flower-like. Not so healthy or so loved as the boys, but still miraculously her own proud and cherished possession.

So there was no time for the pursuit of beauty, or for the uplifting of other harassed and teeming women, or for the instruction of their neglected children.

Her husband was still, as he had always been, deferentially kind and incredulously proud of her—and verbally encouraging. Helga tried not to see that he had rather lost any personal interest in her, except for the short spaces between the times when she was preparing for or recovering from childbirth. She shut her eyes to the fact that his encouragement had become a little platitudinous, limited mostly to "The Lord will look out for you," "We must accept what God sends," or "My mother had nine children and was thankful for every one." If she was inclined to wonder a little just how they were to manage with another child on the way, he would point out to her that her doubt and uncertainty were a stupendous ingratitude. Had not the good God saved her soul from hell-fire and eternal damnation? Had He not in His great kindness given her three small lives to raise up for His glory? Had He not showered her with numerous other mercies (evidently too numerous to be named separately)?

"You must," the Reverend Mr. Pleasant Green would say unctuously, "trust the Lord more fully, Helga."

This pabulum did not irritate her. Perhaps it was the fact that the preacher was, now, not so much at home that even lent to it a measure of real comfort. For the adoring women of his flock, noting how with increasing frequency their pastor's house went unswept and undusted, his children unwashed, and his wife untidy, took pleasant pity on him and invited him often to tasty orderly meals, specially prepared for him, in their own clean houses.

Helga, looking about in helpless dismay and sick disgust at the disorder around her, the permanent assembly of partly emptied medicine bottles on the clock-shelf, the perpetual array of drying baby-clothes on the chair-backs, the constant debris of broken toys on the floor, the unceasing litter of half-dead flowers on the table, dragged in by the toddling twins from the forlorn garden, failed to blame him for the thoughtless selfishness of these absences. And, she was thankful, whenever possible, to be relieved from the ordeal of cooking. There were times when, having had to retreat from the kitchen in lumbering haste with her sensitive nose gripped between tightly squeezing fingers, she had been sure that the greatest kindness that God could ever show to her would be to free her forever from the sight and smell of food.

How, she wondered, did other women, other mothers, manage? Could it be possible that, while presenting such smiling and contented faces, they were all always on the edge of health? All always worn out and apprehensive? Or was it only she, a poor weak city-bred thing, who felt that the strain of what the Reverend Mr. Pleasant Green had so often gently and patiently reminded her was a natural thing, an act of God, was almost unendurable?

One day on her round of visiting—a church duty, to be done no matter how miserable one was—she summoned up sufficient boldness to ask several women how they felt, how they managed. The answers were a resigned shrug, or an amused snort, or an upward rolling of eyeballs with a mention of "de Lawd" looking after us all.

" 'Tain't nothin', nothin' at all, chile," said one, Sary Jones, who, as Helga knew, had had six children in about as many years. "Yuh all takes it too ha'd. Jes' remembah et's natu'al fo' a 'oman to hab chilluns an' don' fret so."

"But," protested Helga, "I'm always so tired and half sick. That can't be natural."

"Laws, chile, we's all ti'ed. An' Ah reckons we's all gwine a be ti'ed till kingdom come. Jes' make de bes' of et, honey. Jes' make de bes' yuh can."

Helga sighed, turning her nose away from the steaming coffee which her hostess had placed for her and against which her squeamish stomach was about to revolt. At the moment the compensations of immortality seemed very shadowy and very far away.

"Jes' remembah," Sary went on, staring sternly into Helga's thin face, "we all gits ouah res' by an' by. In de nex' worl' we's all recompense'. Jes' put yo' trus' in de Sabioah."

Looking at the confident face of the little bronze figure on the opposite side of the immaculately spread table, Helga had a sensation of shame that she should be less than content. Why couldn't she be as trusting and as certain that her troubles would not overwhelm her as Sary Jones was? Sary, who in all likelihood had toiled every day of her life since early childhood except on those days, totalling perhaps sixty, following the birth of her six children. And who by dint of superhuman saving had somehow succeeded in feeding and clothing them and sending them all to school. Before her Helga felt humbled and oppressed by the sense of her own unworthiness and lack of sufficient faith.

"Thanks, Sary," she said, rising in retreat from the coffee, "you've done me a world of good. I'm really going to try to be more patient."

So, though with growing yearning she longed for the great ordinary things of life, hunger, sleep, freedom from pain, she resigned herself to the doing without them. The possibility of alleviating her burdens by a greater faith became lodged in her mind. She gave herself up to it. It *did* help. And the beauty of leaning on the wisdom of God, of trusting, gave to her a queer sort of satisfaction. Faith was really quite easy. One had only to yield. To ask no questions. The more weary, the more weak, she became, the easier it was. Her religion was to her a kind of protective coloring, shielding her from the cruel light of an unbearable reality.

This utter yielding in faith to what had been sent her found her favor, too, in the eyes of her neighbors. Her husband's flock began to approve and commend this submission and humility to a superior wisdom. The womenfolk spoke more kindly and more affectionately of the preacher's Northern wife. "Pore Mis' Green, wid all dem small chilluns at once. She suah do hab it ha'd. An' she don' nebah complains an' frets no mo'e. Jes' trus' in de Lawd lak de Good Book say. Mighty sweet lil' 'oman too."

Helga didn't bother much about the preparations for the coming child. Actually and metaphorically she bowed her head before God, trusting in Him to see her through. Secretly she was glad that she had not to worry about herself or anything. It was a relief to be able to put the entire responsibility on someone else.

Twenty-four

It began, this next child-bearing, during the morning services of a breathless hot Sunday while the fervent choir soloist was singing: "Ah am freed of mah sorrow," and lasted far into the small hours of Tuesday morning. It seemed, for some reason, not to go off just right. And when, after that long frightfulness, the fourth little dab of amber humanity which Helga had contributed to a despised race was held before her for maternal approval, she failed entirely to respond properly to this sop of consolation for the suffering and horror through which she had passed. There was from her no pleased, proud smile, no loving, possessive gesture, no manifestation of interest in the important matters of sex and weight. Instead she deliberately closed her eyes, mutely shutting out the sickly infant, its smiling father, the soiled midwife, the curious neighbors, and the tousled room.

A week she lay so. Silent and listless. Ignoring food, the clamoring children, the comings and goings of solicitous, kind-hearted women, her hovering husband, and all of life about her. The neighbors were puzzled. The Reverend Mr. Pleasant Green was worried. The midwife was frightened.

On the floor, in and out among the furniture and under her bed, the twins played. Eager to help, the church-women crowded in and, meeting there others on the same laudable errand, stayed to gossip and to wonder. Anxiously the preacher sat, Bible in hand, beside his wife's bed, or in a nervous half-guilty manner invited the congregated parishioners to join him in prayer for the healing of their sister. Then, kneeling, they would beseech God to stretch out His all-powerful hand on behalf of the afflicted one, softly at first, but with rising vehemence, accompanied by moans and tears, until it seemed that the God to whom they prayed must in mercy to the sufferer grant relief. If only so that she might rise up and escape from the tumult, the heat, and the smell.

Helga, however, was unconcerned, undisturbed by the commotion about her. It was all part of the general unreality. Nothing reached her. Nothing penetrated the kind darkness into which her bruised spirit had retreated. Even that red-letter event, the coming to see her of the old white physician from downtown, who had for a long time stayed talking gravely to her husband, drew from her no interest. Nor for days was she aware that a stranger, a nurse from Mobile, had been added to her household, a brusquely efficient woman who produced order out of chaos and quiet out of bedlam. Neither did the absence of the children, removed by good neighbors at Miss Hartley's insistence, impress her. While she had gone down into that appalling blackness of pain, the ballast of her brain had got loose and she hovered for a long time somewhere in that delightful borderland on the edge of unconsciousness, an enchanted and blissful place where peace and incredible quiet encompassed her.

After weeks she grew better, returned to earth, set her reluctant feet to the hard path of life again.

"Well, here you are!" announced Miss Hartley in her slightly harsh voice one afternoon just before the fall of evening. She had for some time been standing at the bedside gazing down at Helga with an intent speculative look.

"Yes," Helga agreed in a thin little voice, "I'm back." The truth was that she had been back for some hours. Purposely she had lain silent and still, wanting to linger forever in that serene haven, that effortless calm where nothing was expected of her. There she could watch the figures of the past drift by. There was her mother, whom she had loved from a distance and finally so scornfully blamed, who appeared as she had always remembered her, unbelievably beautiful, young, and remote. Robert Anderson, questioning, purposely detached, affecting, as she realized now, her life in a remarkably cruel degree; for at last she understood clearly how deeply, how passionately, she must have loved him. Anne, lovely, secure, wise, selfish. Axel Olsen, conceited, worldly, spoiled. Audrey Denney, placid, taking quietly and without fuss the things which she wanted. James Vayle, snobbish, smug, servile. Mrs. Hayes-Rore, important, kind, determined. The Dahls, rich, correct, climbing. Flashingly, fragmentarily, other long-forgotten figures, women in gay fashionable frocks and men in formal black and white, glided by in bright rooms to distant, vaguely familiar music.

It was refreshingly delicious, this immersion in the past. But it was finished now. It was over. The words of her husband, the Reverend Mr. Pleasant Green, who had been standing at the window looking mournfully out at the scorched melon-patch, ruined because Helga had been ill so long and unable to tend it, were confirmation of that.

"The Lord be praised," he said, and came forward. It was distinctly disagreeable. It was even more disagreeable to feel his moist hand on hers. A cold shiver brushed over her. She closed her eyes. Obstinately and with all her small strength she drew her hand away from him. Hid it far down under the bed-covering, and turned her face away to hide a grimace of unconquerable aversion. She cared nothing, at that moment, for his hurt surprise. She knew only that, in the hideous agony that for interminable hours—no, centuries—she had borne, the luster of religion had vanished; that revulsion had come upon her; that she hated this man. Between them the vastness of the universe had come.

Miss Hartley, all-seeing and instantly aware of a situation, as she had been quite aware that her patient had been conscious for some time before she herself had announced the fact, intervened, saying firmly: "I think it might be better if you didn't try to talk to her now. She's terribly sick and weak yet. She's still got some fever and we mustn't excite her or she's liable to slip back. And we don't want that, do we?"

No, the man, her husband, responded, they didn't want that. Reluctantly he went from the room with a last look at Helga, who was lying on her back with one frail, pale hand under her small head, her curly black hair scattered loose on the pillow. She regarded him from behind dropped lids. The day was hot, her breasts were covered only by a nightgown of filmy *crêpe*, a relic of prematrimonial days, which had slipped from one carved shoulder. He flinched. Helga's petulant lip curled, for she well knew that this fresh reminder of her desirability was like the flick of a whip.

Miss Hartley carefully closed the door after the retreating husband. "It's time," she said, "for your evening treatment, and then you've got to try to sleep for a while. No more visitors tonight."

Helga nodded and tried unsuccessfully to make a little smile. She was glad of Miss Hartley's presence. It would, she felt, protect her from so much. She mustn't, she thought to herself, get well too fast. Since it seemed she was going to get well. In bed she could think, could have a certain amount of quiet. Of aloneness.

In that period of racking pain and calamitous fright Helga had learned what passion and credulity could do to one. In her was born angry bitterness and an enormous disgust. The cruel, unrelieved suffering had beaten down her protective wall of artificial faith in the infinite wisdom, in the mercy, of God. For had she not called in her agony on Him? And He had not heard. Why? Because, she knew now, He wasn't there. Didn't exist. Into that yawning gap of unspeakable brutality had gone, too, her belief in the miracle and wonder of life. Only scorn, resentment, and hate remained—and ridicule. Life wasn't a miracle, a wonder. It was, for Negroes at least, only a great disappointment. Something to be got through with as best one could. No one was interested in them or helped them. God! Bah! And they were only a nuisance to other people.

Everything in her mind was hot and cold, beating and swirling about. Within her emaciated body raged disillusion. Chaotic turmoil. With the obscuring curtain of religion rent, she was able to look about her and see with shocked eyes this thing that she had done to herself. She couldn't, she thought ironically, even blame God for it, now that she knew that He didn't exist. No. No more than she could pray to Him for the death of her husband, the Reverend Mr. Pleasant Green. The white man's God. And His great love for all people regardless of race! What idiotic nonsense she had allowed herself to believe. How could she, how could anyone, have been so deluded? How could ten million black folk credit it when daily before their eyes was enacted its contradiction? Not that she at all cared about the ten million. But herself. Her sons. Her daughter. These would grow to manhood, to womanhood, in this vicious, this hypocritical land. The dark eyes filled with tears.

"I wouldn't," the nurse advised, "do that. You've been dreadfully sick, you know. I can't have you worrying. Time enough for that when you're well. Now you must sleep all you possibly can."

Helga did sleep. She found it surprisingly easy to sleep. Aided by Miss Hartley's rather masterful discernment, she took advantage of the ease with which this blessed enchantment stole over her. From her husband's praisings, prayers, and caresses she sought refuge in sleep, and from the neighbors' gifts, advice, and sympathy.

There was that day on which they told her that the last sickly infant, born of such futile torture and lingering torment, had died after a short week of slight living. Just closed his eyes and died. No vitality. On hearing it Helga too had just closed her eyes. Not to die. She was convinced that before her there were years of living. Perhaps of happiness even. For a new idea had come to her. She had closed her eyes to shut in any telltale gleam of the relief which she felt. One less. And she had gone off into sleep.

And there was that Sunday morning on which the Reverent Mr. Pleasant Green had informed her that they were that day to hold a special thanksgiving service for her recovery. There would, he said, be prayers, special testimonies, and songs. Was there anything particular she would like to have said, to have prayed for, to have sung? Helga had smiled from sheer amusement as she replied that there was nothing. Nothing at all. She only hoped that they would enjoy themselves. And, closing her eyes that he might be discouraged from longer tarrying, she had gone off into sleep.

Waking later to the sound of joyous religious abandon floating in through the opened windows, she had asked a little diffidently that she be allowed to read. Miss Hartley's sketchy brows contracted into a dubious frown. After a judicious pause she had answered: "No, I don't think so." Then, seeing the rebellious tears which had sprung into her patient's eyes, she added kindly: "But I'll read to you a little if you like."

That, Helga replied, would be nice. In the next room on a high-up shelf was a book. She'd forgotten the name, but its author was Anatole France. There was a story, "The Procurator of Judea." Would Miss Hartley read that? "Thanks. Thanks awfully."

" 'Lælius Lamia, born in Italy of illustrious parents,' " began the nurse in her slightly harsh voice.

Helga drank it in.

" '. . . For to this day the women bring down doves to the altar as their victims. . . .' "

Helga closed her eyes.

" '. . . Africa and Asia have already enriched us with a considerable number of gods. . . .' "

Miss Hartley looked up. Helga had slipped into slumber while the superbly ironic ending which she had so desired to hear was yet a long way off. A dull tale, was Miss Hartley's opinion, as she curiously turned the pages to see how it turned out.

" 'Jesus? . . . Jesus—of Nazareth? I cannot call him to mind.' "

"Huh! she muttered, puzzled. "Silly." And closed the book.

Twenty-five

During the long process of getting well, between the dreamy intervals when she was beset by the insistent craving for sleep, Helga had had too much time to think. At first she had felt only an astonished anger at the quagmire in which she had engulfed herself. She had ruined her life. Made it impossible ever again to do the things that she wanted, have the things that she loved, mingle with the people she liked. She had, to put it as brutally as anyone could, been a fool. The damnedest kind of a fool. And she had paid for it. Enough. More than enough.

Her mind, swaying back to the protection that religion had afforded her, almost she wished that it had not failed her. An illusion. Yes. But better, far better, than this terrible reality. Religion had, after all, its uses. It blunted the perceptions. Robbed life of its crudest truths. Especially it had its uses for the poor—and the blacks.

For the blacks. The Negroes.

And this, Helga decided, was what ailed the whole Negro race in America, this fatuous belief in the white man's God, this childlike trust in full compensation for all woes and privations in "kingdom come." Sary Jones's absolute conviction, "In de nex' worl' we's all recompense'," came back to her. And ten million souls were as sure of it as was Sary. How the white man's God must laugh at the great joke he had played on them! Bound them to slavery, then to poverty and insult, and made them bear it unresistingly, uncomplainingly almost, by sweet promises of mansions in the sky by and by.

"Pie in the sky," Helga said aloud derisively, forgetting for the moment Miss Hartley's brisk presence, and so was a little startled at hearing her voice from the adjoining room saying severely: "My goodness! No! I should say you can't have pie. It's too indigestible. Maybe when you're better—"

"That," assented Helga, "is what I said. Pie—by and by. That's the trouble."

The nurse looked concerned. Was this an approaching relapse? Coming to the bedside, she felt at her patient's pulse while giving her a searching look. No. "You'd better," she admonished, a slight edge to her tone, "try to get a little nap. You haven't had any sleep today, and you can't get too much of it. You've got to get strong, you know."

With this Helga was in full agreement. It seemed hundreds of years since she had been strong. And she would need strength. For in some way she was determined to get herself out of this bog into which she had strayed. Or—she would have to die. She couldn't endure it. Her suffocation and shrinking loathing were too great. Not to be borne. Again. For she had to admit that it wasn't new, this feeling of dissatisfaction, of asphyxiation. Something like it she had experienced before. In Naxos. In New York. In Copenhagen. This differed only in degree. And it was of the present and therefore seemingly more reasonable. The other revulsions were of the past, and now less explainable.

The thought of her husband roused in her a deep and contemptuous hatred. At his every approach she had forcibly to subdue a furious inclination to scream out in protest. Shame, too, swept over her at every thought of her marriage. Marriage. This sacred thing of which parsons and other Christian folk ranted so sanctimoniously, how immoral—according to their own standards—it could be! But Helga felt also a modicum of pity for him, as for one already abandoned. She meant to leave him. And it was, she had to concede, all of her own doing, this marriage. Nevertheless, she hated him.

The neighbors and churchfolk came in for their share of her all-embracing hatred. She hated their raucous laughter, their stupid acceptance of all things, and their unfailing trust in "de Lawd." And more than all the rest she hated the jangling Clementine Richards, with her provocative smirkings, because she had not succeeded in marrying the preacher and thus saving her, Helga, from that crowning idiocy.

Of the children Helga tried not to think. She wanted not to leave them—if that were possible. The recollection of her own childhood, lonely, unloved, rose too poignantly before her for her to consider calmly such a solution. Though she forced herself to believe that this was different. There was not the element of race, of white and black. They were all black together. And they would have their father. But to leave them would be a tearing agony, a rending of deepest fibers. She felt that through all the rest of her lifetime she would be hearing their cry of "Mummy, Mummy, Mummy," through sleepless nights. No. She couldn't desert them.

How, then, was she to escape from the oppression, the degradation, that her life had become? It was so difficult. It was terribly difficult. It was almost hopeless. So for a while—for the immediate present, she told herself—she put aside the making of any plan for her going. "I'm still," she reasoned, "too weak, too sick. By and by, when I'm really strong—"

It was so easy and so pleasant to think about freedom and cities, about clothes and books, about the sweet mingled smell of Houbigant and cigarettes in softly lighted rooms filled with inconsequential chatter and laughter and sophisticated tuneless music. It was so hard to think out a feasible way of retrieving all these agreeable, desired things. Just then. Later. When she got up. By and by. She must rest. Get strong. Sleep. Then, afterwards, she could work out some arrangement. So she dozed and dreamed in snatches of sleeping and waking, letting time run on. Away.

And hardly had she left her bed and become able to walk again without pain, hardly had the children returned from the homes of the neighbors, when she began to have her fifth child.

LANGSTON HUGHES
Photograph by Edward Weston, 1933.
© 1981 Center for Creative Photography, Arizona Board of Regents.
Courtesy, the National Portrait Gallery, Smithsonian Institution.

LANGSTON HUGHES

1902 TO 1967

S umming up the spirit of creative independence proudly espoused by the rebel-artists of the Harlem Renaissance, Langston Hughes issued a manifesto in 1926 that has served ever since as a touchstone for genuinely African American art:

> We younger Negro artists who create now intend to express our individual dark-skinned selves without fear or shame. If white people are pleased we are glad. If they are not, it doesn't matter. We know we are beautiful. And ugly too. . . . If colored people are pleased we are glad. If they are not, their displeasure doesn't matter either. We build our temples for tomorrow, strong as we know how, and we stand on top of the mountain, free within ourselves.

Hughes's anticipation of the "Black is beautiful" credo of the 1960s and 1970s is only one reason why his work and example, more than that of any other writer of the Harlem Renaissance, have been treasured by succeeding generations of black readers and imitated by many black writers. Hughes always aimed to be a poet of the people, a man of letters who spoke to and for the black everyman. Not surprisingly, his most lasting contribution to African American fiction is the black everyman figure he named Jesse B. Semple, a seasoned Harlem veteran with a down-home past, garrulous and canny, a superb raconteur and commentator on the curious ways of black and white folk alike. The man who came to be known simply as "Simple" was not born in Hughes's writing until 1943. Yet his colorful manner of speaking, indomitable sense of humor, and passion for life despite adversity and injustice are all previewed in Hughes's best poetry and fiction from the Harlem Renaissance.

James Langston Hughes was born in Joplin, Missouri, the only child of an ambitious but frustrated father, who abandoned his family early in his son's life, and a dedicated but impoverished mother. Langston's black forbears included a member of John Brown's insurrection at Harper's Ferry and a former United States congressman. Growing up with a keen sense of the historic African American struggle, Hughes spent his boyhood in Lawrence, Kansas, often unhappy and lonely but emotionally sustained by a nurturing grandmother and intellectually stimulated by a strong love of reading. He began writing poetry in his early teens. He finished high school in Cleveland, Ohio, in 1920, where he read the poetry of Walt Whitman and Carl Sandburg, two major influences on his own verse, and was elected class poet. Soon after graduation Hughes composed one of his most memorable poems, "The Negro Speaks of Rivers," and sent it to Jessie Fauset, literary editor of *The Crisis*, who published it with enthusiasm in 1921.

Encouraged by Fauset's reception of his work, Hughes continued to write for *The Crisis* during his freshman year at Columbia University in 1921. But college life did not suit him, and he soon resolved to go to sea, his voyages taking him to Africa and eventually Paris. Near the end of 1924 Hughes, who had continued to write and publish during his travels, returned to the United States a well-known figure in black poetry circles. In January 1926 Alfred A. Knopf published his first volume of verse *The Weary Blues*. The title poem, which incorporated the "sad raggy tune" of the urban blues in a signature blend of literate and vernacular expression, won first prize for poetry in a 1925 literary contest sponsored by Charles Johnson's *Opportunity* magazine. Unlike the more traditional poetry of Claude McKay and Countee Cullen, Hughes's verse would stretch the structural and tonal boundaries of his form, experimenting through the remainder of the decade with blues, spirituals, jazz, and free verse techniques in a variety of voices and dialects. Controversy followed him when Hughes's second volume, *Fine Clothes to the Jew* (1927), offended the genteel and the pretentious. But Hughes kept on writing what he described in his autobiography as "poems like the songs they sang on Seventh Street—gay songs, because you had to be gay or die; sad songs, because you couldn't help being sad sometimes. But gay or sad, you kept on living and you kept on going." As black America's most popular poet, Hughes kept on going in the spirit of Seventh Street, publishing at least one innovative collection of poems or a verse drama in every remaining decade of his life. As a self-supporting writer he worked productively at his trade in a number of additional genres, including drama, opera, autobiography, social history, and anthologies of African and African American folklore, fiction, and poetry.

One of the many fields of twentieth-century African American literature that Hughes had a hand in cultivating was fiction. He wrote his first novel, *Not Without Laughter* (1930), just as the Harlem Renaissance was winding down. Set in small-town Kansas, Hughes's somewhat autobiographical novel traces a pattern of migration familiar in Harlem Renaissance fiction, except that the protagonist of *Not Without Laughter* makes his way to Chicago, where at the story's end he is poised to undertake a promising future, supported and encouraged by his aunt, a successful blues singer. Not until 1958 would Hughes write another novel, *Tambourines to Glory*, which exposes some of the excesses of the storefront church and popular religion in Harlem. More adept at shorter forms of fiction, Hughes's renditions of the anecdotes and racy folk wisdom of Jesse B. Semple, collected in five volumes beginning in 1950, mark his most enduring contribution to African American storytelling. Yet his first book of short stories, *The Ways of White Folks* (1934), revealed in Hughes a biting psychological realism that must have made many white readers wince at his satirical analysis of white racist paternalism in all its sanctimonious self-deception.

A vintage story from Hughes's first fiction collection, "The Blues I'm Playing" represents its author's parting shot at a rich, eccentric white female patron who oversaw his comings and goings and tried to edit his writing during the last years of the Harlem Renaissance. But in a more general sense "The Blues I'm Playing" asks: To whom does African American art belong and to what ought it owe its supreme allegiance?—fundamental questions that black writers pondered in the early 1930s as they mulled over the passing of the renaissance. In the struggle for power and authority between a folksy black southern-born pianist and the overbearing white lady who imposes her patronage on her "little black friend," Hughes dramatizes his rejection of any sort of art that alienates the artist from his or her people. Oceola Jones must beware of dependency on Mrs. Ellsworth on the one hand, and, on the other, the more seductive trap of alienated modernism, which holds that "you could live on nothing but art." Oceola's commitment to marriage and the blues, as well as to her art, epitomizes Hughes's faith that, the whims of white faddists notwithstanding, African American art could grow and thrive as long as the artist remembered that the soul of her or his creativity was rooted in a community of black people and black expressive traditions that ultimately did not require a renaissance, or its pundits and patrons, to tell them who they were or what art was for.

Barksdale, Richard. *Langston Hughes: The Poet and His Critics*. Chicago: American Library Association, 1977.

Berry, Faith. *Langston Hughes: Before and Beyond Harlem*. Westport, CT: Lawrence Hill, 1983.

Emanuel, James A. *Langston Hughes*. New York: Twayne, 1967.

Hughes, Langston. *The Big Sea*. New York: Knopf, 1940.

————. *I Wonder as I Wander*. New York: Rinehart, 1956.

Miller, R. Baxter. *Langston Hughes and Gwendolyn Brooks: A Reference Guide*. Boston: G. K. Hall, 1978.

O'Daniel, Therman B., ed. *Langston Hughes, Black Genius: A Critical Evaluation*. New York: William Morrow, 1971.

Rampersad, Arnold. *The Life of Langston Hughes*, vol. 1, 1902–1941: I, Too, Sing America; vol. 2, 1941–1967: I Dream a World. New York: Oxford University Press, 1986, 1988.

Tracy, Steven C. *Langston Hughes & the Blues*. Urbana: University of Illinois Press, 1988.

THE BLUES I'M PLAYING

Oceola Jones, pianist, studied under Philippe in Paris. Mrs. Dora Ellsworth paid her bills. The bills included a little apartment on the Left Bank and a grand piano. Twice a year Mrs. Ellsworth came over from New York and spent part of her time with Oceola in the little apartment. The rest of her time abroad she usually spent at Biarritz or Juan les Pins, where she would see the new canvases of Antonio Bas, young Spanish painter who also enjoyed the patronage of Mrs. Ellsworth. Bas and Oceola, the woman thought, both had genius. And whether they had genius or not, she loved them, and took good care of them.

Poor dear lady, she had no children of her own. Her husband was dead. And she had no interest in life now save art, and the young people who created art. She was very rich, and it gave her pleasure to share her richness with beauty. Except that she was sometimes confused as to where beauty lay—in the youngsters or in what they made, in the creators or the creation. Mrs. Ellsworth had been known to help charming young people who wrote terrible poems, blue-eyed young men who painted awful pictures. And she once turned down a garlic-smelling soprano-singing girl who, a few years later, had all the critics in New York at her feet. The girl was so sallow. And she really needed a bath, or at least a mouth wash, on the day when Mrs. Ellsworth went to hear her sing at an East Side settlement house. Mrs. Ellsworth had sent a small check and let it go at that—since, however, living to regret bitterly her lack of musical acumen in the face of garlic.

About Oceola, though, there had been no doubt. The Negro girl had been highly recommended to her by Ormond Hunter, the music critic, who often went to Harlem to hear the church concerts there, and had thus listened twice to Oceola's playing.

"A most amazing tone," he had told Mrs. Ellsworth, knowing her interest in the young and unusual. "A flare for the piano such as I have seldom encountered. All she needs is training—finish, polish, a repertoire."

"Where is she?" asked Mrs. Ellsworth at once. "I will hear her play."

By the hardest, Oceola was found. By the hardest, an appointment was made for her to come to East 63rd Street and play for Mrs. Ellsworth. Oceola had said she was busy every day. It seemed that she had pupils, rehearsed a church choir, and played almost nightly for colored house parties or dances. She made quite a good deal of money. She wasn't tremendously interested, it seemed, in going way downtown to play for some elderly lady she had never heard of, even if the request did come from the white critic, Ormond Hunter, via the pastor of the church whose choir she rehearsed, and to which Mr. Hunter's maid belonged.

It was finally arranged, however. And one afternoon, promptly on time, black Miss Oceola Jones rang the door bell of white Mrs. Dora Ellsworth's grey stone house just off Madison. A butler who actually wore brass buttons opened the door, and she was shown upstairs to the music room. (The butler had been warned of her coming.) Ormond Hunter was already there, and they shook hands. In a moment, Mrs. Ellsworth came in, a tall stately grey-haired lady in black with a scarf that sort of floated behind her. She was tremendously intrigued at meeting Oceola, never having had before amongst all her artists a black one. And she was greatly impressed that Ormond Hunter should have recommended the girl. She began right away, treating her as a protegee; that is, she began asking her a great many questions she would not dare ask anyone else at first meeting, except a protegee. She asked her how old she was and where her mother and father were and how she made her living and whose music she liked best to play and was she married and would she take one lump or two in her tea, with lemon or cream?

After tea, Oceola played. She played the Rachmaninoff *Prelude in C Sharp Minor*. She played from the Liszt *Études*. She played the *St. Louis Blues*. She played Ravel's *Pavanne pour une Enfante Défunte*. And then she said she had to go. She was playing that night for a dance in Brooklyn for the benefit of the Urban League.

Mrs. Ellsworth and Ormond Hunter breathed, "How lovely!"

Mrs. Ellsworth said, "I am quite overcome, my dear. You play so beautifully." She went on further to say, "You must let me help you. Who is your teacher?"

"I have none now," Oceola replied. "I teach pupils myself. Don't have time any more to study—nor money either."

"But you must have time," said Mrs. Ellsworth, "and money, also. Come back to see me on Tuesday. We will arrange it, my dear."

And when the girl had gone, she turned to Ormond Hunter for advice on piano teachers to instruct those who already had genius, and need only to be developed.

Then began one of the most interesting periods in Mrs. Ellsworth's whole experience in aiding the arts. The period of Oceola. For the Negro girl, as time went on, began to occupy a greater and greater place in Mrs. Ellsworth's interests, to take up more and more of her time, and to use up more and more of her money. Not that Oceola ever asked for money, but Mrs. Ellsworth herself seemed to keep thinking of so much more Oceola needed.

At first it was hard to get Oceola to need anything. Mrs. Ellsworth had the feeling that the girl mistrusted her generosity, and Oceola did—for she had never met anybody interested in pure art before. Just to be given things for *art's sake* seemed suspicious to Oceola.

That first Tuesday, when the colored girl came back at Mrs. Ellsworth's request, she answered the white woman's questions with a why-look in her eyes.

"Don't think I'm being personal, dear," said Mrs. Ellsworth, "but I must know your background in order to help you. Now, tell me . . ."

Oceola wondered why on earth the woman wanted to help her. However, since Mrs. Ellsworth seemed interested in her life's history, she brought it forth so as not to hinder the progress of the afternoon, for she wanted to get back to Harlem by six o'clock.

Born in Mobile in 1903. Yes, m'am, she was older than she looked. Papa had a band, that is her step-father. Used to play for all the lodge turn-outs, picnics, dances, barbecues. You could get the best roast pig in the world in Mobile. Her mother used to play the organ in church, and when the deacons bought a piano after the big revival, her mama played that, too. Oceola played by ear for a long while until her mother taught her notes. Oceola played an organ, also, and a cornet.

"My, my," said Mrs. Ellsworth.

"Yes, m'am," said Oceola. She had played and practiced on lots of instruments in the South before her step-father died. She always went to band rehearsals with him.

"And where was your father, dear?" asked Mrs. Ellsworth.

"My step-father had the band," replied Oceola. Her mother left off playing in the church to go with him traveling in Billy Kersands' Minstrels. He had the biggest mouth in the world, Kersands did, and used to let Oceola put both her hands in it at a time and stretch it. Well, she and her mama and step-papa settled down in Houston. Sometimes her parents had jobs and sometimes they didn't. Often they were hungry, but Oceola went to school and had a regular piano-teacher, an old German woman, who gave her what technique she had today.

"A fine old teacher," said Oceola. "She used to teach me half the time for nothing. God bless her."

"Yes," said Mrs. Ellsworth. "She gave you an excellent foundation."

"Sure did. But my step-papa died, got cut, and after that Mama didn't have no more use for Houston so we moved to St. Louis. Mama got a job playing for the movies in a Market Street theater, and I played for a church choir, and saved some money and went to Wilberforce. Studied piano there, too. Played for all the college dances. Graduated. Came to New York and heard Rachmaninoff and was crazy about him. Then Mama died, so I'm keeping the little flat myself. One room is rented out."

"Is she nice?" asked Mrs. Ellsworth, "your roomer?"

"It's not a she," said Oceola. "He's a man. I hate women roomers."

"Oh!" said Mrs. Ellsworth. "I should think all roomers would be terrible."

"He's right nice," said Oceola. "Name's Pete Williams."

"What does he do?" asked Mrs. Ellsworth.

"A Pullman porter," replied Oceola, "but he's saving money to go to Med school. He's a smart fellow."

But it turned out later that he wasn't paying Oceola any rent.

That afternoon, when Mrs. Ellsworth announced that she had made her an appointment with one of the best piano teachers in New York, the black girl seemed pleased. She recognized the name. But how, she wondered, would she find time for study, with her pupils and her choir, and all. When Mrs. Ellsworth said that she would cover her *entire* living expenses, Oceola's eyes were full of that why-look, as though she didn't believe it.

"I have faith in your art, dear," said Mrs. Ellsworth, at parting. But to prove it quickly, she sat down that very evening and sent Oceola the first monthly check so that she would no longer have to take in pupils or drill choirs or play at house parties. And so Oceola would have faith in art, too.

That night Mrs. Ellsworth called up Ormond Hunter and told him what she had done. And she asked if Mr. Hunter's maid knew Oceola, and if she supposed that that man rooming with her were anything to her. Ormond Hunter said he would inquire.

Before going to bed, Mrs. Ellsworth told her housekeeper to order a book called "Nigger Heaven" on the morrow, and also anything else Brentano's had about Harlem. She made a mental note that she must go up there sometime, for she had never yet seen that dark section of New York; and now that she had a Negro protegee, she really ought to know something about it. Mrs. Ellsworth couldn't recall ever having known a single Negro before in her whole life, so she found Oceola fascinating. And just as black as she herself was white.

Mrs. Ellsworth began to think in bed about what gowns would look best on Oceola. Her protegee would have to be well-dressed. She wondered, too, what sort of a place the girl lived in. And who that man was who lived with her. She began to think that really Oceola ought to have a place to herself. It didn't seem quite respectable. . . .

When she woke up in the morning, she called her car and went by her dressmaker's. She asked the good woman what kind of colors looked well with black; not black fabrics, but a black skin.

"I have a little friend to fit out," she said.

"A *black* friend?" said the dressmaker.

"A black friend," said Mrs. Ellsworth.

III

Some days later Ormond Hunter reported on what his maid knew about Oceola. It seemed that the two belonged to the same church, and although the maid did not know Oceola very well, she knew what everybody said about her in the church. Yes, indeed! Oceola were a right nice girl, for sure, but it certainly were a shame she were giving all her money to that man what stayed with her and what she was practically putting through college so he could be a doctor.

"Why," gasped Mrs. Ellsworth, "the poor child is being preyed upon."

"It seems to me so," said Ormond Hunter.

"I must get her out of Harlem," said Mrs. Ellsworth, "at once. I believe it's worse than Chinatown."

"She might be in a more artistic atmosphere," agreed Ormond Hunter. "And with her career launched, she probably won't want that man anyhow."

"She won't need him," said Mrs. Ellsworth. "She will have her art."

But Mrs. Ellsworth decided that in order to increase the rapprochement between art and Oceola, something should be done now, at once. She asked the girl to come down to see her the next day, and when it was time to go home, the white woman said, "I have a half-hour before dinner. I'll drive you up. You know I've never been to Harlem."

"All right," said Oceola. "That's nice of you."

But she didn't suggest the white lady's coming in, when they drew up before a rather sad-looking apartment house in 134th Street. Mrs. Ellsworth had to ask could she come in.

"I live on the fifth floor," said Oceola, "and there isn't any elevator."

"It doesn't matter, dear," said the white woman, for she meant to see the inside of this girl's life, elevator or no elevator.

The apartment was just as she thought it would be. After all, she had read Thomas Burke on Limehouse. And here was just one more of those holes in the wall, even if it was five stories high. The windows looked down on slums. There were only four rooms, small as maids' rooms, all of them. An upright piano almost filled the parlor. Oceola slept in the dining-room. The roomer slept in the bed-chamber beyond the kitchen.

"Where is he, darling?"

"He runs on the road all summer," said the girl. "He's in and out."

"But how do you breathe in here?" asked Mrs. Ellsworth. "It's so small. You must have more space for your soul, dear. And for a grand piano. Now, in the Village . . ."

"I do right well here," said Oceola.

"But in the Village where so many nice artists live we can get . . ."

"But I don't want to move yet. I promised my roomer he could stay till fall."

"Why till fall?"

"He's going to Meharry then."

"To marry?"

"Meharry, yes m'am. That's a colored Medicine school in Nash-ville."

"Colored? Is it good?"

"Well, it's cheap," said Oceola. "After he goes, I don't mind moving."

"But I wanted to see you settled before I go away for the summer."

"When you come back is all right. I can do till then."

"Art is long," reminded Mrs. Ellsworth, "and time is fleeting, my dear."

"Yes, m'am," said Oceola, "but I gets nervous if I start worrying about time."

So Mrs. Ellsworth went off to Bar Harbor for the season, and left the man with Oceola.

I V

That was some years ago. Eventually art and Mrs. Ellsworth triumphed. Oceola moved out of Harlem. She lived in Gay Street west of Washington Square where she met Genevieve Taggard, and Ernestine Evans, and two or three sculptors, and a cat-painter who was also a protegee of Mrs. Ellsworth. She spent her days practicing, playing for friends of her patron, going to concerts, and reading books about music. She no longer had pupils or rehearsed the choir, but she still loved to play for Harlem house parties—for nothing—now that she no longer needed the money, out of sheer love of jazz. This rather disturbed Mrs. Ellsworth, who still believed in art of the old school, portraits that really and truly looked like people, poems about nature, music that had soul in it, not syncopation. And she felt the dignity of art. Was it in keeping with genius, she wondered, for Oceola to have a studio full of white and colored people every Saturday night (some of them actually drinking gin *from bottles*) and dancing to the most tomtom-like music she had ever heard coming out of a grand piano? She wished she could lift Oceola up bodily and take her away from all that, for art's sake.

So in the spring, Mrs. Ellsworth organized weekends in the upstate mountains where she had a little lodge and where Oceola could look from the high places at the stars, and fill her soul with the vastness of the eternal, and forget about jazz. Mrs. Ellsworth really began to hate jazz—especially on a grand piano.

If there were a lot of guests at the lodge, as there sometimes were, Mrs. Ellsworth might share the bed with Oceola. Then she would read aloud Tennyson or Browning before turning out the light, aware all the time of the electric strength of that brown-black body beside her, and of the deep drowsy voice asking what the poems were about. And then Mrs. Ellsworth would feel very motherly toward this dark girl whom she had taken under her wing on the wonderful road of art, to nurture and love until she became a great interpreter of the piano. At such times the elderly white woman was glad her late husband's money, so well invested, furnished her with a large surplus to devote to the needs of her protegees, especially to Oceola, the blackest—and most interesting of all.

Why the most interesting?

Mrs. Ellsworth didn't know, unless it was that Oceola really was talented, terribly alive, and that she looked like nothing Mrs. Ellsworth had ever been near before. Such a rich velvet black, and such a hard young body! The teacher of the piano raved about her strength.

"She can stand a great career," the teacher said. "She has everything for it."

"Yes," agreed Mrs. Ellsworth, thinking, however, of the Pullman porter at Meharry, "but she must learn to sublimate her soul."

So for two years then, Oceola lived abroad at Mrs. Ellsworth's expense. She studied with Philippe, had the little apartment on the Left Bank, and learned about Debussy's African background. She met many black Algerian and French West Indian students, too, and listened to their interminable arguments ranging from Garvey to Picasso to Spengler to Jean Cocteau, and thought they all must be crazy. Why did they or anybody argue so much about life or art? Oceola merely lived—and loved it. Only the Marxian students seemed sound to her for they, at least, wanted people to have enough to eat. That was important, Oceola thought, remembering, as she did, her own sometimes hungry years. But the rest of the controversies, as far as she could fathom, were based on air.

Oceola hated most artists, too, and the word *art* in French or English. If you wanted to play the piano or paint pictures or write books, go ahead! But why talk so much about it? Montparnasse was worse in that respect than the Village. And as for the cultured Negroes who were always saying art would break down color lines, art could save the race and prevent lynchings! "Bunk!" said Oceola. "My ma and pa were both artists when it came to making music, and the white folks ran them out of town for being dressed up in Alabama. And look at the Jews! Every other artist in the world's a Jew, and still folks hate them."

She thought of Mrs. Ellsworth (dear soul in New York), who never made uncomplimentary remarks about Negroes, but frequently did about Jews. Of little Menuhin she would say, for instance, "He's a *genius*—not a Jew," hating to admit his ancestry.

In Paris, Oceola especially loved the West Indian ball rooms where the black colonials danced the beguin. And she liked the entertainers at Bricktop's. Sometimes late at night there, Oceola would take the piano and beat out a blues for Brick and the assembled guests. In her playing of Negro folk music, Oceola never doctored it up, or filled it full of classical runs, or fancy falsities. In the blues she made the bass notes throb like tom-toms, the trebles cry like little flutes, so deep in the earth and so high in the sky that they understood everything. And when the night club crowd would get up and dance to her blues, and Bricktop would yell, "Hey! Hey!" Oceola felt as happy as if she were performing a Chopin étude for the nicely gloved Oh's and Ah-ers in a Crillon salon.

Music, to Oceola, demanded movement and expression, dancing

and living to go with it. She liked to teach, when she had the choir, the singing of those rhythmical Negro spirituals that possessed the power to pull colored folks out of their seats in the amen corner and make them prance and shout in the aisles for Jesus. She never liked those fashionable colored churches where shouting and movement were discouraged and looked down upon, and where New England hymns instead of spirituals were sung. Oceola's background was too well-grounded in Mobile, and Billy Kersands' Minstrels, and the Sanctified churches where religion was a joy, to stare mystically over the top of a grand piano like white folks and imagine that Beethoven had nothing to do with life, or that Schubert's love songs were only sublimations.

Whenever Mrs. Ellsworth came to Paris, she and Oceola spent hours listening to symphonies and string quartettes and pianists. Oceola enjoyed concerts, but seldom felt, like her patron, that she was floating on clouds of bliss. Mrs. Ellsworth insisted, however, that Oceola's spirit was too moved for words at such times—therefore she understood why the dear child kept quiet. Mrs. Ellsworth herself was often too moved for words, but never by pieces like Ravel's *Bolero* (which Oceola played on the phonograph as a dance record) or any of the compositions of *les Six*.

What Oceola really enjoyed most with Mrs. Ellsworth was not going to concerts, but going for trips on the little river boats in the Seine; or riding out to old chateaux in her patron's hired Renault; or to Versailles, and listening to the aging white lady talk about the romantic history of France, the wars and uprising, the loves and intrigues of princes and kings and queens, about guillotines and lace handkerchiefs, snuff boxes and daggers. For Mrs. Ellsworth had loved France as a girl, and had made a study of its life and lore. Once she used to sing simple little French songs rather well, too. And she always regretted that her husband never understood the lovely words— or even tried to understand them.

Oceola learned the accompaniments for all the songs Mrs. Ellsworth knew and sometimes they tried them over together. The middle-aged white woman loved to sing when the colored girl played, and she even tried spirituals. Often, when she stayed at the little Paris apartment, Oceola would go into the kitchen and cook something good for late supper, maybe an oyster soup, or fried apples and bacon. And sometimes Oceola had pigs' feet.

"There's nothing quite so good as a pig's foot," said Oceola, "after playing all day."

"Then you must have pigs' feet," agreed Mrs. Ellsworth.

And all this while Oceola's development at the piano blossomed into perfection. Her tone became a singing wonder and her interpretations warm and individual. She gave a concert in Paris, one in Brussels, and another in Berlin. She got the press notices all pianists crave. She had her picture in lots of European papers. And she came home to New York a year after the stock market crashed and nobody had any money—except folks like Mrs. Ellsworth who had so much it would be hard to ever lose it all.

Oceola's one time Pullman porter, now a coming doctor, was graduating from Meharry that spring. Mrs. Ellsworth saw her dark protegee go South to attend his graduation with tears in her eyes. She thought that by now music would be enough, after all those years under the best teachers, but alas, Oceola was not yet sublimated, even by Philippe. She wanted to see Pete.

Oceola returned North to prepare for her New York concert in the fall. She wrote Mrs. Ellsworth at Bar Harbor that her doctor boyfriend was putting in one more summer on the railroad, then in the autumn he would intern at Atlanta. And Oceola said that he had asked her to marry him. Lord, she was happy!

It was a long time before she heard from Mrs. Ellsworth. When the letter same, it was full of long paragraphs about the beautiful music Oceola had within her power to give the world. Instead, she wanted to marry and be burdened with children! Oh, my dear, my dear!

Oceola, when she read it, thought she had done pretty well knowing Pete this long and not having children. But she wrote back that she didn't see why children and music couldn't go together. Anyway, during the present depression, it was pretty hard for a beginning artist like herself to book a concert tour—so she might just as well be married awhile. Pete, on his last run in from St. Louis, had suggested that they have the wedding Christmas in the South. "And he's impatient, at that. He needs me."

This time Mrs. Ellsworth didn't answer by letter at all. She was back in town in late September. In November, Oceola played at Town Hall. The critics were kind, but they didn't go wild. Mrs. Ellsworth swore it was because of Pete's influence on her protegee.

"But he was in Atlanta," Oceola said.

"His spirit was here," Mrs. Ellsworth insisted. "All the time you were playing on that stage, he was here, the monster! Taking you out of yourself, taking you away from the piano."

"Why, he wasn't," said Oceola. "He was watching an operation in Atlanta."

But from then on, things didn't go well between her and her patron. The white lady grew distinctly cold when she received Oceola in her beautiful drawing room among the jade vases and amber cups worth thousands of dollars. When Oceola would have to wait there for Mrs. Ellsworth, she was afraid to move for fear she might knock something over—that would take ten years of a Harlemite's wages to replace, if broken.

Over the tea cups, the aging Mrs. Ellsworth did not talk any longer about the concert tour she had once thought she might finance for Oceola, if no recognized bureau took it up. Instead, she spoke of that something she believed Oceola's fingers had lost since her return from Europe. And she wondered why any one insisted on living in Harlem.

"I've been away from my own people so long," said the girl, "I want to live right in the middle of them again."

Why, Mrs. Ellsworth wondered farther, did Oceola, at her last concert in a Harlem church, not stick to the classical items listed on the program. Why did she insert one of her own variations on the spirituals, a syncopated variation from the Sanctified Church, that made an old colored lady rise up and cry out from her pew, "Glory to God this evenin'! Yes! Hallelujah! Whooo-oo!" right at the concert? Which seemed most undignified to Mrs. Ellsworth, and unworthy of the teachings of Philippe. And furthermore, why was Pete coming up to New York for Thanksgiving? And who had sent him the money to come?

"Me," said Oceola. "He doesn't make anything interning."

"Well," said Mrs. Ellsworth, "I don't think much of him." But Oceola didn't seem to care what Mrs. Ellsworth thought, for she made no defense.

Thanksgiving evening, in bed, together in a Harlem apartment, Pete and Oceola talked about their wedding to come. They would have a big one in a church with lots of music. And Pete would give her a ring. And she would have on a white dress, light and fluffy, not silk. "I hate silk," she said. "I hate expensive things." (She thought of her mother being buried in a cotton dress, for they were all broke when she died. Mother would have been glad about her marriage.) "Pete," Oceola said, hugging him in the dark, "let's live in Atlanta, where there are lots of colored people, like us."

"What about Mrs. Ellsworth?" Pete asked. "She coming down to Atlanta for our wedding?"

"I don't know," said Oceola.

"I hope not, 'cause if she stops at one of them big hotels. I won't have you going to the back door to see her. That's one thing I hate about the South—where there're white people, you have to go to the back door."

"Maybe she can stay with us," said Oceola. "I wouldn't mind."

"I'll be damned," said Pete. "You want to get lynched?"

But it happened that Mrs. Ellsworth didn't care to attend the wedding, anyway. When she saw how love had triumphed over art, she decided she could no longer influence Oceola's life. The period of Oceola was over. She would send checks, occasionally, if the girl needed them, besides, of course, something beautiful for the wedding, but that would be all. These things she told her the week after Thanksgiving.

"And Oceola, my dear, I've decided to spend the whole winter in Europe. I sail on December eighteenth. Christmas—while you are marrying—I shall be in Paris with my precious Antonio Bas. In January, he has an exhibition of oils in Madrid. And in the spring, a new young poet is coming over whom I want to visit Florence, to really know Florence. A charming white-haired boy from Omaha whose soul has been crushed in the West. I want to try to help him. He, my dear, is one of the few people who live for their art—and nothing else. . . . Ah, such a beautiful life! . . . You will come and play for me once before I sail?"

"Yes, Mrs. Ellsworth," said Oceola, genuinely sorry that the end had come. Why did white folks think you could live on nothing but art? Strange! Too strange! Too strange!

V

The Persian vases in the music room were filled with long-stemmed lilies that night when Oceola Jones came down from Harlem for the last time to play for Mrs. Dora Ellsworth. Mrs. Ellsworth had on a gown of black velvet, and a collar of pearls about her neck. She was very kind and gentle to Oceola, as one would be to a child who has done a great wrong but doesn't know any better. But to the black girl from Harlem, she looked very cold and white, and her grand piano seemed like the biggest and heaviest in the world—as Oceola sat down to play it with the technique for which Mrs. Ellsworth had paid.

As the rich and aging white woman listened to the great roll of Beethoven sonatas and to the sea and moonlight of the Chopin nocturnes, as she watched the swaying dark strong shoulders of Oceola Jones, she began to reproach the girl aloud for running away from art and music, for burying herself in Atlanta and love—love for a man unworthy of lacing up her boot straps, as Mrs. Ellsworth put it.

"You could shake the stars with your music, Oceola. Depression or no depression, I could make you great. And yet you propose to dig a grave for yourself. Art is bigger than love."

"I believe you, Mrs. Ellsworth," said Oceola, not turning away from the piano. "But being married won't keep me from making tours, or being an artist."

"Yes, it will," said Mrs. Ellsworth. "He'll take all the music out of you."

"No, he won't," said Oceola.

"You don't know, child," said Mrs. Ellsworth, "what men are like."

"Yes, I do," said Oceola simply. And her fingers began to wander slowly up and down the keyboard, flowing into the soft and lazy syncopation of a Negro blues, a blues that deepened and grew into rollicking jazz, then into an earth-throbbing rhythm that shook the lilies in the Persian vases of Mrs. Ellsworth's music room. Louder than the voice of the white woman who cried that Oceola was deserting beauty, deserting her real self, deserting her hope in life, the flood of wild syncopation filled the house, then sank into the slow and singing blues with which it had begun.

The girl at the piano heard the white woman saying, "Is this what I spent thousands of dollars to teach you?"

"No," said Oceola simply. "This is mine. . . . Listen! . . . How sad and gay it is. Blue and happy—laughing and crying. . . . How white like you and black like me. . . . How much like a man. . . . And how like a woman. . . . Warm as Pete's mouth. . . . These are the blues. . . . I'm playing."

Mrs. Ellsworth sat very still in her chair looking at the lilies trembling delicately in the priceless Persian vases, while Oceola made the bass notes throb like tom-toms deep in the earth.

> *O, if I could holler*

Sang the blues,

> *Like a mountain jack,*
> *I'd go up on de mountain*

sang the blues,

> *And call my baby back.*

"And I," said Mrs. Ellsworth rising from her chair, "would stand looking at the stars."

WALLACE THURMAN
By permission of the Beinecke Library, Yale University.

WALLACE THURMAN

1902 TO 1934

I n *Infants of the Spring* (1932), Wallace Thurman's satirical roman à clef about the Harlem Renaissance, the protagonist, a budding black novelist named Raymond Taylor, announces: "I don't expect to be a great writer. I don't think the Negro race can produce one now, any more than can America. I know of only one Negro who has the elements of greatness, and that's Jean Toomer. The rest of us are merely journeymen, planting seed for someone else to harvest. We all get sidetracked sooner or later." Nowhere in *Infants of the Spring* does Raymond Taylor serve more plainly as his creator's mouthpiece than in this confession of his own shortcomings and this depreciation of the artistic movement to which Thurman contributed so much.

Langston Hughes remembered Thurman as "a strangely brilliant black boy" who "wanted to be a *very* great writer" but who could not fairly credit anything he had written because it did not measure up to what he so admired in his voluminous reading of revered white authors like Proust, Melville, and Tolstoy. Thurman's high ideals for African American writing combined with a jaundiced insider's estimate of what he felt that he and other black writers had actually achieved in their heyday made him an excellent debunker of the pretensions and self-deceptions of the Harlem Renaissance. But was Thurman's penchant for satire and invective the sign of a consciousness artistically crippled by self-contempt? Or would he have turned away from the excesses of his own mordant style in favor of a more nuanced way of harnessing criticism and comedy in future writing? The author's death from tuberculosis at the age of thirty-two leaves unanswered these and many other intriguing questions about the potential of the best-read and most uncompromising of the writers of the Harlem Renaissance.

Wallace Thurman arrived in Harlem in 1925 brimming with energy and ambition. Since his birth in Salt Lake City, Utah, he had spent most of his time in school or college, graduating from the University of Southern California in 1925 after a brief stint as a medical student at the University of Utah. Thurman's socialist politics and slashing writing style appealed to the owners of *The Messenger*, a black radical monthly, which hired him as an editor in 1926. Later that year Thurman joined with Hughes, Zora Neale Hurston, and a handful of other young black writers and artists to publish *Fire!!*, the most iconoclastic literary magazine black America had ever seen. Its many scandalized critics helped to extinguish *Fire!!* after one issue, leaving Thurman to pay the magazine's publication bills. Strapped financially and suffering from a variety of ailments exacerbated by too much drinking, Thurman labored as a journalist, a ghostwriter for various "true confessions" magazines, and a reader and editor for a prosperous white-owned publishing house. He simultaneously pursued careers as a dramatist and novelist.

Thurman's greatest success on the stage came in 1929 when his play *Harlem* opened at the Apollo Theater on Broadway to considerable applause and enjoyed a run of over ninety performances. As a novelist Thurman made his debut with *The Blacker the Berry* (1929), an exploration of a subject taboo in most earlier African American fiction: intraracial color prejudice and the self-hatred spawned by it. In 1932 Thurman's last major works appeared, *The Interne* (co-authored with A. L. Furman), a problem novel about medical abuses in a large city hospital, and *Infants of the Spring*, a flawed but unflinching post-mortem on the Harlem Renaissance itself.

Having coined the term *niggeratti* in derisive reference to the self-impressed Harlem literati, Wallace Thurman left no doubts as to the direction of his satire when he made the setting of *Infants of the Spring* an artists' colony in a refurbished Harlem residence dubbed by its inhabitants "Niggeratti Manor." Thurman's uncertainty about where the Harlem Renaissance was headed is reflected in his novel's lack of purposeful action. The writers and artists of Niggeratti Manor do little besides ridicule each other's foibles, engage in long-winded social and aesthetic arguments, and drink a prodigious amount of gin. Thurman is at his best in his rapid-fire sketches of the Harlem "niggeratti" and the motley assembly of poseurs, hustlers, and hangers-on that find their natural habitat in the parties and drinking bouts the "niggeratti" sponsor.

The liveliest and most comically revealing incident in the novel centers on the abortive attempt of Raymond Taylor and his cohorts to form a literary salon ostensibly "for the purpose of exchanging ideas and expressing and criticizing individual theories." Presided over by the pompous Dr. A. L. Parkes, whose vapid auguries of a new racial millenium parody the prophecies of Alain Locke, the salon attracts practically everybody who was anybody among Harlem's literati. The gathering is hosted by Raymond Taylor (Thurman) and two of his neurotic fellow-residents at Niggeratti Manor, Eustace Savoy, a singer who aspires to performing Schubert rather than spirituals, and Paul Arbian, a bohemian painter and devotee of Oscar Wilde. Among the literary lights who attend the salon are Sweetie May Carr (Zora Neale Hurston), Tony Crews (Langston Hughes), DeWitt Clinton (Countee Cullen), Cedric Williams (Eric Walrond), and Dr. Manfred Trout (Rudolph Fisher). The cynicism, pettiness, and tunnel vision unmasked by the clash of egos unleashed by the salon testifies to Thurman's pessimistic assessment of the malaise into which the Harlem Renaissance had fallen by the early 1930s. About all a disheartened Raymond Taylor can offer as a remedy is a vague prescription for the individual black artist to find his or her own way. Unfortunately Wallace Thurman was unable to follow his own advice.

SUGGESTIONS FOR FURTHER READING

There are no book-length studies of Wallace Thurman's life or edited collections of his work. The best resources for criticism of Thurman's writing are the books on African American fiction and the histories of the Harlem Renaissance listed in the "Suggestions for Further Reading" following the introduction to this anthology.

INFANTS OF THE SPRING

L ⌐─── ⌐

XXI

. . . Raymond seemed to have developed a new store of energy. For three days and nights, he had secluded himself in his room, and devoted all his time to the continuance of his novel. For three years it had remained a project. Now he was making rapid progress. The ease with which he could work once he set himself to it amazed him, and at the same time he was suspicious of this unexpected facility. Nevertheless, his novel was progressing, and he intended to let nothing check him.

In line with this resolution, he insisted that Paul and Eustace hold their nightly gin parties without his presence, and they were also abjured to steer all company clear of his studio. . . .

Having withdrawn from every activity connected with Niggeratti Manor, Raymond had also forgotten that Dr. Parkes had promised to communicate with him, concerning some mysterious idea, and he was taken by surprise when Eustace came into the room one morning, bearing a letter from Dr. Parkes.

"Well, I'm plucked," Raymond exclaimed.

"What's the matter?" Eustace queried.

"Will you listen to this?" He read the letter aloud.

"My dear Raymond:

I will be in New York on Thursday night. I want you to do me a favor. It seems to me that with the ever increasing number of younger Negro artists and intellectuals gathering in Harlem, some effort should be made to establish what well might become a distinguished salon. All of you engaged in creative work, should, I believe, welcome the chance to meet together once every fortnight, for the purpose of exchanging ideas and expressing and criticizing individual theories. This might prove to be both stimulating and profitable. And it might also bring into active being a concerted movement which would establish the younger Negro talent once and for all as a vital artistic force. With this in mind, I would appreciate your inviting as many of your colleagues as possible to your studio on Thursday evening. I will be there to preside. I hope you are intrigued by the idea and willing to coöperate. Please wire me your answer. Collect, of course.

Very sincerely yours,
Dr. A. L. Parkes."

"Are you any more good?" Raymond asked as he finished reading.

"Sounds like a great idea," Eustace replied enthusiastically.

"It *is* great. Too great to miss," Raymond acquiesced mischievously. "Come on, let's get busy on the telephone."

Thursday night came and so did the young hopefuls. The first to arrive was Sweetie May Carr. Sweetie May was a short story writer, more noted for her ribald wit and personal effervescence than for any actual literary work. She was a great favorite among those whites who went in for Negro prodigies. Mainly because she lived up to their conception of what a typical Negro should be. It seldom occurred to any of her patrons that she did this with tongue in cheek. Given a paleface audience, Sweetie May would launch forth into a saga of the little all-colored Mississippi town where she claimed to have been born. Her repertoire of tales was earthy, vulgar and funny. Her darkies always smiled through their tears, sang spirituals on the slightest provocation, and performed buck dances when they should have been working. Sweetie May was a master of southern dialect, and an able raconteur, but she was too indifferent to literary creation to transfer to paper that which she told so well. The intricacies of writing bored her, and her written work was for the most part turgid and unpolished. But Sweetie May knew her white folks.

"It's like this," she had told Raymond. "I have to eat. I also wish to finish my education. Being a Negro writer these days is a racket and I'm going to make the most of it while it lasts. Sure I cut the fool. But I enjoy it, too. I don't know a tinker's damn about art. I care less about it. My ultimate ambition, as you know, is to become a gynecologist. And the only way I can live easily until I have the requisite training is to pose as a writer of potential ability. *Voila!* I get my tuition paid at Columbia. I rent an apartment and have all the furniture contributed by kind hearted o'fays. I receive bundles of groceries from various sources several times a week . . . all accomplished by dropping a discreet hint during an evening's festivities. I find queer places for whites to go in Harlem . . . out of the way primitive churches, sidestreet speakeasies. They fall for it. About twice a year I manage to sell a story. It is acclaimed. I am a genius in the making. Thank God for this Negro literary renaissance! Long may it flourish!"

Sweetie May was accompanied by two young girls, recently emigrated from Boston. They were the latest to be hailed as incipient immortals. Their names were Doris Westmore and Hazel Jamison. Doris wrote short stories. Hazel wrote poetry. Both had become known through a literary contest fostered by one of the leading Negro magazines. Raymond liked them more than he did most of the younger recruits to the movement. For one thing, they were characterized by a freshness and naïveté which he and his cronies had lost. And, surprisingly enough for Negro prodigies, they actually gave promise of possessing literary talent. He was most pleased to see them. He was also amused by their interest and excitement. A salon! A literary gathering! It was one of the civilized institutions they had dreamed of finding in New York, one of the things they had longed and hoped for.

As time passed, others came in. Tony Crews, smiling and self-effacing, a mischievous boy, grateful for the chance to slip away from the backwoods college he attended. Raymond had never been able to analyze this young poet. His work was interesting and unusual. It was also spotty. Spasmodically he gave promise of developing into a first rate poet. Already he had published two volumes, prematurely, Raymond thought. Both had been excessively praised by whites and universally damned by Negroes. Considering the nature of his work this was to be expected. The only unknown quantity was the poet himself. Would he or would he not fulfill the promise exemplified in some of his work? Raymond had no way of knowing and even an intimate friendship with Tony himself had failed to enlighten him. For Tony was the most close-mouthed and cagey individual Raymond had ever known when it came to personal matters. He fended off every attempt to probe into his inner self and did this with such an unconscious and naïve air that the prober soon came to one of two conclusions: Either Tony had no depth whatsoever, or else he was too deep for plumbing by ordinary mortals.

DeWitt Clinton, the Negro poet laureate, was there, too, accompanied, as usual, by his *fideles achates*, David Holloway. David had been acclaimed the most handsome Negro in Harlem by a certain group of whites. He was in great demand by artists who wished to paint him. He had become a much touted romantic figure. In reality he was a fairly intelligent school teacher, quite circumspect in his habits, a rather timid beau, who imagined himself to be bored with life.

Dr. Parkes finally arrived, accompanied by Carl Denny, the artist, and Carl's wife, Annette. Next to arrive was Cedric Williams, a West Indian, whose first book, a collection of short stories with a Caribbean background, in Raymond's opinion, marked him as one of the three Negroes writing who actually had something to say, and also some concrete idea of style. Cedric was followed by Austin Brown, a portrait painter whom Raymond personally despised, a Dr. Manfred Trout, who practiced medicine and also wrote exceptionally good short stories, Glenn Madison, who was a Communist, and a long, lean professorial person, Allen Fenderson, who taught school and had ambitions to become a crusader modeled after W. E. B. Du Bois.

The roster was now complete. There was an hour of small talk and drinking of mild cocktails in order to induce ease and allow the various guests to become acquainted and voluble. Finally, Dr. Parkes ensconced himself in Raymond's favorite chair, where he could get a good view of all in the room, and clucked for order.

Raymond observed the professor closely. Paul's description never seemed more apt. He was a mother hen clucking at her chicks. Small, dapper, with sensitive features, graying hair, a dominating head, and restless hands and feet, he smiled benevolently at his brood. Then, in his best continental manner, which he had acquired during four years at European Universities, he began to speak.

"You are," he perorated, "the outstanding personalities in a new generation. On you depends the future of your race. You are not, as were your predecessors, concerned with donning armor, and clashing swords with the enemy in the public square. You are finding both an escape and a weapon in beauty, which beauty when created by you will cause the American white man to reëstimate the Negro's value to his civilization, cause him to realize that the American black man is too valuable, too potential of utilitarian accomplishment, to be kept downtrodden and segregated.

"Because of your concerted storming up Parnassus, new vistas will be spread open to the entire race. The Negro in the south will no more know peonage, Jim Crowism, or loss of the ballot, and the Negro everywhere in America will know complete freedom and equality.

"But," and here his voice took on a more serious tone, "to accomplish this, your pursuit of beauty must be vital and lasting. I am somewhat fearful of the decadent strain which seems to have filtered into most of your work. Oh, yes, I know you are children of the age and all that, but you must not, like your paleface contemporaries, wallow in the mire of post-Victorian license. You have too much at stake. You must have ideals. You should become . . . well, let me suggest your going back to your racial roots, and cultivating a healthy paganism based on African traditions.

"For the moment that is all I wish to say. I now want you all to give expression to your own ideas. Perhaps we can reach a happy mean for guidance."

He cleared his throat and leaned contentedly back in his chair. No one said a word. Raymond was full of contradictions, which threatened to ooze forth despite his efforts to remain silent. But he knew that once the ooze began there would be no stopping the flood, and he was anxious to hear what some of the others might have to say.

However, a glance at the rest of the people in the room assured him that most of them had not the slightest understanding of what had been said, nor any ideas on the subject, whatsoever. Once more Dr. Parkes clucked for discussion. No one ventured a word. Raymond could see that Cedric, like himself, was full of argument, and also like him, did not wish to appear contentious at such an early stage in the discussion. Tony winked at Raymond when he caught his eye, but the expression on his face was as inscrutable as ever. Sweetie May giggled behind her handkerchief. Paul amused himself by sketching the various people in the room. The rest were blank.

"Come, come, now," Dr. Parkes urged somewhat impatiently, "I'm not to do all the talking. What have you to say, DeWitt?"

All eyes sought out the so-called Negro poet laureate. For a moment he stirred uncomfortably in his chair, then in a high pitched, nasal voice proceeded to speak.

"I think, Dr. Parkes, that you have said all there is to say. I agree with you. The young Negro artist must go back to his pagan heritage for inspiration and to the old masters for form."

Raymond could not suppress a snort. For DeWitt's few words had given him a vivid mental picture of that poet's creative hours—eyes on a page of Keats, fingers on typewriter, mind frantically conjuring African scenes. And there would of course be a Bible nearby.

Paul had ceased being intent on his drawing long enough to hear "pagan heritage," and when DeWitt finished he inquired inelegantly:

"What old black pagan heritage?"

DeWitt gasped, surprised and incredulous.

"Why, from your ancestors."

"Which ones?" Paul pursued dumbly.

"Your African ones, of course." DeWitt's voice was full of disdain.

"What about the rest?"

"What rest?" He was irritated now.

"My German, English and Indian ancestors," Paul answered willingly. "How can I go back to African ancestors when their blood is so diluted and their country and times so far away? I have no conscious affinity for them at all."

Dr. Parkes intervened: "I think you've missed the point, Paul."

"And I," Raymond was surprised at the suddenness with which he joined in the argument, "think he has hit the nail right on the head. Is there really any reason why *all* Negro artists should consciously and deliberately dig into African soil for inspiration and material unless they actually wish to do so?"

"I don't mean that. I mean you should develop your inherited spirit."

DeWitt beamed. The doctor had expressed his own hazy theory. Raymond was about to speak again, when Paul once more took the bit between his own teeth.

"I ain't got no African spirit."

Sweetie May giggled openly at this, as did Carl Denny's wife, Annette. The rest looked appropriately sober, save for Tony, whose eyes continued to telegraph mischievously to Raymond. Dr. Parkes tried to squelch Paul with a frown. He should have known better.

"I'm not an African," the culprit continued. "I'm an American and a perfect product of the melting pot."

"That's nothing to brag about." Cedric spoke for the first time.

"And I think you're all on the wrong track." All eyes were turned toward this new speaker, Allen Fenderson. "Dr. Du Bois has shown us the way. We must be militant fighters. We must not hide away in ivory towers and prate of beauty. We must fashion cudgels and bludgeons rather than sensitive plants. We must excoriate the white man, and make him grant us justice. We must fight for complete social and political and economic equality."

"What we ought to do," Glenn Madison growled intensely, "is to join hands with the workers of the world and overthrow the present capitalistic régime. We are of the proletariat and must fight our battles allied with them, rather than singly and selfishly."

"All of us?" Raymond inquired quietly.

"All of us who have a trace of manhood and are more interested in the rights of human beings than in gin parties and neurotic capitalists."

"I hope you're squelched," Paul stage whispered to Raymond.

"And how!" Raymond laughed. Several joined in. Dr. Parkes spoke quickly to Fenderson, ignoring the remarks of the Communist.

"But, Fenderson . . . this is a new generation and must make use of new weapons. Some of us will continue to fight in the old way, but there are other things to be considered, too. Remember, a beautiful sonnet can be as effectual, nay even more effectual, than a rigorous hymn of hate."

"The man who would understand and be moved by a hymn of hate would not bother to read your sonnet and, even if he did, he would not know what it was all about."

"I don't agree. Your progress must be a boring in from the top, not a battle from the bottom. Convert the higher beings and the lower orders will automatically follow."

"Spoken like a true capitalistic minion," Glenn Madison muttered angrily.

Fenderson prepared to continue his argument, but he was forestalled by Cedric.

"What does it matter," he inquired diffidently, "what any of you do so long as you remain true to yourselves? There is no necessity for this movement becoming standardized. There is ample room for everyone to follow his own individual track. Dr. Parkes wants us all to go back to Africa and resurrect our pagan heritage, become atavistic. In this he is supported by Mr. Clinton. Fenderson here wants us all to be propagandists and yell at the top of our lungs at every conceivable injustice. Madison wants us all to take a cue from Leninism and fight the capitalistic bogey. Well . . . why not let each young hopeful choose his own path? Only in that way will anything at all be achieved."

"Which is just what I say," Raymond smiled gratefully at Cedric. "One cannot make movements nor can one plot their course. When the work of a given number of individuals during a given period is looked at in retrospect, then one can identify a movement and evaluate its distinguishing characteristics. Individuality is what we should strive for. Let each seek his own salvation. To me, a wholesale flight back to Africa or a wholesale allegiance to Communism or a wholesale adherence to an antiquated and for the most part ridiculous propagandistic program are all equally futile and unintelligent."

Dr. Parkes gasped and sought for an answer. Cedric forestalled him.

"To talk of an African heritage among American Negroes *is* unintelligent. It is only in the West Indies that you can find direct descendents from African ancestors. Your primitive instincts among all but the extreme proletariat have been ironed out. You're standardized Americans."

"Oh, no," Carl Denny interrupted suddenly. "You're wrong. It's

in our blood. It's . . ." he fumbled for a word, "fixed. Why . . ."
he stammered again, "remember Cullen's poem, *Heritage*:

> " 'So I lie who find no peace
> Night or day, no slight release
> From the unremittant beat
> Made by cruel padded feet
> Walking through my body's street.
> Up and down they go, and back,
> Treading out a jungle track.'

"We're all like that. Negroes are the only people in America not
standardized. The feel of the African jungle is in their blood. Its
rhythms surge through their bodies. Look how Negroes laugh and
dance and sing, all spontaneous and individual."

"Exactly," Dr. Parkes and DeWitt nodded assent.

"I have yet to see an intelligent or middle class American Negro
laugh and sing and dance spontaneously. That's an illusion, a pretty
sentimental fiction. Moreover your songs and dances are not individual. Your spirituals are mediocre folk songs, ignorantly culled from
Methodist hymn books. There are white men who can sing them just
as well as Negroes, if not better, should they happen to be untrained
vocalists like Robeson, rather than highly trained technicians like
Hayes. And as for dancing spontaneously and feeling the rhythms of
the jungle . . . humph!"

Sweetie May jumped into the breach.

"I can do the Charleston better than any white person."

"I particularly stressed . . . intelligent people. The lower orders of
any race have more vim and vitality than the illuminated tenth."

Sweetie May leaped to her feet.

"Why, you West Indian . . ."

"Sweetie, Sweetie," Dr. Parkes was shocked by her polysyllabic expletive.

Pandemonium reigned. The master of ceremonies could not cope
with the situation. Cedric called Sweetie an illiterate southern hussy.
She called him all types of profane West Indian monkey chasers.
DeWitt and David were shocked and showed it. The literary doctor,
the Communist and Fenderson moved uneasily around the room.
Annette and Paul giggled. The two child prodigies from Boston
looked on wide-eyed, utterly bewildered and dismayed. Raymond
leaned back in his chair, puffing on a cigarette, detached and
amused. Austin, the portrait painter, audibly repeated over and over

to himself: "Just like niggers . . . just like niggers." Carl Denny interposed himself between Cedric and Sweetie May. Dr. Parkes clucked for civilized behavior, which came only when Cedric stalked angrily out of the room.

After the alien had been routed and peace restored, Raymond passed a soothing cocktail. Meanwhile Austin and Carl had begun arguing about painting. Carl did not possess a facile tongue. He always had difficulty formulating in words the multitude of ideas which seethed in his mind. Austin, to quote Raymond, was an illiterate cad. Having examined one of Carl's pictures on Raymond's wall, he had disparaged it. Raymond listened attentively to their argument. He despised Austin mainly because he spent most of his time imploring noted white people to give him a break by posing for a portrait. Having the gift of making himself pitiable, and having a glib tongue when it came to expatiating on the trials and tribulations of being a Negro, he found many sitters, all of whom thought they were encouraging a handicapped Negro genius. After one glimpse at the completed portrait, they invariably changed their minds.

"I tell you," he shouted, "your pictures are distorted and grotesque. Art is art, I say. And art holds a mirror up to nature. No mirror would reflect a man composed of angles. God did not make man that way. Look at Sargent's portraits. He was an artist."

"But he wasn't," Carl expostulated. "We . . . we of this age . . . we must look at Matisse, Gauguin, Picasso and Renoir for guidance. They get the feel of the age. . . . They . . ."

"Are all crazy and so are you," Austin countered before Carl could proceed.

Paul rushed to Carl's rescue. He quoted Wilde in rebuttal: Nature imitates art, then went on to blaspheme Sargent. Carl, having found some words to express a new idea fermenting in his brain, forgot the argument at hand, went off on a tangent and began telling the dazed Dr. Parkes about the Negroid quality in his drawings. DeWitt yawned and consulted his watch. Raymond mused that he probably resented having missed the prayer meeting which he attended every Thursday night. In another corner of the room the Communist and Fenderson had locked horns over the ultimate solution of the Negro problem. In loud voices each contended for his own particular solution. Karl Marx and Lenin were pitted against Du Bois and his disciples. The writing doctor, bored to death, slipped quietly from the room without announcing his departure or even saying good night. Being more intelligent than most of the others, he had wisely kept silent. Tony and Sweetie May had taken adjoining chairs, and were soon engaged in comparing their versions of original verses to the St. James Infirmary, which Tony contended was soon to become as epical as the St. Louis Blues. Annette and Howard began gossiping about various outside personalities. The child prodigies looked from one to the other, silent, perplexed, uncomfortable, not knowing what to do or say. Dr. Parkes visibly recoiled from Carl's incoherent expository barrage, and wilted in his chair, willing but unable to effect a courteous exit. Raymond sauntered around the room, dispensing cocktails, chuckling to himself.

Such was the first and last salon.

AN INTRODUCTION TO CONTEMPORARY HARLEMESE

EXPURGATED AND ABRIDGED

RUDOLPH FISHER

AIN'T GOT 'EM
Possesses no virtues—is no good.

ASK FOR
Challenge to battle in terms that don't mean maybe.

BELLY-RUB
An indelicate but accurate designation of any sexy dance, the *bump* being the popular current example.

BIGGY
Sarcastic abbreviation of *big boy*.

BOOGY
Negro. A contraction of *Booker T.*, used only of and by members of the race. My own favorite among all the synonyms of Negro, of which the following are current: *Cloud, crow, darky, dinge, dinky, eight-ball, hunk, hunky, ink, jap, jasper, jig, jigaboo, jigwalker, joker, kack, Mose, race-man, race-woman, Sam, shade, shine, smoke, spade, zigaboo.*

BOY
Friend and ally. Buddy.

BRING MUD
To fall below expectations, disappoint. He who escorts a homely *sheba* to a *dickty shout brings mud*.

BROTHER
A form of address, usually ironic. A bystander, witnessing the arrest of some offender, may observe: "It's *too bad now, brother.*"

BUMP
BUMPTY-BUMP
BUMP-THE-BUMP
A *shout* characterized by a forward and backward swaying of the hips. Said to be an excellent aphrodisiac. Also said to be the despair of *fays*.

BUTT
Buttocks.

CAN
Buttocks.

CATCH AIR
To take leave, usually under urgent pressure.

CHOKE
To defeat. To *turn one's damper down*.

CHORINE
A chorus girl.

CHORAT
A chorus man.

CLOUD
See *boogy*.

CROW
See *boogy*.

DADDY
Provider of affection and other more tangible delights.

DARKEY
See *boogy*.

DICKTY
Adj.—Swell.
Noun—High-toned person.

DINGE
See *boogy*.

DINKY
See *boogy*.

DOG
Any extraordinary person, thing, or event. *"Ain't this a dog?"* is a comment on anything unusual.

DO IT!
DO THAT THING!
DO YOUR STUFF!
"More power to ye!"

DOWN THE WAY
Designation of some place familiar to both parties talking.

DO ONE'S STUFF
Exhibit one's best. Show off.

EIGHT-BALL
The number 8 pool ball is black.

EVERMORE
Extremely, as an *evermore red-hot mamma.*

DRUNK DOWN
Plumbing the nadir of inebriation. Soused to helplessness.

FAY
OFAY
A person who, so far as is known, is white. *Fay* is said to be the original term and *ofay* a contraction of "old" and "fay."

FREEBY
Something for nothing, as complimentary tickets to a theater.

FROM WAY BACK
Of extraordinary experience and skill.

GET AWAY
I.e., with something. Escape unpunished for audacity; to triumph, as does the successful *jiver* or the winner at blackjack.

GIVE ONE AIR
To dismiss one with finality. To "give one the gate."

GRAVY
Unearned increment. *Freeby.*

GREAT DAY IN THE MORNING!
Exclamation of wonder.

HAUL IT
Haul hiney. Depart in great haste. *Catch air. It,* without an obvious antecedent, usually has pelvic significance. "Put *it* in the chair" means "Sit down."

HIGH

Enjoying the elevated spirits of moderately advanced inebriation. "Tight" in the usual slang sense. Cf. *tight* in the Harlemese sense.

HINEY

Affectionate diminutive for hind-quarters. "It's your hiney" means "It will cost you your hiney," i.e., "You are undone."

HOT

Kindling admiration. As overdone among jigs as is "marvelous" among fays.

HOT YOU!

Pronounced hot-choo. Equivalent to *Oh, no, now!* q.v.

HOW COME?

Why?

HUNK, HUNKY

See *boogy*.

I MEAN

"You said it." Ex. "Some *sheba*, huh?"—"*I mean.*"

INK

See *boogy*.

JAP

See *boogy*.

JASPER

See *boogy*.

JAZZ

1. The modern American musical idiom, of course.
2. Sometimes synonymous with *jive*, q.v.

JIG, JIGABOO, JIGWALKER

See *boogy*.

JIVE

1. Pursuit in love or any device thereof. Usually flattery with intent to win.
2. Capture.
In either sense this word implies passing fancy, hence, deceit.

JIVER

One who *jives*.

JOHN-BROWN

Dog-gone.

JOKER
See *boogy*.

KACK
Extreme sarcasm for *dickty*, q.v.

K.M.
Kitchen mechanic, i.e., cook, girl, scullion, menial.

LONG-GONE
Lost. State in which *it's one's hiney*.

LORD TODAY!
Exclamation of wonder.

MAMMA
Potential or actual sweetheart.

MARTIN
Jocose designation of death. Derived from Bert Williams' story: *Wait Till Martin Comes*.

MISS
Fail. A question is characteristically answered by use of *miss* or some equivalent expression. Ex. "Did you win money?"—"I didn't miss" or "Nothing different." "Do you mean me?"—"I don't mean your brother" and so on.

MONKEY-BACK
Dude.

MONKEY-MAN
"Cake-eater."

MOSE
See *boogy*.

MISS ANNE
MR. CHARLIE
Non-specific designation of "swell" whites. Ex. "Boy, boot-legging pays. That boogy's got a straight-eight just like *Mr. Charlie's*."—"Yea, and his *mamma's* got a fur coat just like *Miss Anne's*, too."

MUD
See *bring mud*.

NO LIE
You said it. *I mean*.

OFAY
See *fay*.

OH, NO, NOW!
Exclamation of admiration.

OSCAR
Dumb-bell.

OUT (OF) THIS WORLD
Beyond mortal experience or belief.

PAPA
1. See *daddy*.
2. Equivalent to *brother*.

PLAY THAT
I.e., play that game, hence, to countenance or tolerate.

POKE OUT
Be distinguished, excel.

PREVIOUS
Premature, hence, presumptuous. He who tries to break into a ticket-line is likely to be warned, "Don't get too *previous, brother*."

PUT ONE IN
To report one to some enemy or authority in order to have one punished.

PUT (GET, HAVE) THE LOCKS ON
To handcuff. Hence to render helpless. Most frequently heard in reference to some form of gambling, such as card games and love affairs.

PUT IT ON ONE
To injure one deliberately.

RACE-MAN (WOMAN)
See *boogy*.

RED-HOT
Somewhat hotter than *hot*. Extremely striking.

RIGHT
Somewhat in excess of perfection.

RIGHT ON
Nevertheless.

RAT
Antithesis of *dickty*.

SALTY DOG
Stronger than *dog*.

SAM
See *boogy*.

SEE ONE GO
Give one aid. *"See me go for* breakfast?" means "Pay for my breakfast?" It is the answerer's privilege to interpret the query literally, thus: "See you go—to hell."

SHARP
Striking "Keen." A beautifully dressed woman is *"sharp out this world."*

SHEBA
Queen. Frail. Broad.

SHOUT
1. Ball. Prom.
2. A slow one-step in which all the company gets happy.

SLIP
1. To kid.
2. *To slip in the dozens, to disparage one's family.*

SMOKE
See *boogy*.

SMOKE OVER
"Give the once over." Observe critically.

SMOOTHE
Verb—To calm, to quell anger. What *sweet mamma* does to *cruel papa* when he gets *tight*, q.v.
Adj.—1. Cunning, "slick," as a *smoothe jiver*. 2.—Faultless, as a *smoothe brown*.

STRUT ONE'S STUFF
See *do one's stuff*.

STUFF
1. Talent, as above.
2. Hokum. Boloney. Banana oil. Ex. "They tell me that *sheba* tried to commit suicide over her *daddy*."—"Huh. That's a lot o' *stuff*."

TELL 'EM!
TELL 'EM 'BOUT IT!
Exclamation of agreement and approval.

THE MAN
Designation of abstract authority. He who trespasses where a sign forbids is asked: "Say, biggy, can't you read *the man's* sign?"

THERE AIN'T NOTHING TO THAT
This signifies complete agreement with a previous assertion. It is equivalent to saying, "That is beyond question."

TIGHT
Tough. Redoubtable. Hard. Not "drunk" in the usual sense, for which the Harlemese is *high*.

TO BE HAD
To be bested.

TO BE ON
To bear actual or pretended malice against.

TOO BAD
1. Marvelous.
2. Extremely unfortunate.

TOOTIN'
Right. Unquestionable. Full remark is "You are dog-gone tootin'."

TURN 'EM ON
Strut one's stuff.

TURN ONE'S DAMPER DOWN
To reduce the temperature of one who is *hot*, q.v. Hence, to *choke*.

UH-HUH
Yes.

UH-UH
No.

UPPITY
High-hat.

WHAT DO YOU SAY?
How do you do?

CAN'T SAY IT
No complaint.

ZIGABOO
See *boogy*.